Orley Farm
Volume I

by

Anthony Trollope

Orley Farm
Volume I
by Anthony Trollope

Copyright © 2024

All Rights reserved.

No part of this publication may be reproduced, stored in a retrieval system, or transmitted in any form or by any means, electronic, mechanical, photocopying or Otherwise, without the written permission of the publisher.
The author/editor asserts the moral right to be identified as the author/editor of this work.

ISBN: 978-93-64284-37-0

Published by

DOUBLE 9 BOOKS

2/13-B, Ansari Road
Daryaganj, New Delhi – 110002
info@double9books.com
www.double9books.com
Tel. 011-40042856

This book is under public domain

ABOUT THE AUTHOR

Anthony Trollope (1815-1882) was a renowned English novelist of the Victorian era, best known for his insightful and richly detailed portrayals of 19th-century English society. His prolific writing career produced a vast array of novels, many of which have become classics of English literature. First Novels: Trollope's debut novel, "The Macdermots of Ballycloran", was published in 1847. However, it was not until the publication of "The Warden" in 1855 that he gained significant recognition. Trollope's writing is known for its realism, detailed character development, and exploration of social issues. His characters are often complex and multifaceted, reflecting the diverse nature of human experiences. He employed a straightforward narrative style, often interjecting his own commentary and opinions, which adds a distinctive voice to his works. Trollope's works remain significant in the study of Victorian literature. His keen observations of society, human relationships, and institutional behaviors continue to be appreciated for their depth and insight. Many of his novels have been adapted for television, radio, and stage, keeping his stories and characters alive for new generations. Anthony Trollope's contribution to literature is marked by his ability to combine detailed social critique with engaging storytelling, making him one of the enduring figures of English literature.

CONTENTS

CHAPTER I
THE COMMENCEMENT OF THE
GREAT ORLEY FARM CASE

It is not true that a rose by any other name will smell as sweet. Were it true, I should call this story "The Great Orley Farm Case." But who would ask for the ninth number of a serial work burthened with so very uncouth an appellation? Thence, and therefore,—Orley Farm.

I say so much at commencing in order that I may have an opportunity of explaining that this book of mine will not be devoted in any special way to rural delights. The name might lead to the idea that new precepts were to be given, in the pleasant guise of a novel, as to cream-cheeses, pigs with small bones, wheat sown in drills, or artificial manure. No such aspirations are mine. I make no attempts in that line, and declare at once that agriculturists will gain nothing from my present performance. Orley Farm, my readers, will be our scene during a portion of our present sojourn together, but the name has been chosen as having been intimately connected with certain legal questions which made a considerable stir in our courts of law.

It was twenty years before the date at which this story will be supposed to commence that the name of Orley Farm first became known to the wearers of the long robe. At that time had died an old gentleman, Sir Joseph Mason, who left behind him a landed estate in Yorkshire of considerable extent and value. This he bequeathed, in a proper way, to his eldest son, the Joseph Mason, Esq., of our date. Sir Joseph had been a London merchant; had made his own money, having commenced the world, no doubt, with half a crown; had become, in turn, alderman, mayor, and knight; and in the fulness of time was gathered to his fathers. He had purchased this estate in Yorkshire late in life—we may as well become acquainted with the name, Groby Park—and his eldest son had lived there with such enjoyment of the privileges of an English country gentleman as he had been able to master for himself. Sir Joseph had also had three daughters, full sisters of Joseph of Groby, whom he endowed sufficiently and gave over to three respective loving husbands. And then shortly before his death, three years or so, Sir

Joseph had married a second wife, a lady forty-five years his junior, and by her he also left one son, an infant only two years old when he died.

For many years this prosperous gentleman had lived at a small country house, some five-and-twenty miles from London, called Orley Farm. This had been his first purchase of land, and he had never given up his residence there, although his wealth would have entitled him to the enjoyment of a larger establishment. On the birth of his youngest son, at which time his eldest was nearly forty years old, he made certain moderate provision for the infant, as he had already made moderate provision for his young wife; but it was then clearly understood by the eldest son that Orley Farm was to go with the Groby Park estate to him as the heir. When, however, Sir Joseph died, a codicil to his will, executed with due legal formalities, bequeathed Orley Farm to his youngest son, little Lucius Mason.

Then commenced those legal proceedings which at last developed themselves into the great Orley Farm Case. The eldest son contested the validity of the codicil; and indeed there were some grounds on which it appeared feasible that he should do so. This codicil not only left Orley Farm away from him to baby Lucius, but also interfered in another respect with the previous will. It devised a sum of two thousand pounds to a certain Miriam Usbech, the daughter of one Jonathan Usbech who was himself the attorney who had attended upon Sir Joseph for the making out of this very will, and also of this very codicil. This sum of two thousand pounds was not, it is true, left away from the surviving Joseph, but was to be produced out of certain personal property which had been left by the first will to the widow. And then old Jonathan Usbech had died, while Sir Joseph Mason was still living.

All the circumstances of the trial need not be detailed here. It was clearly proved that Sir Joseph had during his whole life expressed his intention of leaving Orley Farm to his eldest son; that he was a man void of mystery, and not given to secrets in his money matters, and one very little likely to change his opinion on such subjects. It was proved that old Jonathan Usbech at the time in which the will was made was in very bad circumstances, both as regards money and health. His business had once not been bad, but he had eaten and drunk it, and at this period was feeble and penniless, overwhelmed both by gout and debt. He had for many years been much employed by Sir Joseph in money matters, and it was known that he was so employed almost up to the day of his death. The question was whether he had been employed to make this codicil.

The body of the will was in the handwriting of the widow, as was also the codicil. It was stated by her at the trial that the words were dictated to her by Usbech in her husband's hearing, and that the document was then signed by her husband in the presence of them both, and also in the presence of two other persons—a young man employed by her husband as a clerk, and by a servant-maid. These two last, together with Mr. Usbech, were the three witnesses whose names appeared in the codicil. There had been no secrets between Lady Mason and her husband as to his will. She had always, she said, endeavoured to induce him to leave Orley Farm to her child from the day of the child's birth, and had at last succeeded. In agreeing to this Sir Joseph had explained to her, somewhat angrily, that he wished to provide for Usbech's daughter, and that now he would do so out of moneys previously intended for her, the widow, and not out of the estate which would go to his eldest son. To this she had assented without a word, and had written the codicil in accordance with the lawyer's dictation, he, the lawyer, suffering at the time from gout in his hand. Among other things Lady Mason proved that on the date of the signatures Mr. Usbech had been with Sir Joseph for sundry hours.

Then the young clerk was examined. He had, he said, witnessed in his time four, ten, twenty, and, under pressure, he confessed to as many as a hundred and twenty business signatures on the part of his employer, Sir Joseph. He thought he had witnessed a hundred and twenty, but would take his oath he had not witnessed a hundred and twenty-one. He did remember witnessing a signature of his master about the time specified by the date of the codicil, and he remembered the maid-servant also signing at the same time. Mr. Usbech was then present; but he did not remember Mr. Usbech having the pen in his hand. Mr. Usbech, he knew, could not write at that time, because of the gout; but he might, no doubt, have written as much as his own name. He swore to both the signatures—his own and his master's; and in cross-examination swore that he thought it probable that they might be forgeries. On re-examination he was confident that his own name, as there appearing, had been written by himself; but on re-cross-examination, he felt sure that there was something wrong. It ended in the judge informing him that his word was worth nothing, which was hard enough on the poor young man, seeing that he had done his best to tell all that he remembered. Then the servant-girl came into the witness-box. She was sure it was her own handwriting. She remembered being called in to write her name, and seeing the master write his. It had all been explained to her at the time, but she admitted that she had not understood the explanation. She had also seen the clerk write his name, but she was not sure that she had seen Mr. Usbech write. Mr. Usbech had had a pen in his hand; she was sure of that.

The last witness was Miriam Usbech, then a very pretty, simple girl of seventeen. Her father had told her once that he hoped Sir Joseph would make provision for her. This had been shortly before her father's death. At her father's death she had been sent for to Orley Farm, and had remained there till Sir Joseph died. She had always regarded Sir Joseph and Lady Mason as her best friends. She had known Sir Joseph all her life, and did not think it unnatural that he should provide for her. She had heard her father say more than once that Lady Mason would never rest till the old gentleman had settled Orley Farm upon her son.

Not half the evidence taken has been given here, but enough probably for our purposes. The will and codicil were confirmed, and Lady Mason continued to live at the farm. Her evidence was supposed to have been excellently given, and to have been conclusive. She had seen the signature, and written the codicil, and could explain the motive. She was a woman of high character, of great talent, and of repute in the neighbourhood; and, as the judge remarked, there could be no possible reason for doubting her word. Nothing also could be simpler or prettier than the evidence of Miriam Usbech, as to whose fate and destiny people at the time expressed much sympathy. That stupid young clerk was responsible for the only weak part of the matter; but if he proved nothing on one side, neither did he prove anything on the other.

This was the commencement of the great Orley Farm Case, and having been then decided in favour of the infant it was allowed to slumber for nearly twenty years. The codicil was confirmed, and Lady Mason remained undisturbed in possession of the house, acting as guardian for her child till he came of age, and indeed for some time beyond that epoch. In the course of a page or two I shall beg my readers to allow me to introduce this lady to their acquaintance.

Miriam Usbech, of whom also we shall see something, remained at the farm under Lady Mason's care till she married a young attorney, who in process of time succeeded to such business as her father left behind him. She suffered some troubles in life before she settled down in the neighbouring country town as Mrs. Dockwrath, for she had had another lover, the stupid young clerk who had so villainously broken down in his evidence; and to this other lover, whom she had been unable to bring herself to accept, Lady Mason had given her favour and assistance. Poor Miriam was at that time a soft, mild-eyed girl, easy to be led, one would have said; but in this matter Lady Mason could not lead her. It was in vain to tell her that the character of young Dockwrath did not stand high, and that young Kenneby, the clerk, should be promoted to all manner of good things. Soft and mild-eyed as Miriam was, Love was still the lord of all. In this matter she would not be persuaded; and eventually she gave her two thousand pounds to Samuel Dockwrath, the young attorney with the questionable character.

This led to no breach between her and her patroness. Lady Mason, wishing to do the best for her young friend, had favoured John Kenneby, but she was not a woman at all likely to quarrel on such a ground as this. "Well, Miriam," she had said, "you must judge for yourself, of course, in such a matter as this. You know my regard for you."

"Oh yes, ma'am," said Miriam, eagerly.

"And I shall always be glad to promote your welfare as Mrs. Dockwrath, if possible. I can only say that I should have had more satisfaction in attempting to do so for you as Mrs. Kenneby." But, in spite of the seeming coldness of these words, Lady Mason had been constant to her friend for many years, and had attended to her with more or less active kindness in all the sorrows arising from an annual baby and two sets of twins—a progeny which before the commencement of my tale reached the serious number of sixteen, all living.

Among other solid benefits conferred by Lady Mason had been the letting to Mr. Dockwrath of certain two fields, lying at the extremity of the farm property, and quite adjacent to the town of Hamworth in which old Mr. Usbech had resided. These had been let by the year, at a rent not considered to be too high at that period, and which had certainly become much lower in proportion to the value of the land, as the town of Hamworth had increased. On these fields Mr. Dockwrath expended some money, though probably not so much as he averred; and when noticed to give them up at the period of young Mason's coming of age, expressed himself terribly aggrieved.

"Surely, Mr. Dockwrath, you are very ungrateful," Lady Mason had said to him. But he had answered her with disrespectful words; and hence had arisen an actual breach between her and poor Miriam's husband. "I must say, Miriam, that Mr. Dockwrath is unreasonable," Lady Mason had said. And what could a poor wife answer? "Oh! Lady Mason, pray let it bide a time till it all comes right." But it never did come right; and the affair of those two fields created the great Orley Farm Case, which it will be our business to unravel.

And now a word or two as to this Orley Farm. In the first place let it be understood that the estate consisted of two farms. One, called the Old Farm, was let to an old farmer named Greenwood, and had been let to him and to his father for many years antecedent to the days of the Masons. Mr. Greenwood held about three hundred acres of land, paying with admirable punctuality over four hundred a year in rent, and was regarded by all the Orley people as an institution on the property. Then there was the farm-house and the land attached to it. This was the residence in which Sir Joseph had lived, keeping in his own hands this portion of the property. When first inhabited by him the house was not fitted for more than the requirements of an ordinary farmer, but he had gradually added to it and ornamented it till it was commodious, irregular, picturesque, and straggling. When he died, and during the occupation of his widow, it consisted of three buildings of various heights, attached to each other, and standing in a row. The lower contained a large kitchen, which had been the living-room of the farm-house, and was surrounded by bake-house, laundry, dairy, and servants' room, all of fair dimensions. It was two stories high, but the rooms were low, and the roof steep and covered with tiles. The next portion had been added by Sir Joseph, then Mr. Mason, when he first thought of living at the place. This also was tiled, and the rooms were nearly as low; but there were three stories, and the building therefore was considerably higher. For five-and-twenty years the farm-house, so arranged, had sufficed for the common wants of Sir Joseph and his family; but when he determined to give up his establishment in the City, he added on another step to the house at Orley Farm. On this occasion he built a good dining-room, with a drawing-room over it, and bed-room over that; and this portion of the edifice was slated.

The whole stood in one line fronting on to a large lawn which fell steeply away from the house into an orchard at the bottom. This lawn was cut in terraces, and here and there upon it there stood apple-trees of ancient growth; for here had been the garden of the old farm-house. They were large, straggling trees, such as do not delight the eyes of modern gardeners; but they produced fruit by the bushel, very sweet to the palate, though probably not so perfectly round, and large, and handsome as those which the horticultural skill of the present day requires. The face of the house from one end to the other was covered with vines and passion-flowers, for the aspect was due south; and as the whole of the later addition was faced by a verandah, which also, as regarded the ground-floor, ran along the middle building, the place in summer was pretty enough. As I have said before, it was irregular and straggling, but at the same time roomy and picturesque. Such was Orley Farm-house.

There were about two hundred acres of land attached to it, together with a large old-fashioned farm-yard, standing not so far from the house as most gentlemen farmers might perhaps desire. The farm buildings, however, were well hidden, for Sir Joseph, though he would at no time go to the expense of constructing all anew, had spent more money than such a proceeding would have cost him doctoring existing evils and ornamenting the standing edifices. In doing this he had extended the walls of a brewhouse, and covered them with creepers, so as to shut out from the hall door the approach to the farm-yard, and had put up a quarter of a mile of high ornamental paling for the same purpose. He had planted an extensive shrubbery along the brow of the hill at one side of the house, had built summer-houses, and sunk a ha-ha fence below the orchard, and had contrived to give to the place the unmistakable appearance of an English gentleman's country-house. Nevertheless, Sir Joseph had never bestowed upon his estate, nor had it ever deserved, a more grandiloquent name than that which it had possessed of old.

Orley Farm-house itself is somewhat more than a mile distant from the town of Hamworth, but the land runs in the direction of the town, not skirting the high road, but stretching behind the cottages which stand along the pathway; and it terminates in those two fields respecting which Mr. Dockwrath the attorney became so irrationally angry at the period of which we are now immediately about to treat. These fields lie on the steep slope of Hamworth Hill, and through them runs the public path from the hamlet of Roxeth up to Hamworth church; for, as all the world knows, Hamworth church stands high, and is a landmark to the world for miles and miles around.

Within a circuit of thirty miles from London no land lies more beautifully circumstanced with regard to scenery than the country about Hamworth; and its most perfect loveliness commences just beyond the slopes of Orley Farm. There is a little village called Coldharbour, consisting of some half-dozen cottages, situated immediately outside Lady Mason's gate,—and it may as well be stated here that this gate is but three hundred yards from the house, and is guarded by no lodge. This village stands at the foot of Cleeve Hill. The land hereabouts ceases to be fertile, and breaks away into heath and common ground. Round the foot of the hill there are extensive woods, all of which belong to Sir Peregrine Orme, the lord of the manor. Sir Peregrine is not a rich man, not rich, that is, it being borne in mind that he is a baronet, that he represented his county in parliament for three or four sessions, and that his ancestors have owned The Cleeve estate for the last four hundred years; but he is by general repute the greatest man in these parts. We may expect to hear more of him also as the story makes its way.

I know many spots in England and in other lands, world-famous in regard to scenery, which to my eyes are hardly equal to Cleeve Hill. From the top of it you are told that you may see into seven counties; but to me that privilege never possessed any value. I should not care to see into seventeen counties, unless the country which spread itself before my view was fair and lovely. The country which is so seen from Cleeve Hill is exquisitely fair and lovely;—very fair, with glorious fields of unsurpassed fertility, and lovely with oak woods and brown open heaths which stretch away, hill after hill, down towards the southern coast. I could greedily fill a long chapter with the well-loved glories of Cleeve Hill; but it may be that we must press its heather with our feet more than once in the course of our present task, and if so, it will be well to leave something for those coming visits.

"Ungrateful! I'll let her know whether I owe her any gratitude. Haven't I paid her her rent every half-year as it came due? what more would she have? Ungrateful, indeed! She is one of those women who think that you ought to go down on your knees to them if they only speak civilly to you. I'll let her know whether I'm ungrateful."

These words were spoken by angry Mr. Samuel Dockwrath to his wife, as he stood up before his parlour-fire after breakfast, and the woman to whom he referred was Lady Mason. Mr. Samuel Dockwrath was very angry as he so spoke, or at any rate he seemed to be so. There are men who take a delight in abusing those special friends whom their wives best love, and Mr. Dockwrath was one of these. He had never given his cordial consent to the intercourse which had hitherto existed between the lady of Orley Farm and his household, although he had not declined the substantial benefits which had accompanied it. His pride had rebelled against the feeling of patronage, though his interest had submitted to the advantages thence derived. A family of sixteen children is a heavy burden for a country attorney with a small practice, even though his wife may have had a fortune of two thousand pounds; and thus Mr. Dockwrath, though he had never himself loved Lady Mason, had permitted his wife to accept all those numberless kindnesses which a lady with comfortable means and no children is always able to bestow on a favoured neighbour who has few means and many children. Indeed, he himself had accepted a great favour with reference to the holding of those two fields, and had acknowledged as much when first he took them into his hands some sixteen or seventeen years back. But all that was forgotten now; and having held them for so long a period, he bitterly felt the loss, and resolved that it would ill become him as a man and an attorney to allow so deep an injury to pass unnoticed. It may be, moreover, that Mr. Dockwrath was now doing somewhat better in the world than formerly, and that he could afford to give up Lady Mason, and to demand also that his wife should give her up. Those trumpery presents from Orley Farm were very well while he was struggling for bare bread, but now, now that he had turned the corner,—now that by his divine art and mystery of law he had managed to become master of that beautiful result of British perseverance, a balance at his banker's, he could afford to indulge his natural antipathy to a lady who had endeavoured in early life to divert from him the little fortune which had started him in the world.

Miriam Dockwrath, as she sat on this morning, listening to her husband's anger, with a sick little girl on her knee, and four or five others clustering round her, half covered with their matutinal bread and milk, was mild-eyed and soft as ever. Hers was a nature in which softness would ever prevail;—softness, and that tenderness of heart, always leaning, and sometimes almost crouching, of which a mild eye is the outward sign. But her comeliness and prettiness were gone. Female beauty of the sterner, grander sort may support the burden of sixteen children, all living,—and still survive. I have known it to do so, and to survive with much of its youthful glory. But that mild-eyed, soft, round, plumpy prettiness gives way beneath such a weight as that: years alone tell on it quickly; but children and limited means combined with years leave to it hardly a chance.

"I'm sure I'm very sorry," said the poor woman, worn with her many cares.

"Sorry; yes, and I'll make her sorry, the proud minx. There's an old saying, that those who live in glass houses shouldn't throw stones."

"But, Samuel, I don't think she means to be doing you any harm. You know she always did say— Don't, Bessy; how can you put your fingers into the basin in that way?"

"Sam has taken my spoon away, mamma."

"I'll let her know whether she's doing any harm or no. And what signifies what was said sixteen years ago? Has she anything to show in writing? As far as I know, nothing of the kind was said."

"Oh, I remember it, Samuel; I do indeed!"

"Let me tell you then that you had better not try to remember anything about it. If you ain't quiet, Bob, I'll make you, pretty quick; d'ye hear that? The fact is, your memory is not worth a curse. Where are you to get milk for all those children, do you think, when the fields are gone?"

"I'm sure I'm very sorry, Samuel."

"Sorry; yes, and somebody else shall be sorry too. And look here, Miriam, I won't have you going up to Orley Farm on any pretence whatever; do you hear that?" and then, having given that imperative command to his wife and slave, the lord and master of that establishment walked forth into his office.

On the whole Miriam Usbech might have done better had she followed the advice of her patroness in early life, and married the stupid clerk.

CHAPTER II
LADY MASON AND HER SON

I trust that it is already perceived by all persistent novel readers that very much of the interest of this tale will be centred in the person of Lady Mason. Such educated persons, however, will probably be aware that she is not intended to be the heroine. The heroine, so called, must by a certain fixed law be young and marriageable. Some such heroine in some future number shall be forthcoming, with as much of the heroic about her as may be found convenient; but for the present let it be understood that the person and character of Lady Mason is as important to us as can be those of any young lady, let her be ever so gracious or ever so beautiful.

In giving the details of her history, I do not know that I need go back beyond her grandfather and grandmother, who were thoroughly respectable people in the hardware line; I speak of those relatives by the father's side. Her own parents had risen in the world,—had risen from retail to wholesale, and considered themselves for a long period of years to be good representatives of the commercial energy and prosperity of Great Britain. But a fall had come upon them,—as a fall does come very often to our excellent commercial representatives—and Mr. Johnson was in the "Gazette." It would be long to tell how old Sir Joseph Mason was concerned in these affairs, how he acted as the principal assignee, and how ultimately he took to his bosom as his portion of the assets of the estate, young Mary Johnson, and made her his wife and mistress of Orley Farm. Of the family of the Johnsons there were but three others, the father, the mother, and a brother. The father did not survive the disgrace of his bankruptcy, and the mother in process of time settled herself with her son in one of the Lancashire manufacturing towns, where John Johnson raised his head in business to some moderate altitude, Sir Joseph having afforded much valuable assistance. There for the present we will leave them.

I do not think that Sir Joseph ever repented of the perilous deed he did in marrying that young wife. His home for many years had been desolate and solitary; his children had gone from him, and did not come to visit him very frequently in his poor home at the farm. They had become grander people than him, had been gifted with aspiring minds, and in every turn and twist which they took, looked to do something towards washing themselves clean from the dirt of the counting-house. This was specially the case with Sir Joseph's son, to whom the father had made over lands and money sufficient to enable him to come before the world as a country gentleman with a coat of arms on his coach-panel. It would be inconvenient for us to run off to Groby Park at the present moment, and I will therefore say no more just now as to Joseph junior, but will explain that Joseph senior was not made angry by this neglect. He was a grave, quiet, rational man, not however devoid of some folly; as indeed what rational man is so devoid? He was burdened with an ambition to establish a family as the result of his success in life; and having put forth his son into the world with these views, was content that that son should act upon them persistently. Joseph Mason, Esq., of Groby Park, in Yorkshire, was now a county magistrate, and had made some way towards a footing in the county society around him. With these hopes, and ambition such as this, it was probably not expedient that he should spend much of his time at Orley Farm. The three daughters were circumstanced much in the same way: they had all married gentlemen, and were bent on rising in the world; moreover, the steadfast resolution of purpose which characterised their father was known by them all,—and by their husbands: they had received their fortunes, with some settled contingencies to be forthcoming on their father's demise; why, then, trouble the old gentleman at Orley Farm?

Under such circumstances the old gentleman married his young wife,— to the great disgust of his four children. They of course declared to each other, corresponding among themselves by letter, that the old gentleman had positively disgraced himself. It was impossible that they should make any visits whatever to Orley Farm while such a mistress of the house was there;—and the daughters did make no such visits. Joseph, the son, whose monetary connection with his father was as yet by no means fixed and settled in its nature, did make one such visit, and then received his father's assurance—so at least he afterwards said and swore—that this marriage should by no means interfere with the expected inheritance of the Orley Farm acres. But at that time no young son had been born,—nor, probably, was any such young son expected.

The farm-house became a much brighter abode for the old man, for the few years which were left to him, after he had brought his young wife home. She was quiet, sensible, clever, and unremitting in her attention. She burthened him with no requests for gay society, and took his home as she found it, making the best of it for herself, and making it for him much better than he had ever hitherto known it. His own children had always looked down upon him, regarding him merely as a coffer from whence money might be had; and he, though he had never resented this contempt, had in a certain measure been aware of it. But there was no such feeling shown by his wife. She took the benefits which he gave her graciously and thankfully, and gave back to him in return, certainly her care and time, and apparently her love. For herself, in the way of wealth and money, she never asked for anything.

And then the baby had come, young Lucius Mason, and there was of course great joy at Orley Farm. The old father felt that the world had begun again for him, very delightfully, and was more than ever satisfied with his wisdom in regard to that marriage. But the very genteel progeny of his early youth were more than ever dissatisfied, and in their letters among themselves dealt forth harder and still harder words upon poor Sir Joseph. What terrible things might he not be expected to do now that his dotage was coming on? Those three married ladies had no selfish fears—so at least they declared, but they united in imploring their brother to look after his interests at Orley Farm. How dreadfully would the young heir of Groby be curtailed in his dignities and seignories if it should be found at the last day that Orley Farm was not to be written in his rent-roll!

And then, while they were yet bethinking themselves how they might best bestir themselves, news arrived that Sir Joseph had suddenly died. Sir Joseph was dead, and the will when read contained a codicil by which that young brat was made the heir to the Orley Farm estate. I have said that Lady Mason during her married life had never asked of her husband anything for herself; but in the law proceedings which were consequent upon Sir Joseph's death, it became abundantly evident that she had asked him for much for her son,—and that she had been specific in her requests, urging him to make a second heir, and to settle Orley Farm upon her own boy, Lucius. She herself stated that she had never done this except in the presence of a third person. She had often done so in the presence of Mr. Usbech the attorney,—as to which Mr. Usbech was not alive to testify; and she had also done so more than once in the presence of Mr. Furnival, a barrister,—as to which Mr. Furnival, being alive, did testify—very strongly.

As to that contest nothing further need now be said. It resulted in the favour of young Lucius Mason, and therefore, also, in the favour of the widow;—in the favour moreover of Miriam Usbech, and thus ultimately in the favour of Mr. Samuel Dockwrath, who is now showing himself to be so signally ungrateful. Joseph Mason, however, retired from the battle nothing convinced. His father, he said, had been an old fool, an ass, an idiot, a vulgar, ignorant fool; but he was not a man to break his word. That signature to the codicil might be his or might not. If his, it had been obtained by fraud. What could be easier than to cheat an old doting fool? Many men agreed with Joseph Mason, thinking that Usbech the attorney had perpetrated this villainy on behalf of his daughter; but Joseph Mason would believe, or say that he believed—a belief in which none but his sisters joined him,—that Lady Mason herself had been the villain. He was minded to press the case on to a Court of Appeal, up even to the House of Lords; but he was advised that in doing so he would spend more money than Orley Farm was worth, and that he would, almost to a certainty, spend it in vain. Under this advice he cursed the laws of his country, and withdrew to Groby Park.

Lady Mason had earned the respect of all those around her by the way in which she bore herself in the painful days of the trial, and also in those of her success,—especially also by the manner in which she gave her evidence. And thus, though she had not been much noticed by her neighbours during the short period of her married life, she was visited as a widow by many of the more respectable people round Hamworth. In all this she showed no feeling of triumph; she never abused her husband's relatives, or spoke much of the harsh manner in which she had been used. Indeed, she was not given to talk about her own personal affairs; and although, as I have said, many of her neighbours visited her, she did not lay herself out for society. She accepted and returned their attention, but for the most part seemed to be willing that the matter should so rest. The people around by degrees came to know her ways, they spoke to her when they met her, and occasionally went through the ceremony of a morning call; but did not ask her to their tea-parties, and did not expect to see her at picnic and archery meetings.

Among those who took her by the hand in the time of her great trouble was Sir Peregrine Orme of The Cleeve,—for such was the name which had belonged time out of mind to his old mansion and park. Sir Peregrine was a gentleman now over seventy years of age, whose family consisted of the widow of his only son, and the only son of that widow, who was of course the heir to his estate and title. Sir Peregrine was an excellent old man, as I trust may hereafter be acknowledged; but his regard for Lady Mason was perhaps in the first instance fostered by his extreme dislike to her stepson, Joseph Mason of Groby. Mr. Joseph Mason of Groby was quite as rich a man as Sir Peregrine, and owned an estate which was nearly as large as The Cleeve property; but Sir Peregrine would not allow that he was a gentleman, or that he could by any possible transformation become one. He had not probably ever said so in direct words to any of the Mason family, but his opinion on the matter had in some way worked its way down to Yorkshire, and therefore there was no love to spare between these two county magistrates. There had been a slight acquaintance between Sir Peregrine and Sir Joseph; but the ladies of the two families had never met till after the death of the latter. Then, while that trial was still pending, Mrs. Orme had come forward at the instigation of her father-in-law, and by degrees there had grown up an intimacy between the two widows. When the first offers of assistance were made and accepted, Sir Peregrine no doubt did not at all dream of any such result as this. His family pride, and especially the pride which he took in his widowed daughter-in-law, would probably have been shocked by such a surmise; but, nevertheless, he had seen the friendship grow and increase without alarm. He himself had become attached to Lady Mason, and had gradually learned to excuse in her that want of gentle blood and early breeding which as a rule he regarded as necessary to a gentleman, and from which alone, as he thought, could spring many of those excellences which go to form the character of a lady.

It may therefore be asserted that Lady Mason's widowed life was successful. That it was prudent and well conducted no one could doubt. Her neighbours of course did say of her that she would not drink tea with Mrs. Arkwright of Mount Pleasant villa because she was allowed the privilege of entering Sir Peregrine's drawing-room; but such little scandal as this was a matter of course. Let one live according to any possible or impossible rule, yet some offence will be given in some quarter. Those who knew anything of Lady Mason's private life were aware that she did not encroach on Sir Peregrine's hospitality. She was not at The Cleeve as much as circumstances would have justified, and at one time by no means so much as Mrs. Orme would have desired.

In person she was tall and comely. When Sir Joseph had brought her to his house she had been very fair,—tall, slight, fair, and very quiet,—not possessing that loveliness which is generally most attractive to men, because the beauty of which she might boast depended on form rather than on the brightness of her eye, or the softness of her cheek and lips. Her face too, even at that age, seldom betrayed emotion, and never showed signs either of anger or of joy. Her forehead was high, and though somewhat narrow, nevertheless gave evidence of considerable mental faculties; nor was the evidence false, for those who came to know Lady Mason well, were always ready to acknowledge that she was a woman of no ordinary power. Her eyes were large and well formed, but somewhat cold. Her nose was long and regular. Her mouth also was very regular, and her teeth perfectly beautiful; but her lips were straight and thin. It would sometimes seem that she was all teeth, and yet it is certain that she never made an effort to show them. The great fault of her face was in her chin, which was too small and sharp, thus giving on occasions something of meanness to her countenance. She was now forty-seven years of age, and had a son who had reached man's estate; and yet perhaps she had more of woman's beauty at this present time than when she stood at the altar with Sir Joseph Mason. The quietness and repose of her manner suited her years and her position; age had given fulness to her tall form; and the habitual sadness of her countenance was in fair accordance with her condition and character. And yet she was not really sad,—at least so said those who knew her. The melancholy was in her face rather than in her character, which was full of energy,—if energy may be quiet as well as assured and constant.

Of course she had been accused a dozen times of matrimonial prospects. What handsome widow is not so accused? The world of Hamworth had been very certain at one time that she was intent on marrying Sir Peregrine Orme. But she had not married, and I think I may say on her behalf that she had never thought of marrying. Indeed, one cannot see how such a woman could make any effort in that line. It was impossible to conceive that a lady so staid in her manner should be guilty of flirting; nor was there any man within ten miles of Hamworth who would have dared to make the attempt. Women for the most part are prone to love-making—as nature has intended that they should be; but there are women from whom all such follies seem to be as distant as skittles and beer are distant from the dignity of the Lord Chancellor. Such a woman was Lady Mason.

At this time—the time which is about to exist for us as the period at which our narrative will begin—Lucius Mason was over twenty-two years old, and was living at the farm. He had spent the last three or four years of his life in Germany, where his mother had visited him every year, and had now come home intending to be the master of his own destiny. His mother's care for him during his boyhood, and up to the time at which he became of age, had been almost elaborate in its thoughtfulness. She had consulted Sir Peregrine as to his school, and Sir Peregrine, looking to the fact of the lad's own property, and also to the fact, known by him, of Lady Mason's means for such a purpose, had recommended Harrow. But the mother had hesitated, had gently discussed the matter, and had at last persuaded the baronet that such a step would be injudicious. The boy was sent to a private school of a high character, and Sir Peregrine was sure that he had been so sent at his own advice. "Looking at the peculiar position of his mother," said Sir Peregrine to his young daughter-in-law, "at her very peculiar position, and that of his relatives, I think it will be better that he should not appear to assume anything early in life; nothing can be better conducted than Mr. Crabfield's establishment, and after much consideration I have had no hesitation in recommending her to send her son to him." And thus Lucius Mason had been sent to Mr. Crabfield, but I do not think that the idea originated with Sir Peregrine.

"And perhaps it will be as well," added the baronet, "that he and Perry should not be together at school, though I have no objection to their meeting in the holidays. Mr. Crabfield's vacations are always timed to suit the Harrow holidays." The Perry here mentioned was the grandson of Sir Peregrine—the young Peregrine who in coming days was to be the future lord of The Cleeve. When Lucius Mason was modestly sent to Mr. Crabfield's establishment at Great Marlow, young Peregrine Orme, with his prouder hopes, commenced his career at the public school.

Mr. Crabfield did his duty by Lucius Mason, and sent him home at seventeen a handsome, well-mannered lad, tall and comely to the eye, with soft brown whiskers sprouting on his cheek, well grounded in Greek, Latin, and Euclid, grounded also in French and Italian, and possessing many more acquirements than he would have learned at Harrow. But added to these, or rather consequent on them, was a conceit which public-school education would not have created. When their mothers compared them in the holidays, not openly with outspoken words, but silently in their hearts, Lucius Mason was found by each to be the superior both in manners and knowledge; but each acknowledged also that there was more of ingenuous boyhood about Peregrine Orme.

Peregrine Orme was a year the younger, and therefore his comparative deficiencies were not the cause of any intense sorrow at The Cleeve; but his grandfather would probably have been better satisfied—and perhaps also so would his mother—had he been less addicted to the catching of rats, and better inclined towards Miss Edgeworth's novels and Shakespeare's plays, which were earnestly recommended to him by the lady and the gentleman. But boys generally are fond of rats, and very frequently are not fond of reading; and therefore, all this having been duly considered, there was not much deep sorrow in those days at The Cleeve as to the boyhood of the heir.

But there was great pride at Orley Farm, although that pride was shown openly to no one. Lady Mason in her visits at The Cleeve said but little as to her son's present exeellences. As to his future career in life she did say much both to Sir Peregrine and to Mrs. Orme, asking the council of the one and expressing her fears to the other; and then, Sir Peregrine having given his consent, she sent the lad to Germany.

He was allowed to come of age without any special signs of manhood, or aught of the glory of property; although, in his case, that coming of age did put him into absolute possession of his inheritance. On that day, had he been so minded, he could have turned his mother out of the farm-house, and taken exclusive possession of the estate; but he did in fact remain in Germany for a year beyond this period, and returned to Orley Farm only in time to be present at the celebration of the twenty-first birthday of his friend Peregrine Orme. This ceremony, as may be surmised, was by no means slurred over without due rejoicing. The heir at the time was at Christchurch; but at such a period a slight interruption to his studies was not to be lamented. There had been Sir Peregrine Ormes in those parts ever since the days of James I; and indeed in days long antecedent to those there had been knights bearing that name, some of whom had been honourably beheaded for treason, others imprisoned for heresy; and one made away with on account of a supposed royal amour,—to the great glorification of all his descendants. Looking to the antecedents of the family, it was only proper that the coming of age of the heir should be duly celebrated; but Lucius Mason had had no antecedents; no great-great-grandfather of his had knelt at the feet of an improper princess; and therefore Lady Mason, though she had been at The Cleeve, had not mentioned the fact that on that very day her son had become a man. But when Peregrine Orme became a man—though still in his manhood too much devoted to rats—she gloried greatly in her quiet way, and whispered a hope into the baronet's ear that the young heir would not imitate the ambition of his ancestor. "No, by Jove! it would not do now at all," said Sir Peregrine, by no means displeased at the allusion.

And then that question as to the future life of Lucius Mason became one of great importance, and it was necessary to consult, not only Sir Peregrine Orme, but the young man himself. His mother had suggested to him first the law: the great Mr. Furnival, formerly of the home circuit, but now practising only in London, was her very special friend, and would give her and her son all possible aid in this direction. And what living man could give better aid than the great Mr. Furnival? But Lucius Mason would have none of the law. This resolve he pronounced very clearly while yet in Germany, whither his mother visited him, bearing with her a long letter written by the great Mr. Furnival himself. But nevertheless young Mason would have none of the law. "I have an idea," he said, "that lawyers are all liars." Whereupon his mother rebuked him for his conceited ignorance and want of charity; but she did not gain her point.

She had, however, another string to her bow. As he objected to be a lawyer, he might become a civil engineer. Circumstances had made Sir Peregrine Orme very intimate with the great Mr. Brown. Indeed, Mr. Brown was under great obligations to Sir Peregrine, and Sir Peregrine had promised to use his influence. But Lucius Mason said that civil engineers were only tradesmen of an upper class, tradesmen with intellects; and he, he said, wished to use his intellect, but he did not choose to be a tradesman. His mother rebuked him again, as well he deserved that she should,—and then asked him of what profession he himself had thought. "Philology," said he; "or as a profession, perhaps literature. I shall devote myself to philology and the races of man. Nothing considerable has been done with them as a combined pursuit." And with these views he returned home—while Peregrine Orme at Oxford was still addicted to the hunting of rats.

But with philology and the races of man he consented to combine the pursuit of agriculture. When his mother found that he wished to take up his abode in his own house, she by no means opposed him, and suggested that, as such was his intention, he himself should farm his own land. He was very ready to do this, and had she not represented that such a step was in every way impolitic, he would willingly have requested Mr. Greenwood of the Old Farm to look elsewhere, and have spread himself and his energies over the whole domain. As it was he contented himself with desiring that Mr. Dockwrath would vacate his small holding, and as he was imperative as to that his mother gave way without making it the cause of a battle. She would willingly have left Mr. Dockwrath in possession, and did say a word or two as to the milk necessary for those sixteen children. But Lucius Mason was ducal in his ideas, and intimated an opinion that he had a right to do what he liked with his own. Had not Mr. Dockwrath been told, when the fields were surrendered to him as a favour, that he would only have them in possession till the heir should come of age? Mr. Dockwrath had been so told; but tellings such as these are easily forgotten by men with sixteen children. And thus Mr. Mason became an agriculturist with special scientific views as to chemistry, and a philologist with the object of making that pursuit bear upon his studies with reference to the races of man. He was convinced that by certain admixtures of ammonia and earths he could produce cereal results hitherto unknown to the farming world, and that by tracing out the roots of words he could trace also the wanderings of man since the expulsion of Adam from the garden. As to the latter question his mother was not inclined to contradict him. Seeing that he would sit at the feet neither of Mr. Furnival nor of Mr. Brown, she had no objection to the races of man. She could endure to be talked to about the Oceanic Mongolidae and the Iapetidae of the Indo-Germanic class, and had perhaps her own ideas that such matters, though somewhat foggy, were better than rats. But when he came to the other subject, and informed her that the properly plentiful feeding of the world was only kept waiting for the chemists, she certainly did have her fears. Chemical agriculture is expensive; and though the results may possibly be remunerative, still, while we are thus kept waiting by the backwardness of the chemists, there must be much risk in making any serious expenditure with such views.

"Mother," he said, when he had now been at home about three months, and when the fiat for the expulsion of Samuel Dockwrath had already gone forth, "I shall go to Liverpool to-morrow."

"To Liverpool, Lucius?"

"Yes. That guano which I got from Walker is adulterated. I have analyzed it, and find that it does not contain above thirty-two and a half hundredths of—of that which it ought to hold in a proportion of seventy-five per cent. of the whole."

"Does it not?"

"No; and it is impossible to obtain results while one is working with such fictitious materials. Look at that bit of grass at the bottom of Greenwood's Hill."

"The fifteen-acre field? Why, Lucius, we always had the heaviest crops of hay in the parish off that meadow."

"That's all very well, mother; but you have never tried,—nobody about here ever has tried, what the land can really produce. I will throw that and the three fields beyond it into one; I will get Greenwood to let me have that bit of the hill-side, giving him compensation of course—"

"And then Dockwrath would want compensation."

"Dockwrath is an impertinent rascal, and I shall take an opportunity of telling him so. But as I was saying, I will throw those seventy acres together, and then I will try what will be the relative effects of guano and the patent blood, But I must have real guano, and so I shall go to Liverpool."

"I think I would wait a little, Lucius. It is almost too late for any change of that kind this year."

"Wait! Yes, and what has come of waiting? We don't wait at all in doubling our population every thirty-three years; but when we come to the feeding of them we are always for waiting. It is that waiting which has reduced the intellectual development of one half of the human race to its present terribly low state—or rather prevented its rising in a degree proportionate to the increase of the population. No more waiting for me, mother, if I can help it."

"But, Lucius, should not such new attempts as that be made by men with large capital?" said the mother.

"Capital is a bugbear," said the son, speaking on this matter quite *ex cathedrâ*, as no doubt he was entitled to do by his extensive reading at a German university—"capital is a bugbear. The capital that is really wanting is thought, mind, combination, knowledge."

"But, Lucius—"

"Yes, I know what you are going to say, mother. I don't boast that I possess all these things; but I do say that I will endeavour to obtain them."

"I have no doubt you will; but should not that come first?"

"That is waiting again. We all know as much as this, that good manure will give good crops if the sun be allowed full play upon the land, and nothing but the crop be allowed to grow. That is what I shall attempt at first, and there can be no great danger in that." And so he went to Liverpool.

Lady Mason during his absence began to regret that she had not left him in the undisturbed and inexpensive possession of the Mongolidae and the Iapetidae. His rent from the estate, including that which she would have paid him as tenant of the smaller farm, would have enabled him to live with all comfort; and, if such had been his taste, he might have become a philosophical student, and lived respectably without adding anything to his income by the sweat of his brow. But now the matter was likely to become serious enough. For a gentleman farmer determined to wait no longer for the chemists, whatever might be the results, an immediate profitable return per acre could not be expected as one of them. Any rent from that smaller farm would now be out of the question, and it would be well if the payments made so punctually by old Mr. Greenwood were not also swallowed up in the search after unadulterated guano. Who could tell whether in the pursuit of science he might not insist on chartering a vessel, himself, for the Peruvian coast?

CHAPTER III
THE CLEEVE

I have said that Sir Peregrine Orme was not a rich man, meaning thereby that he was not a rich man considering his acknowledged position in the county. Such men not uncommonly have their tens, twelves, and twenty thousands a year; but Sir Peregrine's estate did not give him above three or four. He was lord of the manor of Hamworth, and possessed seignorial rights, or rather the skeleton and remembrance of such rights with reference to a very large district of country; but his actual property—that from which he still received the substantial benefits of ownership—was not so large as those of some of his neighbours. There was, however, no place within the county which was so beautifully situated as The Cleeve, or which had about it so many of the attractions of age. The house itself had been built at two periods,—a new set of rooms having been added to the remains of the old Elizabethan structure in the time of Charles II. It had not about it anything that was peculiarly grand or imposing, nor were the rooms large or even commodious; but everything was old, venerable, and picturesque. Both the dining-room and the library were panelled with black wainscoating; and though the drawing-rooms were papered, the tall, elaborately-worked wooden chimney-pieces still stood in them, and a wooden band or belt round the rooms showed that the panels were still there, although hidden by the modern paper.

But it was for the beauty and wildness of its grounds that The Cleeve was remarkable. The land fell here and there into narrow, wild ravines and woody crevices. The soil of the park was not rich, and could give but little assistance to the chemists in supplying the plentiful food expected by Mr. Mason for the coming multitudes of the world; it produced in some parts heather instead of grass, and was as wild and unprofitable as Cleeve Common, which stretched for miles outside the park palings; but it seemed admirably adapted for deer and for the maintenance of half-decayed venerable oaks. Young timber also throve well about the place, and in this respect Sir Peregrine was a careful landlord. There ran a river through the park,—the River Cleeve, from which the place and parish are said to have taken their names;—a river, or rather a stream, very narrow and inconsiderable as to its volume of water, but which passed for some two miles through so narrow a passage as to give to it the appearance of a cleft or fissure in the rocks. The water tumbled over stones through this entire course, making it seem to be fordable almost everywhere without danger of wet feet; but in truth there was hardly a spot at which it could be crossed without a bold leap from rock to rock. Narrow as was the aperture through which the water had cut its way, nevertheless a path had been contrived now on one side of the stream and now on the other, crossing it here and there by slight hanging wooden bridges. The air here was always damp with spray, and the rocks on both sides were covered with long mosses, as were also the overhanging boughs of the old trees. This place was the glory of The Cleeve, and as far as picturesque beauty goes it was very glorious. There was a spot in the river from whence a steep path led down from the park to the water, and at this spot the deer would come to drink. I know nothing more beautiful than this sight, when three or four of them could be so seen from one of the wooden bridges towards the hour of sunset in the autumn.

Sir Peregrine himself at this time was an old man, having passed his seventieth year. He was a fine, handsome English gentleman with white hair, keen gray eyes, a nose slightly aquiline, and lips now too closely pressed together in consequence of the havoc which time had made among his teeth. He was tall, but had lost something of his height from stooping,— was slight in his form, but well made, and vain of the smallness of his feet and the whiteness of his hands. He was generous, quick tempered, and opinionated; generally very mild to those who would agree with him and submit to him, but intolerant of contradiction, and conceited as to his experience of the world and the wisdom which he had thence derived. To those who were manifestly his inferiors he was affable, to his recognised equals he was courteous, to women he was almost always gentle;—but to men who claimed an equality which he would not acknowledge, he could make himself particularly disagreeable. In judging the position which a man should hold in the world, Sir Peregrine was very resolute in ignoring all claims made by wealth alone. Even property in land could not in his eyes create a gentleman. A gentleman, according to his ideas, should at any rate have great-grandfathers capable of being traced in the world's history; and the greater the number of such, and the more easily traceable they might be on the world's surface, the more unquestionable would be the status of the claimant in question. Such being the case, it may be imagined that Joseph Mason, Esq., of Groby Park did not rank high in the estimation of Sir Peregrine Orme.

I have said that Sir Peregrine was fond of his own opinion; but nevertheless he was a man whom it was by no means difficult to lead. In the first place he was singularly devoid of suspicion. The word of a man or of a woman was to him always credible, until full proof had come home to him that it was utterly unworthy of credit. After that such a man or woman might as well spare all speech as regards the hope of any effect on the mind of Sir Peregrine Orme. He did not easily believe a fellow-creature to be a liar, but a liar to him once was a liar always. And then he was amenable to flattery, and few that are so are proof against the leading-strings of their flatterers. All this was well understood of Sir Peregrine by those about him. His gardener, his groom, and his woodman all knew his foibles. They all loved him, respected him, and worked for him faithfully; but each of them had his own way in his own branch.

And there was another person at The Cleeve who took into her own hands a considerable share of the management and leading of Sir Peregrine, though, in truth, she made no efforts in that direction. This was Mrs. Orme, the widow of his only child, and the mother of his heir. Mrs. Orme was a younger woman than Mrs. Mason of Orley Farm by nearly five years, though her son was but twelve months junior to Lucius Mason. She had been the daughter of a brother baronet, whose family was nearly as old as that of the Ormes; and therefore, though she had come penniless to her husband, Sir Peregrine had considered that his son had married well. She had been a great beauty, very small in size and delicate of limb, fair haired, with soft blue wondering eyes, and a dimpled cheek. Such she had been when young Peregrine Orme brought her home to The Cleeve, and the bride at once became the darling of her father-in-law. One year she had owned of married joy, and then all the happiness of the family had been utterly destroyed, and for the few following years there had been no sadder household in all the country-side than that of Sir Peregrine Orme. His son, his only son, the pride of all who knew him, the hope of his political party in the county, the brightest among the bright ones of the day for whom the world was just opening her richest treasures, fell from his horse as he was crossing into a road, and his lifeless body was brought home to The Cleeve.

All this happened now twenty years since, but the widow still wears the colours of mourning. Of her also the world of course said that she would soon console herself with a second love; but she too has given the world the lie. From that day to the present she has never left the house of her father-in-law; she has been a true child to him, and she has enjoyed all a child's privileges. There has been but little favour for any one at The Cleeve who has been considered by the baronet to disregard the wishes of the mistress of the establishment. Any word from her has been law to him, and he has of course expected also that her word should be law to others. He has yielded to her in all things, and attended to her will as though she were a little queen, recognizing in her feminine weakness a sovereign power, as some men can and do; and having thus for years indulged himself in a quixotic gallantry to the lady of his household, he has demanded of others that they also should bow the knee.

During the last twenty years The Cleeve has not been a gay house. During the last ten those living there have been contented, and in the main happy; but there has seldom been many guests in the old hall, and Sir Peregrine has not been fond of going to other men's feasts. He inherited the property very early in life, and then there were on it some few encumbrances. While yet a young man he added something to these, and now, since his own son's death, he has been setting his house in order, that his grandson should receive the family acres intact. Every shilling due on the property has been paid off; and it is well that this should be so, for there is reason to fear that the heir will want a helping hand out of some of youth's difficulties, — perhaps once or twice before his passion for rats gives place to a good English gentleman-like resolve to hunt twice a week, look after his timber, and live well within his means.

The chief fault in the character of young Peregrine Orme was that he was so young. There are men who are old at one-and-twenty, —are quite fit for Parliament, the magistrate's bench, the care of a wife, and even for that much sterner duty, the care of a balance at the bankers; but there are others who at that age are still boys, —whose inner persons and characters have not begun to clothe themselves with the "toga virilis." I am not sure that those whose boyhoods are so protracted have the worst of it, if in this hurrying and competitive age they can be saved from being absolutely trampled in the dust before they are able to do a little trampling on their own account. Fruit that grows ripe the quickest is not the sweetest; nor when housed and garnered will it keep the longest. For young Peregrine there was no need of competitive struggles. The days have not yet come, though they are no doubt coming, when "detur digniori" shall be the rule of succession to all titles, honours, and privileges whatsoever. Only think what a life it would give to the education of the country in general, if any lad from seventeen to twenty-one could go in for a vacant dukedom; and if a goodly inheritance could be made absolutely incompatible with incorrect spelling and doubtful proficiency in rule of three!

Luckily for Peregrine junior these days are not yet at hand, or I fear that there would be little chance for him. While Lucius Mason was beginning to think that the chemists might be hurried, and that agriculture might be beneficially added to philology, our friend Peregrine had just been rusticated, and the head of his college had intimated to the baronet that it would be well to take the young man's name off the college books. This accordingly had been done, and the heir of The Cleeve was at present at home with his mother and grandfather. What special act of grace had led to this severity we need not inquire, but we may be sure that the frolics of which he had been guilty had been essentially young in their nature. He had assisted in driving a farmer's sow into the man's best parlour, or had daubed the top of the tutor's cap with white paint, or had perhaps given liberty to a bag full of rats in the college hall at dinner-time. Such were the youth's academical amusements, and as they were pursued with unremitting energy it was thought well that he should be removed from Oxford.

Then had come the terrible question of his university bills. One after another, half a score of them reached Sir Peregrine, and then took place that terrible interview,—such as most young men have had to undergo at least once,—in which he was asked how he intended to absolve himself from the pecuniary liabilities which he had incurred.

"I am sure I don't know," said young Orme, sadly.

"But I shall be glad, sir, if you will favour me with your intentions," said Sir Peregrine, with severity. "A gentleman does not, I presume, send his orders to a tradesman without having some intention of paying him for his goods."

Sir Peregrine and his heir.

"I intended that they should all be paid, of course."

"And how, sir? by whom?"

"Well, sir,—I suppose I intended that you should pay them;" and the scapegrace as he spoke looked full up into the baronet's face with his bright blue eyes,—not impudently, as though defying his grandfather, but with a bold confidence which at once softened the old man's heart.

Sir Peregrine turned away and walked twice the length of the library; then, returning to the spot where the other stood, he put his hand on his grandson's shoulder. "Well, Peregrine, I will pay them," he said. "I have no doubt that you did so intend when you incurred them;—and that was perhaps natural. I will pay them; but for your own sake, and for your dear mother's sake, I hope that they are not very heavy. Can you give me a list of all that you owe?"

Young Peregrine said that he thought he could, and sitting down at once he made a clean breast of it. With all his foibles, follies, and youthful ignorances, in two respects he stood on good ground. He was neither false nor a coward. He continued to scrawl down items as long as there were any of which he could think, and then handed over the list in order that his grandfather might add them up. It was the last he ever heard of the matter; and when he revisited Oxford some twelve months afterwards, the tradesmen whom he had honoured with his custom bowed to him as low as though he had already inherited twenty thousand a year.

Peregrine Orme was short in stature as was his mother, and he also had his mother's wonderfully bright blue eyes; but in other respects he was very like his father and grandfather;—very like all the Ormes who had lived for ages past. His hair was light; his forehead was not large, but well formed and somewhat prominent; his nose had something, though not much, of the eagle's beak; his mouth was handsome in its curve, and his teeth were good, and his chin was divided by a deep dimple. His figure was not only short, but stouter than that of the Ormes in general. He was very strong on his legs; he could wrestle, and box, and use the single-stick with a quickness and precision that was the terror of all the freshmen who had come in his way.

Mrs. Orme, his mother, no doubt thought that he was perfect. Looking at the reflex of her own eyes in his, and seeing in his face so sweet a portraiture of the nose and mouth and forehead of him whom she had loved so dearly and lost so soon, she could not but think him perfect. When she was told that the master of Lazarus had desired that her son should be removed from his college, she had accused the tyrant of unrelenting, persecuting tyranny; and the gentle arguments of Sir Peregrine had no effect towards changing her ideas. On that disagreeable matter of the bills little or nothing was said to her. Indeed, money was a subject with which she was never troubled. Sir Peregrine conceived that money was a man's business, and that the softness of a woman's character should be preserved by a total absence of all pecuniary thoughts and cares.

And then there arose at The Cleeve a question as to what should immediately be done with the heir. He himself was by no means so well prepared with an answer as had been his friend Lucius Mason. When consulted by his grandfather, he said that he did not know. He would do anything that Sir Peregrine wished. Would Sir Peregrine think it well that he should prepare himself for the arduous duties of a master of hounds? Sir Peregrine did not think this at all well, but it did not appear that he himself was prepared with any immediate proposition. Then Peregrine discussed the matter with his mother, explaining that he had hoped at any rate to get the next winter's hunting with the H.H.;—which letters have represented the Hamworth Fox Hunt among sporting men for many years past. To this his mother made no objection, expressing a hope, however, that he would go abroad in the spring. "Home-staying youths have ever homely wits," she said to him, smiling on him ever so sweetly.

"That's quite true, mother," he said. "And that's why I should like to go to Leicestershire this winter." But going to Leicestershire this winter was out of the question.

CHAPTER IV
THE PERILS OF YOUTH

Going to Leicestershire was quite out of the question for young Orme at this period of his life, but going to London unfortunately was not so. He had become acquainted at Oxford with a gentleman of great skill in his peculiar line of life, whose usual residence was in the metropolis; and so great had been the attraction found in the character and pursuits of this skilful gentleman, that our hero had not been long at The Cleeve, after his retirement from the university, before he visited his friend. Cowcross Street, Smithfield, was the site of this professor's residence, the destruction of rats in a barrel was his profession, and his name was Carroty Bob. It is not my intention to introduce the reader to Carroty Bob in person, as circumstances occurred about this time which brought his intimacy with Mr. Orme to an abrupt conclusion. It would be needless to tell how our hero was induced to back a certain terrier, presumed to be the pride of Smithfield; how a great match came off, second only in importance to a contest for the belt of England; how money was lost and quarrels arose, and how Peregrine Orme thrashed one sporting gent within an inch of his life, and fought his way out of Carroty Bob's house at twelve o'clock at night. The tale of the row got into the newspapers, and of course reached The Cleeve. Sir Peregrine sent for his grandson into his study, and insisted on knowing everything;—how much money there was to pay, and what chance there might be of an action and damages. Of an action and damages there did not seem to be any chance, and the amount of money claimed was not large. Rats have this advantage, that they usually come cheaper than race-horses; but then, as Sir Peregrine felt sorely, they do not sound so well.

"Do you know, sir, that you are breaking your mother's heart?" said Sir Peregrine, looking very sternly at the young man—as sternly as he was able to look, let him do his worst.

Peregrine the younger had a very strong idea that he was not doing anything of the kind. He had left her only a quarter of an hour since; and though she had wept during the interview, she had forgiven him with many caresses, and had expressed her opinion that the chief fault had lain with Carroty Bob and those other wretched people who had lured her dear child into their villainous den. She had altogether failed to conceal her pride at his having fought his way out from among them, and had ended by supplying his pocket out of her own immediate resources. "I hope not, sir," said Peregrine the younger, thinking over some of these things.

"But you will, sir, if you go on with this shameless career. I do not speak of myself. I do not expect you to sacrifice your tastes for me; but I did think that you loved your mother!"

"So I do;—and you too."

"I am not speaking about myself sir. When I think what your father was at your age;—how nobly—" And then the baronet was stopped in his speech, and wiped his eyes with his handkerchief. "Do you think that your father, sir, followed such pursuits as these? Do you think that he spent his time in the pursuit of—rats?"

"Well; I don't know; I don't think he did. But I have heard you say, sir, that you sometimes went to cockfights when you were young."

"To cockfights! well, yes. But let me tell you, sir, that I always went in the company of gentlemen—that is, when I did go, which was very seldom." The baronet in some after-dinner half-hour had allowed this secret of his youth to escape from him, imprudently.

"And I went to the house in Cowcross Street with Lord John Fitzjoly."

"The last man in all London with whom you ought to associate! But I am not going to argue with you, sir. If you think, and will continue to think, that the slaughtering of vermin is a proper pursuit—"

"But, sir, foxes are vermin also."

"Hold your tongue, sir, and listen to me. You know very well what I mean, sir. If you think that—rats are a proper pursuit for a gentleman in your sphere of life, and if all that I can say has no effect in changing your opinion—I shall have done. I have not many years of life before me, and when I shall be no more, you can squander the property in any vile pursuits that may be pleasing to you. But, sir, you shall not do it while I am living; nor, if I can help it, shall you rob your mother of such peace of mind as is left for her in this world. I have only one alternative for you, sir—." Sir Peregrine did not stop to explain what might be the other branch of this alternative. "Will you give me your word of honour as a gentleman that you will never again concern yourself in this disgusting pursuit?"

"Never, grandfather!" said Peregrine, solemnly.

Sir Peregrine before he answered bethought himself that any pledge given for a whole life-time must be foolish; and he bethought himself also that if he could wean his heir from rats for a year or so, the taste would perish from lack of nourishment. "I will say for two years," said Sir Peregrine, still maintaining his austere look.

"For two years!" repeated Peregrine the younger; "and this is the fourth of October."

"Yes, sir; for two years," said the baronet, more angry than ever at the young man's pertinacity, and yet almost amused at his grandson's already formed resolve to go back to his occupation at the first opportunity allowed.

"Couldn't you date it from the end of August, sir? The best of the matches always come off in September."

"No, sir; I will not date it from any other time than the present. Will you give me your word of honour as a gentleman, for two years?"

Peregrine thought over the proposition for a minute or two in sad anticipation of all that he was to lose, and then slowly gave his adhesion to the terms. "Very well, sir;—for two years." And then he took out his pocket-book and wrote in it slowly.

It was at any rate manifest that he intended to keep his word, and that was much; so Sir Peregrine accepted the promise for what it was worth. "And now," said he, "if you have got nothing better to do, we will ride down to Crutchley Wood."

"I should like it of all things," said his grandson.

"Samson wants me to cut a new bridle-path through from the larches at the top of the hill down to Crutchley Bottom; but I don't think I'll have it done. Tell Jacob to let us have the nags; I'll ride the gray pony. And ask your mother if she'll ride with us."

It was the manner of Sir Peregrine to forgive altogether when he did forgive; and to commence his forgiveness in all its integrity from the first moment of the pardon. There was nothing he disliked so much as being on bad terms with those around him, and with none more so than with his grandson. Peregrine well knew how to make himself pleasant to the old man, and when duly encouraged would always do so. And thus the family party, as they rode on this occasion through the woods of The Cleeve, discussed oaks and larches, beech and birches, as though there were no such animal as a rat in existence, and no such place known as Cowcross Street.

"Well, Perry, as you and Samson are both of one mind, I suppose the path must be made," said Sir Peregrine, as he got off his horse at the entrance of the stable-yard, and prepared to give his feeble aid to Mrs. Orme.

Shortly after this the following note was brought up to The Cleeve by a messenger from Orley Farm:—

> My dear Sir Peregrine,
>
> If you are quite disengaged at twelve o'clock to-morrow, I will walk over to The Cleeve at that hour. Or if it would suit you better to call here as you are riding, I would remain within till you come. I want your kind advice on a certain matter.
>
> Most sincerely yours,
>
> Mary Mason.
>
> Thursday.

Lady Mason, when she wrote this note, was well aware that it would not be necessary for her to go to The Cleeve. Sir Peregrine's courtesy would not permit him to impose any trouble on a lady when the alternative of taking that trouble on himself was given to him. Moreover, he liked to have some object for his daily ride; he liked to be consulted "on certain matters;" and he especially liked being so consulted by Lady Mason. So he sent word back that he would be at the farm at twelve on the following day, and exactly at that hour his gray pony or cob might have been seen slowly walking up the avenue to the farm-house.

The Cleeve was not distant from Orley Farm more than two miles by the nearest walking-path, although it could not be driven much under five. With any sort of carriage one was obliged to come from The Cleeve House down to the lodge on the Hamworth and Alston road, and then to drive through the town of Hamworth, and so back to the farm. But in walking one would take the path along the river for nearly a mile, thence rise up the hill to the top of Crutchley Wood, descend through the wood to Crutchley Bottom, and, passing along the valley, come out at the foot of Cleeve Hill, just opposite to Orley Farm Gate. The distance for a horseman was somewhat greater, seeing that there was not as yet any bridle-way through Crutchley Wood. Under these circumstances the journey between the two houses was very frequently made on foot; and for those walking from The Cleeve House to Hamworth the nearest way was by Lady Mason's gate.

Lady Mason's drawing-room was very pretty, though it was by no means fashionably furnished. Indeed, she eschewed fashion in all things, and made no pretence of coming out before the world as a great lady. She had never kept any kind of carriage, though her means, combined with her son's income, would certainly have justified her in a pony-chaise. Since Lucius had become master of the house he had presented her with such a vehicle, and also with the pony and harness complete; but as yet she had never used it, being afraid, as she said to him with a smile, of appearing ambitious before the stern citizens of Hamworth. "Nonsense, mother," he had replied, with a considerable amount of young dignity in his face. "We are all entitled to those comforts for which we can afford to pay without injury to any one. I shall take it ill of you if I do not see you using it."

"Oh, Sir Peregrine, this is so kind of you," said Lady Mason, coming forward to meet her friend. She was plainly dressed, without any full exuberance of costume, and yet everything about her was neat and pretty, and everything had been the object of feminine care. A very plain dress may occasion as much study as the most elaborate, — and may be quite as worthy of the study it has caused. Lady Mason, I am inclined to think, was by no means indifferent to the subject, but then to her belonged the great art of hiding her artifice.

"Not at all; not at all," said Sir Peregrine, taking her hand and pressing it, as he always did. "What is the use of neighbours if they are not neighbourly?" This was all very well from Sir Peregrine in the existing case; but he was not a man who by any means recognised the necessity of being civil to all who lived near him. To the great and to the poor he was neighbourly; but it may be doubted whether he would have thought much of Lady Mason if she had been less good looking or less clever.

"Ah! I know how good you always are to me. But I'll tell you why I am troubling you now. Lucius went off two days since to Liverpool."

"My grandson told me that he had left home."

"He is an excellent young man, and I am sure that I have every reason to be thankful." Sir Peregrine, remembering the affair in Cowcross Street, and certain other affairs of a somewhat similar nature, thought that she had; but for all that he would not have exchanged his own bright-eyed lad for Lucius Mason with all his virtues and all his learning.

"And indeed I am thankful," continued the widow. "Nothing can be better than his conduct and mode of life; but—"

"I hope he has no attraction at Liverpool, of which you disapprove."

"No, no; there is nothing of that kind. His attraction is —; but perhaps I had better explain the whole matter. Lucius, you know, has taken to farming."

"He has taken up the land which you held yourself, has he not?"

"Yes, and a little more; and he is anxious to add even to that. He is very energetic about it, Sir Peregrine."

"Well; the life of a gentleman farmer is not a bad one; though in his special circumstances I would certainly have recommended a profession."

"Acting upon your advice I did urge him to go to the bar. But he has a will of his own, and a mind altogether made up as to the line of life which he thinks will suit him best. What I fear now is, that he will spend more money upon experiments than he can afford."

"Experimental farming is an expensive amusement," said Sir Peregrine, with a very serious shake of his head.

"I am afraid it is; and now he has gone to Liverpool to buy — guano," said the widow, feeling some little shame in coming to so inconsiderable a conclusion after her somewhat stately prologue.

"To buy guano! Why could he not get his guano from Walker, as my man Symonds does?"

"He says it is not good. He analyzed it, and —"

"Fiddlestick! Why didn't he order it in London, if he didn't like Walker's. Gone to Liverpool for guano! I'll tell you what it is, Lady Mason; if he intends to farm his land in that way, he should have a very considerable capital at his back. It will be a long time before he sees his money again." Sir Peregrine had been farming all his life, and had his own ideas on the subject. He knew very well that no gentleman, let him set to work as he might with his own land, could do as well with it as a farmer who must make a living out of his farming besides paying the rent; — who must do that or else have no living; and he knew also that such operations as those which his young friend was now about to attempt was an amusement fitted only for the rich. It may be also that he was a little old-fashioned, and therefore prejudiced against new combinations between agriculture and chemistry. "He must put a stop to that kind of work very soon, Lady Mason; he must indeed; or he will bring himself to ruin—and you with him."

Lady Mason's face became very grave and serious. "But what can I say to him, Sir Peregrine? In such a matter as that I am afraid that he would not mind me. If you would not object to speaking to him?"

Sir Peregrine was graciously pleased to say that he would not object. It was a disagreeable task, he said, that of giving advice to a young man who was bound by no tie either to take it or even to receive it with respect.

"You will not find him at all disrespectful; I think I can promise that," said the frightened mother; and that matter was ended by a promise on the part of the baronet to take the case in hand, and to see Lucius immediately on his return from Liverpool. "He had better come and dine at The Cleeve," said Sir Peregrine, "and we will have it out after dinner." All of which made Lady Mason very grateful.

CHAPTER V
SIR PEREGRINE MAKES A SECOND PROMISE

We left Lady Mason very grateful at the end of the last chapter for the promise made to her by Sir Peregrine with reference to her son; but there was still a weight on Lady Mason's mind. They say that the pith of a lady's letter is in the postscript, and it may be that that which remained for Lady Mason to say, was after all the matter as to which she was most anxious for assistance. "As you are here," she said to the baronet, "would you let me mention another subject?"

"Surely," said he, again putting down his hat and riding-stick.

Sir Peregrine was not given to close observation of those around him, or he might have seen by the heightened colour of the lady's face, and by the slight nervous hesitation with which she began to speak, that she was much in earnest as to this other matter. And had he been clever in his powers of observation he might have seen also that she was anxious to hide this feeling. "You remember the circumstances of that terrible lawsuit?" she said, at last.

"What; as to Sir Joseph's will? Yes; I remember them well."

"I know that I shall never forget all the kindness that you showed me," said she. "I don't know how I should have lived through it without you and dear Mrs. Orme."

"But what about it now?"

"I fear I am going to have further trouble."

"Do you mean that the man at Groby Park is going to try the case again? It is not possible after such a lapse of time. I am no lawyer, but I do not think that he can do it."

"I do not know—I do not know what he intends, or whether he intends anything; but I am sure of this,—that he will give me trouble if he can. But I will tell you the whole story, Sir Peregrine. It is not much, and perhaps after all may not be worth attention. You know the attorney in Hamworth who married Miriam Usbech?"

"What, Samuel Dockwrath? Oh, yes; I know him well enough; and to tell the truth I do not think very well of him. Is he not a tenant of yours?"

"Not at present." And then Lady Mason explained the manner in which the two fields had been taken out of the lawyer's hands by her son's order.

"Ah! he was wrong there," said the baronet. "When a man has held land so long it should not be taken away from him except under pressing circumstances; that is if he pays his rent."

"Mr. Dockwrath did pay his rent, certainly; and now, I fear, he is determined to do all he can to injure us."

"But what injury can Mr. Dockwrath do you?"

"I do not know, but he has gone down to Yorkshire,—to Mr. Mason's place; I know that; and he was searching through some papers of old Mr. Usbech's before he went. Indeed, I may say that I know as a fact that he has gone to Mr. Mason with the hope that these law proceedings may be brought on again."

"You know it as a fact?"

"I think I may say so."

"But, dear Lady Mason, may I ask you how you know this as a fact?"

"His wife was with me yesterday," she said, with some feeling of shame as she disclosed the source from whence she had obtained her information.

"And did she tell the tale against her own husband?"

"Not as meaning to say anything against him, Sir Peregrine; you must not think so badly of her as that; nor must you think that I would willingly obtain information in such a manner. But you must understand that I have always been her friend; and when she found that Mr. Dockwrath had left home on a matter in which I am so nearly concerned, I cannot but think it natural that she should let me know."

To this Sir Peregrine made no direct answer. He could not quite say that he thought it was natural, nor could he give any expressed approval of any such intercourse between Lady Mason and the attorney's wife. He thought it would be better that Mr. Dockwrath should be allowed to do his worst, if he had any intention of doing evil, and that Lady Mason should pass it by without condescending to notice the circumstance. But he made allowances for her weakness, and did not give utterance to his disapproval in words.

"I know you think that I have done wrong," she then said, appealing to him; and there was a tone of sorrow in her voice which went to his heart.

"No, not wrong; I cannot say that you have done wrong. It may be a question whether you have done wisely."

"Ah! if you only condemn my folly, I will not despair. It is probable I may not have done wisely, seeing that I had not you to direct me. But what shall I do now? Oh, Sir Peregrine, say that you will not desert me if all this trouble is coming on me again!"

"No, I will not desert you, Lady Mason; you may be sure of that."

"Dearest friend!"

"But I would advise you to take no notice whatever of Mr. Dockwrath and his proceedings. I regard him as a person entirely beneath your notice, and if I were you I should not move at all in this matter unless I received some legal summons which made it necessary for me to do so. I have not the honour of any personal acquaintance with Mr. Mason of Groby Park." It was in this way that Sir Peregrine always designated his friend's stepson — "but if I understand the motives by which he may probably be actuated in this or in any other matter, I do not think it likely that he will expend money on so very unpromising a case."

"He would do anything for vengeance."

"I doubt if he would throw away his money even for that, unless he were very sure of his prey. And in this matter, what can he possibly do? He has the decision of the jury against him, and at the time he was afraid to carry the case up to a court of appeal."

"But, Sir Peregrine, it is impossible to know what documents he may have obtained since that."

"What documents can do you any harm;—unless, indeed, there should turn out to be a will subsequent to that under which your son inherits the property?"

"Oh, no; there was no subsequent will."

"Of course there was not; and therefore you need not frighten yourself. It is just possible that some attempt may be made now that your son is of age, but I regard even that as improbable."

"And you would not advise me then to say anything to Mr. Furnival?"

"No; certainly not—unless you receive some legal notice which may make it necessary for you to consult a lawyer. Do nothing; and if Mrs. Dockwrath comes to you again, tell her that you are not disposed to take any notice of her information. Mrs. Dockwrath is, I am sure, a very good sort of woman. Indeed I have always heard so. But, if I were you, I don't think that I should feel inclined to have much conversation with her about my private affairs. What you tell her you tell also to her husband." And then the baronet, having thus spoken words of wisdom, sat silent in his arm-chair; and Lady Mason, still looking into his face, remained silent also for a few minutes.

"I am so glad I asked you to come," she then said.

"I am delighted, if I have been of any service to you."

"Of any service! oh, Sir Peregrine, you cannot understand what it is to live alone as I do,—for of course I cannot trouble Lucius with these matters; nor can a man, gifted as you are, comprehend how a woman can tremble at the very idea that those law proceedings may possibly be repeated."

Sir Peregrine could not but remember as he looked at her that during all those law proceedings, when an attack was made, not only on her income but on her honesty, she had never seemed to tremble. She had always been constant to herself, even when things appeared to be going against her. But years passing over her head since that time had perhaps told upon her courage.

"But I will fear nothing now, as you have promised that you will still be my friend."

"You may be very sure of that, Lady Mason. I believe that I may fairly boast that I do not easily abandon those whom I have once regarded with esteem and affection; among whom Lady Mason will, I am sure, allow me to say that she is reckoned as by no means the least." And then taking her hand, the old gentleman bowed over it and kissed it.

"My dearest, dearest friend!" said she; and lifting Sir Peregrine's beautifully white hand to her lips she also kissed that. It will be remembered that the gentleman was over seventy, and that this pretty scene could therefore be enacted without impropriety on either side. Sir Peregrine then went, and as he passed out of the door Lady Mason smiled on him very sweetly. It is quite true that he was over seventy; but nevertheless the smile of a pretty woman still had charms for him, more especially if there was a tear in her eye the while;—for Sir Peregrine Orme had a soft heart.

As soon as the door was closed behind him Lady Mason seated herself in her accustomed chair, and all trace of the smile vanished from her face. She was alone now, and could allow her countenance to be a true index of her mind. If such was the case her heart surely was very sad. She sat there perfectly still for nearly an hour, and during the whole of that time there was the same look of agony on her brow. Once or twice she rubbed her hands across her forehead, brushing back her hair, and showing, had there been any one by to see it, that there was many a gray lock there mixed with the brown hairs. Had there been any one by, she would, it may be surmised, have been more careful.

There was no smile in her face now, neither was there any tear in her eye. The one and the other emblem were equally alien to her present mood. But there was sorrow at her heart, and deep thought in her mind. She knew that her enemies were conspiring against her,—against her and against her son; and what steps might she best take in order that she might baffle them?

**There was sorrow in her heart, and
deep thought in her mind.**

"I have got that woman on the hip now." Those were the words which Mr. Dockwrath had uttered into his wife's ears, after two days spent in searching through her father's papers. The poor woman had once thought of burning all those papers—in old days before she had become Mrs. Dockwrath. Her friend, Lady Mason, had counselled her to do so, pointing out to her that they were troublesome, and could by no possibility lead to profit; but she had consulted her lover, and he had counselled her to burn nothing. "Would that she had been guided by her friend!" she now said to herself with regard to that old trunk, and perhaps occasionally with regard to some other things.

"I have got that woman on the hip at last!" and there had been a gleam of satisfaction in Samuel's eye as he uttered the words which had convinced his wife that it was not an idle threat. She knew nothing of what the box had contained; and now, even if it had not been kept safe from her under Samuel's private key, the contents which were of interest had of course gone. "I have business in the north, and shall be away for about a week," Mr. Dockwrath had said to her on the following morning.

"Oh, very well; then I'll put up your things," she had answered in her usual mild, sad, whining, household voice. Her voice at home was always sad and whining, for she was overworked, and had too many cares, and her lord was a tyrant to her rather than a husband.

"Yes, I must see Mr. Mason immediately. And look here, Miriam, I positively insist that you do not go to Orley Farm, or hold any intercourse whatever with Lady Mason. D'ye hear?"

Mrs. Dockwrath said that she did hear, and promised obedience. Mr. Dockwrath probably guessed that the moment his back was turned all would be told at the farm, and probably also had no real objection to her doing so. Had he in truth wished to keep his proceedings secret from Lady Mason he would not have divulged them to his wife. And then Mr. Dockwrath did start for the north, bearing certain documents with him; and soon after his departure Mrs. Dockwrath did pay a visit to Orley Farm.

Lady Mason sat there perfectly still for about an hour thinking what she would do. She had asked Sir Peregrine, and had the advantage of his advice; but that did not weigh much with her. What she wanted from Sir Peregrine was countenance and absolute assistance in the day of trouble,—not advice. She had desired to renew his interest in her favour, and to receive from him his assurance that he would not desert her; and that she had obtained. It was of course also necessary that she should consult him; but in turning over within her own mind this and that line of conduct, she did not, consciously, attach any weight to Sir Peregrine's opinion. The great question for her to decide was this;—should she put herself and her case into the hands of her friend Mr. Furnival now at once, or should she wait till she had received some certain symptom of hostile proceedings? If she did see Mr. Furnival, what could she tell him? Only this, that Mr. Dockwrath had found some document among the papers of old Mr. Usbech, and had gone off with the same to Groby Park in Yorkshire. What that document might be she was as ignorant as the attorney's wife.

When the hour was ended she had made up her mind that she would do nothing more in the matter, at any rate on that day.

CHAPTER VI
THE COMMERCIAL ROOM, BULL INN, LEEDS

Mr. Samuel Dockwrath was a little man, with sandy hair, a pale face, and stone-blue eyes. In judging of him by appearance only and not by the ear, one would be inclined to doubt that he could be a very sharp attorney abroad and a very persistent tyrant at home. But when Mr. Dockwrath began to talk, one's respect for him began to grow. He talked well and to the point, and with a tone of voice that could command where command was possible, persuade where persuasion was required, mystify when mystification was needed, and express with accuracy the tone of an obedient humble servant when servility was thought to be expedient. We will now accompany him on his little tour into Yorkshire.

Groby Park is about seven miles from Leeds, and as Mr. Dockwrath had in the first instance to travel from Hamworth up to London, he did not reach Leeds till late in the evening. It was a nasty, cold, drizzling night, so that the beauties and marvels of the large manufacturing town offered him no attraction, and at nine o'clock he had seated himself before the fire in the commercial room at The Bull, had called for a pair of public slippers, and was about to solace all his cares with a glass of mahogany-coloured brandy and water and a cigar. The room had no present occupant but himself, and therefore he was able to make the most of all its comforts. He had taken the solitary arm-chair, and had so placed himself that the gas would fall direct from behind his head on to that day's Leeds and Halifax Chronicle, as soon as he should choose to devote himself to local politics.

The waiter had looked at him with doubtful eyes when he asked to be shown into the commercial room, feeling all but confident that such a guest had no right to be there. He had no bulky bundles of samples, nor any of those outward characteristics of a commercial "gent" with which all men conversant with the rail and road are acquainted, and which the accustomed eye of a waiter recognises at a glance. And here it may be well to explain that ordinary travellers are in this respect badly treated by the customs of England, or rather by the hotel-keepers. All inn-keepers have commercial rooms, as certainly as they have taps and bars, but all of them do not have commercial rooms in the properly exclusive sense. A stranger, therefore, who has asked for and obtained his mutton-chop in the commercial room of The Dolphin, The Bear, and The George, not unnaturally asks to be shown into the same chamber at the King's Head. But the King's Head does a business with real commercials, and the stranger finds himself—out of his element.

"'Mercial, sir?" said the waiter at The Bull Inn, Leeds, to Mr. Dockwrath, in that tone of doubt which seemed to carry an answer to his own question. But Mr. Dockwrath was not a man to be put down by a waiter. "Yes," said he. "Didn't you hear me say so?" And then the waiter gave way. None of those lords of the road were in the house at the moment, and it might be that none would come that night.

Mr. Dockwrath had arrived by the 8.22 p.m. down, but the 8.45 p.m. up from the north followed quick upon his heels, and he had hardly put his brandy and water to his mouth before a rush and a sound of many voices were heard in the hall. There is a great difference between the entrance into an inn of men who are not known there and of men who are known. The men who are not known are shy, diffident, doubtful, and anxious to propitiate the chambermaid by great courtesy. The men who are known are loud, jocular, and assured;—or else, in case of deficient accommodation, loud, angry, and full of threats. The guests who had now arrived were well known, and seemed at present to be in the former mood. "Well, Mary, my dear, what's the time of day with you?" said a rough, bass voice, within the hearing of Mr. Dockwrath. "Much about the old tune, Mr. Moulder," said the girl at the bar. "Time to look alive and keep moving. Will you have them boxes up stairs, Mr. Kantwise?" and then there were a few words about the luggage, and two real commercial gentlemen walked into the room.

Mr. Dockwrath resolved to stand upon his rights, so he did not move his chair, but looked up over his shoulder at the new comers. The first man who entered was short and very fat;—so fat that he could not have seen his own knees for some considerable time past. His face rolled with fat, as also did all his limbs. His eyes were large, and bloodshot. He wore no beard, and therefore showed plainly the triple bagging of his fat chin. In spite of his overwhelming fatness, there was something in his face that was masterful and almost vicious. His body had been overcome by eating, but not as yet his spirit—one would be inclined to say. This was Mr. Moulder, well known on the road as being in the grocery and spirit line; a pushing man, who understood his business, and was well trusted by his firm in spite of his habitual intemperance. What did the firm care whether or no he killed himself by eating and drinking? He sold his goods, collected his money, and made his remittances. If he got drunk at night that was nothing to them, seeing that he always did his quota of work the next day. But Mr. Moulder did not get drunk. His brandy and water went into his blood, and into his eyes, and into his feet, and into his hands,—but not into his brain.

The other was a little square man in the hardware line, of the name of Kantwise. He disposed of fire-irons, grates, ovens, and kettles, and was at the present moment heavily engaged in the sale of certain newly-invented metallic tables and chairs lately brought out by the Patent Steel Furniture Company, for which Mr. Kantwise did business. He looked as though a skin rather too small for the purpose had been drawn over his head and face so that his forehead and cheeks and chin were tight and shiny. His eyes were small and green, always moving about in his head, and were seldom used by Mr. Kantwise in the ordinary way. At whatever he looked he looked sideways; it was not that he did not look you in the face, but he always looked at you with a sidelong glance, never choosing to have you straight in front of him. And the more eager he was in conversation— the more anxious he might be to gain his point, the more he averted his face and looked askance; so that sometimes he would prefer to have his antagonist almost behind his shoulder. And then as he did this, he would thrust forward his chin, and having looked at you round the corner till his eyes were nearly out of his head, he would close them both and suck in his lips, and shake his head with rapid little shakes, as though he were saying to himself, "Ah, sir! you're a bad un, a very bad un." His nose—for I should do Mr. Kantwise injustice if I did not mention this feature—seemed to have been compressed almost into nothing by that skin-squeezing operation. It was long enough, taking the measurement down the bridge, and projected sufficiently, counting the distance from the upper lip; but it had all the properties of a line; it possessed length without breadth. There was nothing in it from side to side. If you essayed to pull it, your fingers would meet. When I shall have also said that the hair on Mr. Kantwise's head stood up erect all round to the height of two inches, and that it was very red, I shall have been accurate enough in his personal description.

That Mr. Moulder represented a firm good business, doing tea, coffee, and British brandy on a well-established basis of capital and profit, the travelling commercial world in the north of England was well aware. No one entertained any doubt about his employers, Hubbles and Grease of Houndsditch. Hubbles and Grease were all right, as they had been any time for the last twenty years. But I cannot say that there was quite so strong a confidence felt in the Patent Steel Furniture Company generally, or in the individual operations of Mr. Kantwise in particular. The world in Yorkshire and Lancashire was doubtful about metallic tables, and it was thought that Mr. Kantwise was too eloquent in their praise.

Mr. Moulder when he had entered the room, stood still, to enable the waiter to peel off from him his greatcoat and the large shawl with which his neck was enveloped, and Mr. Kantwise performed the same operation for himself, carefully folding up the articles of clothing as he took them off. Then Mr. Moulder fixed his eyes on Mr. Dockwrath, and stared at him very hard. "Who's the party, James?" he said to the waiter, speaking in a whisper that was plainly heard by the attorney.

"Gen'elman by the 8.22 down," said James.

"Commercial?" asked Mr. Moulder, with angry frown.

"He says so himself, anyways," said the waiter.

"Gammon!" replied Mr. Moulder, who knew all the bearings of a commercial man thoroughly, and could have put one together if he were only supplied with a little bit—say the mouth, as Professor Owen always does with the Dodoes. Mr. Moulder now began to be angry, for he was a stickler for the rights and privileges of his class, and had an idea that the world was not so conservative in that respect as it should be. Mr. Dockwrath, however, was not to be frightened, so he drew his chair a thought nearer to the fire, took a sup of brandy and water, and prepared himself for war if war should be necessary.

"Cold evening, sir, for the time of year," said Mr. Moulder, walking up to the fireplace, and rolling the lumps of his forehead about in his attempt at a frown. In spite of his terrible burden of flesh, Mr. Moulder could look angry on occasions, but he could only do so when he was angry. He was not gifted with a command of his facial muscles.

"Yes," said Mr. Dockwrath, not taking his eyes from off the Leeds and Halifax Chronicle. "It is coldish. Waiter, bring me a cigar."

This was very provoking, as must be confessed. Mr. Moulder had not been prepared to take any step towards turning the gentleman out, though doubtless he might have done so had he chosen to exercise his prerogative. But he did expect that the gentleman would have acknowledged the weakness of his footing, by moving himself a little towards one side of the fire, and he did not expect that he would have presumed to smoke without asking whether the practice was held to be objectionable by the legal possessors of the room. Mr. Dockwrath was free of any such pusillanimity. "Waiter," he said again, "bring me a cigar, d'ye hear?"

The great heart of Moulder could not stand this unmoved. He had been an accustomed visitor to that room for fifteen years, and had always done his best to preserve the commercial code unsullied. He was now so well known, that no one else ever presumed to take the chair at the four o'clock commercial dinner if he were present. It was incumbent on him to stand forward and make a fight, more especially in the presence of Kantwise, who was by no means stanch to his order. Kantwise would at all times have been glad to have outsiders in the room, in order that he might puff his tables, and if possible effect a sale;—a mode of proceeding held in much aversion by the upright, old-fashioned, commercial mind.

"Sir," said Mr. Moulder, having become very red about the cheeks and chin, "I and this gentleman are going to have a bit of supper, and it ain't accustomed to smoke in commercial rooms during meals. You know the rules no doubt if you're commercial yourself;—as I suppose you are, seeing you in this room."

Now Mr. Moulder was wrong in his law, as he himself was very well aware. Smoking is allowed in all commercial rooms when the dinner has been some hour or so off the table. But then it was necessary that he should hit the stranger in some way, and the chances were that the stranger would know nothing about commercial law. Nor did he; so he merely looked Mr. Moulder hard in the face. But Mr. Kantwise knew the laws well enough, and as he saw before him a possible purchaser of metallic tables, he came to the assistance of the attorney.

"I think you are a little wrong there, Mr. Moulder; eh; ain't you?" said he.

"Wrong about what?" said Moulder, turning very sharply upon his base-minded compatriot.

"Well, as to smoking. It's nine o'clock, and if the gentleman—"

"I don't care a brass farthing about the clock," said the other, "but when I'm going to have a bit of steak with my tea, in my own room, I chooses to have it comfortable."

"Goodness me, Mr. Moulder, how many times have I seen you sitting there with a pipe in your mouth, and half a dozen gents eating their teas the while in this very room? The rule of the case I take it to be this; when—"

"Bother your rules."

"Well; it was you spoke of them."

"The question I take to be this," said Moulder, now emboldened by the opposition he had received. "Has the gentleman any right to be in this room at all, or has he not? Is he commercial, or is he—miscellaneous? That's the chat, as I take it."

"You're on the square there, I must allow," said Kantwise.

"James," said Moulder, appealing with authority to the waiter, who had remained in the room during the controversy;—and now Mr. Moulder was determined to do his duty and vindicate his profession, let the consequences be what they might. "James, is that gentleman commercial, or is he not?"

It was clearly necessary now that Mr. Dockwrath himself should take his own part, and fight his own battle. "Sir," said he, turning to Mr. Moulder, "I think you'll find it extremely difficult to define that word;—extremely difficult. In this enterprising country all men are more or less commercial."

"Hear! hear!" said Mr. Kantwise.

"That's gammon," said Mr. Moulder.

"Gammon it may be," said Mr. Dockwrath, "but nevertheless it's right in law. Taking the word in its broadest, strictest, and most intelligible sense, I am a commercial gentleman; and as such I do maintain that I have a full right to the accommodation of this public room."

"That's very well put," said Mr. Kantwise.

"Waiter," thundered out Mr. Moulder, as though he imagined that that functionary was down the yard at the taproom instead of standing within three feet of his elbow. "Is this gent a commercial, or is he not? Because if not,—then I'll trouble you to send Mr. Crump here. My compliments to Mr. Crump, and I wish to see him." Now Mr. Crump was the landlord of the Bull Inn.

"Master's just stepped out, down the street," said James.

"Why don't you answer my question, sir?" said Moulder, becoming redder and still more red about his shirt-collars.

"The gent said as how he was 'mercial," said the poor man. "Was I to go to contradict a gent and tell him he wasn't when he said as how he was?"

"If you please," said Mr. Dockwrath, "we will not bring the waiter into this discussion. I asked for the commercial room, and he did his duty in showing me to the door of it. The fact I take to be this; in the south of England the rules to which you refer are not kept so strictly as in these more mercantile localities."

"I've always observed that," said Kantwise.

"I travelled for three years in Devonshire, Somersetshire, and Wiltshire," said Moulder, "and the commercial rooms were as well kept there as any I ever see."

"I alluded to Surrey and Kent," said Mr. Dockwrath.

"They're uncommonly miscellaneous in Surrey and Kent," said Kantwise. "There's no doubt in the world about that."

"If the gentleman means to say that he's come in here because he didn't know the custom of the country, I've no more to say, of course," said Moulder. "And in that case, I, for one, shall be very happy if the gentleman cam make himself comfortable in this room as a stranger, and I may say guest;—paying his own shot, of course."

"And as for me, I shall be delighted," said Kantwise. "I never did like too much exclusiveness. What's the use of bottling oneself up? that's what I always say. Besides, there's no charity in it. We gents as are always on the road should show a little charity to them as ain't so well accustomed to the work."

At this allusion to charity Mr. Moulder snuffled through his nose to show his great disgust, but he made no further answer. Mr. Dockwrath, who was determined not to yield, but who had nothing to gain by further fighting, bowed his head, and declared that he felt very much obliged. Whether or no there was any touch of irony in his tone, Mr. Moulder's ears were not fine enough to discover. So they now sat round the fire together, the attorney still keeping his seat in the middle. And then Mr. Moulder ordered his little bit of steak with his tea. "With the gravy in it, James," he said, solemnly. "And a bit of fat, and a few slices of onion, thin mind, put on raw, not with all the taste fried out; and tell the cook if she don't do it as it should be done, I'll be down into the kitchen and do it myself. You'll join me, Kantwise, eh?"

"Well, I think not; I dined at three, you know."

"Dined at three! What of that? a dinner at three won't last a man for ever. You might as well join me."

"No, I think not. Have you got such a thing as a nice red herring in the house, James?"

"Get one round the corner, sir."

"Do, there's a good fellow; and I'll take it for a relish with my tea. I'm not so fond of your solids three times a day. They heat the blood too much."

"Bother," grunted Moulder; and then they went to their evening meal, over which we will not disturb them. The steak, we may presume, was cooked aright, as Mr. Moulder did not visit the kitchen, and Mr. Kantwise no doubt made good play with his unsubstantial dainty, as he spoke no further till his meal was altogether finished.

"Did you ever hear anything of that Mr. Mason who lives near Bradford?" asked Mr. Kantwise, addressing himself to Mr. Moulder, as soon as the things had been cleared from the table, and that latter gentleman had been furnished with a pipe and a supply of cold without.

"I remember his father when I was a boy," said Moulder, not troubling himself to take his pipe from his mouth, "Mason and Martock in the Old Jewry; very good people they were too."

"He's decently well off now, I suppose, isn't he?" said Kantwise, turning away his face, and looking at his companion out of the corners of his eyes.

"I suppose he is. That place there by the road-side is all his own, I take it. Have you been at him with some of your rusty, rickety tables and chairs?"

"Mr. Moulder, you forget that there is a gentleman here who won't understand that you're at your jokes. I was doing business at Groby Park, but I found the party uncommon hard to deal with."

"Didn't complete the transaction?"

"Well, no; not exactly; but I intend to call again. He's close enough himself, is Mr. Mason. But his lady, Mrs. M.! Lord love you, Mr. Moulder, that is a woman!"

"She is; is she? As for me, I never have none of these private dealings. It don't suit my book at all; nor it ain't what I've been accustomed to. If a man's wholesale, let him be wholesale." And then, having enunciated this excellent opinion with much energy, he took a long pull at his brandy and water.

"Very old fashioned, Mr. Moulder," said Kantwise, looking round the corner, then shutting his eyes and shaking his head.

"May be," said Moulder, "and yet none the worse for that. I call it hawking and peddling, that going round the country with your goods on your back. It ain't trade." And then there was a lull in the conversation, Mr. Kantwise, who was a very religious gentleman, having closed his eyes, and being occupied with some internal anathema against Mr. Moulder.

"Begging your pardon, sir, I think you were talking about one Mr. Mason who lives in these parts," said Dockwrath.

"Exactly. Joseph Mason, Esq., of Groby Park," said Mr. Kantwise, now turning his face upon the attorney.

"I suppose I shall be likely to find him at home to-morrow, if I call?"

"Certainly, sir; certainly; leastwise I should say so. Any personal acquaintance with Mr. Mason, sir? If so, I meant nothing offensive by my allusion to the lady, sir; nothing at all, I can assure you."

"The lady's nothing to me, sir; nor the gentleman either;—only that I have a little business with him."

"Shall be very happy to join you in a gig, sir, to-morrow, as far as Groby Park; or fly, if more convenient. I shall only take a few patterns with me, and they're no weight at all,—none in the least, sir. They go on behind, and you wouldn't know it, sir." To this, however, Mr. Dockwrath would not assent. As he wanted to see Mr. Mason very specially, he should go early, and preferred going by himself.

"No offence, I hope," said Mr. Kantwise.

"None in the least," said Mr. Dockwrath.

"And if you would allow me, sir, to have the pleasure of showing you a few of my patterns, I'm sure I should be delighted." This he said observing that Mr. Moulder was sitting over his empty glass with the pipe in his hand, and his eyes fast closed. "I think, sir, I could show you an article that would please you very much. You see, sir, that new ideas are coming in every day, and wood, sir, is altogether going out,—altogether going out as regards furniture. In another twenty years, sir, there won't be such a thing as a wooden table in the country, unless with some poor person that can't afford to refurnish. Believe me, sir, iron's the thing now-a-days."

"And indian-rubber," said Dockwrath.

"Yes; indian-rubber's wonderful too. Are you in that line, sir?"

"Well; no; not exactly."

"It's not like iron, sir. You can't make a dinner-table for fourteen people out of indian-rubber, that will shut up into a box 3-6 by 2-4 deep, and 2-6 broad. Why, sir, I can let you have a set of drawing-room furniture for fifteen ten that you've never seen equalled in wood for three times the money;— ornamented in the tastiest way, sir, and fit for any lady's drawing-room or boodoor. The ladies of quality are all getting them now for their boodoors. There's three tables, eight chairs, easy rocking-chair, music-stand, stool to match, and pair of stand-up screens, all gilt in real Louey catorse; and it goes in three boxes 4-2 by 2-1 and 2-3. Think of that, sir. For fifteen ten and the boxes in." Then there was a pause, after which Mr. Kantwise added—"If ready money, the carriage paid." And then he turned his head very much away, and looked back very hard at his expected customer.

"I'm afraid the articles are not in my line," said Mr. Dockwrath.

"It's the tastiest present for a gentleman to make to his lady that has come out since—since those sort of things have come out at all. You'll let me show you the articles, sir. It will give me the sincerest pleasure." And Mr.

Kantwise proposed to leave the room in order that he might introduce the three boxes in question.

"They would not be at all in my way," said Mr. Dockwrath.

"The trouble would be nothing," said Mr. Kantwise, "and it gives me the greatest pleasure to make them known when I find any one who can appreciate such undoubted luxuries;" and so saying Mr. Kantwise skipped out of the room, and soon returned with James and Boots, each of the three bearing on his shoulder a deal box nearly as big as a coffin, all of which were deposited in different parts of the room. Mr. Moulder in the meantime snored heavily, his head falling on to his breast every now and again. But nevertheless he held fast by his pipe.

Mr. Kantwise skipped about the room with wonderful agility, unfastening the boxes, and taking out the contents, while Joe the boots and James the waiter stood by assisting. They had never yet seen the glories of these chairs and tables, and were therefore not unwilling to be present. It was singular to see how ready Mr. Kantwise was at the work, how recklessly he threw aside the whitey-brown paper in which the various pieces of painted iron were enveloped, and with what a practised hand he put together one article after another. First there was a round loo-table, not quite so large in its circumference as some people might think desirable, but, nevertheless, a round loo-table. The pedestal with its three claws was all together. With a knowing touch Mr. Kantwise separated the bottom of what looked like a yellow stick, and, lo! there were three legs, which he placed carefully on the ground. Then a small bar was screwed on to the top, and over the bar was screwed the leaf, or table itself, which consisted of three pieces unfolding with hinges. These, when the screw had been duly fastened in the centre, opened out upon the bar, and there was the table complete.

It was certainly a "tasty" article, and the pride with which Mr. Kantwise glanced back at it was quite delightful. The top of the table was blue, with a red bird of paradise in the middle; and the edges of the table, to the breadth of a couple of inches, were yellow. The pillar also was yellow, as were the three legs. "It's the real Louey catorse," said Mr. Kantwise, stooping down to go on with table number two, which was, as he described it, a "chess," having the proper number of blue and light-pink squares marked upon it; but this also had been made Louey catorse with reference to its legs and edges. The third table was a "sofa," of proper shape, but rather small in size. Then, one after another, he brought forth and screwed up the chairs, stools, and sundry screens, and within a quarter of an hour he had put up the whole set complete. The red bird of paradise and the blue ground appeared on all, as did also the yellow legs and edgings which gave to them their peculiarly fashionable character. "There," said Mr. Kantwise, looking at them with fond admiration, "I don't mind giving a personal guarantee that there's nothing equal to that for the money either in England or in France."

"They are very nice," said Mr. Dockwrath. When a man has had produced before him for his own and sole delectation any article or articles, how can he avoid eulogium? Mr. Dockwrath found himself obliged to pause, and almost feared that he should find himself obliged to buy.

"Nice! I should rather think they are," said Mr. Kantwise, becoming triumphant,—"and for fifteen ten, delivered, boxes included. There's nothing like iron, sir, nothing; you may take my word for that. They're so strong, you know. Look here, sir." And then Mr. Kantwise, taking two of the pieces of whitey-brown paper which had been laid aside, carefully spread one on the centre of the round table, and the other on the seat of one of the chairs. Then lightly poising himself on his toe, he stepped on to the chair, and from thence on to the table. In that position he skillfully brought his feet together, so that his weight was directly on the leg, and gracefully waved his hands over his head. James and Boots stood by admiring, with open mouths, and Mr. Dockwrath, with his hands in his pockets, was meditating whether he could not give the order without complying with the terms as to ready money.

"There is nothing like iron, Sir; nothing."

"Look at that for strength," said Mr. Kantwise from his exalted position. "I don't think any lady of your acquaintance, sir, would allow you to stand on her rosewood or mahogany loo-table. And if she did, you would not like to adventure it yourself. But look at this for strength," and he waved his arms abroad, still keeping his feet skilfully together in the same exact position.

At that moment Mr. Moulder awoke. "So you've got your iron traps out, have you?" said he. "What; you're there, are you? Upon my word I'd sooner you than me."

"I certainly should not like to see you up here, Mr. Moulder. I doubt whether even this table would bear five-and-twenty stone. Joe, lend me your shoulder, there's a good fellow." And then Mr. Kantwise, bearing very lightly on the chair, descended to the ground without accident.

"Now, that's what I call gammon," said Moulder.

"What is gammon, Mr. Moulder?" said the other, beginning to be angry.

"It's all gammon. The chairs and tables is gammon, and so is the stools and the screens."

"Mr. Moulder, I didn't call your tea and coffee and brandy gammon."

"You can't; and you wouldn't do any harm if you did. Hubbles and Grease are too well known in Yorkshire for you to hurt them. But as for all that show-off and gimcrack-work, I tell you fairly it ain't what I call trade, and it ain't fit for a commercial room. It's gammon, gammon, gammon! James, give me a bedcandle." And so Mr. Moulder took himself off to bed.

"I think I'll go too," said Mr. Dockwrath.

"You'll let me put you up the set, eh?" said Mr. Kantwise.

"Well; I'll think about it," said the attorney. "I'll not just give you an answer to-night. Good night, sir; I'm very much obliged to you." And he too went, leaving Mr. Kantwise to repack his chairs and tables with the assistance of James the waiter.

CHAPTER VII
THE MASONS OF GROBY PARK

Groby Park is about seven miles from Leeds, in the direction of Bradford, and thither on the morning after the scene described in the last chapter Mr. Dockwrath was driven in one of the gigs belonging to the Bull Inn. The park itself is spacious, but is flat and uninteresting, being surrounded by a thin belt of new-looking fir-trees, and containing but very little old or handsome timber. There are on the high road two very important lodges, between which is a large ornamented gate, and from thence an excellent road leads to the mansion, situated in the very middle of the domain. The house is Greek in its style of architecture,—at least so the owner says; and if a portico with a pediment and seven Ionic columns makes a house Greek, the house in Groby Park undoubtedly is Greek.

Here lived Mr. and Mrs. Mason, the three Misses Mason, and occasionally the two young Messrs. Mason; for the master of Groby Park was blessed with five children. He himself was a big, broad, heavy-browed man, in whose composition there was nothing of tenderness, nothing of poetry, and nothing of taste; but I cannot say that he was on the whole a bad man. He was just in his dealings, or at any rate endeavoured to be so. He strove hard to do his duty as a county magistrate against very adverse circumstances. He endeavoured to enable his tenants and labourers to live. He was severe to his children, and was not loved by them; but nevertheless they were dear to him, and he endeavoured to do his duty by them. The wife of his bosom was not a pleasant woman, but nevertheless he did his duty by her; that is, he neither deserted her, nor beat her, nor locked her up. I am not sure that he would not have been justified in doing one of these three things, or even all the three; for Mrs. Mason of Groby Park was not a pleasant woman.

But yet he was a bad man in that he could never forget and never forgive. His mind and heart were equally harsh and hard and inflexible. He was a man who considered that it behoved him as a man to resent all injuries, and to have his pound of flesh in all cases. In his inner thoughts he had ever boasted to himself that he had paid all men all that he owed. He had, so he thought, injured no one in any of the relations of life. His tradesmen got their money regularly. He answered every man's letter. He exacted nothing from any man for which he did not pay. He never ill-used a servant either by bad language or by over-work. He never amused himself, but devoted his whole time to duties. He would fain even have been hospitable, could he have gotten his neighbours to come to him and have induced his wife to put upon the table sufficient food for them to eat.

Such being his virtues, what right had any one to injure him? When he got from his grocer adulterated coffee,—he analyzed the coffee, as his half-brother had done the guano,—he would have flayed the man alive if the law would have allowed him. Had he not paid the man monthly, giving him the best price as though for the best article? When he was taken in with a warranty for a horse, he pursued the culprit to the uttermost. Maid-servants who would not come from their bedrooms at six o'clock, he would himself disturb while enjoying their stolen slumbers. From his children he exacted all titles of respect, because he had a right to them. He wanted nothing that belonged to any one else, but he could not endure that aught should be kept from him which he believed to be his own. It may be imagined, therefore, in what light he esteemed Lady Mason and her son, and how he regarded their residence at Orley Farm, seeing that he firmly believed that Orley Farm was his own, if all the truth were known.

I have already hinted that Mrs. Mason was not a delightful woman. She had been a beauty, and still imagined that she had not lost all pretension to be so considered. She spent, therefore, a considerable portion of her day in her dressing-room, spent a great deal of money for clothes, and gave herself sundry airs. She was a little woman with long eyes, and regular eyelashes, with a straight nose, and thin lips and regular teeth. Her face was oval, and her hair was brown. It had at least once been all brown, and that which was now seen was brown also. But, nevertheless, although she was possessed of all these charms, you might look at her for ten days together, and on the eleventh you would not know her if you met her in the streets.

But the appearance of Mrs. Mason was not her forte. She had been a beauty; but if it had been her lot to be known in history, it was not as a beauty that she would have been famous. Parsimony was her great virtue, and a power of saving her strong point. I have said that she spent much money in dress, and some people will perhaps think that the two points of character are not compatible. Such people know nothing of a true spirit of parsimony. It is from the backs and bellies of other people that savings are made with the greatest constancy and the most satisfactory results.

The parsimony of a mistress of a household is best displayed on matters eatable;—on matters eatable and drinkable; for there is a fine scope for domestic savings in tea, beer, and milk. And in such matters chiefly did Mrs. Mason operate, going as far as she dared towards starving even her husband. But nevertheless she would feed herself in the middle of the day, having a roast fowl with bread sauce in her own room. The miser who starves himself and dies without an ounce of flesh on his bones, while his skinny head lies on a bag of gold, is after all, respectable. There has been a grand passion in his life, and that grandest work of man, self-denial. You cannot altogether despise one who has clothed himself with rags and fed himself with bone-scrapings, while broadcloth and ortolans were within his easy reach. But there are women, wives and mothers of families, who would give the bone-scrapings to their husbands and the bones to their servants, while they hide the ortolans for themselves; and would dress children in rags, while they cram chests, drawers, and boxes with silks and satins for their own backs. Such a woman one can thoroughly despise, and even hate; and such a woman was Mrs. Mason of Groby Park.

I shall not trouble the reader at present with much description of the young Masons. The eldest son was in the army, and the younger at Cambridge, both spending much more money than their father allowed them. Not that he, in this respect, was specially close-fisted. He ascertained what was sufficient,—amply sufficient as he was told by the colonel of the regiment and the tutor of the college,—and that amount he allowed, assuring both Joseph and John that if they spent more, they would themselves have to pay for it out of the moneys which should enrich them in future years. But how could the sons of such a mother be other than spendthrifts? Of course they were extravagant; of course they spent more than they should have done; and their father resolved that he would keep his word with them religiously.

The daughters were much less fortunate, having no possible means of extravagance allowed to them. Both the father and mother decided that they should go out into the county society, and therefore their clothing was not absolutely of rags. But any young lady who does go into society, whether it be of county or town, will fully understand the difference between a liberal and a stingy wardrobe. Girls with slender provisions of millinery may be fit to go out,—quite fit in their father's eyes; and yet all such going out may be matter of intense pain. It is all very well for the world to say that a girl should be happy without reference to her clothes. Show me such a girl, and I will show you one whom I should be very sorry that a boy of mine should choose as his sweetheart.

The three Misses Mason, as they always were called by the Groby Park people, had been christened Diana, Creusa, and Penelope, their mother having a passion for classic literature, which she indulged by a use of

Lemprière's dictionary. They were not especially pretty, nor were they especially plain. They were well grown and healthy, and quite capable of enjoying themselves in any of the amusements customary to young ladies, — if only the opportunities were afforded them.

Mr. Dockwrath had thought it well to write to Mr. Mason, acquainting that gentleman with his intended visit. Mr. Mason, he said to himself, would recognise his name, and know whence he came, and under such circumstances would be sure to see him, although the express purpose of the proposed interview should not have been explained to him. Such in result was exactly the case. Mr. Mason did remember the name of Dockwrath, though he had never hitherto seen the bearer of it; and as the letter was dated from Hamworth, he felt sufficient interest in the matter to await at home the coming of his visitor.

"I know your name, Mr. Mason, sir, and have known it long," said Mr. Dockwrath, seating himself in the chair which was offered to him in the magistrate's study; "though I never had the pleasure of seeing you before, — to my knowledge. My name is Dockwrath, sir, and I am a solicitor. I live at Hamworth, and I married the daughter of old Mr. Usbech, sir, whom you will remember."

Mr. Mason listened attentively as these details were uttered before him so clearly, but he said nothing, merely bowing his head at each separate statement. He knew all about old Usbech's daughter nearly as well as Mr. Dockwrath did himself, but he was a man who knew how to be silent upon occasions.

"I was too young, sir," continued Dockwrath, "when you had that trial about Orley Farm to have anything to do with the matter myself, but nevertheless I remember all the circumstances as though it was yesterday. I suppose, sir, you remember them also?"

"Yes, Mr. Dockwrath, I remember them very well."

"Well, sir, my impression has always been that—" And then the attorney stopped. It was quite his intention to speak out plainly before Mr. Mason, but he was anxious that that gentleman should speak out too. At any rate it might be well that he should be induced to express some little interest in the matter.

"Your impression, you say, has always been—" said Mr. Mason, repeating the words of his companion, and looking as ponderous and grave as ever. His countenance, however, expressed nothing but his usual ponderous solemnity.

"My impression always was—that there was something that had not been as yet found out."

"What sort of thing, Mr. Dockwrath?"

"Well; some secret. I don't think that your lawyers managed the matter well, Mr. Mason."

"You think you would have done it better, Mr. Dockwrath?"

"I don't say that, Mr. Mason. I was only a lad at the time, and could not have managed it at all. But they didn't ferret about enough. Mr. Mason, there's a deal better evidence than any that is given by word of mouth. A clever counsel can turn a witness pretty nearly any way he likes, but he can't do that with little facts. He hasn't the time, you see, to get round them. Your lawyers, sir, didn't get up the little facts as they should have done."

"And you have got them up since, Mr. Dockwrath?"

"I don't say that, Mr. Mason. You see all my interest lies in maintaining the codicil. My wife's fortune came to her under that deed. To be sure that's gone and spent long since, and the Lord Chancellor with all the judges couldn't enforce restitution; but, nevertheless, I wouldn't wish that any one should have a claim against me on that account."

"Perhaps you will not object to say what it is that you do wish?"

"I wish to see right done, Mr. Mason; that's all. I don't think that Lady Mason or her son have any right to the possession of that place. I don't think that that codicil was a correct instrument; and in that case of Mason versus Mason I don't think that you and your friends got to the bottom of it." And then Mr. Dockwrath leaned back in his chair with an inward determination to say nothing more, until Mr. Mason should make some sign.

That gentleman, however, still remained ponderous and heavy, and therefore there was a short period of silence—"And have you got to the bottom of it since, Mr. Dockwrath?" at last he said.

"I don't say that I have," said the attorney.

"Might I ask then what it is you propose to effect by the visit with which you have honoured me? Of course you are aware that these are very private matters; and although I should feel myself under an obligation to you, or to any man who might assist me to arrive at any true facts which have hitherto been concealed, I am not disposed to discuss the affair with a stranger on grounds of mere suspicion."

"I shouldn't have come here, Mr. Mason, at very great expense, and personal inconvenience to myself in my profession, if I had not some good reason for doing so. I don't think that you ever got to the bottom of that matter, and I can't say that I have done so now; I haven't even tried. But I tell you what, Mr. Mason; if you wish it, I think I could put you in the way of—trying."

"My lawyers are Messrs. Round and Crook of Bedford Row. Will it not be better that you should go to them, Mr. Dockwrath?"

"No, Mr. Mason. I don't think it will be better that I should go to them. I know Round and Crook well, and don't mean to say a word against them; but if I go any farther into this affair I must do it with the principal. I am not going to cut my own throat for the sake of mending any man's little finger. I have a family of sixteen children, Mr. Mason, and I have to look about very sharp,—very sharp indeed." Then there was another pause, and Mr. Dockwrath began to perceive that Mr. Mason was not by nature an open, demonstrative, or communicative man. If anything further was to be done, he himself must open out a little. "The fact is, Mr. Mason, that I have come across documents which you should have had at that trial. Round and Crook ought to have had them, only they weren't half sharp. Why, sir, Mr. Usbech had been your father's man of business for years upon years, and yet they didn't half go through his papers. They turned 'em over and looked at 'em; but never thought of seeing what little facts might be proved."

"And these documents are with you now, here?"

"No, Mr. Mason, I am not so soft as that. I never carry about original documents unless when ordered to prove. Copies of one or two items I have made; not regular copies, Mr. Mason, but just a line or two to refresh my memory." And Mr. Dockwrath took a small letter-case out of his breast coat pocket.

By this time Mr. Mason's curiosity had been roused, and he began to think it possible that his visitor had discovered information which might be of importance to him. "Are you going to show me any document?" said he.

"That's as may be," said the attorney. "I don't know as yet whether you care to see it. I have come a long way to do you a service, and it seems to me you are rather shy of coming forward to meet me. As I said before, I've a very heavy family, and I'm not going to cut the nose off my own face to put money into any other man's pocket. What do you think my journey down here will cost me, including loss of time, and interruption to my business?"

"Look here, Mr. Dockwrath; if you are really able to put me into possession of any facts regarding the Orley Farm estate which I ought to know, I will see that you are compensated for your time and trouble. Messrs. Round and Crook—"

"I'll have nothing to do with Round and Crook. So that's settled, Mr. Mason."

"Then, Mr. Dockwrath—"

"Half a minute, Mr. Mason. I'll have nothing to do with Round and Crook; but as I know you to be a gentleman and a man of honour, I'll put you in possession of what I've discovered, and leave it to you afterwards to do what you think right about my expenses, time, and services. You won't forget that it is a long way from Hamworth to Groby Park. And if you should succeed—"

"If I am to look at this document, I must do so without pledging myself to anything," said Mr. Mason, still with much solemnity. He had great doubts as to his new acquaintance, and much feared that he was derogating from his dignity as a county magistrate and owner of Groby Park in holding any personal intercourse with him; but nevertheless he could not resist the temptation. He most firmly believed that that codicil had not expressed the genuine last will and fair disposition of property made by his father, and it might certainly be the case that proof of all that he believed was to be found among the papers of the old lawyer. He hated Lady Mason with all his power of hatred, and if there did, even yet, exist for him a chance of upsetting her claims and ruining her before the world, he was not the man to forego that chance.

"Well, sir, you shall see it," said Mr. Dockwrath; "or rather hear it, for there is not much to see." And so saying he extracted from his pocket-book a very small bit of paper.

"I should prefer to read it, if it's all the same to you, Mr. Dockwrath. I shall understand it much better in that way."

"As you like, Mr. Mason," said the attorney, handing him the small bit of paper. "You will understand, sir, that it's no real copy, but only a few dates and particulars, just jotted down to assist my own memory." The document, supported by which Mr. Dockwrath had come down to Yorkshire, consisted of half a sheet of note paper, and the writing upon this covered hardly the half of it. The words which Mr. Mason read were as follows:—

Date of codicil. 14th July 18—.

Witnesses to the instrument. John Kenneby; Bridget Bolster; Jonathan Usbech. N.B. Jonathan Usbech died before the testator.

Mason and Martock. Deed of separation; dated 14th July 18—.

Executed at Orley Farm.

Witnesses John Kenneby; and Bridget Bolster. Deed was prepared in the office of Jonathan Usbech, and probably executed in his presence.

That was all that was written on the paper, and Mr. Mason read the words to himself three times before he looked up, or said anything concerning them. He was not a man quick at receiving new ideas into his mind, or of understanding new points; but that which had once become intelligible to him and been made his own, remained so always. "Well," said he, when he read the above words for the third time.

"You don't see it, sir?" said Mr. Dockwrath.

"See what?" said Mr. Mason, still looking at the scrap of paper.

"Why; the dates, to begin with."

"I see that the dates are the same;—the 14th of July in the same year."

"Well," said Mr. Dockwrath, looking very keenly into the magistrate's face.

"Well," said Mr. Mason, looking over the paper at his boot.

"John Kenneby and Bridget Bolster were witnesses to both the instruments," said the attorney.

"So I see," said the magistrate.

"But I don't remember that it came out in evidence that either of them recollected having been called on for two signatures on the same day."

"No; there was nothing of that came out;—or was even hinted at."

"No; nothing even hinted at, Mr. Mason,—as you justly observe. That is what I mean by saying that Round and Crook's people didn't get up their little facts. Believe me, sir, there are men in the profession out of London who know quite as much as Round and Crook. They ought to have had those facts, seeing that the very copy of the document was turned over by their hands." And Mr. Dockwrath hit the table heavily in the warmth of his indignation against his professional brethren. Earlier in the interview Mr. Mason would have been made very angry by such freedom, but he was not angry now.

"Yes; they ought to have known it," said he. But he did not even yet see the point. He merely saw that there was a point worth seeing.

"Known it! Of course they ought to have known it. Look here, Mr. Mason! If I had it on my mind that I'd thrown over a client of mine by such carelessness as that, I'd — I'd strike my own name off the rolls; I would indeed. I never could look a counsel in the face again, if I'd neglected to brief him with such facts as those. I suppose it was carelessness; eh, Mr. Mason?"

"Oh, yes; I'm afraid so," said Mr. Mason, still rather in the dark.

"They could have had no object in keeping it back, I should say."

"No; none in life. But let us see, Mr. Dockwrath; how does it bear upon us? The dates are the same, and the witnesses the same."

"The deed of separation is genuine. There is no doubt about that."

"Oh; you're sure of that?"

"Quite certain. I found it entered in the old office books. It was the last of a lot of such documents executed between Mason and Martock after the old man gave up the business. You see she was always with him, and knew all about it."

"About the partnership deed?"

"Of course she did. She's a clever woman, Mr. Mason; very clever, and it's almost a pity that she should come to grief. She has carried it on so well; hasn't she?"

Mr. Mason's face now became very black. "Why," said he, "if what you seem to allege be true, she must be a — a — a —. What do you mean, sir, by pity?"

Mr. Dockwrath shrugged his shoulders. "It is very blue," said he, "uncommon blue."

"She must be a swindler; a common swindler. Nay, worse than that."

"Oh, yes, a deal worse than that, Mr. Mason. And as for common; — according to my way of thinking there's nothing at all common about it. I look upon it as about the best got-up plant I ever remember to havē heard of. I do, indeed, Mr. Mason." The attorney during the last ten minutes of the conversation had quite altered his tone, understanding that he had already achieved a great part of his object; but Mr. Mason in his intense anxiety did not observe this. Had Mr. Dockwrath, in commencing the conversation, talked about "plants" and "blue," Mr. Mason would probably have rung his bell for the servant. "If it's anything, it's forgery," said Mr. Dockwrath, looking his companion full in the face.

"I always felt sure that my father never intended to sign such a codicil as that."

"He never did sign it, Mr. Mason."

"And,—and the witnesses!" said Mr. Mason, still not enlightened as to the true extent of the attorney's suspicion.

"They signed the other deed; that is two of them did. There is no doubt about that;—on that very day. They certainly did witness a signature made by the old gentleman in his own room on that 14th of July. The original of that document, with the date and their names, will be forthcoming soon enough."

"Well," said Mr. Mason.

"But they did not witness two signatures."

"You think not, eh!"

"I'm sure of it. The girl Bolster would have remembered it, and would have said so. She was sharp enough."

"Who wrote all the names then at the foot of the will?" said Mr. Mason.

"Ah! that's the question. Who did write them? We know very well, Mr. Mason, you and I that is, who did not. And having come to that, I think we may give a very good guess who did."

And then they both sat silent for some three or four minutes. Mr. Dockwrath was quite at his ease, rubbing his chin with his hand, playing with a paper-knife which he had taken from the study table, and waiting till it should please Mr. Mason to renew the conversation. Mr. Mason was not at his ease, though all idea of affecting any reserve before the attorney had left him. He was thinking how best he might confound and destroy the woman who had robbed him for so many years; who had defied him, got the better of him, and put him to terrible cost; who had vexed his spirit through his whole life, deprived him of content, and had been to him as a thorn ever present in a festering sore. He had always believed that she had defrauded him, but this belief had been qualified by the unbelief of others. It might have been, he had half thought, that the old man had signed the codicil in his dotage, having been cheated and bullied into it by the woman. There had been no day in her life on which he would not have ruined her, had it been in his power to do so. But now—now, new and grander ideas were breaking in upon his mind. Could it be possible that he might live to see her, not merely deprived of her ill-gained money, but standing in the dock as a felon to receive sentence for her terrible misdeeds? If that might be so, would he not receive great compensation for all that he had suffered? Would it not be sweet to his sense of justice that both of them should thus at last have their own? He did not even yet understand all that Mr. Dockwrath suspected. He did not fully perceive why the woman was supposed to have chosen as the date of her forgery, the date of that other genuine deed. But he did understand, he did perceive—at least so he thought,—that new and perhaps conclusive evidence of her villainy was at last within his reach.

"And what shall we do now, Mr. Dockwrath?" he said at last.

"Well; am I to understand that you do me the honour of asking my advice upon that question as being your lawyer?"

This question immediately brought Mr. Mason back to business that he did understand. "A man in my position cannot very well change his legal advisers at a moment's notice. You must be very well aware of that, Mr. Dockwrath. Messrs. Round and Crook—"

"Messrs. Round and Crook, sir, have neglected your business in a most shameful manner. Let me tell you that, sir."

"Well; that's as may be. I'll tell you what I'll do, Mr. Dockwrath; I'll think over this matter in quiet, and then I'll come up to town. Perhaps when there I may expect the honour of a further visit from you."

"And you won't mention the matter to Round and Crook?"

"I can't undertake to say that, Mr. Dockwrath. I think it will perhaps be better that I should mention it, and then see you afterwards."

"And how about my expenses down here?"

Just at this moment there came a light tap at the study door, and before the master of the house could give or withhold permission the mistress of the house entered the room. "My dear," she said, "I didn't know that you were engaged."

"Yes, I am engaged," said the gentleman.

"Oh, I'm sure I beg pardon. Perhaps this is the gentleman from Hamworth?"

"Yes, ma'am," said Mr. Dockwrath. "I am the gentleman from Hamworth. I hope I have the pleasure of seeing you very well, ma'am?" And getting up from his chair he bowed politely.

"Mr. Dockwrath, Mrs. Mason," said the lady's husband, introducing them; and then Mrs. Mason curtsied to the stranger. She too was very anxious to know what might be the news from Hamworth.

"Mr. Dockwrath will lunch with us, my dear," said Mr. Mason. And then the lady, on hospitable cares intent, left them again to themselves.

CHAPTER VIII
MRS. MASON'S HOT LUNCHEON

Though Mr. Dockwrath was somewhat elated by this invitation to lunch, he was also somewhat abashed by it. He had been far from expecting that Mr. Mason of Groby Park would do him any such honour, and was made aware by it of the great hold which he must have made upon the attention of his host. But nevertheless he immediately felt that his hands were to a certain degree tied. He, having been invited to sit down at Mr. Mason's table, with Mrs. M. and the family,—having been treated as though he were a gentleman, and thus being for the time being put on a footing of equality with the county magistrate, could not repeat that last important question: "How about my expenses down here?" nor could he immediately go on with the grand subject in any frame of mind which would tend to further his own interests. Having been invited to lunch, he could not haggle with due persistency for his share of the business in crushing Lady Mason, nor stipulate that the whole concern should not be trusted to the management of Round and Crook. As a source of pride this invitation to eat was pleasant to him, but he was forced to acknowledge to himself that it interfered with business.

Nor did Mr. Mason feel himself ready to go on with the conversation in the manner in which it had been hitherto conducted. His mind was full of Orley Farm and his wrongs, and he could bring himself to think of nothing else; but he could no longer talk about it to the attorney sitting there in his study. "Will you take a turn about the place while the lunch is getting ready?" he said. So they took their hats and went out into the garden.

"It is dreadful to think of," said Mr. Mason, after they had twice walked in silence the length of a broad gravel terrace.

"What; about her ladyship?" said the attorney.

"Quite dreadful!" and Mr. Mason shuddered. "I don't think I ever heard of anything so shocking in my life. For twenty years, Mr. Dockwrath, think of that. Twenty years!" and his face as he spoke became almost black with horror.

"It is very shocking," said Mr. Dockwrath; "very shocking. What on earth will be her fate if it be proved against her? She has brought it on herself; that is all that one can say of her."

"D— — her! d— — her!" exclaimed the other, gnashing his teeth with concentrated wrath. "No punishment will be bad enough for her. Hanging would not be bad enough."

"They can't hang her, Mr. Mason," said Mr. Dockwrath, almost frightened by the violence of his companion.

"No; they have altered the laws, giving every encouragement to forgers, villains, and perjurers. But they can give her penal servitude for life. They must do it."

"She is not convicted yet, you know."

"D— — her!" repeated the owner of Groby Park again, as he thought of his twenty years of loss. Eight hundred a year for twenty years had been taken away from him; and he had been worsted before the world after a hard fight. "D— — her!" he continued to growl between his teeth. Mr. Dockwrath when he had first heard his companion say how horrid and dreadful the affair was, had thought that Mr. Mason was alluding to the condition in which the lady had placed herself by her assumed guilt. But it was of his own condition that he was speaking. The idea which shocked him was the thought of the treatment which he himself had undergone. The dreadful thing at which he shuddered was his own ill usage. As for her;—pity for her! Did a man ever pity a rat that had eaten into his choicest dainties?

"The lunch is on the table, sir," said the Groby Park footman in the Groby Park livery. Under the present household arrangement of Groby Park all the servants lived on board wages. Mrs. Mason did not like this system, though it had about it certain circumstances of economy which recommended it to her; it interfered greatly with the stringent aptitudes of her character and the warmest passion of her heart; it took away from her the delicious power of serving out the servants' food, of locking up the scraps of meat, and of charging the maids with voracity. But, to tell the truth, Mr. Mason had been driven by sheer necessity to take this step, as it had been found impossible to induce his wife to give out sufficient food to enable the servants to live and work. She knew that in not doing so she injured herself; but she could not do it. The knife in passing through the loaf would make the portion to be parted with less by one third than the portion to be retained. Half a pound of salt butter would reduce itself to a quarter of a pound. Portions of meat would become infinitesimal. When standing with viands before her, she had not free will over her hands. She could not bring herself to part with victuals, though she might ruin herself by retaining them. Therefore, by the order of the master, were the servants placed on board wages.

Mr. Dockwrath soon found himself in the dining-room, where the three young ladies with their mamma were already seated at the table. It was a handsome room, and the furniture was handsome; but nevertheless it was a heavy room, and the furniture was heavy. The table was large enough for a party of twelve, and might have borne a noble banquet; as it was the promise was not bad, for there were three large plated covers concealing hot viands, and in some houses lunch means only bread and cheese.

Mr. Mason went through the form of introduction between Mr. Dockwrath and his daughters. "That is Miss Mason, that Miss Creusa Mason, and this Miss Penelope. John, remove the covers." And the covers were removed, John taking them from the table with a magnificent action of his arm which I am inclined to think was not innocent of irony. On the dish before the master of the house,—a large dish which must I fancy have been selected by the cook with some similar attempt at sarcasm,—there reposed three scraps, as to the nature of which Mr. Dockwrath, though he looked hard at them, was unable to enlighten himself. But Mr. Mason knew them well, as he now placed his eyes on them for the third time. They were old enemies of his, and his brow again became black as he looked at them. The scraps in fact consisted of two drumsticks of a fowl and some indescribable bone out of the back of the same. The original bird had no doubt first revealed all its glories to human eyes,—presuming the eyes of the cook to be inhuman—in Mrs. Mason's "boodoor." Then, on the dish before the lady, there were three other morsels, black-looking and very suspicious to the eye, which in the course of conversation were proclaimed to be ham,—broiled ham. Mrs. Mason would never allow a ham in its proper shape to come into the room, because it is an article upon which the guests are themselves supposed to operate with the carving-knife. Lastly, on the dish before Miss Creusa there reposed three potatoes.

The face of Mr. Mason became very black as he looked at the banquet which was spread upon his board, and Mrs. Mason, eyeing him across the table, saw that it was so. She was not a lady who despised such symptoms in her lord, or disregarded in her valour the violence of marital storms. She had quailed more than once or twice under rebuke occasioned by her great domestic virtue, and knew that her husband, though he might put up with much as regarded his own comfort, and that of his children, could be very angry at injuries done to his household honour and character as a hospitable English country gentleman.

Consequently the lady smiled and tried to look self-satisfied as she invited her guest to eat. "This is ham," said she with a little simper, "broiled ham, Mr. Dockwrath; and there is chicken at the other end; I think they call it—devilled."

"Shall I assist the young ladies to anything first?" said the attorney, wishing to be polite.

"Nothing, thank you," said Miss Penelope, with a very stiff bow. She also knew that Mr. Dockwrath was an attorney from Hamworth, and considered herself by no means bound to hold any sort of conversation with him.

"My daughters only eat bread and butter in the middle of the day," said the lady. "Creusa, my dear, will you give Mr. Dockwrath a potato. Mr. Mason, Mr. Dockwrath will probably take a bit of that chicken."

"I would recommend him to follow the girls' example, and confine himself to the bread and butter," said the master of the house, pushing about the scraps with his knife and fork. "There is nothing here for him to eat."

"My dear!" exclaimed Mrs. Mason.

"There is nothing here for him to eat," repeated Mr. Mason. "And as far as I can see there is nothing there either. What is it you pretend to have in that dish?"

"My dear!" again exclaimed Mrs. Mason.

"What is it?" repeated the lord of the house in an angry tone.

"Broiled ham, Mr. Mason."

"Then let the ham be brought in," said he. "Diana, ring the bell."

"But the ham is not cooked, Mr. Mason," said the lady. "Broiled ham is always better when it has not been first boiled."

"Is there no cold meat in the house?" he asked.

"I am afraid not," she replied, now trembling a little in anticipation of what might be coming after the stranger should have gone. "You never like large joints yourself, Mr. Mason; and for ourselves we don't eat meat at luncheon."

"Nor anybody else either, here," said Mr. Mason in his anger.

"Pray don't mind me, Mr. Mason," said the attorney, "pray don't, Mr. Mason. I am a very poor fist at lunch; I am indeed."

"I am sure I am very sorry, very sorry, Mr. Mason," continued the lady. "If I had known that an early dinner was required, it should have been provided;—although the notice given was so very short."

"I never dine early," said Mr. Dockwrath, thinking that some imputation of a low way of living was conveyed in this supposition that he required a dinner under the pseudonym of a lunch. "I never do, upon my word—we are quite regular at home at half-past five, and all I ever take in the middle of the day is a biscuit and a glass of sherry,—or perhaps a bite of bread and cheese. Don't be uneasy about me, Mrs. Mason."

The three young ladies, having now finished their repast, got up from the table and retired, following each other out of the room in a line. Mrs. Mason remained for a minute or two longer, and then she also went. "The carriage has been ordered at three, Mr. M.," she said. "Shall we have the pleasure of your company?" "No," growled the husband. And then the lady went, sweeping a low curtsy to Mr. Dockwrath as she passed out of the room.

There was again a silence between the host and his guest for some two or three minutes, during which Mr. Mason was endeavouring to get the lunch out of his head, and to redirect his whole mind to Lady Mason and his hopes of vengeance. There is nothing perhaps so generally consoling to a man as a well-established grievance; a feeling of having been injured, on which his mind can brood from hour to hour, allowing him to plead his own cause in his own court, within his own heart,—and always to plead it successfully. At last Mr. Mason succeeded, and he could think of his enemy's fraud and forget his wife's meanness. "I suppose I may as well order my gig now," said Mr. Dockwrath, as soon as his host had arrived at this happy frame of mind.

"Your gig? ah, well. Yes. I do not know that I need detain you any longer. I can assure you that I am much obliged to you, Mr. Dockwrath, and I shall hope to see you in London very shortly."

"You are determined to go to Round and Crook, I suppose?"

"Oh, certainly."

"You are wrong, sir. They'll throw you over again as sure as your name is Mason."

"Mr. Dockwrath, you must if you please allow me to judge of that myself."

"Oh, of course, sir, of course. But I'm sure that a gentleman like you, Mr. Mason, will understand—"

"I shall understand that I cannot expect your services, Mr. Dockwrath,— your valuable time and services,—without remunerating you for them. That shall be fully explained to Messrs. Round and Crook."

"Very well, sir; very well. As long as I am paid for what I do, I am content. A professional gentleman of course expects that. How is he to get along else; particular with sixteen children?" And then Mr. Dockwrath got into the gig, and was driven back to the Bull at Leeds.

CHAPTER IX
A CONVIVIAL MEETING

On the whole Mr. Dockwrath was satisfied with the results of his trip to Groby Park, and was in a contented frame of mind as he was driven back to Leeds. No doubt it would have been better could he have persuaded Mr. Mason to throw over Messrs. Round and Crook, and put himself altogether into the hands of his new adviser; but this had been too much to expect. He had not expected it, and had made the suggestion as the surest means of getting the best terms in his power, rather than with a hope of securing the actual advantage named. He had done much towards impressing Mr. Mason with an idea of his own sharpness, and perhaps something also towards breaking the prestige which surrounded the names of the great London firm. He would now go to that firm and make his terms with them. They would probably be quite as ready to acquiesce in the importance of his information as had been Mr. Mason.

Before leaving the inn after breakfast he had agreed to join the dinner in the commercial room at five o'clock, and Mr. Mason's hot lunch had by no means induced him to alter his purpose. "I shall dine here," he had said when Mr. Moulder was discussing with the waiter the all-important subject of dinner. "At the commercial table sir?" the waiter had asked, doubtingly. Mr. Dockwrath had answered boldly in the affirmative, whereat Mr. Moulder had growled; but Mr. Kantwise had expressed satisfaction. "We shall be extremely happy to enjoy your company," Mr. Kantwise had said, with a graceful bow, making up by his excessive courtesy for the want of any courtesy on the part of his brother-traveller. With reference to all this Mr. Moulder said nothing; the stranger had been admitted into the room, to a certain extent even with his own consent, and he could not now be turned out; but he resolved within his own mind that for the future he would be more firm in maintaining the ordinances and institutes of his profession.

On his road home, Mr. Dockwrath had encountered Mr. Kantwise going to Groby Park, intent on his sale of a drawing-room set of the metallic furniture; and when he again met him in the commercial room he asked after his success. "A wonderful woman that, Mr. Dockwrath," said Mr. Kantwise, "a really wonderful woman; no particular friend of yours I think you say?"

"None in the least, Mr. Kantwise,"

"Then I may make bold to assert that for persevering sharpness she beats all that I ever met, even in Yorkshire;" and Mr. Kantwise looked at his new friend over his shoulder, and shook his head as though lost in wonder and admiration. "What do you think she's done now?"

"She didn't give you much to eat, I take it."

"Much to eat! I'll tell you what it is, Mr. Dockwrath; my belief is that woman would have an absolute pleasure in starving a Christian; I do indeed. I'll tell you what she has done; she has made me put her up a set of them things at twelve, seventeen, six! I needn't tell you that they were never made for the money."

"Why, then, did you part with them at a loss?"

"Well; that's the question. I was soft, I suppose. She got round me, badgering me, till I didn't know where I was. She wanted them as a present for the curate's wife, she said. Whatever should induce her to make a present!"

"She got them for twelve, seventeen, six; did she?" said Dockwrath, thinking that it might be as well to remember this, if he should feel inclined to make a purchase himself.

"But they was strained, Mr. Dockwrath; I must admit they was strained,—particularly the loo."

"You had gone through your gymnastics on it a little too often?" asked the attorney. But this Mr. Kantwise would not acknowledge. The strength of that table was such that he could stand on it for ever without injury to it; but nevertheless, in some other way it had become strained, and therefore he had sold the set to Mrs. Mason for £12 17s. 6d., that lady being minded to make a costly present to the wife of the curate of Groby.

When dinner-time came Mr. Dockwrath found that the party was swelled to the number of eight, five other undoubted commercials having brought themselves to anchor at the Bull Inn during the day. To all of these, Mr. Kantwise introduced him. "Mr. Gape, Mr. Dockwrath," said he, gracefully moving towards them the palm of his hand, and eyeing them over his shoulder. "Mr. Gape is in the stationery line," he added, in a whisper to the attorney, "and does for Cumming and Jibber of St. Paul's Churchyard. Mr. Johnson, Mr. Dockwrath. Mr. J. is from Sheffield. Mr. Snengkeld, Mr. Dockwrath;" and then he imparted in another whisper the necessary information as to Mr. Snengkeld. "Soft goods, for Brown Brothers, of Snow Hill," and so on through the whole fraternity. Each member bowed as his name was mentioned; but they did not do so very graciously, as Mr. Kantwise was not a great man among them. Had the stranger been introduced to them by Moulder,—Moulder the patriarch,—his reception among them would have been much warmer. And then they sat down to dinner, Mr. Moulder taking the chair as president, and Mr. Kantwise sitting opposite to him, as being the longest sojourner at the inn. Mr. Dockwrath sat at the right hand of Kantwise, discreetly avoiding the neighbourhood of Moulder, and the others ranged themselves according to fancy at the table. "Come up along side of me, old fellow," Moulder said to Snengkeld. "It ain't the first time that you and I have smacked our lips together over the same bit of roast beef." "Nor won't, I hope, be the last by a long chalk, Mr. Moulder," said Snengkeld, speaking with a deep, hoarse voice which seemed to ascend from some region of his body far below his chest. Moulder and Snengkeld were congenial spirits; but the latter, though the older man, was not endowed with so large a volume of body or so highly dominant a spirit. Brown Brothers, of Snow Hill, were substantial people, and Mr. Snengkeld travelled in strict accordance with the good old rules of trade which Moulder loved so well.

The politeness and general good manners of the company were something very pretty to witness. Mr. Dockwrath, as a stranger, was helped first, and every courtesy was shown to him. Even Mr. Moulder carved the beef for him with a loving hand, and Mr. Kantwise was almost subservient in his attention. Mr. Dockwrath thought that he had certainly done right in coming to the commercial table, and resolved on doing so on all occasions of future journeys. So far all was good. The commercial dinner, as he had ascertained, would cost him only two shillings, and a much inferior repast eaten by himself elsewhere would have stood in his bill for three. So far all was good; but the test by which he was to be tried was now approaching him.

When the dinner was just half over,—Mr. Moulder well knew how to mark the time,—that gentleman called for the waiter, and whispered an important order into that functionary's ears. The functionary bowed, retired from the room, and reappeared again in two minutes, bearing a bottle of sherry in each hand; one of these he deposited at the right hand of Mr. Moulder; and the other at the right hand of Mr. Kantwise.

"Sir," said Mr. Moulder, addressing himself with great ceremony to Mr. Dockwrath, "the honour of a glass of wine with you, sir," and the president, to give more importance to the occasion, put down his knife and fork, leaned back in his chair, and put both his hands upon his waistcoat, looking intently at the attorney out of his little eyes.

Mr. Dockwrath was immediately aware that a crisis had come upon him which demanded an instant decision. If he complied with the president's invitation he would have to pay his proportion of all the wine bill that might be incurred that evening by the seven commercial gentlemen at the table, and he knew well that commercial gentlemen do sometimes call for bottle after bottle with a reckless disregard of expense. But to him, with his sixteen children, wine at an hotel was terrible. A pint of beer and a glass of brandy and water were the luxuries which he had promised himself, and with manly fortitude he resolved that he would not be coerced into extravagance by any president or any Moulder.

"Sir," said he, "I'm obliged by the honour, but I don't drink wine to my dinner." Whereupon Mr. Moulder bowed his head very solemnly, winked at Snengkeld, and then drank wine with that gentleman.

"It's the rule of the room," whispered Mr. Kantwise into Mr. Dockwrath's ear; but Mr. Dockwrath pretended not to hear him, and the matter was allowed to pass by for the time.

But Mr. Snengkeld asked him for the honour, as also did Mr. Gape, who sat at Moulder's left hand; and then Mr. Dockwrath began to wax angry. "I think I remarked before that I don't drink wine to my dinner," he said; and then the three at the president's end of the table all looked at each other very solemnly, and they all winked; and after that there was very little conversation during the remainder of the meal, for men knew that the goddess of discord was in the air.

The cheese came, and with that a bottle of port wine, which was handed round, Mr. Dockwrath of course refusing to join in the conviviality; and then the cloth was drawn, and the decanters were put before the president. "James, bring me a little brandy-and-water," said the attorney, striving to put a bold face on the matter, but yet speaking with diminished voice.

"Half a moment, if you please, sir," said Moulder; and then he exclaimed with stentorian voice, "James, the dinner bill." "Yes, sir," said the waiter, and disappeared without any thought towards the requisition for brandy-and-water from Mr. Dockwrath.

For the next five minutes they all remained silent, except that Mr. Moulder gave the Queen's health as he filled his glass and pushed the bottles from him. "Gentlemen, the Queen," and then he lifted his glass of port up to the light, shut one eye as he looked at it, and immediately swallowed the contents as though he were taking a dose of physic. "I'm afraid they'll charge you for the wine," said Mr. Kantwise, again whispering to his neighbour. But Mr. Dockwrath paid no apparent attention to what was said to him. He was concentrating his energies with a view to the battle.

James, the waiter, soon returned. He also knew well what was about to happen, and he trembled as he handed in the document to the president. "Let's have it, James," said Moulder, with much pleasantry, as he took the paper in his hand. "The old ticket I suppose; five bob a head." And then he read out the bill, the total of which, wine and beer included, came to forty shillings. "Five shillings a head, gentlemen, as I said. You and I can make a pretty good guess as to the figure; eh, Snengkeld?" And then he put down his two half-crowns on the waiter, as also did Mr. Snengkeld, and then Mr. Gape, and so on till it came to Mr. Kantwise.

"I think you and I will leave it, and settle at the bar," said Kantwise, appealing to Dockwrath, and intending peace if peace were still possible.

"No," shouted Moulder, from the other end of the table; "let the man have his money now, and then his troubles will be over. If there's to be any fuss about it, let's have it out. I like to see the dinner bill settled as soon as the dinner is eaten. Then one gets an appetite for one's supper."

"I don't think I have the change," said Kantwise, still putting off the evil day.

"I'll lend, it you," said Moulder, putting his hand into his trousers-pockets. But the money was forthcoming out of Mr. Kantwise's own proper repositories, and with slow motion he put down the five shillings one after the other.

And then the waiter came to Mr. Dockwrath. "What's this?" said the attorney, taking up the bill and looking at it. The whole matter had been sufficiently explained to him, but nevertheless Mr. Moulder explained it again. "In commercial rooms, sir, as no doubt you must be well aware, seeing that you have done us the honour of joining us here, the dinner bill is divided equally among all the gentlemen as sit down. It's the rule of the room, sir. You has what you like, and you calls for what you like, and conwiviality is thereby encouraged. The figure generally comes to five shillings, and you afterwards gives what you like to the waiter. That's about it, ain't it, James?"

"That's the rule, sir, in all commercial rooms as I ever see," said the waiter.

The matter had been so extremely well put by Mr. Moulder, and that gentleman's words had carried with them so much conviction, that Dockwrath felt himself almost tempted to put down the money; as far as his sixteen children and general ideas of economy were concerned he would have done so; but his legal mind could not bear to be beaten. The spirit of litigation within him told him that the point was to be carried. Moulder,

Gape, and Snengkeld together could not make him pay for wine he had neither ordered nor swallowed. His pocket was guarded by the law of the land, and not by the laws of any special room in which he might chance to find himself. "I shall pay two shillings for my dinner," said he, "and sixpence for my beer;" and then he deposited the half-crown.

"Do you mean us to understand," said Moulder, "that after forcing your way into this room, and sitting down along with gentlemen at this table, you refuse to abide by the rules of the room?" And Mr. Moulder spoke and looked as though he thought that such treachery must certainly lead to most disastrous results. The disastrous result which a stranger might have expected at the moment would be a fit of apoplexy on the part of the worthy president.

"I neither ordered that wine nor did I drink it," said Mr. Dockwrath, compressing his lips, leaning back in his chair, and looking up into one corner of the ceiling.

"The gentleman certainly did not drink the wine," said Kantwise, "I must acknowledge that; and as for ordering it, why that was done by the president, in course."

"Gammon!" said Mr. Moulder, and he fixed his eyes steadfastly upon his Vice. "Kantwise, that's gammon. The most of what you says is gammon."

"Mr. Moulder, I don't exactly know what you mean by that word gammon, but it's objectionable. To my feelings it's very objectionable. I say that the gentleman did not drink the wine, and I appeal to the gentleman who sits at the gentleman's right, whether what I say is not correct. If what I say is correct, it can't be—gammon. Mr. Busby, did that gentleman drink the wine, or did he not?"

"Not as I see," said Mr. Busby, somewhat nervous at being thus brought into the controversy. He was a young man just commencing his travels, and stood in awe of the great Moulder.

"Gammon!" shouted Moulder, with a very red face. "Everybody at the table knows he didn't drink the wine. Everybody saw that he declined the honour when proposed, which I don't know that I ever saw a gentleman do at a commercial table till this day, barring that he was a teetotaller, which is gammon too. But its P.P. here, as every commercial gentleman knows, Kantwise as well as the best of us."

"P.P., that's the rule," growled Snengkeld, almost from under the table.

"In commercial rooms, as the gentleman must be aware, the rule is as stated by my friend on my right," said Mr. Gape. "The wine is ordered by the president or chairman, and is paid for in equal proportions by the company or guests," and in his oratory Mr. Gape laid great stress on the word "or." "The gentleman will easily perceive that such a rule as this is necessary in such a society; and unless—"

But Mr. Gape was apt to make long speeches, and therefore Mr. Moulder interrupted him. "You had better pay your five shillings, sir, and have no jaw about it. The man is standing idle there."

"It's not the value of the money," said Dockwrath, "but I must decline to acknowledge that I am amenable to the jurisdiction."

"There has clearly been a mistake," said Johnson from Sheffield, "and we had better settle it among us; anything is better than a row." Johnson from Sheffield was a man somewhat inclined to dispute the supremacy of Moulder from Houndsditch.

"No, Johnson," said the president. "Anything is not better than a row. A premeditated infraction of our rules is not better than a row."

"Did you say premeditated?" said Kantwise. "I think not premeditated."

"I did say premeditated, and I say it again."

"It looks uncommon like it," said Snengkeld.

"When a gentleman," said Gape, "who does not belong to a society—"

"It's no good having more talk," said Moulder, "and we'll soon bring this to an end. Mr.—; I haven't the honour of knowing the gentleman's name."

"My name is Dockwrath, and I am a solicitor."

"Oh, a solicitor; are you? and you said last night you was commercial! Will you be good enough to tell us, Mr. Solicitor—for I didn't just catch your name, except that it begins with a dock—and that's where most of your clients are to be found, I suppose—"

"Order, order, order!" said Kantwise, holding up both his hands.

"It's the chair as is speaking," said Mr. Gape, who had a true Englishman's notion that the chair itself could not be called to order.

"You shouldn't insult the gentleman because he has his own ideas," said Johnson.

"I don't want to insult no one," continued Moulder; "and those who know me best, among whom I can't as yet count Mr. Johnson, though hopes I shall some day, won't say it of me." "Hear—hear—hear!" from both Snengkeld and Gape; to which Kantwise added a little "hear—hear!" of his own, of which Mr. Moulder did not quite approve. "Mr. Snengkeld and Mr. Gape, they're my old friends, and they knows me. And they knows the way of a commercial room—which some gentlemen don't seem as though they do. I don't want to insult no one; but as chairman here at this conwivial meeting, I asks that gentleman who says he is a solicitor whether he means to pay his dinner bill according to the rules of the room, or whether he don't?"

"I've paid for what I've had already," said Dockwrath, "and I don't mean to pay for what I've not had."

"James," exclaimed Moulder,—and all the chairman was in his voice as he spoke,—"my compliments to Mr. Crump, and I will request his attendance for five minutes;" and then James left the room, and there was silence for a while, during which the bottles made their round of the table.

"Hadn't we better send back the pint of wine which Mr. Dockwrath hasn't used?" suggested Kantwise.

"I'm d—— if we do!" replied Moulder, with much energy; and the general silence was not again broken till Mr. Crump made his appearance; but the chairman whispered a private word or two to his friend Snengkeld. "I never sent back ordered liquor to the bar yet, unless it was bad; and I'm not going to begin now."

And then Mr. Crump came in. Mr. Crump was a very clean-looking person, without any beard; and dressed from head to foot in black. He was about fifty, with grizzly gray hair, which stood upright on his head, and his face at the present moment wore on it an innkeeper's smile. But it could also assume an innkeeper's frown, and on occasions did so—when bills were disputed, or unreasonable strangers thought that they knew the distance in posting miles round the neighbourhood of Leeds better than did he, Mr. Crump, who had lived at the Bull Inn all his life. But Mr. Crump rarely frowned on commercial gentlemen, from whom was derived the main stay of his business and the main prop of his house.

"Mr. Crump," began Moulder, "here has occurred a very unpleasant transaction."

"I know all about it, gentlemen," said Mr. Crump. "The waiter has acquainted me, and I can assure you, gentlemen, that I am extremely sorry that anything should have arisen to disturb the harmony of your dinner-table."

"We must now call upon you, Mr. Crump," began Mr. Moulder, who was about to demand that Dockwrath should be turned bodily out of the room.

"If you'll allow me one moment, Mr. Moulder," continued Mr. Crump, "and I'll tell you what is my suggestion. The gentleman here, who I understand is a lawyer, does not wish to comply with the rules of the commercial room."

"I certainly don't wish or intend to pay for drink that I didn't order and haven't had," said Dockwrath.

"Exactly," said Mr. Crump. "And therefore, gentlemen, to get out of the difficulty, we'll presume, if you please, that the bill is paid."

"The lawyer, as you call him, will have to leave the room," said Moulder.

"Perhaps he will not object to step over to the coffee-room on the other side," suggested the landlord.

"I can't think of leaving my seat here under such circumstances," said Dockwrath.

"You can't," said Moulder. "Then you must be made, as I take it."

"Let me see the man that will make me," said Dockwrath.

Mr. Crump looked very apologetic and not very comfortable. "There is a difficulty, gentlemen; there is a difficulty, indeed," he said. "The fact is, the gentleman should not have been showed into the room at all;" and he looked very angrily at his own servant, James.

"He said he was 'mercial," said James. "So he did. Now he says as how he's a lawyer. What's a poor man to do?"

"I'm a commercial lawyer," said Dockwrath.

"He must leave the room, or I shall leave the house," said Moulder.

"Gentlemen, gentlemen!" said Crump. "This kind of thing does not happen often, and on this occasion I must try your kind patience. If Mr. Moulder would allow me to suggest that the commercial gentlemen should take their wine in the large drawing-room up stairs this evening, Mrs. C.

will do her best to make it comfortable for them in five minutes. There of course they can be private."

There was something in the idea of leaving Mr. Dockwrath alone in his glory which appeased the spirit of the great Moulder. He had known Crump, moreover, for many years, and was aware that it would be a dangerous, and probably an expensive proceeding to thrust out the attorney by violence. "If the other gentlemen are agreeable, I am," said he. The other gentlemen were agreeable, and, with the exception of Kantwise, they all rose from their chairs.

"I must say I think you ought to leave the room as you don't choose to abide by the rules," said Johnson, addressing himself to Dockwrath.

"That's your opinion," said Dockwrath.

"Yes, it is," said Johnson. "That's my opinion."

"My own happens to be different," said Dockwrath; and so he kept his chair.

"There, Mr. Crump," said Moulder, taking half a crown from his pocket and throwing it on the table. "I sha'n't see you at a loss."

"Thank you, sir," said Mr. Crump; and he very humbly took up the money.

"I keep a little account for charity at home," said Moulder.

"It don't run very high, do it?" asked Snengkeld, jocosely.

"Not out of the way, it don't. But now I shall have the pleasure of writing down in it that I paid half a crown for a lawyer who couldn't afford to settle his own dinner bill. Sir, we have the pleasure of wishing you a good night."

"I hope you'll find the large drawing-room up stairs quite comfortable," said Dockwrath.

And then they all marched out of the room, each with his own glass, Mr. Moulder leading the way with stately step. It was pleasant to see them as they all followed their leader across the open passage of the gateway, in by the bar, and so up the chief staircase. Mr. Moulder walked slowly, bearing the bottle of port and his own glass, and Mr. Snengkeld and Mr. Gape followed in line, bearing also their own glasses, and maintaining the dignity of their profession under circumstances of some difficulty.

And then they all marched out of the room, each with his own glass.

"Gentlemen, I really am sorry for this little accident," said Mr. Crump, as they were passing the bar; "but a lawyer, you know—"

"And such a lawyer, eh, Crump?" said Moulder.

"It might be five-and-twenty pound to me to lay a hand on him!" said the landlord.

When the time came for Mr. Kantwise to move, he considered the matter well. The chances, however, as he calculated them, were against any profitable business being done with the attorney, so he also left the room. "Good night, sir," he said as he went. "I wish you a very good night."

"Take care of yourself," said Dockwrath; and then the attorney spent the rest of the evening alone.

CHAPTER X
MR., MRS., AND MISS FURNIVAL

I will now ask my readers to come with me up to London, in order that I may introduce them to the family of the Furnivals. We shall see much of the Furnivals before we reach the end of our present undertaking, and it will be well that we should commence our acquaintance with them as early as may be done.

Mr. Furnival was a lawyer—I mean a barrister—belonging to Lincoln's Inn, and living at the time at which our story is supposed to commence in Harley Street. But he had not been long a resident in Harley Street, having left the less fashionable neighbourhood of Russell Square only two or three years before that period. On his marriage he had located himself in a small house in Keppel Street, and had there remained till professional success, long waited for, enabled him to move further west, and indulge himself with the comforts of larger rooms and more servants. At the time of which I am now speaking Mr. Furnival was known, and well known, as a successful man; but he had struggled long and hard before that success had come to him, and during the earliest years of his married life had found the work of keeping the wolf from the door to be almost more than enough for his energies.

Mr. Furnival practised at the common law bar, and early in life had attached himself to the home circuit. I cannot say why he obtained no great success till he was nearer fifty than forty years of age. At that time I fancy that barristers did not come to their prime till a period of life at which other men are supposed to be in their decadence. Nevertheless, he had married on nothing, and had kept the wolf from the door. To do this he had been constant at his work in season and out of season, during the long hours of day and the long hours of night. Throughout his term times he had toiled in court, and during the vacations he had toiled out of court. He had reported volumes of cases, having been himself his own short-hand writer,—as it is well known to most young lawyers, who as a rule always fill an upper shelf in their law libraries with Furnival and Staples' seventeen volumes in calf. He had worked for the booksellers, and for the newspapers, and for the attorneys,—always working, however, with reference to the law; and though he had worked for years with the lowest pay, no man had heard him complain. That no woman had heard him do so, I will not say; as it is more than probable that into the sympathising ears of Mrs. Furnival he did pour forth plaints as to the small wages which the legal world meted out to him in return for his labours. He was a constant, hard, patient man, and at last there came to him the full reward of all his industry. What was the special case by which Mr. Furnival obtained his great success no man could say. In all probability there was no special case. Gradually it began to be understood that he was a safe man, understanding his trade, true to his clients, and very damaging as an opponent. Legal gentlemen are, I believe, quite as often bought off as bought up. Sir Richard and Mr. Furnival could not both be required on the same side, seeing what a tower of strength each was in himself; but then Sir Richard would be absolutely neutralized if Mr. Furnival were employed on the other side. This is a system well understood by attorneys, and has been found to be extremely lucrative by gentlemen leading at the bar.

Mr. Furnival was now fifty-five years of age, and was beginning to show in his face some traces of his hard work. Not that he was becoming old, or weak, or worn; but his eye had lost its fire—except the fire peculiar to his profession; and there were wrinkles in his forehead and cheeks; and his upper lip, except when he was speaking, hung heavily over the lower; and the loose skin below his eye was forming into saucers; and his hair had become grizzled; and on his shoulders, except when in court, there was a slight stoop. As seen in his wig and gown he was a man of commanding presence,—and for ten men in London who knew him in this garb, hardly one knew him without it. He was nearly six feet high, and stood forth prominently, with square, broad shoulders and a large body. His head also was large; his forehead was high, and marked strongly by signs of intellect; his nose was long and straight, his eyes were very gray, and capable to an extraordinary degree both of direct severity and of concealed sarcasm. Witnesses have been heard to say that they could endure all that Mr. Furnival could say to them, and continue in some sort to answer all his questions, if only he would refrain from looking at them. But he would never refrain; and therefore it was now well understood how great a thing it was to secure the services of Mr. Furnival. "Sir," an attorney would say to an unfortunate client doubtful as to the expenditure, "your witnesses will not be able to stand in the box if we allow Mr. Furnival to be engaged on the other side." I am inclined to think that Mr. Furnival owed to this power of his eyes his almost unequalled perfection in that peculiar branch of his profession. His voice was powerful, and not unpleasant when used within the precincts of a court, though it grated somewhat harshly on the ears in the smaller compass of a private room. His flow of words was free and good, and seemed to come from him without the slightest effort. Such at least was always the case with him when standing wigged and gowned before a judge. Latterly, however, he had tried his eloquence on another arena, and not altogether with equal success. He was now in Parliament, sitting as member for the Essex Marshes, and he had not as yet carried either the country or the House with him, although he had been frequently on his legs. Some men said that with a little practice he would yet become very serviceable as an honourable and learned member; but others expressed a fear that he had come too late in life to these new duties.

I have spoken of Mr. Furnival's great success in that branch of his profession which required from him the examination of evidence, but I would not have it thought that he was great only in this, or even mainly in this. There are gentlemen at the bar, among whom I may perhaps notice my old friend Mr. Chaffanbrass as the most conspicuous, who have confined their talents to the browbeating of witnesses,—greatly to their own profit, and no doubt to the advantage of society. But I would have it understood that Mr. Furnival was by no means one of these. He had been no Old Bailey lawyer, devoting himself to the manumission of murderers, or the security of the swindling world in general. He had been employed on abstruse points of law, had been great in will cases, very learned as to the rights of railways, peculiarly apt in enforcing the dowries of married women, and successful above all things in separating husbands and wives whose lives had not been passed in accordance with the recognised rules of Hymen. Indeed there is no branch of the Common Law in which he was not regarded as great and powerful, though perhaps his proficiency in damaging the general characters of his opponents has been recognised as his especial forte. Under these circumstances I should grieve to have him confounded with such men as Mr. Chaffanbrass, who is hardly known by the profession beyond the precincts of his own peculiar court in the City. Mr. Furnival's reputation has spread itself wherever stuff gowns and horsehair wigs are held in estimation.

Mr. Furnival when clothed in his forensic habiliments certainly possessed a solemn and severe dignity which had its weight even with the judges. Those who scrutinised his appearance critically might have said that it was in some respects pretentious; but the ordinary jurymen of this country are not critical scrutinisers of appearance, and by them he was never held in light estimation. When in his addresses to them, appealing to their intelligence, education, and enlightened justice, he would declare that the property of his clients was perfectly safe in their hands, he looked to be such an advocate as a litigant would fain possess when dreading the soundness of his own cause. Any cause was sound to him when once he had been feed for its support, and he carried in his countenance his assurance of this soundness,—and the assurance of unsoundness in the cause of his opponent. Even he did not always win; but on the occasion of his losing, those of the uninitiated who had heard the pleadings would express their astonishment that he should not have been successful.

When he was divested of his wig his appearance was not so perfect. There was then a hard, long straightness about his head and face, giving to his countenance the form of a parallelogram, to which there belonged a certain meanness of expression. He wanted the roundness of forehead, the short lines, and the graceful curves of face which are necessary to unadorned manly comeliness. His whiskers were small, grizzled, and ill grown, and required the ample relief of his wig. In no guise did he look other than a clever man; but in his dress as a simple citizen he would perhaps be taken as a clever man in whose tenderness of heart and cordiality of feeling one would not at first sight place implicit trust.

As a poor man Mr. Furnival had done his duty well by his wife and family,—for as a poor man he had been blessed with four children. Three of these had died as they were becoming men and women, and now, as a rich man, he was left with one daughter, an only child. As a poor man Mr. Furnival had been an excellent husband, going forth in the morning to his work, struggling through the day, and then returning to his meagre dinner and his long evenings of unremitting drudgery. The bodily strength which had supported him through his work in those days must have been immense, for he had allowed himself no holidays. And then success and money had come,—and Mrs. Furnival sometimes found herself not quite so happy as she had been when watching beside him in the days of their poverty.

The equal mind,—as mortal Delius was bidden to remember, and as Mr. Furnival might also have remembered had time been allowed him to cultivate the classics,—the equal mind should be as sedulously maintained when things run well, as well as when they run hardly; and perhaps the maintenance of such equal mind is more difficult in the former than in the latter stage of life. Be that as it may, Mr. Furnival could now be very cross on certain domestic occasions, and could also be very unjust. And there was worse than this,—much worse behind. He, who in the heyday of his youth would spend night after night poring over his books, copying out reports, and never asking to see a female habiliment brighter or more attractive than his wife's Sunday gown, he, at the age of fifty-five, was now running after strange goddesses! The member for the Essex Marshes, in these his latter days, was obtaining for himself among other successes the character of a Lothario; and Mrs. Furnival, sitting at home in her genteel drawing-room near Cavendish Square, would remember with regret the small dingy parlour in Keppel Street.

Mrs. Furnival in discussing her grievances would attribute them mainly to port wine. In his early days Mr. Furnival had been essentially an abstemious man. Young men who work fifteen hours a day must be so. But now he had a strong opinion about certain Portuguese vintages, was convinced that there was no port wine in London equal to the contents of his own bin, saving always a certain green cork appertaining to his own club, which was to be extracted at the rate of thirty shillings a cork. And Mrs. Furnival attributed to these latter studies not only a certain purple hue which was suffusing his nose and cheeks, but also that unevenness of character and those supposed domestic improprieties to which allusion has been made. It may, however, be as well to explain that Mrs. Ball, the old family cook and housekeeper, who had ascended with the Furnivals in the world, opined that made-dishes did the mischief. He dined out too often, and was a deal too particular about his dinner when he dined at home. If Providence would see fit to visit him with a sharp attack of the gout, it would—so thought Mrs. Ball—be better for all parties.

Whether or no it may have been that Mrs. Furnival at fifty-five—for she and her lord were of the same age—was not herself as attractive in her husband's eyes as she had been at thirty, I will not pretend to say. There can have been no just reason for any such change in feeling, seeing that the two had grown old together. She, poor woman, would have been quite content with the attentions of Mr. Furnival, though his hair was grizzled and his nose was blue; nor did she ever think of attracting to herself the admiration of any swain whose general comeliness might be more free from all taint of age. Why then should he wander afield—at the age of fifty-five? That he did wander afield, poor Mrs. Furnival felt in her agony convinced; and among those ladies whom on this account she most thoroughly detested was our friend Lady Mason of Orley Farm. Lady Mason and the lawyer had first become acquainted in the days of the trial, now long gone by, on which occasion Mr. Furnival had been employed as the junior counsel; and that acquaintance had ripened into friendship, and now flourished in full vigour,—to Mrs. Furnival's great sorrow and disturbance.

Mrs. Furnival herself was a stout, solid woman, sensible on most points, but better adapted, perhaps, to the life in Keppel Street than that to which she had now been promoted. As Kitty Blacker she had possessed feminine charms which would have been famous had they been better known. Mr. Furnival had fetched her from farther East—from the region of Great Ormond street and the neighbourhood of Southampton Buildings. Her cherry cheeks, and her round eye, and her full bust, and her fresh lip, had conquered the hard-tasked lawyer; and so they had gone forth to fight the world together. Her eye was still round, and her cheek red, and her bust full,—there had certainly been no falling off there; nor will I say that her lip had lost its freshness. But the bloom of her charms had passed away, and she was now a solid, stout, motherly woman, not bright in converse, but by no means deficient in mother-wit, recognizing well the duties which she owed to others, but recognizing equally well those which others owed to her. All the charms of her youth—had they not been given to him, and also all her solicitude, all her anxious fighting with the hard world? When they had been poor together, had she not patched and turned and twisted, sitting silently by his side into the long nights, because she would not ask him for the price of a new dress? And yet now, now that they were rich—? Mrs. Furnival, when she put such questions within her own mind, could hardly answer this latter one with patience. Others might be afraid of the great Mr. Furnival in his wig and gown; others might be struck dumb by his power of eye and mouth; but she, she, the wife of his bosom, she could catch him without his armour. She would so catch him and let him know what she thought of all her wrongs. So she said to herself many a day, and yet the great deed, in all its explosiveness, had never yet been done. Small attacks of words there had been many, but hitherto the courage to speak out her griefs openly had been wanting to her.

I can now allow myself but a small space to say a few words of Sophia Furnival, and yet in that small space must be confined all the direct description which can be given of one of the principal personages of this story. At nineteen Miss Furnival was in all respects a young woman. She was forward in acquirements, in manner, in general intelligence, and in powers of conversation. She was a handsome, tall girl, with expressive gray eyes and dark-brown hair. Her mouth, and hair, and a certain motion of her neck and turn of her head, had come to her from her mother, but her eyes were those of her father: they were less sharp perhaps, less eager after their prey; but they were bright as his had been bright, and sometimes had in them more of absolute command than he was ever able to throw into his own.

Their golden days had come on them at a period of her life which enabled her to make a better use of them than her mother could do. She never felt herself to be struck dumb by rank or fashion, nor did she in the drawing-rooms of the great ever show signs of an Eastern origin. She could adapt herself without an effort to the manners of Cavendish Square;—ay, and if need were, to the ways of more glorious squares even than that. Therefore was her father never ashamed to be seen with her on his arm in the houses of his new friends, though on such occasions he was willing enough to go out without disturbing the repose of his wife. No mother could have loved her children with a warmer affection than that which had warmed the heart of poor Mrs. Furnival; but under such circumstances as these was it singular that she should occasionally become jealous of her own daughter?

Sophia Furnival was, as I have said, a clever, attractive girl, handsome, well-read, able to hold her own with the old as well as with the young, capable of hiding her vanity if she had any, mild and gentle to girls less gifted, animated in conversation, and yet possessing an eye that could fall softly to the ground, as a woman's eye always should fall upon occasions.

Nevertheless she was not altogether charming. "I don't feel quite sure that she is real," Mrs. Orme had said of her, when on a certain occasion Miss Furnival had spent a day and a night at The Cleeve.

CHAPTER XI
MRS. FURNIVAL AT HOME

Lucius Mason on his road to Liverpool had passed through London, and had found a moment to call in Harley Street. Since his return from Germany he had met Miss Furnival both at home at his mother's house — or rather his own — and at The Cleeve. Miss Furnival had been in the neighbourhood, and had spent two days with the great people at The Cleeve, and one day with the little people at Orley Farm. Lucius Mason had found that she was a sensible girl, capable of discussing great subjects with him; and had possibly found some other charms in her. Therefore he had called in Harley Street.

On that occasion he could only call as he passed through London without delay; but he received such encouragement as induced him to spend a night in town on his return, in order that he might accept an invitation to drink tea with the Furnivals. "We shall be very happy to see you," Mrs. Furnival had said, backing the proposition which had come from her daughter without any very great fervour; "but I fear Mr. Furnival will not be at home. Mr. Furnival very seldom is at home now." Young Mason did not much care for fervour on the part of Sophia's mother, and therefore had accepted the invitation, though he was obliged by so doing to curtail by some hours his sojourn among the guano stores of Liverpool.

It was the time of year at which few people are at home in London, being the middle of October; but Mrs. Furnival was a lady of whom at such periods it was not very easy to dispose. She could have made herself as happy as a queen even at Margate, if it could have suited Furnival and Sophia to be happy at Margate with her. But this did not suit Furnival or Sophia. As regards money, any or almost all other autumnal resorts were open to her, but she could be contented at none of them because Mr. Furnival always pleaded that business — law business or political business — took him elsewhere. Now Mrs. Furnival was a woman who did not like to be deserted, and who could not, in the absence of those social joys which Providence had vouchsafed to her as her own, make herself happy with the society of other women such as herself. Furnival was her husband, and she wanted him to carve for her, to sit opposite to her at the breakfast table, to tell her the news of the day, and to walk to church with her on Sundays. They had been made one flesh and one bone, for better and worse, thirty years since; and now in her latter days she could not put up with disseveration and dislocation.

She had gone down to Brighton in August, soon after the House broke up, and there found that very handsome apartments had been taken for her—rooms that would have made glad the heart of many a lawyer's wife. She had, too, the command of a fly, done up to look like a private brougham, a servant in livery, the run of the public assembly-rooms, a sitting in the centre of the most fashionable church in Brighton—all that the heart of woman could desire. All but the one thing was there; but, that one thing being absent, she came moodily back to town at the end of September. She would have exchanged them all with a happy heart for very moderate accommodation at Margate, could she have seen Mr. Furnival's blue nose on the other side of the table every morning and evening as she sat over her shrimps and tea.

Men who had risen in the world as Mr. Furnival had done do find it sometimes difficult to dispose of their wives. It is not that the ladies are in themselves more unfit for rising than their lords, or that if occasion demanded they would not as readily adapt themselves to new spheres. But they do not rise, and occasion does not demand it. A man elevates his wife to his own rank, and when Mr. Brown, on becoming solicitor-general, becomes Sir Jacob, Mrs. Brown also becomes my lady. But the whole set among whom Brown must be more or less thrown do not want her ladyship. On Brown's promotion she did not become part of the bargain. Brown must henceforth have two existences—a public and a private existence; and it will be well for Lady Brown, and well also for Sir Jacob, if the latter be not allowed to dwindle down to a minimum.

If Lady B. can raise herself also, if she can make her own occasion—if she be handsome and can flirt, if she be impudent and can force her way, if she have a daring mind and can commit great expenditure, if she be clever and can make poetry, if she can in any way create a separate glory for herself, then, indeed, Sir Jacob with his blue nose may follow his own path, and all will be well. Sir Jacob's blue nose seated opposite to her will not be her summum bonum.

But worthy Mrs. Furnival—and she was worthy—had created for herself no such separate glory, nor did she dream of creating it; and therefore she had, as it were, no footing left to her. On this occasion she had gone to Brighton, and had returned from it sulky and wretched, bringing her daughter back to London at the period of London's greatest desolation. Sophia had returned uncomplaining, remembering that good things were in store for her. She had been asked to spend her Christmas with the Staveleys at Noningsby—the family of Judge Staveley, who lives near Alston, at a very pretty country place so called. Mr. Furnival had been for many years acquainted with Judge Staveley,—had known the judge when he was a leading counsel; and now that Mr. Furnival was a rising man, and now that he had a pretty daughter, it was natural that the young Staveleys and Sophia Furnival should know each other. But poor Mrs. Furnival was too ponderous for this mounting late in life, and she had not been asked to Noningsby. She was much too good a mother to repine at her daughter's promised gaiety. Sophia was welcome to go; but by all the laws of God and man it would behove her lord and husband to eat his mincepie at home.

"Mr. Furnival was to be back in town this evening," the lady said, as though apologizing to young Mason for her husband's absence, when he entered the drawing-room, "but he has not come, and I dare say will not come now."

Mason did not care a straw for Mr. Furnival. "Oh! won't he?" said he. "I suppose business keeps him."

"Papa is very busy about politics just at present," said Sophia, wishing to make matters smooth in her mother's mind. "He was obliged to be at Romford in the beginning of the week, and then he went down to Birmingham. There is some congress going on there, is there not?"

"All that must take a great deal of time," said Lucius.

"Yes; and it is a terrible bore," said Sophia. "I know papa finds it so."

"Your papa likes it, I believe," said Mrs. Furnival, who would not hide even her grievances under a bushel.

"I don't think he likes being so much from home, mamma. Of course he likes excitement, and success. All men do. Do they not, Mr. Mason?"

"They all ought to do so, and women also."

"Ah! but women have no sphere, Mr. Mason."

"They have minds equal to those of men," said Lucius, gallantly, "and ought to be able to make for themselves careers as brilliant."

"Women ought not to have any spheres," said Mrs. Furnival.

"I don't know that I quite agree with you there, mamma."

"The world is becoming a great deal too fond of what you call excitement and success. Of course it is a good thing for a man to make money by his profession, and a very hard thing when he can't do it," added Mrs. Furnival, thinking of the olden days. "But if success in life means rampaging about, and never knowing what it is to sit quiet over his own fireside, I for one would as soon manage to do without it."

"But, mamma, I don't see why success should always be rampageous."

"Literary women who have achieved a name bear their honours quietly," said Lucius.

"I don't know," said Mrs. Furnival. "I am told that some of them are as fond of gadding as the men. As regards the old maids, I don't care so much about it; people who are not married may do what they like with themselves, and nobody has anything to say to them. But it is very different for married people. They have no business to be enticed away from their homes by any success."

"Mamma is all for a Darby and Joan life," said Sophia, laughing.

"No I am not, my dear; and you should not say so. I don't advocate anything that is absurd. But I do say that life should be lived at home. That is the best part of it. What is the meaning of home if it isn't that?"

Poor Mrs. Furnival! she had no idea that she was complaining to a stranger of her husband. Had any one told her so she would have declared that she was discussing world-wide topics; but Lucius Mason, young as he was, knew that the marital shoe was pinching the lady's domestic corn, and he made haste to change the subject.

"You know my mother, Mrs. Furnival?"

Mrs. Furnival said that she had the honour of acquaintance with Lady Mason; but on this occasion also she exhibited but little fervour.

"I shall meet her up in town to-morrow," said Lucius. "She is coming up for some shopping."

"Oh! indeed," said Mrs. Furnival.

"And then we go down home together. I am to meet her at the chymist's at the top of Chancery Lane."

Now this was a very unnecessary communication on the part of young Mason, and also an unfortunate one. "Oh! indeed," said Mrs. Furnival again, throwing her head a little back. Poor woman! she could not conceal what was in her mind, and her daughter knew all about it immediately. The truth was this. Mr. Furnival had been for some days on the move, at Birmingham and elsewhere, and had now sent up sudden notice that he should probably be at home that very night. He should probably be at home that night, but in such case would be compelled to return to his friends at Birmingham on the following afternoon. Now if it were an ascertained fact that he was coming to London merely with the view of meeting Lady Mason, the wife of his bosom would not think it necessary to provide for him the warmest welcome. This of course was not an ascertained fact; but were there not terrible grounds of suspicion? Mr. Furnival's law chambers were in Old Square, Lincoln's Inn, close to Chancery Lane, and Lady Mason had made her appointment with her son within five minutes' walk of that locality. And was it not in itself a strange coincidence that Lady Mason, who came to town so seldom, should now do so on the very day of Mr. Furnival's sudden return? She felt sure that they were to meet on the morrow, but yet she could not declare even to herself that it was an ascertained fact.

"Oh! indeed," she said; and Sophia understood all about it, though Lucius did not.

Then Mrs. Furnival sank into silence; and we need not follow, word for word, the conversation between the young lady and the young gentleman. Mr. Mason thought that Miss Furnival was a very nice girl, and was not at all ill pleased to have an opportunity of passing an evening in her company; and Miss Furnival thought—. What she thought, or what young ladies may think generally about young gentlemen, is not to be spoken openly; but it seemed as though she also were employed to her own satisfaction, while her mother sat moody in her own arm-chair. In the course of the evening the footman in livery brought in tea, handing it round on a big silver salver, which also added to Mrs. Furnival's unhappiness. She would have liked to sit behind her tea-tray as she used to do in the good old hard-working days, with a small pile of buttered toast on the slop-bowl, kept warm by hot water below. In those dear old hard-working days, buttered toast had been a much-loved delicacy with Furnival; and she, kind woman, had never begrudged her eyes, as she sat making it for him over the parlour fire. Nor would she have begrudged them now, neither her eyes nor the work of her hands, nor all the thoughts of her heart, if he would have consented to accept of her handiwork; but in these days Mr. Furnival had learned a relish for other delicacies.

She also had liked buttered toast, always, however, taking the pieces with the upper crust, in order that the more luscious morsels might be left for him; and she had liked to prepare her own tea leisurely, putting in slowly the sugar and cream—skimmed milk it had used to be, dropped for herself with a sparing hand, in order that his large breakfast-cup might be whitened to his liking; but though the milk had been skimmed and scanty, and though the tea itself had been put in with a sparing hand, she had then been mistress of the occasion. She had had her own way, and in stinting herself had found her own reward. But now—the tea had no flavour now that it was made in the kitchen and brought to her, cold and vapid, by a man in livery whom she half feared to keep waiting while she ministered to her own wants.

And so she sat moody in her arm-chair, cross and sulky, as her daughter thought. But yet there was a vein of poetry in her heart, as she sat there, little like a sibyl as she looked. Dear old days, in which her cares and solicitude were valued; in which she could do something for the joint benefit of the firm into which she had been taken as a partner! How happy she had been in her struggles, how piteously had her heart yearned towards him when she thought that he was struggling too fiercely, how brave and constant he had been; and how she had loved him as he sat steady as a rock at his grinding work! Now had come the great success of which they had both dreamed together, of which they had talked as arm in arm they were taking the exercise that was so needful to him, walking quickly round Russell Square, quickly round Bloomsbury Square and Bedford Square, and so back to the grinding work in Keppel Street. It had come now—all of which they had dreamed, and more than all they had dared to hope. But of what good was it? Was he happy? No; he was fretful, bilious, and worn with toil which was hard to him because he ate and drank too much; he was ill at ease in public, only half understanding the political life which he was obliged to assume in his new ambition; and he was sick in his conscience—she was sure that must be so: he could not thus neglect her, his loving, constant wife, without some pangs of remorse. And was she happy? She might have revelled in silks and satins, if silks and satins would have done her old heart good. But they would do her no good. How she had joyed in a new dress when it had been so hard to come by, so slow in coming, and when he would go with her to the choosing of it! But her gowns now were hardly of more interest to her than the joints of meat which the butcher brought to the door with the utmost regularity. It behoved the butcher to send good beef and the milliner to send good silk, and there was an end of it.

Not but what she could have been ecstatic about a full skirt on a smart body if he would have cared to look at it. In truth she was still soft and young enough within, though stout, and solid, and somewhat aged without. Though she looked cross and surly that night, there was soft poetry within her heart. If Providence, who had bountifully given, would now by chance mercifully take away those gifts, would she not then forgive everything and toil for him again with the same happiness as before? Ah! yes; she could forgive everything, anything, if he would only return and be contented to sit opposite to her once again. "O mortal Delius, dearest lord and husband!" she exclaimed within her own breast, in language somewhat differing from that of the Roman poet, "why hast thou not remembered to maintain a mind equal in prosperity as it was always equal and well poised in adversity? Oh my Delius, since prosperity has been too much for thee, may the Lord bless thee once more with the adversity which thou canst bear—which thou canst bear, and I with thee!" Thus did she sing sadly within her own bosom,— sadly, but with true poetic cadence; while Sophia and Lucius Mason, sitting by, when for a moment they turned their eyes upon her, gave her credit only for the cross solemnity supposed to be incidental to obese and declining years.

And then there came a ring at the bell and a knock at the door, and a rush along the nether passages, and the lady knew that he of whom she had been thinking had arrived. In olden days she had ever met him in the narrow passage, and, indifferent to the maid, she had hung about his neck and kissed him in the hall. But now she did not stir from the chair. She could forgive him all and run again at the sound of his footstep, but she must first know that such forgiveness and such running would be welcome.

"That's papa," said Sophia.

"Don't forget that I have not met him since I have been home from Germany," said Lucius. "You must introduce me."

In a minute or two Mr. Furnival opened the door and walked into the room. Men when they arrive from their travels now-a-days have no strippings of greatcoats, no deposits to make of thick shawls and double gloves, no absolutely necessary changes of raiment. Such had been the case when he had used to come back cold and weary from the circuits; but now he had left Birmingham since dinner by the late express, and enjoyed his nap in the train for two hours or so, and walked into his own drawing-room as he might have done had he dined in his own dining-room.

"How are you, Kitty?" he said to his wife, handing to her the forefinger of his right hand by way of greeting. "Well, Sophy, my love;" and he kissed his daughter. "Oh! Lucius Mason. I am very glad to see you. I can't say I should have remembered you unless I had been told. You are very welcome in Harley Street, and I hope you will often be here."

Mr. Furnival's welcome home.

"It's not very often he'd find you at home, Mr. Furnival," said the aggrieved wife.

"Not so often as I could wish just at present; but things will be more settled, I hope, before very long. How's your mother, Lucius?"

"She's pretty well, thank you, sir. I've to meet her in town to-morrow, and go down home with her."

There was then silence in the room for a few seconds, during which Mrs. Furnival looked very sharply at her husband. "Oh! she's to be in town, is she?" said Mr. Furnival, after a moment's consideration. He was angry with Lady Mason at the moment for having put him into this position. Why had she told her son that she was to be up in London, thus producing conversation and tittle-tattle which made deceit on his part absolutely necessary? Lady Mason's business in London was of a nature which would not bear much open talking. She herself, in her earnest letter summoning Mr. Furnival up from Birmingham, had besought him that her visit to his chambers might not be made matter of discussion. New troubles might be coming on her, but also they might not; and she was very anxious that no one should know that she was seeking a lawyer's advice on the matter. To all this Mr. Furnival had given in his adhesion; and yet she had put it into her son's power to come to his drawing-room and chatter there of her whereabouts. For a moment or two he doubted; but at the expiration of those moments he saw that the deceit was necessary. "She's to be in town, is she?" said he. The reader will of course observe that this deceit was practised, not as between husband and wife with reference to an assignation with a lady, but between the lawyer and the outer world with reference to a private meeting with a client. But then it is sometimes so difficult to make wives look at such matters in the right light.

"She's coming up for some shopping," said Lucius.

"Oh! indeed," said Mrs. Furnival. She would not have spoken if she could have helped it, but she could not help it; and then there was silence in the room for a minute or two, which Lucius vainly endeavoured to break by a few indifferent observations to Miss Furnival. The words, however, which he uttered would not take the guise of indifferent observations, but fell flatly on their ears, and at the same time solemnly, as though spoken with the sole purpose of creating sound.

"I hope you have been enjoying yourself at Birmingham," said Mrs. Furnival.

"Enjoyed myself! I did not exactly go there for enjoyment."

"Or at Romford, where you were before?"

"Women seem to think that men have no purpose but amusement when they go about their daily work," said Mr. Furnival; and then he threw himself back in his arm-chair, and took up the last Quarterly.

Lucius Mason soon perceived that all the harmony of the evening had in some way been marred by the return of the master of the house, and that he might be in the way if he remained; he therefore took his leave.

"I shall want breakfast punctually at half-past eight to-morrow morning," said Mr. Furnival, as soon as the stranger had withdrawn. "I must be in chambers before ten;" and then he took his candle and withdrew to his own room.

Sophia rang the bell and gave the servant the order; but Mrs. Furnival took no trouble in the matter whatever. In the olden days she would have bustled down before she went to bed, and have seen herself that everything was ready, so that the master of the house might not be kept waiting. But all this was nothing to her now.

CHAPTER XII
MR. FURNIVAL'S CHAMBERS

Mr. Furnival's chambers were on the first floor in a very dingy edifice in Old Square, Lincoln's Inn. This square was always dingy, even when it was comparatively open and served as the approach from Chancery Lane to the Lord Chancellor's Court; but now it has been built up with new shops for the Vice-Chancellor, and to my eyes it seems more dingy than ever.

He there occupied three rooms, all of them sufficiently spacious for the purposes required, but which were made oppressive by their general dinginess and by a smell of old leather which pervaded them. In one of them sat at his desk Mr. Crabwitz, a gentleman who had now been with Mr. Furnival for the last fifteen years, and who considered that no inconsiderable portion of the barrister's success had been attributable to his own energy and genius. Mr. Crabwitz was a genteel-looking man, somewhat over forty years of age, very careful as to his gloves, hat, and umbrella, and not a little particular as to his associates. As he was unmarried, fond of ladies' society, and presumed to be a warm man in money matters, he had his social successes, and looked down from a considerable altitude on some men who from their professional rank might have been considered as his superiors. He had a small bachelor's box down at Barnes, and not unfrequently went abroad in the vacations. The door opening into the room of Mr. Crabwitz was in the corner fronting you on the left-hand side as you entered the chambers. Immediately on your left was a large waiting-room, in which an additional clerk usually sat at an ordinary table. He was not an authorised part of the establishment, being kept only from week to week; but nevertheless, for the last two or three years he had been always there, and Mr. Crabwitz intended that he should remain, for he acted as fag to Mr. Crabwitz. This waiting-room was very dingy, much more so than the clerk's room, and boasted of no furniture but eight old leathern chairs and two old tables. It was surrounded by shelves which were laden with books and dust, which by no chance were ever disturbed. But to my ideas the most dingy of the three rooms was that large one in which the great man himself sat; the door of which directly fronted you as you entered. The furniture was probably better than that in the other chambers, and the place had certainly the appearance of warmth and life which comes from frequent use; but nevertheless, of all the rooms in which I ever sat I think it was the most gloomy. There were heavy curtains to the windows, which had once been ruby but were now brown; and the ceiling was brown, and the thick carpet was brown, and the books which covered every portion of the wall were brown, and the painted wood-work of the doors and windows was of a dark brown. Here, on the morning with which we have now to deal, sat Mr. Furnival over his papers from ten to twelve, at which latter hour Lady Mason was to come to him. The holidays of Mr. Crabwitz had this year been cut short in consequence of his patron's attendance at the great congress which was now sitting, and although all London was a desert, as he had piteously complained to a lady of his acquaintance whom he had left at Boulogne, he was there in the midst of the desert, and on this morning was sitting in attendance at his usual desk.

Why Mr. Furnival should have breakfasted by himself at half-past eight in order that he might be at his chambers at ten, seeing that the engagement for which he had come to town was timed for twelve, I will not pretend to say. He did not ask his wife to join him, and consequently she did not come down till her usual time. Mr. Furnival breakfasted by himself, and at ten o'clock he was in his chambers. Though alone for two hours he was not idle, and exactly at twelve Mr. Crabwitz opened his door and announced Lady Mason.

When we last parted with her after her interview with Sir Peregrine Orme, she had resolved not to communicate with her friend the lawyer,—at any rate not to do so immediately. Thinking on that resolve she had tried to sleep that night; but her mind was altogether disturbed, and she could get no rest. What, if after twenty years of tranquillity all her troubles must now be recommenced? What if the battle were again to be fought,—with such termination as the chances might send to her? Why was it that she was so much greater a coward now than she had been then? Then she had expected defeat, for her friends had bade her not to be sanguine; but in spite of that she had borne up and gone gallantly through the ordeal. But now she felt that if Orley Farm were hers to give she would sooner abandon it than renew the contest. Then, at that former period of her life, she had prepared her mind to do or die in the cause. She had wrought herself up for the work, and had carried it through. But having done that work, having accomplished her terrible task, she had hoped that rest might be in store for her.

As she rose from her bed on the morning after her interview with Sir Peregrine, she determined that she would seek counsel from him in whose counsel she could trust. Sir Peregrine's friendship was more valuable to her than that of Mr. Furnival, but a word of advice from Mr. Furnival was worth all the spoken wisdom of the baronet, ten times over. Therefore she wrote her letter, and proposed an appointment; and Mr. Furnival, tempted as I have said by some evil spirit to stray after strange goddesses in these his blue-nosed days, had left his learned brethren at their congress in Birmingham, and had hurried up to town to assist the widow. He had left that congress, though the wisest Rustums of the law from all the civilised countries of Europe were there assembled, with Boanerges at their head, that great, old, valiant, learned, British Rustum, inquiring with energy, solemnity, and caution, with much shaking of ponderous heads and many sarcasms from those which were not ponderous, whether any and what changes might be made in the modes of answering that great question, "Guilty or not guilty?" and that other equally great question, "Is it meum or is it tuum?" To answer which question justly should be the end and object of every lawyer's work. There were great men there from Paris, very capable, the Ulpians, Tribonians, and Papinians of the new empire, armed with the purest sentiments expressed in antithetical and magniloquent phrases, ravishing to the ears, and armed also with a code which, taken in its integrity, would necessarily, as the logical consequence of its clauses, drive all injustice from the face of the earth. And there were great practitioners from Germany, men very skilled in the use of questions, who profess that the tongue of man, if adequately skilful, may always prevail on guilt to disclose itself; who believe in the power of their own craft to produce truth, as our forefathers believed in torture; and sometimes with the same result. And of course all that was great on the British bench, and all that was famous at the British bar was there,—men very unlike their German brethren, men who thought that guilt never should be asked to tell of itself,—men who were customarily but unconsciously shocked whenever unwary guilt did tell of itself. Men these were, mostly of high and noble feeling, born and bred to live with upright hearts and clean hands, but taught by the peculiar tenets of their profession to think that that which was high and noble in their private intercourse with the world need not also be so esteemed in their legal practice. And there were Italians there, good-humoured, joking, easy fellows, who would laugh their clients in and out of their difficulties; and Spaniards, very grave and serious, who doubted much in their minds whether justice might not best be bought and sold; and our brethren from the United States were present also, very eager to show that in this country law, and justice also, were clouded and nearly buried beneath their wig and gown.

All these and all this did Mr. Furnival desert for the space of twenty-four hours in order that he might comply with the request of Lady Mason. Had she known what it was that she was calling on him to leave, no doubt she would have borne her troubles for another week, — for another fortnight, till those Rustums at Birmingham had brought their labours to a close. She would not have robbed the English bar of one of the warmest supporters of its present mode of practice, even for a day, had she known how much that support was needed at the present moment. But she had not known; and Mr. Furnival, moved by her woman's plea, had not been hard enough in his heart to refuse her.

When she entered the room she was dressed very plainly as was her custom, and a thick veil covered her face; but still she was dressed with care. There was nothing of the dowdiness of the lone lorn woman about her, none of that lanky, washed-out appearance which sorrow and trouble so often give to females. Had she given way to dowdiness, or suffered herself to be, as it were, washed out, Mr. Furnival, we may say, would not have been there to meet her; — of which fact Lady Mason was perhaps aware.

"I am so grateful to you for this trouble," she said, as she raised her veil, and while he pressed her hand between both his own. "I can only ask you to believe that I would not have troubled you unless I had been greatly troubled myself."

Mr. Furnival, as he placed her in an arm-chair by the fireside, declared his sorrow that she should be in grief, and then he took the other arm-chair himself, opposite to her, or rather close to her, — much closer to her than he ever now seated himself to Mrs. F. "Don't speak of my trouble," said he, "it is nothing if I can do anything to relieve you." But though he was so tender, he did not omit to tell her of her folly in having informed her son that she was to be in London. "And have you seen him?" asked Lady Mason.

"He was in Harley Street with the ladies last night. But it does not matter. It is only for your sake that I speak, as I know that you wish to keep this matter private. And now let us hear what it is. I cannot think that there can be anything which need really cause you trouble." And he again took her hand, — that he might encourage her. Lady Mason let him keep her hand for a minute or so, as though she did not notice it; and yet as she turned her eyes to him it might appear that his tenderness had encouraged her.

Sitting there thus, with her hand in his, — with her hand in his during the first portion of the tale, — she told him all that she wished to tell. Something more she told now to him than she had done to Sir Peregrine. "I learned from her," she said, speaking about Mrs. Dockwrath and her husband, "that he had found out something about dates which the lawyers did not find out before."

"Something about dates," said Mr. Furnival, looking with all his eyes into the fire. "You do not know what about dates?"

"No; only this; that he said that the lawyers in Bedford Row—"

"Round and Crook."

"Yes; he said that they were idiots not to have found it out before; and then he went off to Groby Park. He came back last night; but of course I have not seen her since."

By this time Mr. Furnival had dropped the hand, and was sitting still, meditating, looking earnestly at the fire while Lady Mason was looking earnestly at him. She was trying to gather from his face whether he had seen signs of danger, and he was trying to gather from her words whether there might really be cause to apprehend danger. How was he to know what was really inside her mind; what were her actual thoughts and inward reasonings on this subject; what private knowledge she might have which was still kept back from him? In the ordinary intercourse of the world when one man seeks advice from another, he who is consulted demands in the first place that he shall be put in possession of all the circumstances of the case. How else will it be possible that he should give advice? But in matters of law it is different. If I, having committed a crime, were to confess my criminality to the gentleman engaged to defend me, might he not be called on to say: "Then, O my friend, confess it also to the judge; and so let justice be done. Ruat cœlum, and the rest of it?" But who would pay a lawyer for counsel such as that?

In this case there was no question of payment. The advice to be given was to a widowed woman from an experienced man of the world; but, nevertheless, he could only make his calculations as to her peculiar case in the way in which he ordinarily calculated. Could it be possible that anything had been kept back from him? Were there facts unknown to him, but known to her, which would be terrible, fatal, damning to his sweet friend if proved before all the world? He could not bring himself to ask her, but yet it was so material that he should know! Twenty years ago, at the time of the trial, he had at one time thought,—it hardly matters to tell what, but those thoughts had not been favourable to her cause. Then his mind had altered, and he had learned,—as lawyers do learn,—to believe in his own case. And when the day of triumph had come, he had triumphed loudly, commiserating his dear friend for the unjust suffering to which she had been subjected, and speaking in no low or modified tone as to the grasping, greedy cruelty of that man of Groby Park. Nevertheless, through it all, he had felt that Round and Crook had not made the most of their case.

And now he sat, thinking, not so much whether or no she had been in any way guilty with reference to that will, as whether the counsel he should give her ought in any way to be based on the possibility of her having been thus guilty. Nothing might be so damning to her cause as that he should make sure of her innocence, if she were not innocent; and yet he would not ask her the question. If innocent, why was it that she was now so much moved, after twenty years of quiet possession?

"It was a pity," he said, at last, "that Lucius should have disturbed that fellow in the possession of his fields."

"It was; it was!" she said. "But I did not think it possible that Miriam's husband should turn against me. Would it be wise, do you think, to let him have the land again?"

"No, I do not think that. It would be telling him, and telling others also, that you are afraid of him. If he has obtained any information that may be considered of value by Joseph Mason, he can sell it at a higher price than the holding of these fields is worth."

"Would it be well—?" She was asking a question and then checked herself.

"Would what be well?"

"I am so harassed that I hardly know what I am saying. Would it be wise, do you think, if I were to pay him anything, so as to keep him quiet?"

"What; buy him off, you mean?"

"Well, yes;—if you call it so. Give him some sum of money in compensation for his land; and on the understanding, you know—," and then she paused.

"That depends on what he may have to sell," said Mr. Furnival, hardly daring to look at her.

"Ah; yes," said the widow. And then there was another pause.

"I do not think that that would be at all discreet," said Mr. Furnival. "After all, the chances are that it is all moonshine."

"You think so?"

"Yes; I cannot but think so. What can that man possibly have found among the old attorney's papers that may be injurious to your interests?"

"Ah! I do not know; I understand so little of these things. At the time they told me,—you told me that the law might possibly go against my boy's rights. It would have been bad then, but it would be ten times more dreadful now."

"But there were many questions capable of doubt then, which were definitely settled at the trial. As to your husband's intellect on that day, for instance."

"There could be no doubt as to that."

"No; so it has been proved; and they will not raise that point again. Could he have possibly have made a later will?"

"No; I am sure he did not. Had he done so it could not have been found among Mr. Usbech's papers; for, as far as I remember, the poor man never attended to any business after that day."

"What day?"

"The 14th of July, the day on which he was with Sir Joseph."

It was singular, thought the barrister, with how much precision she remembered the dates and circumstances. That the circumstances of the trial should be fresh on her memory was not wonderful; but how was it that she knew so accurately things which had occurred before the trial,—when no trial could have been expected? But as to this he said nothing.

"And you are sure he went to Groby Park?"

"Oh, yes; I have no doubt of it. I am quite sure."

"I do not know that we can do anything but wait. Have you mentioned this to Sir Peregrine?" It immediately occurred to Lady Mason's mind that it would be by no means expedient, even if it were possible, to keep Mr. Furnival in ignorance of anything that she really did; and therefore explained that she had seen Sir Peregrine. "I was so troubled at the first moment that I hardly knew where to turn," she said.

"You were quite right to go to Sir Peregrine."

"I am so glad you are not angry with me as to that."

"And did he say anything—anything particular?"

"He promised that he would not desert me, should there be any new difficulty."

"That is well. It is always good to have the countenance of such a neighbour as he is."

"And the advice of such a friend as you are." And she again put out her hand to him.

"Well; yes. It is my trade, you know, to give advice," and he smiled as he took it.

"How should I live through such troubles without you?"

"We lawyers are very much abused now-a-days," said Mr. Furnival, thinking of what was going on down at Birmingham at that very moment; "but I hardly know how the world would get on without us."

"Ah! but all lawyers are not like you."

"Some perhaps worse, and a great many much better. But, as I was saying, I do not think I would take any steps at present. The man Dockwrath is a vulgar, low-minded, revengeful fellow; and I would endeavour to forget him."

"Ah, if I could!"

"And why not? What can he possibly have learned to your injury?" And then as it seemed to Lady Mason that Mr. Furnival expected some reply to this question, she forced herself to give him one. "I suppose that he cannot know anything."

"I tell you what I might do," said Mr. Furnival, who was still musing. "Round himself is not a bad fellow, and I am acquainted with him. He was the junior partner in that house at the time of the trial, and I know that he persuaded Joseph Mason not to appeal to the Lords. I will contrive, if possible, to see him. I shall be able to learn from him at any rate whether anything is being done."

"And then if I hear that there is not, I shall be comforted."

"Of course; of course."

"But if there is—"

"I think there will be nothing of the sort," said Mr. Furnival, leaving his seat as he spoke.

"But if there is—I shall have your aid?" and she slowly rose from her chair as she spoke.

Mr. Furnival gave her a promise of this, as Sir Peregrine had done before; and then with her handkerchief to her eyes she thanked him. Her tears were not false as Mr. Furnival well saw; and seeing that she wept, and seeing that she was beautiful, and feeling that in her grief and in her beauty she had come to him for aid, his heart was softened towards her, and he put out his arms as though he would take her to his heart—as a daughter. "Dearest friend," he said, "trust me that no harm shall come to you."

"I will trust you," she said, gently stopping the motion of his arm. "I will trust you, altogether. And when you have seen Mr. Round, shall I hear from you?"

At this moment, as they were standing close together, the door opened, and Mr. Crabwitz introduced another lady—who indeed had advanced so quickly towards the door of Mr. Furnival's room, that the clerk had been hardly able to reach it before her.

"Mrs. Furnival, if you please, sir," said Mr. Crabwitz.

CHAPTER XIII
GUILTY, OR NOT GUILTY

Unfortunately for Mr. Furnival, the intruder was Mrs. Furnival—whether he pleased or whether he did not please. There she was in his law chamber, present in the flesh, a sight pleasing neither to her husband nor to her husband's client. She had knocked at the outside door, which, in the absence of the fag, had been opened by Mr. Crabwitz, and had immediately walked across the passage towards her husband's room, expressing her knowledge that Mr. Furnival was within. Mr. Crabwitz had all the will in the world to stop her progress, but he found that he lacked the power to stay it for a moment.

The advantages of matrimony are many and great,—so many and so great, that all men, doubtless, ought to marry. But even matrimony may have its drawbacks; among which unconcealed and undeserved jealousy on the part of the wife is perhaps as disagreeable as any. What is a man to do when he is accused before the world,—before any small fraction of the world, of making love to some lady of his acquaintance? What is he to say? What way is he to look? "My love, I didn't. I never did, and wouldn't think of it for worlds. I say it with my hand on my heart. There is Mrs. Jones herself, and I appeal to her." He is reduced to that! But should any innocent man be so reduced by the wife of his bosom?

I am speaking of undeserved jealousy, and it may therefore be thought that my remarks do not apply to Mrs. Furnival. They do apply to her as much as to any woman. That general idea as to the strange goddesses was on her part no more than a suspicion: and all women who so torment themselves and their husbands may plead as much as she could. And for this peculiar idea as to Lady Mason she had no ground whatever. Lady Mason may have had her faults, but a propensity to rob Mrs. Furnival of her husband's affections had not hitherto been one of them. Mr. Furnival was a clever lawyer, and she had great need of his assistance; therefore she had come to his chambers, and therefore she had placed her hand in his. That Mr. Furnival liked his client because she was good looking may be true. I like my horse, my picture, the view from my study window for the same reason. I am inclined to think that there was nothing more in it than that.

"My dear!" said Mr. Furnival, stepping back a little, and letting his hands fall to his sides. Lady Mason also took a step backwards, and then with considerable presence of mind recovered herself and put out her hand to greet Mrs. Furnival.

"How do you do, Lady Mason?" said Mrs. Furnival, without any presence of mind at all. "I hope I have the pleasure of seeing you very well. I did hear that you were to be in town—shopping; but I did not for a moment expect the—gratification of finding you here." And every word that the dear, good, heart-sore woman spoke, told the tale of her jealousy as plainly as though she had flown at Lady Mason's cap with all the bold demonstrative energy of Spitalfields or St. Giles.

"I came up on purpose to see Mr. Furnival about some unfortunate law business," said Lady Mason.

"Oh, indeed! Your son Lucius did say—shopping."

"Your son Lucius did say—shopping."

"Yes; I told him so. When a lady is unfortunate enough to be driven to a lawyer for advice, she does not wish to make it known. I should be very sorry if my dear boy were to guess that I had this new trouble; or, indeed, if any one were to know it. I am sure that I shall be as safe with you, dear Mrs. Furnival, as I am with your husband." And she stepped up to the angry matron, looking earnestly into her face.

To a true tale of woman's sorrow Mrs. Furnival's heart could be as snow under the noonday sun. Had Lady Mason gone to her and told her all her fears and all her troubles, sought counsel and aid from her, and appealed to her motherly feelings, Mrs. Furnival would have been urgent night and day in persuading her husband to take up the widow's case. She would have bade him work his very best without fee or reward, and would herself have shown Lady Mason the way to Old Square, Lincoln's Inn. She would have been discreet too, speaking no word of idle gossip to any one. When he, in their happy days, had told his legal secrets to her, she had never gossiped,— had never spoken an idle word concerning them. And she would have been constant to her friend, giving great consolation in the time of trouble, as one woman can console another. The thought that all this might be so did come across her for a moment, for there was innocence written in Lady Mason's eyes. But then she looked at her husband's face; and as she found no innocence there, her heart was again hardened. The woman's face could lie;—"the faces of such women are all lies," Mrs. Furnival said to herself;— but in her presence his face had been compelled to speak the truth.

"Oh dear, no; I shall say nothing of course," she said. "I am quite sorry that I intruded. Mr. Furnival, as I happened to be in Holborn—at Mudie's for some books—I thought I would come down and ask whether you intend to dine at home to-day. You said nothing about it either last night or this morning; and nowadays one really does not know how to manage in such matters."

"I told you that I should return to Birmingham this afternoon; I shall dine there," said Mr. Furnival, very sulkily.

"Oh, very well. I certainly knew that you were going out of town. I did not at all expect that you would remain at home; but I thought that you might, perhaps, like to have your dinner before you went. Good morning, Lady Mason; I hope you may be successful in your—lawsuit." And then, curtsying to her husband's client, she prepared to withdraw.

"I believe that I have said all that I need say, Mr. Furnival," said Lady Mason; "so that if Mrs. Furnival wishes—," and she also gathered herself up as though she were ready to leave the room.

"I hardly know what Mrs. Furnival wishes," said the husband.

"My wishes are nothing," said the wife, "and I really am quite sorry that I came in." And then she did go, leaving her husband and the woman of whom she was jealous once more alone together. Upon the whole I think that Mr. Furnival was right in not going home that day to his dinner.

As the door closed somewhat loudly behind the angry lady—Mr. Crabwitz having rushed out hardly in time to moderate the violence of the slam—Lady Mason and her imputed lover were left looking at each other. It was certainly hard upon Lady Mason, and so she felt it. Mr. Furnival was fifty-five, and endowed with a bluish nose; and she was over forty, and had lived for twenty years as a widow without incurring a breath of scandal.

"I hope I have not been to blame," said Lady Mason in a soft, sad voice; "but perhaps Mrs. Furnival specially wished to find you alone."

"No, no; not at all."

"I shall be so unhappy if I think that I have been in the way. If Mrs. Furnival wished to speak to you on business I am not surprised that she should be angry, for I know that barristers do not usually allow themselves to be troubled by their clients in their own chambers."

"Nor by their wives," Mr. Furnival might have added, but he did not.

"Do not mind it," he said; "it is nothing. She is the best-tempered woman in the world; but at times it is impossible to answer even for the best-tempered."

"I will trust you to make my peace with her."

"Yes, of course; she will not think of it after to-day; nor must you, Lady Mason."

"Oh, no; except that I would not for the world be the cause of annoyance to my friends. Sometimes I am almost inclined to think that I will never trouble any one again with my sorrows, but let things come and go as they may. Were it not for poor Lucius I should do so."

Mr. Furnival, looking into her face, perceived that her eyes were full of tears. There could be no doubt as to their reality. Her eyes were full of genuine tears, brimming over and running down; and the lawyer's heart was melted. "I do not know why you should say so," he said. "I do not think your friends begrudge any little trouble they may take for you. I am sure at least that I may so say for myself."

"You are too kind to me; but I do not on that account the less know how much it is I ask of you."

"'The labour we delight in physics pain,'" said Mr. Furnival gallantly. "But, to tell the truth, Lady Mason, I cannot understand why you should be so much out of heart. I remember well how brave and constant you were twenty years ago, when there really was cause for trembling."

"Ah, I was younger then."

"So the almanac tells us; but if the almanac did not tell us I should never know. We are all older, of course. Twenty years does not go by without leaving its marks, as I can feel myself."

"Men do not grow old as women do, who live alone and gather rust as they feed on their own thoughts."

"I know no one whom time has touched so lightly as yourself, Lady Mason; but if I may speak to you as a friend—"

"If you may not, Mr. Furnival, who may?"

"I should tell you that you are weak to be so despondent, or rather so unhappy."

"Another lawsuit would kill me, I think. You say that I was brave and constant before, but you cannot understand what I suffered. I nerved myself to bear it, telling myself that it was the first duty that I owed to the babe that was lying on my bosom. And when standing there in the Court, with that terrible array around me, with the eyes of all men on me, the eyes of men who thought that I had been guilty of so terrible a crime, for the sake of that child who was so weak I could be brave. But it nearly killed me. Mr. Furnival, I could not go through that again; no, not even for his sake. If you can save me from that, even though it be by the buying off of that ungrateful man—"

"You must not think of that."

"Must I not? ah me!"

"Will you tell Lucius all this, and let him come to me?"

"No; not for worlds. He would defy every one, and glory in the fight; but after all it is I that must bear the brunt. No; he shall not know it;—unless it becomes so public that he must know it."

And then, with some further pressing of the hand, and further words of encouragement which were partly tender as from the man, and partly forensic as from the lawyer, Mr. Furnival permitted her to go, and she found her son at the chemist's shop in Holborn as she had appointed. There were no traces of tears or of sorrow in her face as she smiled on Lucius while giving him her hand, and then when they were in a cab together she asked him as to his success at Liverpool.

"I am very glad that I went," said he, "very glad indeed. I saw the merchants there who are the real importers of the article, and I have made arrangements with them."

"Will it be cheaper so, Lucius?"

"Cheaper! not what women generally call cheaper. If there be anything on earth that I hate, it is a bargain. A man who looks for bargains must be a dupe or a cheat, and is probably both."

"Both, Lucius. Then he is doubly unfortunate."

"He is a cheat because he wants things for less than their value; and a dupe because, as a matter of course, he does not get what he wants. I made no bargain at Liverpool,—at least, no cheap bargain; but I have made arrangements for a sufficient supply of a first-rate unadulterated article at its proper market price, and I do not fear but the results will be remunerative." And then, as they went home in the railway carriage the mother talked to her son about his farming as though she had forgotten her other trouble, and she explained to him how he was to dine with Sir Peregrine.

"I shall be delighted to dine with Sir Peregrine," said Lucius, "and very well pleased to have an opportunity of talking to him about his own way of managing his land; but, mother, I will not promise to be guided by so very old-fashioned a professor."

Mr. Furnival, when he was left alone, sat thinking over the interview that had passed. At first, as was most natural, he bethought himself of his wife; and I regret to say that the love which he bore to her, and the gratitude which he owed to her, and the memory of all that they had suffered and enjoyed together, did not fill his heart with thoughts towards her as tender as they should have done. A black frown came across his brow as he meditated on her late intrusion, and he made some sort of resolve that that kind of thing should be prevented for the future. He did not make up his mind how he would prevent it,—a point which husbands sometimes overlook in their marital resolutions. And then, instead of counting up her virtues, he counted up his own. Had he not given her everything; a house such as she had not dreamed of in her younger days? servants, carriages, money, comforts, and luxuries of all sorts? He had begrudged her nothing, had let her have her full share of all his hard-earned gains; and yet she could be ungrateful for all this, and allow her head to be filled with whims and fancies as though she were a young girl,—to his great annoyance and confusion. He would let her know that his chambers, his law chambers, should be private even from her. He would not allow himself to become a laughing-stock to his own clerks and his own brethren through the impertinent folly of a woman who owed to him everything;—and so on! I regret to say that he never once thought of those lonely evenings in Harley Street, of those long days which the poor woman was doomed to pass without the only companionship which was valuable to her. He never thought of that vow which they had both made at the altar, which she had kept so loyally, and which required of him a cherishing, comforting, enduring love. It never occurred to him that in denying her this he as much broke his promise to her as though he had taken to himself in very truth some strange goddess, leaving his wedded wife with a cold ceremony of alimony or such-like. He had been open-handed to her as regards money, and therefore she ought not to be troublesome! He had done his duty by her, and therefore he would not permit her to be troublesome! Such, I regret to say, were his thoughts and resolutions as he sat thinking and resolving about Mrs. Furnival.

And then, by degrees, his mind turned away to that other lady, and they became much more tender. Lady Mason was certainly both interesting and comely in her grief. Her colour could still come and go, her hand was still soft and small, her hair was still brown and smooth. There were no wrinkles in her brow though care had passed over it; her step could still fall lightly, though it had borne a heavy weight of sorrow. I fear that he made a wicked comparison—a comparison that was wicked although it was made unconsciously.

But by degrees he ceased to think of the woman and began to think of the client, as he was in duty bound to do. What was the real truth of all this? Was it possible that she should be alarmed in that way because a small country attorney had told his wife that he had found some old paper, and because the man had then gone off to Yorkshire? Nothing could be more natural than her anxiety, supposing her to be aware of some secret which would condemn her if discovered;—but nothing more unnatural if there were no such secret. And she must know! In her bosom, if in no other, must exist the knowledge whether or no that will were just. If that will were just, was it possible that she should now tremble so violently, seeing that its justice had been substantially proved in various courts of law? But if it were not just—if it were a forgery, a forgery made by her, or with her cognizance—and that now this truth was to be made known! How terrible would that be! But terrible is not the word which best describes the idea as it entered Mr. Furnival's mind. How wonderful would it be; how wonderful would it all have been! By whose hand in such case had those signatures been traced? Could it be possible that she, soft, beautiful, graceful as she was now, all but a girl as she had then been, could have done it, unaided,—

by herself?—that she could have sat down in the still hour of the night, with that old man on one side and her baby in his cradle on the other, and forged that will, signatures and all, in such a manner as to have carried her point for twenty years,—so skilfully as to have baffled lawyers and jurymen and resisted the eager greed of her cheated kinsman? If so, was it not all wonderful! Had not she been a woman worthy of wonder!

And then Mr. Furnival's mind, keen and almost unerring at seizing legal points, went eagerly to work, considering what new evidence might now be forthcoming. He remembered at once the circumstances of those two chief witnesses, the clerk who had been so muddle-headed, and the servant-girl who had been so clear. They had certainly witnessed some deed, and they had done so on that special day. If there had been a fraud, if there had been a forgery, it had been so clever as almost to merit protection! But if there had been such fraud, the nature of the means by which it might be detected became plain to the mind of the barrister,—plainer to him without knowledge of any circumstances than it had done to Mr. Mason after many of such circumstances had been explained to him.

But it was impossible. So said Mr. Furnival to himself, out loud;—speaking out loud in order that he might convince himself. It was impossible, he said again; but he did not convince himself. Should he ask her? No; it was not on the cards that he should do that. And perhaps, if a further trial were forthcoming, it might be better for her sake that he should be ignorant. And then, having declared again that it was impossible, he rang his bell. "Crabwitz," said he, without looking at the man, "just step over to Bedford Row, with my compliments, and learn what is Mr. Round's present address;—old Mr. Round, you know."

Mr. Crabwitz stood for a moment or two with the door in his hand, and Mr. Furnival, going back to his own thoughts, was expecting the man's departure. "Well," he said, looking up and seeing that his myrmidon still stood there.

Mr. Crabwitz was not in a very good humour, and had almost made up his mind to let his master know that such was the case. Looking at his own general importance in the legal world, and the inestimable services which he had rendered to Mr. Furnival, he did not think that that gentleman was treating him well. He had been summoned back to his dingy chamber almost without an excuse, and now that he was in London was not permitted to join even for a day the other wise men of the law who were assembled at the great congress. For the last four days his heart had been yearning to go to Birmingham, but had yearned in vain; and now his master was sending him about town as though he were an errand-lad.

"Shall I step across to the lodge and send the porter's boy to Round and Crook's?" asked Mr. Crabwitz.

"The porter's boy! no; go yourself; you are not busy. Why should I send the porter's boy on my business?" The fact probably was, that Mr. Furnival forgot his clerk's age and standing. Crabwitz had been ready to run anywhere when his employer had first known him, and Mr. Furnival did not perceive the change.

"Very well, sir; certainly I will go if you wish it;—on this occasion that is. But I hope, sir, you will excuse my saying—"

"Saying what?"

"That I am not exactly a messenger, sir. Of course I'll go now, as the other clerk is not in."

"Oh, you're too great a man to walk across to Bedford Row, are you? Give me my hat, and I'll go."

"Oh, no, Mr. Furnival, I did not mean that. I'll step over to Bedford Row, of course;—only I did think—"

"Think what?"

"That perhaps I was entitled to a little more respect, Mr. Furnival. It's for your sake as much as my own that I speak, sir; but if the gentlemen in the Lane see me sent about like a lad of twenty, sir, they'll think—"

"What will they think?"

"I hardly know what they'll think, but I know it will be very disagreeable, sir;—very disagreeable to my feelings. I did think, sir, that perhaps—"

"I'll tell you what it is, Crabwitz, if your situation here does not suit you, you may leave it to-morrow. I shall have no difficulty in finding another man to take your place."

"I am sorry to hear you speak in that way, Mr. Furnival, very sorry—after fifteen years, sir—."

"You find yourself too grand to walk to Bedford Row!"

"Oh, no. I'll go now, of course, Mr. Furnival." And then Mr. Crabwitz did go, meditating as he went many things to himself. He knew his own value, or thought that he knew it; and might it not be possible to find some patron who would appreciate his services more justly than did Mr. Furnival?

CHAPTER XIV
DINNER AT THE CLEEVE

Lady Mason on her return from London found a note from Mrs. Orme asking both her and her son to dine at The Cleeve on the following day. As it had been already settled between her and Sir Peregrine that Lucius should dine there in order that he might be talked to respecting his mania for guano, the invitation could not be refused; but, as for Lady Mason herself, she would much have preferred to remain at home.

Indeed, her uneasiness on that guano matter had been so outweighed by worse uneasiness from another source, that she had become, if not indifferent, at any rate tranquil on the subject. It might be well that Sir Peregrine should preach his sermon, and well that Lucius should hear it; but for herself it would, she thought, have been more comfortable for her to eat her dinner alone. She felt, however, that she could not do so. Any amount of tedium would be better than the danger of offering a slight to Sir Peregrine, and therefore she wrote a pretty little note to say that both of them would be at The Cleeve at seven.

"Lucius, my dear, I want you to do me a great favour," she said as she sat by her son in the Hamworth fly.

"A great favour, mother! of course I will do anything for you that I can."

"It is that you will bear with Sir Peregrine to-night."

"Bear with him! I do not know exactly what you mean. Of course I will remember that he is an old man, and not answer him as I would one of my own age."

"I am sure of that, Lucius, because you are a gentleman. As much forbearance as that a young man, if he be a gentleman, will always show to an old man. But what I ask is something more than that. Sir Peregrine has been farming all his life."

"Yes; and see what are the results! He has three or four hundred acres of uncultivated land on his estate, all of which would grow wheat."

"I know nothing about that," said Lady Mason.

"Ah, but that's the question. My trade is to be that of a farmer, and you are sending me to school. Then comes the question, Of what sort is the schoolmaster?"

"I am not talking about farming now, Lucius."

"But he will talk of it."

"And cannot you listen to him without contradicting him—for my sake? It is of the greatest consequence to me,—of the very greatest, Lucius, that I should have the benefit of Sir Peregrine's friendship."

"If he would quarrel with you because I chanced to disagree with him about the management of land, his friendship would not be worth having."

"I do not say that he will do so; but I am sure you can understand that an old man may be tender on such points. At any rate I ask it from you as a favour. You cannot guess how important it is to me to be on good terms with such a neighbour."

"It is always so in England," said Lucius, after pausing for a while. "Sir Peregrine is a man of family, and a baronet; of course all the world, the world of Hamworth that is, should bow down at his feet. And I too must worship the golden image which Nebuchadnezzar, the King of Fashion, has set up!"

"Lucius, you are unkind to me."

"No, mother, not unkind; but like all men, I would fain act in such matters as my own judgment may direct me."

"My friendship with Sir Peregrine Orme has nothing to do with his rank; but it is of importance to me that both you and I should stand well in his sight." There was nothing more said on the matter; and then they got down at the front door, and were ushered through the low wide hall into the drawing-room.

The three generations of the family were there,—Sir Peregrine, his daughter-in-law, and the heir. Lucius Mason had been at The Cleeve two or three times since his return from Germany, and on going there had always declared to himself that it was the same to him as though he were going into the house of Mrs. Arkwright, the doctor's widow at Hamworth,—or even into the kitchen of Farmer Greenwood. He rejoiced to call himself a democrat, and would boast that rank could have no effect on him. But his boast was an untrue boast, and he could not carry himself at The Cleeve as he would have done and did in Mrs. Arkwright's little drawing-room. There was a majesty in the manner of Sir Peregrine which did awe him; there were tokens of birth and a certain grace of manner about Mrs. Orme which kept down his assumption; and even with young Peregrine he found that though he might be equal he could by no means be more than equal. He had learned more than Peregrine Orme, had ten times more knowledge in his head, had read books of which Peregrine did not even know the names and probably never would know them; but on his side also young Orme possessed something which the other wanted. What that something might be Lucius Mason did not at all understand.

Mrs. Orme got up from her corner on the sofa to greet her friend, and with a soft smile and two or three all but whispered words led her forward to the fire. Mrs. Orme was not a woman given to much speech or endowed with outward warmth of manners, but she could make her few words go very far; and then the pressure of her hand, when it was given, told more than a whole embrace from some other women. There are ladies who always kiss their female friends, and always call them "dear." In such cases one cannot but pity her who is so bekissed. Mrs. Orme did not kiss Lady Mason, nor did she call her dear; but she smiled sweetly as she uttered her greeting, and looked kindness out of her marvellously blue eyes; and Lucius Mason, looking on over his mother's shoulders, thought that he would like to have her for his friend in spite of her rank. If Mrs. Orme would give him a lecture on farming it might be possible to listen to it without contradiction; but there was no chance for him in that respect. Mrs. Orme never gave lectures to any one on any subject.

"So, Master Lucius, you have been to Liverpool, I hear," said Sir Peregrine.

"Yes, sir—I returned yesterday."

"And what is the world doing at Liverpool?"

"The world is wide awake there, sir."

"Oh, no doubt; when the world has to make money it is always wide awake. But men sometimes may be wide awake and yet make no money;—may be wide awake, or at any rate think that they are so."

"Better that, Sir Peregrine, than wilfully go to sleep when there is so much work to be done."

"A man when he's asleep does no harm," said Sir Peregrine.

"What a comfortable doctrine to think of when the servant comes with the hot water at eight o'clock in the morning!" said his grandson.

"It is one that you study very constantly, I fear," said the old man, who at this time was on excellent terms with his heir. There had been no apparent hankering after rats since that last compact had been made, and Peregrine had been doing great things with the H. H.; winning golden opinions from all sorts of sportsmen, and earning a great reputation for a certain young mare which had been bred by Sir Peregrine himself. Foxes are vermin as well as rats, as Perry in his wickedness had remarked; but a young man who can break an old one's heart by a predilection for rat-catching may win it as absolutely and irretrievably by prowess after a fox. Sir Peregrine had told to four different neighbours how a fox had been run into, in the open, near Alston, after twelve desperate miles, and how on that occasion Peregrine had been in at the death with the huntsman and only one other. "And the mare, you know, is only four years old and hardly half trained," said Sir Peregrine, with great exultation. "The young scamp, to have ridden her in that way!" It may be doubted whether he would have been a prouder man or said more about it if his grandson had taken honours.

And then the gong sounded, and, Sir Peregrine led Lady Mason into the dining-room. Lucius, who as we know thought no more of the Ormes than of the Joneses and Smiths, paused in his awe before he gave his arm to Mrs. Orme; and when he did so he led her away in perfect silence, though he would have given anything to be able to talk to her as he went. But he bethought himself that unfortunately he could find nothing to say. And when he sat down it was not much better. He had not dined at The Cleeve before, and I am not sure whether the butler in plain clothes and the two men in livery did not help to create his confusion, — in spite of his well-digested democratic ideas.

The conversation during dinner was not very bright. Sir Peregrine said a few words now and again to Lady Mason, and she replied with a few others. On subjects which did not absolutely appertain to the dinner, she perhaps was the greatest talker; but even she did not say much. Mrs. Orme as a rule never spoke unless she were spoken to in any company consisting of more than herself and one other; and young Peregrine seemed to imagine that carving at the top of the table, asking people if they would take stewed beef, and eating his own dinner, were occupations quite sufficient for his energies. "Have a bit more beef, Mason; do. If you will, I will." So far he went in conversation, but no farther while his work was still before him.

When the servants were gone it was a little better, but not much. "Mason, do you mean to hunt this season?" Peregrine asked.

"No," said the other.

"Well, I would if I were you. You will never know the fellows about here unless you do."

"In the first place I can't afford the time," said Lucius, "and in the next place I can't afford the money." This was plucky on his part, and it was felt to be so by everybody in the room; but perhaps had he spoken all the truth, he would have said also that he was not accustomed to horsemanship.

"To a fellow who has a place of his own as you have, it costs nothing," said Peregrine.

"Oh, does it not?" said the baronet; "I used to think differently."

"Well; not so much, I mean, as if you had everything to buy. Besides, I look upon Mason as a sort of Crœsus. What on earth has he got to do with his money? And then as to time;—upon my word I don't understand what a man means when he says he has not got time for hunting."

"Lucius intends to be a farmer," said his mother.

"So do I," said Peregrine. "By Jove, I should think so. If I had two hundred acres of land in my own hand I should not want anything else in the world, and would never ask any one for a shilling."

"If that be so, I might make the best bargain at once that ever a man made," said the baronet. "If I might take you at your word, Master Perry—."

"Pray don't talk of it, sir," said Mrs. Orme.

"You may be quite sure of this, my dear—that I shall not do more than talk of it." Then Sir Peregrine asked Lady Mason if she would take any more wine; after which the ladies withdrew, and the lecture commenced.

But we will in the first place accompany the ladies into the drawing-room for a few minutes. It was hinted in one of the first chapters of this story that Lady Mason might have become more intimate than she had done with Mrs. Orme, had she so pleased it; and by this it will of course be presumed that she had not so pleased. All this is perfectly true. Mrs. Orme had now been living at The Cleeve the greater portion of her life, and had never while there made one really well-loved friend. She had a sister of her own, and dear old friends of her childhood, who lived far away from her in the northern counties. Occasionally she did see them, and was then very happy; but this was not frequent with her. Her sister, who was married to a peer, might stay at The Cleeve for a fortnight, perhaps once in the year; but Mrs. Orme herself seldom left her own home. She thought, and certainly not without cause, that Sir Peregrine was not happy in her absence, and therefore she never left him. Then, living there so much alone, was it not natural that her heart should desire a friend?

But Lady Mason had been living much more alone. She had no sister to come to her, even though it were but once a year. She had no intimate female friend, none to whom she could really speak with the full freedom of friendship, and it would have been delightful to have bound to her by ties of love so sweet a creature as Mrs. Orme, a widow like herself,—and like herself a widow with one only son. But she, warily picking her steps through life, had learned the necessity of being cautious in all things. The countenance of Sir Peregrine had been invaluable to her, and might it not be possible that she should lose that countenance? A word or two spoken now and then again, a look not intended to be noticed, an altered tone, or perhaps a change in the pressure of the old man's hand, had taught Lady Mason to think that he might disapprove such intimacy. Probably at the moment she was right, for she was quick at reading such small signs. It behoved her to be very careful, and to indulge in no pleasure which might be costly; and therefore she had denied herself in this matter,—as in so many others.

But now it had occurred to her that it might be well to change her conduct. Either she felt that Sir Peregrine's friendship for her was too confirmed to be shaken, or perhaps she fancied that she might strengthen it by means of his daughter-in-law. At any rate she resolved to accept the offer which had once been tacitly made to her, if it were still open to her to do so.

"How little changed your boy is!" she said, when they were seated near to each other, with their coffee-cups between them.

"No; he does not change quickly; and, as you say, he is a boy still in many things. I do not know whether it may not be better that it should be so."

"I did not mean to call him a boy in that sense," said Lady Mason.

"But you might; now your son is quite a man."

"Poor Lucius! yes; in his position it is necessary. His little bit of property is already his own; and then he has no one like Sir Peregrine to look out for him. Necessity makes him manly."

"He will be marrying soon, I dare say," suggested Mrs. Orme.

"Oh, I hope not. Do you think that early marriages are good for young men?"

"Yes, I think so. Why not?" said Mrs. Orme, thinking of her own year of married happiness. "Would you not wish to see Lucius marry?"

"I fancy not. I should be afraid lest I should become as nothing to him. And yet I would not have you think that I am selfish."

"I am sure that you are not that. I am sure that you love him better than all the world besides. I can feel what that is myself."

"But you are not alone with your boy as I am. If he were to send me from him, there would be nothing left for me in this world."

"Send you from him! Ah, because Orley Farm belongs to him. But he would not do that; I am sure he would not."

"He would do nothing unkind; but how could he help it if his wife wished it? But nevertheless I would not keep him single for that reason;—no, nor for any reason if I knew that he wished to marry. But it would be a blow to me."

"I sincerely trust that Peregrine may marry early," said Mrs. Orme, perhaps thinking that babies were preferable either to rats or foxes.

"Yes, it would be well I am sure, because you have ample means, and the house is large; and you would have his wife to love."

"If she were nice it would be so sweet to have her for a daughter. I also am very much alone, though perhaps not so much as you are, Lady Mason."

"I hope not—for I am sometimes very lonely."

"I have often thought that."

"But I should be wicked beyond everything if I were to complain, seeing that Providence has given me so much that I had no right to expect. What should I have done in my loneliness if Sir Peregrine's hand and door had never been opened to me?" And then for the next half-hour the two ladies held sweet converse together, during which we will go back to the gentlemen over their wine.

Over their Wine.

"Are you drinking claret?" said Sir Peregrine, arranging himself and his bottles in the way that was usual to him. He had ever been a moderate man himself, but nevertheless he had a business-like way of going to work after dinner, as though there was a good deal to be done before the drawing-room could be visited.

"No more wine for me, sir," said Lucius.

"No wine!" said Sir Peregrine the elder.

"Why, Mason, you'll never get on if that's the way with you," said Peregrine the younger.

"I'll try at any rate," said the other.

"Water-drinker, moody thinker," and Peregrine sang a word or two from an old drinking-song.

"I am not quite sure of that. We Englishmen I suppose are the moodiest thinkers in all the world, and yet we are not so much given to water-drinking as our lively neighbours across the Channel."

Sir Peregrine said nothing more on the subject, but he probably thought that his young friend would not be a very comfortable neighbour. His present task, however, was by no means that of teaching him to drink, and he struck off at once upon the business he had undertaken. "So your mother tells me that you are going to devote all your energies to farming."

"Hardly that, I hope. There is the land, and I mean to see what I can do with it. It is not much, and I intend to combine some other occupation with it."

"You will find that two hundred acres of land will give you a good deal to do;—that is if you mean to make money by it."

"I certainly hope to do that,—in the long run."

"It seems to me the easiest thing in the world," said Peregrine.

"You'll find out your mistake some day; but with Lucius Mason it is very important that he should make no mistake at the commencement. For a country gentleman I know no prettier amusement than experimental farming;—but then a man must give up all idea of making his rent out of the land."

"I can't afford that," said Lucius.

"No; and that is why I take the liberty of speaking to you. I hope that the great friendship which I feel for your mother will be allowed to stand as my excuse."

"I am very much obliged by your kindness, sir; I am indeed."

"The truth is, I think you are beginning wrong. You have now been to Liverpool, to buy guano, I believe."

"Yes, that and some few other things. There is a man there who has taken out a patent—"

"My dear fellow, if you lay out your money in that way, you will never see it back again. Have you considered in the first place what your journey to Liverpool has cost you?"

"Exactly nine and sixpence per cent. on the money that I laid out there. Now that is not much more than a penny in the pound on the sum expended, and is not for a moment to be taken into consideration in comparison with the advantage of an improved market."

There was more in this than Sir Peregrine had expected to encounter. He did not for a moment doubt the truth of his own experience or the folly and the danger of the young man's proceedings; but he did doubt his own power of proving either the one or the other to one who so accurately computed his expenses by percentages on his outlay. Peregrine opened his eyes and sat by, wondering in silence. What on earth did Mason mean by an improved market?

"I am afraid then," said the baronet, "that you must have laid out a large sum of money."

"A man can't do any good, Sir Peregrine, by hoarding his capital. I don't think very much of capital myself—"

"Don't you?"

"Not of the theory of capital;—not so much as some people do; but if a man has got it, of course it should be expended on the trade to which it is to be applied."

"But some little knowledge—some experience is perhaps desirable before any great outlay is made."

"Yes; some little knowledge is necessary,—and some great knowledge would be desirable if it were accessible;—but it is not, as I take it."

"Long years, perhaps, devoted to such pursuits—"

"Yes, Sir Peregrine; I know what you are going to say. Experience no doubt will teach something. A man who has walked thirty miles a day for thirty years will probably know what sort of shoes will best suit his feet, and perhaps also the kind of food that will best support him through such exertion; but there is very little chance of his inventing any quicker mode of travelling."

"But he will have earned his wages honestly," said Sir Peregrine, almost angrily. In his heart he was very angry, for he did not love to be interrupted.

"Oh, yes; and if that were sufficient we might all walk our thirty miles a day. But some of us must earn wages for other people, or the world will make no progress. Civilization, as I take it, consists in efforts made not for oneself but for others."

"If you won't take any more wine we will join the ladies," said the baronet.

"He has not taken any at all," said Peregrine, filling his own glass for the last time and emptying it.

"That young man is the most conceited puppy it was ever my misfortune to meet," said Sir Peregrine to Mrs. Orme, when she came to kiss him and take his blessing as she always did before leaving him for the night.

"I am sorry for that," said she, "for I like his mother so much."

"I also like her," said Sir Peregrine; "but I cannot say that I shall ever be very fond of her son."

"I'll tell you what, mamma," said young Peregrine, the same evening in his mother's dressing-room. "Lucius Mason was too many for the governor this evening."

"I hope he did not tease your grandfather."

"He talked him down regularly, and it was plain that the governor did not like it."

And then the day was over.

CHAPTER XV
A MORNING CALL AT MOUNT PLEASANT VILLA

On the following day Lady Mason made two visits, using her new vehicle for the first time. She would fain have walked had she dared; but she would have given terrible offence to her son by doing so. He had explained to her, and with some truth, that as their joint income was now a thousand a year, she was quite entitled to such a luxury; and then he went on to say that as he had bought it for her, he should be much hurt if she would not use it. She had put it off from day to day, and now she could put it off no longer.

Her first visit was by appointment at The Cleeve. She had promised Mrs. Orme that she would come up, some special purpose having been named;—but with the real idea, at any rate on the part of the latter, that they might both be more comfortable together than alone. The walk across from Orley Farm to The Cleeve had always been very dear to Lady Mason. Every step of it was over beautiful ground, and a delight in scenery was one of the few pleasures which her lot in life had permitted her to enjoy. But to-day she could not allow herself the walk. Her pleasure and delight must be postponed to her son's wishes! But then she was used to that.

She found Mrs. Orme alone, and sat with her for an hour. I do not know that anything was said between them which deserves to be specially chronicled. Mrs. Orme, though she told her many things, did not tell her what Sir Peregrine had said as he was going up to his bedroom on the preceding evening, nor did Lady Mason say much about her son's farming. She had managed to gather from Lucius that he had not been deeply impressed by anything that had fallen from Sir Peregrine on the subject, and therefore thought it as well to hold her tongue. She soon perceived also, from the fact of Mrs. Orme saying nothing about Lucius, that he had not left behind him any very favourable impression. This was to her cause of additional sorrow, but she knew that it must be borne. Nothing that she could say would induce Lucius to make himself acceptable to Sir Peregrine.

When the hour was over she went down again to her little carriage, Mrs. Orme coming with her to look at it, and in the hall they met Sir Peregrine.

"Why does not Lady Mason stop for lunch?" said he. "It is past half-past one. I never knew anything so inhospitable as turning her out at this moment."

"I did ask her to stay," said Mrs. Orme.

"But I command her to stay," said Sir Peregrine, knocking his stick upon the stone floor of the hall. "And let me see who will dare to disobey me. John, let Lady Mason's carriage and pony stand in the open coach-house till she is ready." So Lady Mason went back and did remain for lunch. She was painfully anxious to maintain the best possible footing in that house, but still more anxious not to have it thought that she was intruding. She had feared that Lucius by his offence might have estranged Sir Peregrine against herself; but that at any rate was not the case.

After lunch she drove herself to Hamworth and made her second visit. On this occasion she called on one Mrs. Arkwright, who was a very old acquaintance, though hardly to be called an intimate friend. The late Mr. Arkwright,—Dr. Arkwright as he used to be styled in Hamworth,—had been Sir Joseph's medical attendant for many years, and therefore there had been room for an intimacy. No real friendship, that is no friendship of confidence, had sprung up; but nevertheless the doctor's wife had known enough of Lady Mason in her younger days to justify her in speaking of things which would not have been mentioned between merely ordinary acquaintance. "I am glad to see you have got promotion," said the old lady, looking out at Lady Mason's little phaeton on the gravel sweep which divided Mrs. Arkwright's house from the street. For Mrs. Arkwright's house was Mount Pleasant Villa, and therefore was entitled to a sweep.

"It was a present from Lucius," said the other, "and as such must be used. But I shall never feel myself at home in my own carriage."

"It is quite proper, my dear Lady Mason, quite proper. With his income and with yours I do not wonder that he insists upon it. It is quite proper, and just at the present moment peculiarly so."

Lady Mason did not understand this; but she would probably have passed it by without understanding it, had she not thought that there was some expression more than ordinary in Mrs. Arkwright's face. "Why peculiarly so at the present moment?" she said.

"Because it shows that this foolish report which is going about has no foundation. People won't believe it for a moment when they see you out and about, and happy-like."

"What rumour, Mrs. Arkwright?" And Lady Mason's heart sunk within her as she asked the question. She felt at once to what it must allude, though she had conceived no idea as yet that there was any rumour on the subject. Indeed, during the last forty-eight hours, since she had left the chambers of Mr. Furnival, she had been more at ease within herself than during the previous days which had elapsed subsequent to the ill-omened visit made to her by Miriam Dockwrath. It had seemed to her that Mr. Furnival anticipated no danger, and his manner and words had almost given her confidence. But now,—now that a public rumour was spoken of, her heart was as low again as ever.

"Sure, haven't you heard?" said Mrs. Arkwright. "Well, I wouldn't be the first to tell you, only that I know that there is no truth in it."

"You might as well tell me now, as I shall be apt to believe worse than the truth after what you have said."

And then Mrs. Arkwright told her. "People have been saying that Mr. Mason is again going to begin those law proceedings about the farm; but I for one don't believe it."

"People have said so!" Lady Mason repeated. She meant nothing; it was nothing to her who the people were. If one said it now, all would soon be saying it. But she uttered the words because she felt herself forced to say something, and the power of thinking what she might best say was almost taken away from her.

"I am sure I don't know where it came from," said Mrs. Arkwright; "but I would not have alluded to it if I had not thought that of course you had heard it. I am very sorry if my saying it has vexed you."

"Oh, no," said Lady Mason, trying to smile.

"As I said before, we all know that there is nothing in it; and your having the pony chaise just at this time will make everybody see that you are quite comfortable yourself."

"Thank you, yes; good-bye, Mrs. Arkwright." And then she made a great effort, feeling aware that she was betraying herself, and that it behoved her to say something which might remove the suspicion which her emotion must have created. "The very name of that lawsuit is so dreadful to me that I can hardly bear it. The memory of it is so terrible to me, that even my enemies would hardly wish that it should commence again."

"Of course it is merely a report," said Mrs. Arkwright, almost trembling at what she had done.

"That is all—at least I believe so. I had heard myself that some such threat had been made, but I did not think that any tidings of it had got abroad."

"It was Mrs. Whiting told me. She is a great busybody, you know." Mrs. Whiting was the wife of the present doctor.

"Dear Mrs. Arkwright, it does not matter in the least. Of course I do not expect that people should hold their tongue on my account. Good-bye, Mrs. Arkwright." And then she got into the little carriage, and did contrive to drive herself home to Orley Farm.

"Dear, dear, dear, dear!" said Mrs. Arkwright to herself when she was left alone. "Only to think of that; that she should be knocked in a heap by a few words—in a moment, as we may say." And then she began to consider of the matter. "I wonder what there is in it! There must be something, or she would never have looked so like a ghost. What will they do if Orley Farm is taken away from them after all!" And then Mrs. Arkwright hurried out on her daily little toddle through the town, that she might talk about and be talked to on the same subject. She was by no means an ill-natured woman, nor was she at all inclined to direct against Lady Mason any slight amount of venom which might alloy her disposition. But then the matter was of such importance! The people of Hamworth had hardly yet ceased to talk of the last Orley Farm trial; and would it not be necessary that they should talk much more if a new trial were really pending? Looking at the matter in that light, would not such a trial be a godsend to the people of Hamworth? Therefore I beg that it may not be imputed to Mrs. Arkwright as a fault that she toddled out and sought eagerly for her gossips.

Lady Mason did manage to drive herself home; but her success in the matter was more owing to the good faith and propriety of her pony, than to any skilful workmanship on her own part. Her first desire had been to get away from Mrs. Arkwright, and having made that effort she was now for a time hardly able to make any other. It was fast coming upon her now. Let Sir Peregrine say what comforting words he might, let Mr. Furnival assure her that she was safe with ever so much confidence, nevertheless she could not but believe, could not but feel inwardly convinced, that that which she so dreaded was to happen. It was written in the book of her destiny that there should be a new trial.

And now, from this very moment, the misery would again begin. People would point at her, and talk of her. Her success in obtaining Orley Farm for her own child would again be canvassed at every house in Hamworth; and not only her success, but the means also by which that success had been obtained. The old people would remember and the young people would inquire; and, for her, tranquillity, repose, and that retirement of life which had been so valuable to her, were all gone.

There could be no doubt that Dockwrath had spread the report immediately on his return from Yorkshire; and had she well thought of the matter she might have taken some comfort from this. Of course he would tell the story which he did tell. His confidence in being able again to drag the case before the Courts would by no means argue that others believed as he believed. In fact the enemies now arraigned against her were only those whom she already knew to be so arraigned. But she had not sufficient command of her thoughts to be able at first to take comfort from such a reflection as this. She felt, as she was being carried home, that the world was going from her, and that it would be well for her, were it possible, that she should die.

But she was stronger when she reached her own door than she had been at Mrs. Arkwright's. There was still within her a great power of self-maintenance, if only time were allowed to her to look about and consider how best she might support herself. Many women are in this respect as she was. With forethought and summoned patience they can endure great agonies; but a sudden pang, unexpected, overwhelms them. She got out of the pony carriage with her ordinary placid face, and walked up to her own room without having given any sign that she was uneasy; and then she had to determine how she should bear herself before her son. It had been with her a great object that both Sir Peregrine and Mr. Furnival should first hear of the tidings from her, and that they should both promise her their aid when they had heard the story as she would tell it. In this she had been successful; and it now seemed to her that prudence would require her to act in the same way towards Lucius. Had it been possible to keep this matter from him altogether, she would have given much to do so; but now it would not be possible. It was clear that Mr. Dockwrath had chosen to make the matter public, acting no doubt with forethought in doing so; and Lucius would be sure to hear words which would become common in Hamworth. Difficult as the task would be to her, it would be best that she should prepare him. So she sat alone till dinner-time planning how she would do this. She had sat alone for hours in the same way planning how she would tell her story to Sir Peregrine; and again as to her second story for Mr. Furnival. Those whose withers are unwrung can hardly guess how absolutely a sore under the collar will embitter every hour for the poor jade who is so tormented!

But she met him at dinner with a smiling face. He loved to see her smile, and often told her so, almost upbraiding her when she would look sad. Why should she be sad, seeing that she had everything that a woman could desire? Her mind was burdened with no heavy thoughts as to feeding coming multitudes. She had no contests to wage with the desultory chemists of the age. His purpose was to work hard during the hours of the day,—

hard also during many hours of the night; and it was becoming that his mother should greet him softly during his few intervals of idleness. He told her so, in some words not badly chosen for such telling; and she, loving mother that she was, strove valiantly to obey him.

During dinner she could not speak to him, nor immediately after dinner. The evil moment she put off from half-hour to half-hour, still looking as though all were quiet within her bosom as she sat beside him with her book in her hand. He was again at work before she began her story; he thought at least that he was at work, for he had before him on the table both Prichard and Latham, and was occupied in making copies from some drawings of skulls which purposed to represent the cerebral development of certain of our more distant Asiatic brethren.

"Is it not singular," said be, "that the jaws of men born and bred in a hunter state should be differently formed from those of the agricultural tribes?"

"Are they?" said Lady Mason.

"Oh yes; the maxillary profile is quite different. You will see this especially with the Mongolians, among the Tartar tribes. It seems to me to be very much the same difference as that between a man and a sheep, but Prichard makes no such remark. Look here at this fellow; he must have been intended to eat nothing but flesh; and that raw, and without any knife or fork."

"I don't suppose they had many knives or forks."

"By close observation I do not doubt that one could tell from a single tooth not only what food the owner of it had been accustomed to eat, but what language he had spoken. I say close observation, you know. It could not be done in a day."

"I suppose not." And then the student again bent over his drawing. "You see it would have been impossible for the owner of such a jaw as that to have ground a grain of corn between his teeth, or to have masticated even a cabbage."

"Lucius," said Lady Mason, becoming courageous on the spur of the moment, "I want you to leave that for a moment and speak to me."

"Well," said he, putting down his pencil and turning round. "Here I am."

"You have heard of the lawsuit which I had with your brother when you were an infant?"

"Of course I have heard of it; but I wish you would not call that man my brother. He would not own me as such, and I most certainly would not own him. As far as I can learn he is one of the most detestable human beings that ever existed."

"You have heard of him from an unfavourable side, Lucius; you should remember that. He is a hard man, I believe; but I do not know that he would do anything which he thought to be unjust."

"Why then did he try to rob me of my property?"

"Because he thought that it should have been his own. I cannot see into his breast, but I presume that it was so."

"I do not presume anything of the kind, and never shall. I was an infant and you were a woman,—a woman at that time without many friends, and he thought that he could rob us under cover of the law. Had he been commonly honest it would have been enough for him to know what had been my father's wishes, even if the will had not been rigidly formal. I look upon him as a robber and a thief."

"I am sorry for that, Lucius, because I differ from you. What I wish to tell you now is this,—that he is thinking of trying the question again."

"What!—thinking of another trial now?" and Lucius Mason pushed his drawings and books from him with a vengeance.

"So I am told."

"And who told you? I cannot believe it, If he intended anything of the kind I must have been the first person to hear of it. It would be my business now, and you may be sure that he would have taken care to let me know his purpose."

And then by degrees she explained to him that the man himself, Mr. Mason of Groby, had as yet declared no such purpose. She had intended to omit all mention of the name of Mr. Dockwrath, but she was unable to do so without seeming to make a mystery with her son. When she came to explain how the rumour had arisen and why she had thought it necessary to tell him this, she was obliged to say that it had all arisen from the wrath of the attorney. "He has been to Groby Park," she said, "and now that he has returned he is spreading this report."

"I shall go to him to-morrow," said Lucius, very sternly.

"No, no; you must not do that. You must promise me that you will not do that."

"But I shall. You cannot suppose that I shall allow such a man as that to tamper with my name without noticing it! It is my business now."

"No, Lucius. The attack will be against me rather than you;—that is, if an attack be made. I have told you because I do not like to have a secret from you."

"Of course you have told me. If you are attacked who should defend you, if I do not?"

"The best defence, indeed the only defence till they take some active step, will be silence. Most probably they will not do anything, and then we can afford to live down such reports as these. You can understand, Lucius, that the matter is grievous enough to me; and I am sure that for my sake you will not make it worse by a personal quarrel with such a man as that."

"I shall go to Mr. Furnival," said he, "and ask his advice."

"I have done that already, Lucius. I thought it best to do so, when first I heard that Mr. Dockwrath was moving in the matter. It was for that that I went up to town."

"And why did you not tell me?"

"I then thought that you might be spared the pain of knowing anything of the matter. I tell you now because I hear to-day in Hamworth that people are talking on the subject. You might be annoyed, as I was just now, if the first tidings had reached you from some stranger."

He sat silent for a while, turning his pencil in his hand, and looking as though he were going to settle the matter off hand by his own thoughts. "I tell you what it is, mother; I shall not let the burden of this fall on your shoulders. You carried on the battle before, but I must do so now. If I can trace any word of scandal to that fellow Dockwrath, I shall indict him for a libel."

"Oh, Lucius!"

"I shall, and no mistake!"

What would he have said had he known that his mother had absolutely proposed to Mr. Furnival to buy off Mr. Dockwrath's animosity, almost at any price?

CHAPTER XVI
MR. DOCKWRATH IN BEDFORD ROW

Mr. Dockwrath, as he left Leeds and proceeded to join the bosom of his family, was not discontented with what he had done. It might not improbably have been the case that Mr. Mason would altogether refuse to see him, and having seen him, Mr. Mason might altogether have declined his assistance. He might have been forced as a witness to disclose his secret, of which he could make so much better a profit as a legal adviser. As it was, Mr. Mason had promised to pay him for his services, and would no doubt be induced to go so far as to give him a legal claim for payment. Mr. Mason had promised to come up to town, and had instructed the Hamworth attorney to meet him there; and under such circumstances the Hamworth attorney had but little doubt that time would produce a considerable bill of costs in his favour.

And then he thought that he saw his way to a great success. I should be painting the Devil too black were I to say that revenge was his chief incentive in that which he was doing. All our motives are mixed; and his wicked desire to do evil to Lady Mason in return for the evil which she had done to him was mingled with professional energy, and an ambition to win a cause that ought to be won—especially a cause which others had failed to win. He said to himself, on finding those names and dates among old Mr. Usbech's papers, that there was still an opportunity of doing something considerable in this Orley Farm Case, and he had made up his mind to do it. Professional energy, revenge, and money considerations would work hand in hand in this matter; and therefore, as he left Leeds in the second-class railway carriage for London, he thought over the result of his visit with considerable satisfaction.

He had left Leeds at ten, and Mr. Moulder had come down in the same omnibus to the station, and was travelling in the same train in a first-class carriage. Mr. Moulder was a man who despised the second-class, and was not slow to say so before other commercials who travelled at a cheaper rate than he did. "Hubbles and Grease," he said, "allowed him respectably, in order that he might go about their business respectable; and he wasn't going to give the firm a bad name by being seen in a second-class carriage, although the difference would go into his own pocket. That wasn't the way he had begun, and that wasn't the way he was going to end." He said nothing to Mr. Dockwrath in the morning, merely bowing in answer to that gentleman's salutation. "Hope you were comfortable last night in the back drawing-room," said Mr. Dockwrath; but Mr. Moulder in reply only looked at him.

At the Mansfield station, Mr. Kantwise, with his huge wooden boxes, appeared on the platform, and he got into the same carriage with Mr. Dockwrath. He had come on by a night train, and had been doing a stroke of business that morning. "Well, Kantwise," Moulder holloaed out from his warm, well-padded seat, "doing it cheap and nasty, eh?"

"Not at all nasty, Mr. Moulder," said the other. "And I find myself among as respectable a class of society in the second-class as you do in the first; quite so;—and perhaps a little better," Mr. Kantwise added, as he took his seat immediately opposite to Mr. Dockwrath. "I hope I have the pleasure of seeing you pretty bobbish this morning, sir." And he shook hands cordially with the attorney.

"Tidy, thank you," said Dockwrath. "My company last night did not do me any harm; you may swear to that."

"Ha! ha! ha! I was so delighted that you got the better of Moulder; a domineering party, isn't he? quite terrible! For myself, I can't put up with him sometimes."

"I didn't have to put up with him last night."

"No, no; it was very good, wasn't it now? very capital, indeed. All the same I wish you'd heard Busby give us 'Beautiful Venice, City of Song!' A charming voice has Busby; quite charming." And there was a pause for a minute or so, after which Mr. Kantwise resumed the conversation. "You'll allow me to put you up one of those drawing-room sets?" he said.

"Well, I am afraid not. I don't think they are strong enough where there are children."

"Dear, dear; dear, dear; to hear you say so, Mr. Dockwrath! Why, they are made for strength. They are the very things for children, because they don't break, you know."

"But they'd bend terribly."

"By no means. They're so elastic that they always recovers themselves. I didn't show you that; but you might turn the backs of them chairs nearly down to the ground, and they will come straight again. You let me send you a set for your wife to look at. If she's not charmed with them I'll—I'll—I'll eat them."

"Women are charmed with anything," said Mr. Dockwrath. "A new bonnet does that."

"They know what they are about pretty well, as I dare say you have found out. I'll send express to Sheffield and have a completely new set put up for you."

"For twelve seventeen six, of course?"

"Oh! dear no, Mr. Dockwrath. The lowest figure for ready money, delivered free, is fifteen ten."

"I couldn't think of paying more than Mrs. Mason."

"Ah! but that was a damaged set; it was, indeed. And she merely wanted it as a present for the curate's wife. The table was quite sprung, and the music-stool wouldn't twist."

"But you'll send them to me new?"

"New from the manufactory; upon my word we will."

"A table that you have never acted upon—have never shown off on; standing in the middle, you know?"

"Yes; upon my honour. You shall have them direct from the workshop, and sent at once; you shall find them in your drawing-room on Tuesday next."

"We'll say thirteen ten."

"I couldn't do it, Mr. Dockwrath—" And so they went on, bargaining half the way up to town, till at last they came to terms for fourteen eleven. "And a very superior article your lady will find them," Mr. Kantwise said as he shook hands with his new friend at parting. ⁻

One day Mr. Dockwrath remained at home in the bosom of his family, saying all manner of spiteful things against Lady Mason, and on the next day he went up to town and called on Round and Crook. That one day he waited in order that Mr. Mason might have time to write; but Mr. Mason had written on the very day of the visit to Groby Park, and Mr. Round junior was quite ready for Mr. Dockwrath when that gentleman called.

Mr. Dockwrath when at home had again cautioned his wife to have no intercourse whatever "with that swindler at Orley Farm," wishing thereby the more thoroughly to imbue poor Miriam with a conviction that Lady Mason had committed some fraud with reference to the will. "You had better say nothing about the matter anywhere; d'you hear? People will talk; all the world will be talking about it before long. But that is nothing to you. If people ask you, say that you believe that I am engaged in the case professionally, but that you know nothing further." As to all which Miriam of course promised the most exact obedience. But Mr. Dockwrath, though he only remained one day in Hamworth before he went to London, took care that the curiosity of his neighbours should be sufficiently excited.

Mr. Dockwrath felt some little trepidation at the heart as he walked into the office of Messrs. Round and Crook in Bedford Row. Messrs. Round and Crook stood high in the profession, and were men who in the ordinary way of business would have had no personal dealings with such a man as Mr. Dockwrath. Had any such intercourse become necessary on commonplace subjects Messrs. Round and Crook's confidential clerk might have seen Mr. Dockwrath, but even he would have looked down upon the Hamworth attorney as from a great moral height. But now, in the matter of the Orley Farm Case, Mr. Dockwrath had determined that he would transact business only on equal terms with the Bedford Row people. The secret was his—of his finding; he knew the strength of his own position, and he would use it. But nevertheless he did tremble inwardly as he asked whether Mr. Round was within;—or if not Mr. Round, then Mr. Crook.

There were at present three members in the firm, though the old name remained unaltered. The Mr. Round and the Mr. Crook of former days were still working partners;—the very Round and the very Crook who had carried on the battle on the part of Mr. Mason of Groby twenty years ago; but to them had been added another Mr. Round, a son of old Round, who, though his name did not absolutely appear in the nomenclature of the firm, was, as a working man, the most important person in it. Old Mr. Round might now be said to be ornamental and communicative. He was a hale man of nearly seventy, who thought a great deal of his peaches up at Isleworth, who came to the office five times a week—not doing very much hard work, and who took the largest share in the profits. Mr. Round senior had enjoyed the reputation of being a sound, honourable man, but was now considered by some to be not quite sharp enough for the practice of the present day.

Mr. Crook had usually done the dirty work of the firm, having been originally a managing clerk; and he still did the same—in a small way. He had been the man to exact penalties, look after costs, and attend to any criminal business, or business partly criminal in its nature, which might chance find its way to them. But latterly in all great matters Mr. Round junior, Mr. Matthew Round,—his father was Richard,—was the member of the firm on whom the world in general placed the greatest dependence. Mr. Mason's letter had in the ordinary way of business come to him, although it had been addressed to his father, and he had resolved on acting on it himself.

When Mr. Dockwrath called Mr. Round senior was at Birmingham, Mr. Crook was taking his annual holiday, and Mr. Round junior was reigning alone in Bedford Row. Instructions had been given to the clerks that if Mr. Dockwrath called he was to be shown in, and therefore he found himself seated, with much less trouble than he had expected, in the private room of Mr. Round junior. He had expected to see an old man, and was therefore somewhat confused, not feeling quite sure that he was in company with one of the principals; but nevertheless, looking at the room, and especially at the arm-chair and carpet, he was aware that the legal gentleman who motioned him to a seat could be no ordinary clerk.

The manner of this legal gentleman was not, as Mr. Dockwrath thought, quite so ceremoniously civil as it might be, considering the important nature of the business to be transacted between them. Mr. Dockwrath intended to treat on equal terms, and so intending would have been glad to have shaken hands with his new ally at the commencement of their joint operations. But the man before him,—a man younger than himself too,—did not even rise from his chair. "Ah! Mr. Dockwrath," he said, taking up a letter from the table, "will you have the goodness to sit down?" And Mr. Matthew Round wheeled his own arm-chair towards the fire, stretching out his legs comfortably, and pointing to a somewhat distant seat as that intended for the accommodation of his visitor. Mr. Dockwrath seated himself in the somewhat distant seat, and deposited his hat upon the floor, not being as yet quite at home in his position; but he made up his mind as he did so that he would be at home before he left the room.

"I find that you have been down in Yorkshire with a client of ours, Mr. Dockwrath," said Mr. Matthew Round.

"Yes, I have," said he of Hamworth.

"Ah! well—; you are in the profession yourself, I believe?"

"Yes; I am an attorney."

"Would it not have been well to have come to us first?"

"No, I think not. I have not the pleasure of knowing your name, sir."

"My name is Round—Matthew Round."

"I beg your pardon, sir; I did not know," said Mr. Dockwrath, bowing. It was a satisfaction to him to learn that he was closeted with a Mr. Round, even if it were not the Mr. Round. "No, Mr. Round, I can't say that I should have thought of that. In the first place I didn't know whether Mr. Mason employed any lawyer, and in the next—"

"Well, well; it does not matter. It is usual among the profession; but it does not in the least signify. Mr. Mason has written to us, and he says that you have found out something about that Orley Farm business."

"Yes; I have found out something. At least, I rather think so."

"Well, what is, it, Mr. Dockwrath?"

"Ah! that's the question. It's rather a ticklish business, Mr. Round; a family affair, as I may say."

"Whose family?"

"To a certain extent my family, and to a certain extent Mr. Mason's family. I don't know how far I should be justified in laying all the facts before you—wonderful facts they are too—in an off-hand way like that. These matters have to be considered a great deal. It is not only the extent of the property. There is much more than that in it, Mr. Round."

"If you don't tell me what there is in it, I don't see what we are to do. I am sure you did not give yourself the trouble of coming up here from Hamworth merely with the object of telling us that you are going to hold your tongue."

"Certainly not, Mr. Round."

"Then what did you come to say?"

"May I ask you, Mr. Round, what Mr. Mason has told you with reference to my interview with him?"

"Yes; I will read you a part of his letter—'Mr. Dockwrath is of opinion that the will under which the estate is now enjoyed is absolutely a forgery.' I presume you mean the codicil, Mr. Dockwrath?"

"Oh yes! the codicil of course."

"'And he has in his possession documents which I have not seen, but which seem to me, as described, to go far to prove that this certainly must have been the case.' And then he goes on with a description of dates, although it is clear that he does not understand the matter himself—indeed he says as much. Now of course we must see these documents before we can give our client any advice." A certain small portion of Mr. Mason's letter Mr. Round did then read, but he did not read those portions in which Mr. Mason expressed his firm determination to reopen the case against Lady Mason, and even to prosecute her for forgery if it were found that he had anything like a fair chance of success in doing so. "I know that you were convinced," he had said, addressing himself personally to Mr. Round senior, "that Lady Mason was acting in good faith. I was always convinced of the contrary, and am more sure of it now than ever." This last paragraph, Mr. Round junior had not thought it necessary to read to Mr. Dockwrath.

"The documents to which I allude are in reference to my confidential family matters; and I certainly shall not produce them without knowing on what ground I am standing."

"Of course you are aware, Mr. Dockwrath, that we could compel you."

"There, Mr. Round, I must be allowed to differ."

"It won't come to that, of course. If you have anything worth showing, you'll show it; and if we make use of you as a witness, it must be as a willing witness."

"I don't think it probable that I shall be a witness in the matter at all."

"Ah, well; perhaps not. My own impression is that no case will be made out; that there will be nothing to take before a jury."

"There again, I must differ from you, Mr. Round."

"Oh, of course! I suppose the real fact is, that it is a matter of money. You want to be paid for what information you have got. That is about the long and the short of it; eh, Mr. Dockwrath?"

"I don't know what you call the long and the short of it, Mr. Round; or what may be your way of doing business. As a professional man, of course I expect to be paid for my work;—and I have no doubt that you expect the same."

"No doubt, Mr. Dockwrath; but—as you have made the comparison, I hope you will excuse me for saying so—we always wait till our clients come to us."

Mr. Dockwrath drew himself up with some intention of becoming angry; but he hardly knew how to carry it out; and then it might be a question whether anger would serve his turn. "Do you mean to say, Mr. Round, if you had found documents such as these, you would have done nothing about them—that you would have passed them by as worthless?"

"I can't say that till I know what the documents are. If I found papers concerning the client of another firm, I should go to that firm if I thought that they demanded attention."

"I didn't know anything about the firm;—how was I to know?"

"Well! you know now, Mr. Dockwrath. As I understand it, our client has referred you to us. If you have anything to say, we are ready to hear it.

If you have anything to show, we are ready to look at it. If you have nothing to say, and nothing to show—"

"Ah, but I have; only—"

"Only you want us to make it worth your while. We might as well have the truth at once. Is not that about it?"

"I want to see my way, of course."

"Exactly. And now, Mr. Dockwrath, I must make you understand that we don't do business in that way."

"Then I shall see Mr. Mason again myself."

"That you can do. He will be in town next week, and, as I believe, wishes to see you. As regards your expenses, if you can show us that you have any communication to make that is worth our client's attention, we will see that you are paid what you are out of pocket, and some fair remuneration for the time you may have lost;—not as an attorney, remember, for in that light we cannot regard you."

"I am every bit as much an attorney as you are."

"No doubt; but you are not Mr. Mason's attorney; and as long as it suits him to honour us with his custom, you cannot be so regarded."

"That's as he pleases."

"No; it is not, Mr. Dockwrath. It is as he pleases whether he employs you or us; but it is not as he pleases whether he employs both on business of the same class. He may give us his confidence, or he may withdraw it."

"Looking at the way the matter was managed before, perhaps the latter may be the better for him."

"Excuse me, Mr. Dockwrath, for saying that that is a question I shall not discuss with you."

Upon this Mr. Dockwrath jumped from his chair, and took up his hat. "Good morning to you, sir," said Mr. Round, without moving from his chair; "I will tell Mr. Mason that you have declined making any communication to us. He will probably know your address—if he should want it."

Mr. Dockwrath paused. Was he not about to sacrifice substantial advantage to momentary anger? Would it not be better that he should carry this impudent young London lawyer with him if it were possible? "Sir," said he, "I am quite willing to tell you all that I know of this matter at present, if you will have the patience to hear it."

"Patience, Mr. Dockwrath! Why I am made of patience. Sit down again, Mr. Dockwrath, and think of it."

Mr. Dockwrath did sit down again, and did think of it; and it ended in his telling to Mr. Round all that he had told to Mr. Mason. As he did so, he looked closely at Mr. Round's face, but there he could read nothing. "Exactly," said Mr. Round. "The fourteenth of July is the date of both. I have taken a memorandum of that. A final deed for closing partnership, was it? I have got that down. John Kenneby and Bridget Bolster. I remember the names,—witnesses to both deeds, were they? I understand; nothing about this other deed was brought up at the trial? I see the point—such as it is. John Kenneby and Bridget Bolster;—both believed to be living. Oh, you can give their address, can you? Decline to do so now? Very well; it does not matter. I think I understand it all now, Mr. Dockwrath; and when we want you again, you shall hear from us. Samuel Dockwrath, is it? Thank you. Good morning. If Mr. Mason wishes to see you, he will write, of course. Good day, Mr. Dockwrath."

And so Mr. Dockwrath went home, not quite contented with his day's work.

CHAPTER XVII
VON BAUHR

It will be remembered that Mr. Crabwitz was sent across from Lincoln's Inn to Bedford Row to ascertain the present address of old Mr. Round. "Mr. Round is at Birmingham," he said, coming back. "Every one connected with the profession is at Birmingham, except—"

"The more fools they," said Mr. Furnival.

"I am thinking of going down myself this evening," said Mr. Crabwitz. "As you will be out of town, sir, I suppose I can be spared?"

"You too!"

"And why not me, Mr. Furnival? When all the profession is meeting together, why should not I be there as well as another? I hope you do not deny me my right to feel an interest in the great subjects which are being discussed."

"Not in the least, Mr. Crabwitz. I do not deny you your right to be Lord Chief Justice, if you can accomplish it. But you cannot be Lord Chief Justice and my clerk at the same time. Nor can you be in my chambers if you are at Birmingham. I rather think I must trouble you to remain here, as I cannot tell at what moment I may be in town again."

"Then, sir, I'm afraid—" Mr. Crabwitz began his speech and then faltered. He was going to tell Mr. Furnival that he must suit himself with another clerk, when he remembered his fees, and paused. It would be very pleasant to him to quit Mr. Furnival, but where could he get such another place? He knew that he himself was invaluable, but then he was invaluable only to Mr. Furnival. Mr. Furnival would be mad to part with him, Mr. Crabwitz thought; but then would he not be almost more mad to part with Mr. Furnival?

"Eh; well?" said Mr. Furnival.

"Oh! of course; if you desire it, Mr. Furnival, I will remain. But I must say I think it is rather hard."

"Look here, Mr. Crabwitz; if you think my service is too hard upon you, you had better leave it. But if you take upon yourself to tell me so again, you must leave it. Remember that." Mr. Furnival possessed the master mind of the two; and Mr. Crabwitz felt this as he slunk back to his own room.

So Mr. Round also was at Birmingham, and could be seen there. This was so far well; and Mr. Furnival, having again with ruthless malice sent Mr. Crabwitz for a cab, at once started for the Euston Square Station. He could master Mr. Crabwitz, and felt a certain pleasure in having done so; but could he master Mrs. F.? That lady had on one or two late occasions shown her anger at the existing state of her domestic affairs, and had once previously gone so far as to make her lord understand that she was jealous of his proceedings with reference to other goddesses. But she had never before done this in the presence of other people;—she had never allowed any special goddess to see that she was the special object of such jealousy. Now she had not only committed herself in this way, but had also committed him, making him feel himself to be ridiculous; and it was highly necessary that some steps should be taken;—if he only knew what step! All which kept his mind active as he journeyed in the cab.

At the station he found three or four other lawyers, all bound for Birmingham. Indeed, during this fortnight the whole line had been alive with learned gentlemen going to and fro, discussing weighty points as they rattled along the iron road, and shaking their ponderous heads at the new ideas which were being ventilated. Mr. Furnival, with many others— indeed, with most of those who were so far advanced in the world as to be making bread by their profession—was of opinion that all this palaver that was going on in the various tongues of Babel would end as it began— in words. "Vox et præterea nihil." To practical Englishmen most of these international congresses seem to arrive at nothing else. Men will not be — talked out of the convictions of their lives. No living orator would convince a grocer that coffee should be sold without chicory; and no amount of eloquence will make an English lawyer think that loyalty to truth should come before loyalty to his client. And therefore our own pundits, though on this occasion they went to Birmingham, summoned by the greatness of the occasion, by the dignity of foreign names, by interest in the question, and by the influence of such men as Lord Boanerges, went there without any doubt on their minds as to the rectitude of their own practice, and fortified with strong resolves to resist all idea of change.

And indeed one cannot understand how the bent of any man's mind should be altered by the sayings and doings of such a congress.

"Well, Johnson, what have you all been doing to-day?" asked Mr. Furnival of a special friend whom he chanced to meet at the club which had been extemporized at Birmingham.

"We have had a paper read by Von Bauhr. It lasted three hours."

"Three hours! heavens! Von Bauhr is, I think, from Berlin."

"Yes; he and Dr. Slotacher. Slotacher is to read his paper the day after to-morrow."

"Then I think I shall go to London again. But what did Von Bauhr say to you during those three hours?"

"Of course it was all in German, and I don't suppose that any one understood him,—unless it was Boanerges. But I believe it was the old story, going to show that the same man might be judge, advocate, and jury."

"No doubt;—if men were machines, and if you could find such machines perfect at all points in their machinery."

"And if the machines had no hearts?"

"Machines don't have hearts," said Mr. Furnival; "especially those in Germany. And what did Boanerges say? His answer did not take three hours more, I hope."

"About twenty minutes; but what he did say was lost on Von Bauhr, who understands as much English as I do German. He said that the practice of the Prussian courts had always been to him a subject of intense interest, and that the general justice of their verdicts could not be impugned."

"Nor ought it, seeing that a single trial for murder will occupy a court for three weeks. He should have asked Von Bauhr how much work he usually got through in the course of a sessions. I don't seem to have lost much by being away. By-the-by, do you happen to know whether Round is here?"

"What, old Round? I saw him in the hall to-day yawning as though he would burst." And then Mr. Furnival strolled off to look for the attorney among the various purlieus frequented by the learned strangers.

"Furnival," said another barrister, accosting him,—an elderly man, small, with sharp eyes and bushy eyebrows, dirty in his attire and poor in his general appearance, "have you seen Judge Staveley?" This was Mr. Chaffanbrass, great at the Old Bailey, a man well able to hold his own in spite of the meanness of his appearance. At such a meeting as this the English bar generally could have had no better representative than Mr. Chaffanbrass.

"No; is he here?"

"He must be here. He is the only man they could find who knows enough Italian to understand what that fat fellow from Florence will say to-morrow."

"We're to have the Italian to-morrow, are we?"

"Yes; and Staveley afterwards. It's as good as a play; only, like all plays, it's three times too long. I wonder whether anybody here believes in it?"

"Yes, Felix Graham does."

"He believes everything—unless it is the Bible. He is one of those young men who look for an instant millennium, and who regard themselves not only as the prophets who foretell it, but as the preachers who will produce it. For myself, I am too old for a new gospel, with Felix Graham as an apostle."

"They say that Boanerges thinks a great deal of him."

"That can't be true, for Boanerges never thought much of any one but himself. Well, I'm off to bed, for I find a day here ten times more fatiguing than the Old Bailey in July."

On the whole the meeting was rather dull, as such meetings usually are. It must not be supposed that any lawyer could get up at will, as the spirit moved him, and utter his own ideas; or that all members of the congress could speak if only they could catch the speaker's eye. Had this been so, a man might have been supported by the hope of having some finger in the pie, sooner or later. But in such case the congress would have lasted for ever. As it was, the names of those who were invited to address the meeting were arranged, and of course men from each country were selected who were best known in their own special walks of their profession. But then these best-known men took an unfair advantage of their position, and were ruthless in the lengthy cruelty of their addresses. Von Bauhr at Berlin was no doubt a great lawyer, but he should not have felt so confident that the legal proceedings of England and of the civilised world in general could be reformed by his reading that book of his from the rostrum in the hall at Birmingham! The civilised world in general, as there represented, had been disgusted, and it was surmised that poor Dr. Slotacher would find but a meagre audience when his turn came.

At last Mr. Furnival succeeded in hunting up Mr. Round, and found him recruiting outraged nature with a glass of brandy and water and a cigar. "Looking for me, have you? Well, here I am; that is to say, what is left of me. Were you in the hall to-day?"

"No; I was up in town."

"Ah! that accounts for your being so fresh. I wish I had been there. Do you ever do anything in this way?" and Mr. Round touched the outside of his glass of toddy with his spoon. Mr. Furnival said that he never did do anything in that way, which was true. Port wine was his way, and it may be doubted whether on the whole it is not the more dangerous way of the two. But Mr. Furnival, though he would not drink brandy and water or smoke cigars, sat down opposite to Mr. Round, and had soon broached the subject which was on his mind.

"Yes," said the attorney, "it is quite true that I had a letter on the subject from Mr. Mason. The lady is not wrong in supposing that some one is moving in the matter."

"And your client wishes you to take up the case again?"

"No doubt he does. He was not a man that I ever greatly liked, Mr. Furnival, though I believe he means well. He thinks that he has been ill used; and perhaps he was ill used—by his father."

"But that can be no possible reason for badgering the life out of his father's widow twenty years after his father's death!"

"Of course he thinks that he has some new evidence. I can't say I looked into the matter much myself. I did read the letter; but that was all, and then I handed it to my son. As far as I remember, Mr. Mason said that some attorney at Hamworth had been to him."

"Exactly; a low fellow whom you would be ashamed to see in your office! He fancies that young Mason has injured him; and though he has received numberless benefits from Lady Mason, this is the way in which he chooses to be revenged on her son."

"We should have nothing to do with such a matter as that, you know. It's not our line."

"No, of course it is not; I am well aware of that. And I am equally well aware that nothing Mr. Mason can do can shake Lady Mason's title, or rather her son's title, to the property. But, Mr. Round, if he be encouraged to gratify his malice—"

"If who be encouraged?"

"Your client, Mr. Mason of Groby;—there can be no doubt that he might harass this unfortunate lady till he brought her nearly to the grave."

"That would be a pity, for I believe she's still an uncommon pretty woman." And the attorney indulged in a little fat inward chuckle; for in these days Mr. Furnival's taste with reference to strange goddesses was beginning to be understood by the profession.

"She is a very old friend of mine," said Mr. Furnival, gravely, "a very old friend indeed; and if I were to desert her now, she would have no one to whom she could look."

"Oh, ah, yes; I'm sure you're very kind;" and Mr. Round altered his face and tone, so that they might be in conformity with those of his companion. "Anything I can do, of course I shall be very happy. I should be slow, myself, to advise my client to try the matter again, but to tell the truth anything of this kind would go to my son now. I did read Mr. Mason's letter, but I immediately handed it to Matthew."

"I will tell you how you can oblige me, Mr. Round."

"Do tell me; I am sure I shall be very happy."

"Look into this matter yourself, and talk it over with Mr. Mason before you allow anything to be done. It is not that I doubt your son's discretion. Indeed we all know what an exceedingly good man of business he is."

"Matthew is sharp enough," said the prosperous father.

"But then young men are apt to be too sharp. I don't know whether you remember the case about that Orley Farm, Mr. Round."

"As well as if it were yesterday," said the attorney.

"Then you must recollect how thoroughly you were convinced that your client had not a leg to stand upon."

"It was I that insisted that he should not carry it before the Chancellor. Crook had the general management of those cases then, and would have gone on; but I said, no. I would not see my client's money wasted in such a wild-goose chase. In the first place the property was not worth it; and in the next place there was nothing to impugn the will. If I remember right it all turned on whether an old man who had signed as witness was well enough to write his name."

"That was the point."

"And I think it was shown that he had himself signed a receipt on that very day—or the day after, or the day before. It was something of that kind."

"Exactly; those were the facts. As regards the result of a new trial, no sane man, I fancy, could have any doubt. You know as well as any one living how great is the strength of twenty years of possession—"

"It would be very strong on her side, certainly."

"He would not have a chance; of course not. But, Mr. Round, he might make that poor woman so wretched that death would be a relief to her. Now it may be possible that something looking like fresh evidence may have been discovered; something of this kind probably has been found, or this man would not be moving; he would not have gone to the expense of a journey to Yorkshire had he not got hold of some new story."

"He has something in his head; you may be sure of that."

"Don't let your son be run away with by this, or advise your client to incur the terrible expense of a new trial, without knowing what you are about. I tell you fairly that I do dread such a trial on this poor lady's account. Reflect what it would be, Mr. Round, to any lady of your own family."

"I don't think Mrs. Round would mind it much; that is, if she were sure of her case."

"She is a strong-minded woman; but poor Lady Mason—."

"She was strong-minded enough too, if I remember right, at the last trial. I shall never forget how composed she was when old Bennett tried to shake her evidence. Do you remember how bothered he was?"

"He was an excellent lawyer,—was Bennett. There are few better men at the bar now-a-days."

"You wouldn't have found him down here, Mr. Furnival, listening to a German lecture three hours long. I don't know how it is, but I think we all used to work harder in those days than the young men do now." And then these eulogists of past days went back to the memories of their youths, declaring how in the old glorious years, now gone, no congress such as this would have had a chance of success. Men had men's work to do then, and were not wont to play the fool, first at one provincial town and then at another, but stuck to their oars and made their fortunes. "It seems to me, Mr. Furnival," said Mr. Round, "that this is all child's play, and to tell the truth I am half ashamed of myself for being here."

"And you'll look into that matter yourself, Mr. Round?"

"Yes, I will, certainly."

"I shall take it as a great favour. Of course you will advise your client in accordance with any new facts which may be brought before you; but as I feel certain that no case against young Mason can have any merits, I do hope that you will be able to suggest to Mr. Mason of Groby that the matter should be allowed to rest." And then Mr. Furnival took his leave, still thinking how far it might be possible that the enemy's side of the question might be supported by real merits. Mr. Round was a good-natured old fellow, and if the case could be inveigled out of his son's hands and into his own, it might be possible that even real merits should avail nothing.

"I confess I am getting rather tired of it," said Felix Graham that evening to his friend young Staveley, as he stood outside his bedroom door at the top of a narrow flight of stairs in the back part of a large hotel at Birmingham.

"Tired of it! I should think you are too."

"But nevertheless I am as sure as ever that good will come from it. I am inclined to think that the same kind of thing must be endured before any improvement is made in anything."

"That all reformers have to undergo Von Bauhr?"

"Yes, all of them that do any good. Von Bauhr's words were very dry, no doubt."

"You don't mean to say that you understood them?"

"Not many of them. A few here and there, for the first half-hour, came trembling home to my dull comprehension, and then—"

"You went to sleep."

"The sounds became too difficult for my ears; but dry and dull and hard as they were, they will not absolutely fall to the ground. He had a meaning in them, and that meaning will reproduce itself in some shape."

"Heaven forbid that it should ever do so in my presence! All the iniquities of which the English bar may be guilty cannot be so intolerable to humanity as Von Bauhr."

"Well, good-night, old fellow; your governor is to give us his ideas to-morrow, and perhaps he will be as bad to the Germans as your Von Bauhr was to us."

"Then I can only say that my governor will be very cruel to the Germans." And so they two went to their dreams.

In the mean time Von Bauhr was sitting alone looking back on the past hours with ideas and views very different from those of the many English lawyers who were at that time discussing his demerits. To him the day had been one long triumph, for his voice had sounded sweet in his own ears as, period after period, he had poured forth in full flowing language the gathered wisdom and experience of his life. Public men in England have so much to do that they cannot give time to the preparation of speeches for such meetings as these, but Von Bauhr had been at work on his pamphlet for months. Nay, taking it in the whole, had he not been at work on it for years? And now a kind Providence had given him the opportunity of pouring it forth before the assembled pundits gathered from all the nations of the civilised world.

As he sat there, solitary in his bedroom, his hands dropped down by his side, his pipe hung from his mouth on to his breast, and his eyes, turned up to the ceiling, were lighted almost with inspiration. Men there at the congress, Mr. Chaffanbrass, young Staveley, Felix Graham, and others, had regarded him as an impersonation of dullness; but through his mind and brain, as he sat there wrapped in his old dressing-gown, there ran thoughts which seemed to lift him lightly from the earth into an elysium of justice and mercy. And at the end of this elysium, which was not wild in its beauty, but trim and orderly in its gracefulness,—as might be a beer-garden at Munich,—there stood among flowers and vases a pedestal, grand above all other pedestals in that garden; and on this there was a bust with an inscription:—"To Von Bauhr, who reformed the laws of nations."

It was a grand thought; and though there was in it much of human conceit, there was in it also much of human philanthropy. If a reign of justice could be restored through his efforts—through those efforts in which on this hallowed day he had been enabled to make so great a progress—how beautiful would it be! And then as he sat there, while the smoke still curled from his unconscious nostrils, he felt that he loved all Germans, all Englishmen, even all Frenchmen, in his very heart of hearts, and especially those who had travelled wearily to this English town that they might listen to the results of his wisdom. He said to himself, and said truly, that he loved the world, and that he would willingly spend himself in these great endeavours for the amelioration of its laws and the perfection of its judicial proceedings. And then he betook himself to bed in a frame of mind that was not unenviable.

Von Bauhr's Dream.

I am inclined, myself, to agree with Felix Graham that such efforts are seldom absolutely wasted. A man who strives honestly to do good will generally do good, though seldom perhaps as much as he has himself anticipated. Let Von Bauhr have his pedestal among the flowers, even though it be small and humble!

CHAPTER XVIII
THE ENGLISH VON BAUHR

On the following morning, before breakfast, Felix Graham and Augustus Staveley prepared themselves for the labours of the coming day by a walk into the country; for even at Birmingham, by perseverance, a walk into the country may be attained,—and very pretty country it is when reached. These congress meetings did not begin before eleven, so that for those who were active time for matutinal exercise was allowed.

Augustus Staveley was the only son of the judge who on that day was to defend the laws of England from such attacks as might be made on them by a very fat advocate from Florence. Of Judge Staveley himself much need not be said now, except that he lived at Noningsby near Alston, distant from The Cleeve about nine miles, and that at his house Sophia Furnival had been invited to pass the coming Christmas. His son was a handsome clever fellow, who had nearly succeeded in getting the Newdegate, and was now a member of the Middle Temple. He was destined to follow the steps of his father, and become a light at the Common Law bar; but hitherto he had not made much essential progress. The world had been too pleasant to him to allow of his giving many of his hours to work. His father was one of the best men in the world, revered on the bench, and loved by all men; but he had not sufficient parental sternness to admit of his driving his son well into harness. He himself had begun the world with little or nothing, and had therefore succeeded; but his son was already possessed of almost everything that he could want, and therefore his success seemed doubtful. His chambers were luxuriously furnished, he had his horse in Piccadilly, his father's house at Noningsby was always open to him, and the society of London spread out for him all its allurements. Under such circumstances how could it be expected that he should work? Nevertheless he did talk of working, and had some idea in his head of the manner in which he would do so. To a certain extent he had worked, and he could talk fluently of the little that he knew. The idea of a *far niente* life would have been intolerable to him; but there were many among his friends who began to think that such a life would nevertheless be his ultimate destiny. Nor did it much matter, they said, for the judge was known to have made money.

But his friend Felix Graham was rowing in a very different boat; and of him also many prophesied that he would hardly be able to push his craft up against the strength of the stream. Not that he was an idle man, but that he would not work at his oars in the only approved method of making progress for his boat. He also had been at Oxford; but he had done little there except talk at a debating society, and make himself notorious by certain ideas on religious subjects which were not popular at the University. He had left without taking a degree, in consequence, as it was believed, of some such notions, and had now been called to the bar with a fixed resolve to open the oyster with such weapons, offensive and defensive, as nature had given to him. But here, as at Oxford, he would not labour on the same terms with other men, or make himself subject to the same conventional rules; and therefore it seemed only too probable that he might win no prize. He had ideas of his own that men should pursue their labours without special conventional regulations, but should be guided in their work by the general great rules of the world,—such for instance as those given in the commandments:—Thou shalt not bear false witness; Thou shalt not steal; and others. His notions no doubt were great, and perhaps were good; but hitherto they had not led him to much pecuniary success in his profession. A sort of a name he had obtained, but it was not a name sweet in the ears of practising attorneys.

And yet it behoved Felix Graham to make money, for none was coming to him ready made from any father. Father or mother he had none, nor uncles and aunts likely to be of service to him. He had begun the world with some small sum, which had grown smaller and smaller, till now there was left to him hardly enough to create an infinitesimal dividend. But he was not a man to become downhearted on that account. A living of some kind he could pick up, and did now procure for himself, from the press of the day. He wrote poetry for the periodicals, and politics for the penny papers with considerable success and sufficient pecuniary results. He would sooner do this, he often boasted, than abandon his great ideas or descend into the arena with other weapons than those which he regarded as fitting for an honest man's hand.

Augustus Staveley, who could be very prudent for his friend, declared that marriage would set him right. If Felix would marry he would quietly slip his neck into the collar and work along with the team, as useful a horse as ever was put at the wheel of a coach. But Felix did not seem inclined to marry. He had notions about that also, and was believed by one or two who knew him intimately to cherish an insane affection for some unknown damsel, whose parentage, education, and future were not likely to assist his views in the outer world. Some said that he was educating this damsel for his wife,—moulding her, so that she might be made fit to suit his taste; but Augustus, though he knew the secret of all this, was of opinion that it would come right at last. "He'll meet some girl in the world with a hatful of money, a pretty face, and a sharp tongue; then he'll bestow his moulded bride on a neighbouring baker with two hundred pounds for her fortune;— and everybody will be happy."

Felix Graham was by no means a handsome man. He was tall and thin, and his face had been slightly marked with the small-pox. He stooped in his gait as he walked, and was often awkward with his hands and legs. But he was full of enthusiasm, indomitable, as far as pluck would make him so, in contests of all kinds, and when he talked on subjects which were near his heart there was a radiance about him which certainly might win the love of the pretty girl with the sharp tongue and the hatful of money. Staveley, who really loved him, had already selected the prize, and she was no other than our friend, Sophia Furnival. The sharp tongue and the pretty face and the hatful of money would all be there; but then Sophia Furnival was a girl who might perhaps expect in return for these things more than an ugly face which could occasionally become radiant with enthusiasm.

The two men had got away from the thickness of the Birmingham smoke, and were seated on the top rung of a gate leading into a stubble field. So far they had gone with mutual consent, but further than this Staveley refused to go. He was seated with a cigar in his mouth. Graham also was smoking, but he was accommodated with a short pipe.

The English Von Bauhr and his pupil.

"A walk before breakfast is all very well," said Staveley, "but I am not going on a pilgrimage. We are four miles from the inn this minute."

"And for your energies that is a good deal. Only think that you should have been doing anything for two hours before you begin to feed."

"I wonder why matutinal labour should always be considered as so meritorious. Merely, I take it, because it is disagreeable."

"It proves that the man can make an effort."

"Every prig who wishes to have it believed that he does more than his neighbours either burns the midnight lamp or gets up at four in the morning. Good wholesome work between breakfast and dinner never seems to count for anything."

"Have you ever tried?"

"Yes; I am trying now, here at Birmingham."

"Not you."

"That's so like you, Graham. You don't believe that anybody is attending to what is going on except yourself. I mean to-day to take in the whole theory of Italian jurisprudence."

"I have no doubt that you may do so with advantage. I do not suppose that it is very good, but it must at any rate be better than our own. Come, let us go back to the town; my pipe is finished."

"Fill another, there's a good fellow. I can't afford to throw away my cigar, and I hate walking and smoking. You mean to assert that our whole system is bad, and rotten, and unjust?"

"I mean to say that I think so."

"And yet we consider ourselves the greatest people in the world,—or at any rate the honestest."

"I think we are; but laws and their management have nothing to do with making people honest. Good laws won't make people honest, nor bad laws dishonest."

"But a people who are dishonest in one trade will probably be dishonest in others. Now, you go so far as to say that all English lawyers are rogues."

"I have never said so. I believe your father to be as honest a man as ever breathed."

"Thank you, sir," and Staveley lifted his hat.

"And I would fain hope that I am an honest man myself."

"Ah, but you don't make money by it."

"What I do mean is this, that from our love of precedent and ceremony and old usages, we have retained a system which contains many of the barbarities of the feudal times, and also many of its lies. We try our culprit as we did in the old days of the ordeal. If luck will carry him through the hot ploughshares, we let him escape though we know him to be guilty. We give him the advantage of every technicality, and teach him to lie in his own defence, if nature has not sufficiently so taught him already."

"You mean as to his plea of not guilty."

"No, I don't; that is little or nothing. We ask him whether or no he confesses his guilt in a foolish way, tending to induce him to deny it; but that is not much. Guilt seldom will confess as long as a chance remains. But we teach him to lie, or rather we lie for him during the whole ceremony of his trial. We think it merciful to give him chances of escape, and hunt him as we do a fox, in obedience to certain laws framed for his protection."

"And should he have no protection?"

"None certainly, as a guilty man; none which may tend towards the concealing of his guilt. Till that be ascertained, proclaimed, and made apparent, every man's hand should be against him."

"But if he is innocent?"

"Therefore let him be tried with every possible care. I know you understand what I mean, though you look as though you did not. For the protection of his innocence let astute and good men work their best, but for the concealing of his guilt let no astute or good man work at all."

"And you would leave the poor victim in the dock without defence?"

"By no means. Let the poor victim, as you call him, — who in ninety-nine cases out of a hundred is a rat who has been preying in our granaries, — let him, I say, have his defender, — the defender of his possible innocence, not the protector of his probable guilt. It, all resolves itself into this. Let every lawyer go into court with a mind resolved to make conspicuous to the light of day that which seems to him to be the truth. A lawyer who does not do that — who does the reverse of that, has in my mind undertaken work which is unfit for a gentleman and impossible for an honest man."

"What a pity it is that you should not have an opportunity of rivalling Von Bauhr at the congress!"

"I have no doubt that Von Bauhr said a great deal of the same nature; and what Von Bauhr said will not wholly be wasted, though it may not yet have reached our sublime understandings."

"Perhaps he will vouchsafe to us a translation."

"It would be useless at present, seeing that we cannot bring ourselves to believe it possible that a foreigner should in any respect be wiser than ourselves. If any such point out to us our follies, we at once claim those follies as the special evidences of our wisdom. We are so self-satisfied with our own customs, that we hold up our hands with surprise at the fatuity of men who presume to point out to us their defects. Those practices in which we most widely depart from the broad and recognised morality of all civilised ages and countries are to us the Palladiums of our jurisprudence. Modes of proceeding which, if now first proposed to us, would be thought to come direct from the devil, have been made so sacred by time that they have lost all the horror of their falseness in the holiness of their age.

We cannot understand that other nations look upon such doings as we regard the human sacrifices of the Brahmins; but the fact is that we drive a Juggernaut's car through every assize town in the country, three times a year, and allow it to be dragged ruthlessly through the streets of the metropolis at all times and seasons. Now come back to breakfast, for I won't wait here any longer." Seeing that these were the ideas of Felix Graham, it is hardly a matter of wonder that such men as Mr. Furnival and Mr. Round should have regarded his success at the bar as doubtful.

"Uncommon bad mutton chops these are," said Staveley, as they sat at their meal in the coffee-room of the Imperial Hotel.

"Are they?" said Graham. "They seem to me much the same as other mutton chops."

"They are uneatable. And look at this for coffee! Waiter, take this away, and have some made fresh."

"Yes, sir," said the waiter, striving to escape without further comment.

"And waiter—"

"Yes, sir;" and the poor overdriven functionary returned.

"Ask them from me whether they know how to make coffee. It does not consist of an unlimited supply of lukewarm water poured over an infinitesimal proportion of chicory. That process, time-honoured in the hotel line, will not produce the beverage called coffee. Will you have the goodness to explain that in the bar as coming from me?"

"Yes, sir," said the waiter; and then he was allowed to disappear.

"How can you give yourself so much trouble with no possible hope of an advantageous result?" said Felix Graham.

"That's what you weak men always say. Perseverance in such a course will produce results. It is because we put up with bad things that hotel-keepers continue to give them to us. Three or four Frenchmen were dining with my father yesterday at the King's Head, and I had to sit at the bottom of the table. I declare to you that I literally blushed for my country; I did indeed. It was useless to say anything then, but it was quite clear that there was nothing that one of them could eat. At any hotel in France you'll get a good dinner; but we're so proud that we are ashamed to take lessons." And thus Augustus Staveley was quite as loud against his own country, and as laudatory with regard to others, as Felix Graham had been before breakfast.

And so the congress went on at Birmingham. The fat Italian from Tuscany read his paper; but as he, though judge in his own country and reformer here in England, was somewhat given to comedy, this morning was not so dull as that which had been devoted to Von Bauhr. After him Judge Staveley made a very elegant, and some said, a very eloquent speech; and so that day was done. Many other days also wore themselves away in this process; numerous addresses were read, and answers made to them, and the newspapers for the time were full of law. The defence of our own system, which was supposed to be the most remarkable for its pertinacity, if not for its justice, came from Mr. Furnival, who roused himself to a divine wrath for the occasion. And then the famous congress at Birmingham was brought to a close, and all the foreigners returned to their own countries.

CHAPTER XIX
THE STAVELEY FAMILY

The next two months passed by without any events which deserve our special notice, unless it be that Mr. Joseph Mason and Mr. Dockwrath had a meeting in the room of Mr. Matthew Round, in Bedford Row. Mr. Dockwrath struggled hard to effect this without the presence of the London attorney; but he struggled in vain. Mr. Round was not the man to allow any stranger to tamper with his client, and Mr. Dockwrath was forced to lower his flag before him. The result was that the document or documents which had been discovered at Hamworth were brought up to Bedford Row; and Dockwrath at last made up his mind that as he could not supplant Matthew Round, he would consent to fight under him as his lieutenant—or even as his sergeant or corporal, if no higher position might be allowed to him.

"There is something in it, certainly, Mr. Mason," said young Round; "but I cannot undertake to say as yet that we are in a position to prove the point."

"It will be proved," said Mr. Dockwrath.

"I confess it seems to me very clear," said Mr. Mason, who by this time had been made to understand the bearings of the question. "It is evident that she chose that day for her date because those two persons had then been called upon to act as witnesses to that other deed."

"That of course is our allegation. I only say that we may have some difficulty in proving it."

"The crafty, thieving swindler!" exclaimed Mr. Mason. "She has been sharp enough if it is as we think," said Round, laughing; and then there was nothing more done in the matter for some time, to the great disgust both of Mr. Dockwrath and Mr. Mason. Old Mr. Round had kept his promise to Mr. Furnival; or, at least, had done something towards keeping it. He had not himself taken the matter into his own hands, but he had begged his son to be cautious. "It's not the sort of business that we care for, Mat," said he; "and as for that fellow down in Yorkshire, I never liked him." To this Mat had answered that neither did he like Mr. Mason; but as the case had about it some very remarkable points, it was necessary to look into it; and then the matter was allowed to stand over till after Christmas.

We will now change the scene to Noningsby, the judge's country seat, near Alston, at which a party was assembled for the Christmas holidays. The judge was there of course,—without his wig; in which guise I am inclined to think that judges spend the more comfortable hours of their existence; and there also was Lady Staveley, her presence at home being altogether a matter of course, inasmuch as she had no other home than Noningsby. For many years past, ever since the happy day on which Noningsby had been acquired, she had repudiated London; and the poor judge, when called upon by his duties to reside there, was compelled to live like a bachelor, in lodgings. Lady Staveley was a good, motherly, warm-hearted woman, who thought a great deal about her flowers and fruit, believing that no one else had them so excellent,—much also about her butter and eggs, which in other houses were, in her opinion, generally unfit to be eaten; she thought also a great deal about her children, who were all swans,—though, as she often observed with a happy sigh, those of her neighbours were so uncommonly like geese. But she thought most of all of her husband, who in her eyes was the perfection of all manly virtues. She had made up her mind that the position of a puisne judge in England was the highest which could fall to the lot of any mere mortal. To become a Lord Chancellor, or a Lord Chief Justice, or a Chief Baron, a man must dabble with Parliament, politics, and dirt; but the bench-fellows of these politicians were selected for their wisdom, high conduct, knowledge, and discretion. Of all such selections, that made by the late king when he chose her husband, was the one which had done most honour to England, and had been in all its results most beneficial to Englishmen. Such was her creed with reference to domestic matters.

The Staveley young people at present were only two in number, Augustus, namely, and his sister Madeline. The eldest daughter was married, and therefore, though she spent these Christmas holidays at Noningsby, must not be regarded as one of the Noningsby family. Of Augustus we have said enough; but as I intend that Madeline Staveley shall, to many of my readers, be the most interesting personage in this story, I must pause to say something of her. I must say something of her; and as, with all women, the outward and visible signs of grace and beauty are those which are thought of the most, or at any rate spoken of the oftenest, I will begin with her exterior attributes. And that the muses may assist me in my endeavour, teaching my rough hands to draw with some accuracy the delicate lines of female beauty, I now make to them my humble but earnest prayer.

Madeline Staveley was at this time about nineteen years of age. That she was perfect in her beauty I cannot ask the muses to say, but that she will some day become so, I think the goddesses may be requested to prophesy. At present she was very slight, and appeared to be almost too tall for her form. She was indeed above the average height of women, and from her brother encountered some ridicule on this head; but not the less were all her movements soft, graceful, and fawnlike as should be those of a young girl. She was still at this time a child in heart and spirit, and could have played as a child had not the instinct of a woman taught to her the expediency of a staid demeanour. There is nothing among the wonders of womanhood more wonderful than this, that the young mind and young heart,—hearts and minds young as youth can make them, and in their natures as gay,— can assume the gravity and discretion of threescore years and maintain it successfully before all comers. And this is done, not as a lesson that has been taught, but as the result of an instinct implanted from the birth. Let us remember the mirth of our sisters in our homes, and their altered demeanours when those homes were opened to strangers; and remember also that this change had come from the inward working of their own feminine natures!

But I am altogether departing from Madeline Staveley's external graces. It was a pity almost that she should ever have become grave, because with her it was her smile that was so lovely. She smiled with her whole face. There was at such moments a peculiar laughing light in her gray eyes, which inspired one with an earnest desire to be in her confidence; she smiled with her soft cheek, the light tints of which would become a shade more pink from the excitement, as they softly rippled into dimples; she smiled with her forehead which would catch the light from her eyes and arch itself in its glory; but above all she smiled with her mouth, just showing, but hardly showing, the beauty of the pearls within. I never saw the face of a woman whose mouth was equal in pure beauty, in beauty that was expressive of feeling, to that of Madeline Staveley. Many have I seen with a richer lip, with a more luxurious curve, much more tempting as baits to the villainy and rudeness of man; but never one that told so much by its own mute eloquence of a woman's happy heart and a woman's happy beauty. It was lovely as I have said in its mirth, but if possible it was still more lovely in its woe; for then the lips would separate, and the breath would come, and in the emotion of her suffering the life of her beauty would be unrestrained.

Her face was oval, and some might say that it was almost too thin; they might say so till they knew it well, but would never say so when they did so know it. Her complexion was not clear, though it would be wrong to call her a brunette. Her face and forehead were never brown, but yet she could not boast the pure pink and the pearly white which go to the formation of a clear complexion. For myself I am not sure that I love a clear complexion.

Pink and white alone will not give that hue which seems best to denote light and life, and to tell of a mind that thinks and of a heart that feels. I can name no colour in describing the soft changing tints of Madeline Staveley's face, but I will make bold to say that no man ever found it insipid or inexpressive.

And now what remains for me to tell? Her nose was Grecian, but perhaps a little too wide at the nostril to be considered perfect in its chiselling. Her hair was soft and brown,—that dark brown which by some lights is almost black; but she was not a girl whose loveliness depended much upon her hair. With some women it is their great charm,—Neæras who love to sit half sleeping in the shade,—but it is a charm that possesses no powerful eloquence. All beauty of a high order should speak, and Madeline's beauty was ever speaking. And now that I have said that, I believe that I have told all that may be necessary to place her outward form before the inward eyes of my readers.

In commencing this description I said that I would begin with her exterior; but it seems to me now that in speaking of these I have sufficiently noted also that which was within. Of her actual thoughts and deeds up to this period it is not necessary for our purposes that anything should be told; but of that which she might probably think or might possibly do, a fair guess may, I hope, be made from that which has been already written.

Such was the Staveley family. Those of their guests whom it is necessary that I should now name, have been already introduced to us. Miss Furnival was there, as was also her father. He had not intended to make any prolonged stay at Noningsby,—at least so he had said in his own drawing-room; but nevertheless he had now been there for a week, and it seemed probable that he might stay over Christmas-day. And Felix Graham was there. He had been asked with a special purpose by his friend Augustus, as we already have heard; in order, namely, that he might fall in love with Sophia Furnival, and by the aid of her supposed hatful of money avoid the evils which would otherwise so probably be the consequence of his highly impracticable turn of mind. The judge was not averse to Felix Graham; but as he himself was a man essentially practical in all his views, it often occurred that, in his mild kindly way, he ridiculed the young barrister. And Sir Peregrine Orme was there, being absent from home as on a very rare occasion; and with him of course were Mrs. Orme and his grandson. Young Perry was making, or was prepared to make, somewhat of a prolonged stay at Noningsby. He had a horse there with him for the hunting, which was changed now and again; his groom going backwards and forwards between that place and The Cleeve. Sir Peregrine, however, intended to return before Christmas, and Mrs. Orme would go with him. He had come for four days, which for him had been a long absence from home, and at the end of the four days he would be gone.

They were all sitting in the dining-room round the luncheon-table on a hopelessly wet morning, listening to a lecture from the judge on the abomination of eating meat in the middle of the day, when a servant came behind young Orme's chair and told him that Mr. Mason was in the breakfast-parlour and wished to see him.

"Who wishes to see you?" said the baronet in a tone of surprise. He had caught the name, and thought at the moment that it was the owner of Groby Park.

"Lucius Mason," said Peregrine, getting up. "I wonder what he can want me for?"

"Oh, Lucius Mason," said the grandfather. Since the discourse about agriculture he was not personally much attached even to Lucius; but for his mother's sake he could be forgiven.

"Pray ask him into lunch," said Lady Staveley. Something had been said about Lady Mason since the Ormes had been at Noningsby, and the Staveley family were prepared to regard her with sympathy, and if necessary with the right hand of fellowship.

"He is the great agriculturist, is he not?" said Augustus. "Bring him in by all means; there is no knowing how much we may not learn before dinner on such a day as this."

"He is an ally of mine; and you must not laugh at him," said Miss Furnival, who was sitting next to Augustus.

But Lucius Mason did not come in. Young Orme remained with him for about a quarter of an hour, and then returned to the room, declaring with rather a serious face, that he must ride to Hamworth and back before dinner.

"Are you going with young Mason?" asked his grandfather.

"Yes, sir; he wishes me to do something for him at Hamworth, and I cannot well refuse him."

"You are not going to fight a duel!" said Lady Staveley, holding up her hands in horror as the idea came across her brain.

"A duel!" screamed Mrs. Orme. "Oh, Peregrine!"

"There can be nothing of the sort," said the judge. "I should think that young Mason is not so foolish; and I am sure that Peregrine Orme is not."

"I have not heard of anything of the kind," said Peregrine, laughing.

"Promise me, Peregrine," said his mother. "Say that you promise me."

"My dearest mother, I have no more thought of it than you have;—indeed I may say not so much."

"You will be back to dinner?" said Lady Staveley.

"Oh yes, certainly."

"And tell Mr. Mason," said the judge, "that if he will return with you we shall be delighted to see him."

The errand which took Peregrine Orme off to Hamworth will be explained in the next chapter, but his going led to a discussion among the gentlemen after dinner as to the position in which Lady Mason was now placed. There was no longer any possibility of keeping the matter secret, seeing that Mr. Dockwrath had taken great care that every one in Hamworth should hear of it. He had openly declared that evidence would now be adduced to prove that Sir Joseph Mason's widow had herself forged the will, and had said to many people that Mr. Mason of Groby had determined to indict her for forgery. This had gone so far that Lucius had declared as openly that he would prosecute the attorney for a libel, and Dockwrath had sent him word that he was quite welcome to do so if he pleased.

"It is a scandalous state of things," said Sir Peregrine, speaking with much enthusiasm, and no little temper, on the subject. "Here is a question which was settled twenty years ago to the satisfaction of every one who knew anything of the case, and now it is brought up again that two men may wreak their vengeance on a poor widow. They are not men; they are brutes."

"But why does she not bring an action against this attorney?" said young Staveley.

"Such actions do not easily lie," said his father. "It may be quite true that Dockwrath may have said all manner of evil things against this lady, and yet it may be very difficult to obtain evidence of a libel. It seems to me from what I have heard that the man himself wishes such an action to be brought."

"And think of the state of poor Lady Mason!" said Mr. Furnival. "Conceive the misery which it would occasion her if she were dragged forward to give evidence on such a matter!"

"I believe it would kill her," said Sir Peregrine.

"The best means of assisting her would be to give her some countenance," said the judge; "and from all that I can hear of her, she deserves it."

"She does deserve it," said Sir Peregrine, "and she shall have it. The people at Hamworth shall see at any rate that my daughter regards her as a fit associate. I am happy to say that she is coming to The Cleeve on my return home, and that she will remain there till after Christmas."

"It is a very singular case," said Felix Graham, who had been thinking over the position of the lady hitherto in silence.

"Indeed it is," said the judge; "and it shows how careful men should be in all matters relating to their wills. The will and the codicil, as it appears, are both in the handwriting of the widow, who acted as an amanuensis not only for her husband but for the attorney. That fact does not in my mind produce suspicion; but I do not doubt that it has produced all this suspicion in the mind of the claimant. The attorney who advised Sir Joseph should have known better."

"It is one of those cases," continued Graham, "in which the sufferer should be protected by the very fact of her own innocence. No lawyer should consent to take up the cudgels against her."

"I am afraid that she will not escape persecution from any such professional chivalry," said the judge.

"All that is moonshine," said Mr. Furnival.

"And moonshine is a very pretty thing if you were not too much afraid of the night air to go and look at it. If the matter be as you all say, I do think that any gentleman would disgrace himself by lending a hand against her."

"Upon my word, sir, I fully agree with you," said Sir Peregrine, bowing to Felix Graham over his glass.

"I will take permission to think, Sir Peregrine," said Mr. Furnival, "that you would not agree with Mr. Graham if you had given to the matter much deep consideration."

"I have not had the advantage of a professional education," said Sir Peregrine, again bowing, and on this occasion addressing himself to the lawyer; "but I cannot see how any amount of learning should alter my views on such a subject."

"Truth and honour cannot be altered by any professional arrangements," said Graham; and then the conversation turned away from Lady Mason, and directed itself to those great corrections of legal reform which had been debated during the past autumn.

The Orley Farm Case, though in other forms and different language, was being discussed also in the drawing-room. "I have not seen much of her," said Sophia Furnival, who by some art had usurped the most prominent part in the conversation, "but what I did see I liked much. She was at The Cleeve when I was staying there, if you remember, Mrs. Orme." Mrs. Orme said that she did remember.

"And we went over to Orley Farm. Poor lady! I think everybody ought to notice her under such circumstances. Papa, I know, would move heaven and earth for her if he could."

"I cannot move the heaven or the earth either," said Lady Staveley; "but if I thought that my calling on her would be any satisfaction to her—"

"It would, Lady Staveley," said Mrs. Orme. "It would be a great satisfaction to her. I cannot tell you how warmly I regard her, nor how perfectly Sir Peregrine esteems her."

"We will drive over there next week, Madeline."

"Do, mamma. Everybody says that she is very nice."

"It will be so kind of you, Lady Staveley," said Sophia Furnival.

"Next week she will be staying with us," said Mrs. Orme. "And that would save you three miles, you know, and we should be so glad to see you."

Lady Staveley declared that she would do both. She would call at The Cleeve, and again at Orley Farm after Lady Mason's return home. She well understood, though she could not herself then say so, that the greater part of the advantage to be received from her kindness would be derived from its being known at Hamworth that the Staveley carriage had been driven up to Lady Mason's door.

"Her son is very clever, is he not?" said Madeline, addressing herself to Miss Furnival.

Sophia shrugged her shoulders and put her head on one side with a pretty grace. "Yes, I believe so. People say so. But who is to tell whether a young man be clever or no?"

"But some are so much more clever than others. Don't you think so?"

"Oh yes, as some girls are so much prettier than others. But if Mr. Mason were to talk Greek to you, you would not think him clever."

"I should not understand him, you know."

"Of course not; but you would understand that he was a blockhead to show off his learning in that way. You don't want him to be clever, you see; you only want him to be agreeable."

"I don't know that I want either the one or the other."

"Do you not? I know I do. I think that young men in society are bound to be agreeable, and that they should not be there if they do not know how to talk pleasantly, and to give something in return for all the trouble we take for them."

"I don't take any trouble for them," said Madeline laughing.

"Surely you must, if you only think of it. All ladies do, and so they ought. But if in return for that a man merely talks Greek to me, I, for my part, do not think that the bargain is fairly carried out."

"I declare you will make me quite afraid of Mr. Mason."

"Oh, he never talks Greek;—at least he never has to me. I rather like him. But what I mean is this, that I do not think a man a bit more likely to be agreeable because he has the reputation of being very clever. For my part I rather think that I like stupid young men."

"Oh, do you? Then now I shall know what you think of Augustus. We think he is very clever; but I do not know any man who makes himself more popular with young ladies."

"Ah, then he is a gay deceiver."

"He is gay enough, but I am sure he is no deceiver. A man may make himself nice to young ladies without deceiving any of them; may he not?"

"You must not take me 'au pied de la lettre,' Miss Staveley, or I shall be lost. Of course he may. But when young gentlemen are so very nice, young ladies are so apt to—"

"To what?"

"Not to fall in love with them exactly, but to be ready to be fallen in love with, and then if a man does do it he is a deceiver. I declare it seems to me that we don't allow them a chance of going right."

"I think that Augustus manages to steer through such difficulties very cleverly."

"He sails about in the open sea, touching at all the most lovely capes and promontories, and is never driven on shore by stress of weather! What a happy sailor he must be!"

"I think he is happy, and that he makes others so."

"He ought to be made an admiral at once But we shall hear some day of his coming to a terrible shipwreck."

"Oh, I hope not!"

"He will return home in desperate plight, with only two planks left together, with all his glory and beauty broken and crumpled to pieces against some rock that he has despised in his pride."

"Why do you prophesy such terrible things for him?"

"I mean that he will get married."

"Get married! of course he will. That's just what we all want. You don't call that a shipwreck; do you?"

"It's the sort of shipwreck that these very gallant barks have to encounter."

"You don't mean that he'll marry a disagreeable wife!"

"Oh, no; not in the least. I only mean to say that like other sons of Adam, he will have to strike his colours. I dare say, if the truth were known, he has done so already."

"I am sure he has not."

"I don't at all ask to know his secrets, and I should look upon you as a very bad sister if you told them."

"But I am sure he has not got any,—of that kind."

"Would he tell you if he had?"

"Oh, I hope so; any serious secret. I am sure he ought, for I am always thinking about him."

"And would you tell him your secrets?"

"I have none."

"But when you have, will you do so?"

"Will I? Well, yes; I think so. But a girl has no such secret," she continued to say, after pausing for a moment. "None, generally, at least, which she tells, even to herself, till the time comes in which she tells it to all whom she really loves." And then there was another pause for a moment.

"I am not quite so sure of that," said Miss Furnival. After which the gentlemen came into the drawing-room.

Augustus Staveley had gone to work in a manner which he conceived to be quite systematic, having before him the praiseworthy object of making a match between Felix Graham and Sophia Furnival. "By George, Graham," he had said, "the finest girl in London is coming down to Noningsby; upon my word I think she is."

"And brought there expressly for your delectation, I suppose."

"Oh no, not at all; indeed, she is not exactly in my style; she is too,— too,—too—in point of fact, too much of a girl for me. She has lots of money, and is very clever, and all that kind of thing."

"I never knew you so humble before."

"I am not joking at all. She is a daughter of old Furnival's, whom by-the-by I hate as I do poison. Why my governor has him down at Noningsby I can't guess. But I tell you what, old fellow, he can give his daughter five-and-twenty thousand pounds. Think of that, Master Brook." But Felix Graham was a man who could not bring himself to think much of such things on the spur of the moment, and when he was introduced to Sophia, he did not seem to be taken with her in any wonderful way.

Augustus had asked his mother to help him, but she had laughed at him. "It would be a splendid arrangement," he had said with energy. "Nonsense, Gus," she had answered. "You should always let those things take their chance. All I will ask of you is that you don't fall in love with her yourself; I don't think her family would be nice enough for you."

But Felix Graham certainly was ungrateful for the friendship spent upon him, and so his friend felt it. Augustus had contrived to whisper into the lady's ear that Mr. Graham was the cleverest young man now rising at the bar, and as far as she was concerned, some amount of intimacy might at any rate have been produced; but he, Graham himself, would not put himself forward. "I will pique him into it," said Augustus to himself, and therefore when on this occasion they came into the drawing-room, Staveley immediately took a vacant seat beside Miss Furnival, with the very friendly object which he had proposed to himself.

There was great danger in this, for Miss Furnival was certainly handsome, and Augustus Staveley was very susceptible. But what will not a man go through for his friend? "I hope we are to have the honour of your company as far as Monkton Grange the day we meet there," he said. The hounds were to meet at Monkton Grange, some seven miles from Noningsby, and all the sportsmen from the house were to be there.

"I shall be delighted," said Sophia, "that is to say if a seat in the carriage can be spared for me."

"But we'll mount you. I know that you are a horsewoman." In answer to which Miss Furnival confessed that she was a horsewoman, and owned also to having brought a habit and hat with her.

"That will be delightful. Madeline will ride also, and you will meet the Miss Tristrams. They are the famous horsewomen of this part of the country."

"You don't mean that they go after the dogs, across the hedges."

"Indeed they do."

"And does Miss Staveley do that?"

"Oh, no—Madeline is not good at a five-barred gate, and would make but a very bad hand at a double ditch. If you are inclined to remain among the tame people, she will be true to your side."

"I shall certainly be one of the tame people, Mr. Staveley."

"I rather think I shall be with you myself; I have only one horse that will jump well, and Graham will ride him. By-the-by, Miss Furnival, what do you think of my friend Graham?"

"Think of him! Am I bound to have thought anything about him by this time?"

"Of course you are;—or at any rate of course you have. I have no doubt that you have composed in your own mind an essay on the character of everybody here. People who think at all always do."

"Do they? My essay upon him then is a very short one."

"But perhaps not the less correct on that account. You must allow me to read it."

"Like all my other essays of that kind, Mr. Staveley, it has been composed solely for my own use, and will be kept quite private."

"I am so sorry for that, for I intended to propose a bargain to you. If you would have shown me some of your essays, I would have been equally liberal with some of mine." And in this way, before the evening was over, Augustus Staveley and Miss Furnival became very good friends.

"Upon my word she is a very clever girl," he said afterwards, as young Orme and Graham were sitting with him in an outside room which had been fitted up for smoking.

"And uncommonly handsome," said Peregrine.

"And they say she'll have lots of money," said Graham. "After all, Staveley, perhaps you could not do better."

"She's not my style at all," said he. "But of course a man is obliged to be civil to girls in his own house." And then they all went to bed.

CHAPTER XX
MR. DOCKWRATH IN HIS OWN OFFICE

In the conversation which had taken place after dinner at Noningsby with regard to the Masons Peregrine Orme took no part, but his silence had not arisen from any want of interest on the subject. He had been over to Hamworth that day on a very special mission regarding it, and as he was not inclined to speak of what he had then seen and done, he held his tongue altogether.

"I want you to do me a great favour," Lucius had said to him, when the two were together in the breakfast-parlour at Noningsby; "but I am afraid it will give you some trouble."

"I sha'n't mind that," said Peregrine, "if that's all."

"You have heard of this row about Joseph Mason and my mother? It has been so talked of that I fear you must have heard it."

"About the lawsuit? Oh yes. It has certainly been spoken of at The Cleeve."

"Of course it has. All the world is talking of it. Now there is a man named Dockwrath in Hamworth—;" and then he went on to explain how it had reached him from various quarters that Mr. Dockwrath was accusing his mother of the crime of forgery; how he had endeavoured to persuade his mother to indict the man for libel; how his mother had pleaded to him with tears in her eyes that she found it impossible to go through such an ordeal; and how he, therefore, had resolved to go himself to Mr. Dockwrath. "But," said he, "I must have some one with me, some gentleman whom I can trust, and therefore I have ridden over to ask you to accompany me as far as Hamworth."

"I suppose he is not a man that you can kick," said Peregrine.

"I am afraid not," said Lucius; "he's over forty years old, and has dozens of children."

"And then he is such a low beast," said Peregrine.

"I have no idea of kicking him, but I think it would be wrong to allow him to go on saying these frightful things of my mother, without showing him that we are not afraid of him." Upon this the two young men got on horseback, and riding into Hamworth, put their horses up at the inn.

"And now I suppose we might as well go at once," said Peregrine, with a very serious face.

"Yes," said the other; "there's nothing to delay us. I cannot tell you how much obliged I am to you for coming with me."

"Oh, don't say anything about that; of course I'm only too happy." But all the same he felt that his heart was beating, and that he was a little nervous. Had he been called upon to go in and thrash somebody, he would have been quite at home; but he did not feel at his ease in making an inimical visit to an attorney's office.

It would have been wise, perhaps, if in this matter Lucius had submitted himself to Lady Mason's wishes. On the previous evening they had talked the matter over with much serious energy. Lucius had been told in the streets of Hamworth by an intermeddling little busybody of an apothecary that it behoved him to do something, as Mr. Dockwrath was making grievous accusations against his mother. Lucius had replied haughtily, that he and his mother would know how to protect themselves, and the apothecary had retreated, resolving to spread the report everywhere. Lucius on his return home had declared to the unfortunate lady that she had now no alternative left to her. She must bring an action against the man, or at any rate put the matter into the hands of a lawyer with a view of ascertaining whether she could do so with any chance of success. If she could not, she must then make known her reason for remaining quiet. In answer to this, Lady Mason had begun by praying her son to allow the matter to pass by.

"But it will not pass by," Lucius had said.

"Yes, dearest, if we leave it, it will,—in a month or two. We can do nothing by interference. Remember the old saying, You cannot touch pitch without being defiled."

But Lucius had replied, almost with anger, that the pitch had already touched him, and that he was defiled. "I cannot consent to hold the property," he had said, "unless something be done." And then his mother had bowed her head as she sat, and had covered her face with her hands.

"I shall go to the man myself," Lucius had declared with energy.

"As your mother, Lucius, I implore you not to do so," she had said to him through her tears.

"I must either do that or leave the country. It is impossible that I should live here, hearing such things said of you, and doing nothing to clear your name." To this she had made no actual reply, and now he was standing at the attorney's door about to do that which he had threatened.

They found Mr. Dockwrath sitting at his desk at the other side of which was seated his clerk. He had not yet promoted himself to the dignity of a private office, but generally used his parlour as such when he was desirous of seeing his clients without disturbance. On this occasion, however, when he saw young Mason enter, he made no offer to withdraw. His hat was on his head as he sat on his stool, and he did not even take it off as he returned the stiff salutation of his visitor. "Keep your hat on your head, Mr. Orme," he said, as Peregrine was about to take his off. "Well, gentlemen, what can I do for you?"

Lucius looked at the clerk, and felt that there would be great difficulty in talking about his mother before such a witness. "We wish to see you in private, Mr. Dockwrath, for a few minutes—if it be convenient."

"Is not this private enough?" said Dockwrath. "There is no one here but my confidential clerk."

"If you could make it convenient—" began Lucius.

"Well, then, Mr. Mason, I cannot make it convenient, and there is the long and the short of it. You have brought Mr. Orme with you to hear what you've got to say, and I choose that my clerk shall remain by to hear it also. Seeing the position in which you stand there is no knowing what may come of such an interview as this."

"In what position do I stand, sir?"

"If you don't know, Mr. Mason, I am not going to tell you. I feel for you, I do upon my word. I feel for you, and I pity you." Mr. Dockwrath as he thus expressed his commiseration was sitting with his high chair tilted back, with his knees against the edge of his desk, with his hat almost down upon his nose as he looked at his visitors from under it, and he amused himself by cutting up a quill pen into small pieces with his penknife. It was not pleasant to be pitied by such a man as that, and so Peregrine Orme conceived.

"Sir, that is nonsense," said Lucius. "I require no pity from you or from any man."

"I don't suppose there is one in all Hamworth that does not feel for you," said Dockwrath.

"He means to be impudent," said Peregrine. "You had better come to the point with him at once."

"No, I don't mean to be impudent, young gentleman. A man may speak his own mind in his own house I suppose without any impudence. You wouldn't stand cap in hand to me if I were to go down to you at The Cleeve."

"I have come here to ask of you," said Lucius, "whether it be true that you are spreading these reports about the town with reference to Lady Mason. If you are a man you will tell me the truth."

"Well; I rather think I am a man."

"It is necessary that Lady Mason should be protected from such infamous falsehoods, and it may be necessary to bring the matter into a court of law—"

"You may be quite easy about that, Mr. Mason. It will be necessary."

"As it may be necessary, I wish to know whether you will acknowledge that these reports have come from you?"

"You want me to give evidence against myself. Well, for once in a way I don't mind if I do. The reports have come from me. Now, is that manly?" And Mr. Dockwrath, as he spoke, pushed his hat somewhat off his nose, and looked steadily across into the face of his opponent.

Lucius Mason was too young for the task which he had undertaken, and allowed himself to be disconcerted. He had expected that the lawyer would deny the charge, and was prepared for what he would say and do in such a case; but now he was not prepared.

"How on earth could you bring yourself to be guilty of such villainy?" said young Orme.

"Highty-tighty! What are you talking about, young man? The fact is, you do not know what you are talking about. But as I have a respect for your grandfather and for your mother I will give you and them a piece of advice, gratis. Don't let them be too thick with Lady Mason till they see how this matter goes."

"Mr. Dockwrath," said Lucius, "you are a mean, low, vile scoundrel."

"Very well, sir. Adams, just take a note of that. Don't mind what Mr. Orme said. I can easily excuse him. He'll know the truth before long, and then he'll beg my pardon."

"I'll take my oath I look upon you as the greatest miscreant that ever I met," said Peregrine, who was of course bound to support his friend.

"You'll change your mind, Mr. Orme, before long, and then you'll find that you have met a worse miscreant than I am. Did you put down those words, Adams?"

"Them as Mr. Mason spoke? Yes; I've got them down."

"Read them," said the master.

And the clerk read them, "Mr. Dockwrath, you are a mean, low, vile scoundrel."

"And now, young gentlemen, if you have got nothing else to observe, as I am rather busy, perhaps you will allow me to wish you good morning."

"Very well, Mr. Dockwrath," said Mason; "you may be sure that you will hear further from me."

"We shall be sure to hear of each other. There is no doubt in the world about that," said the attorney. And then the two young men withdrew with an unexpressed feeling in the mind of each of them, that they had not so completely got the better of their antagonist as the justice of their case demanded.

They then remounted their horses, and Orme accompanied his friend as far as Orley Farm, from whence he got into the Alston road through The Cleeve grounds. "And what do you intend to do now?" said Peregrine as soon as they were mounted.

"I shall employ a lawyer," said he, "on my own footing; not my mother's lawyer, but some one else. Then I suppose I shall be guided by his advice." Had he done this before he made his visit to Mr. Dockwrath, perhaps it might have been better. All this sat very heavily on poor Peregrine's mind; and therefore as the company were talking about Lady Mason after dinner, he remained silent, listening, but not joining in the conversation.

The whole of that evening Lucius and his mother sat together, saying nothing. There was not absolutely any quarrel between them, but on this terrible subject there was an utter want of accordance, and almost of sympathy. It was not that Lucius had ever for a moment suspected his mother of aught that was wrong. Had he done so he might perhaps have been more gentle towards her in his thoughts and words. He not only fully trusted her, but he was quite fixed in his confidence that nothing could shake either her or him in their rights. But under these circumstances he could not understand how she could consent to endure without resistance the indignities which were put upon her. "She should combat them for my sake, if not for her own," he said to himself over and over again. And he had said so also to her, but his words had had no effect.

She, on the other hand, felt that he was cruel to her. She was weighed down almost to the ground by these sufferings which had fallen on her, and yet he would not be gentle and soft to her. She could have borne it all, she thought, if he would have borne with her. She still hoped that if she remained quiet no further trial would take place. At any rate this might be so. That it would be so she had the assurance of Mr. Furnival. And yet all this evil which she dreaded worse than death was to be precipitated on her by her son! So they sat through the long evening, speechless; each seated with the pretence of reading, but neither of them capable of the attention which a book requires.

He did not tell her then that he had been with Mr. Dockwrath, but she knew by his manner that he had taken some terrible step. She waited patiently the whole evening, hoping that he would tell her, but when the hour came for her to go up to her room he had told her nothing. If he now were to turn against her, that would be worse than all! She went up to her room and sat herself down to think. All that passed through her brain on that night I may not now tell; but the grief which pressed on her at this moment with peculiar weight was the self-will and obstinacy of her boy. She said to herself that she would be willing now to die,—to give back her life at once, if such might be God's pleasure; but that her son should bring down her hairs with shame and sorrow to the grave—! In that thought there was a bitterness of agony which she knew not how to endure!

The next morning at breakfast he still remained silent, and his brow was still black. "Lucius," she said, "did you do anything in that matter yesterday?"

"Yes, mother; I saw Mr. Dockwrath."

"Well?"

"I took Peregrine Orme with me that I might have a witness, and I then asked him whether he had spread these reports. He acknowledged that he had done so, and I told him that he was a villain."

Upon hearing this she uttered a long, low sigh, but she said nothing. What use could there now be in her saying aught? Her look of agony went to the young man's heart, but he still thought that he had been right. "Mother," he continued to say, "I am very sorry to grieve you in this way;—very sorry. But I could not hold up my head in Hamworth,—I could not hold up my head anywhere, if I heard these things said of you and did not resent it."

"Ah, Lucius, if you knew the weakness of a woman!"

"And therefore you should let me bear it all. There is nothing I would not suffer; no cost I would not undergo rather than you should endure all this. If you would only say that you would leave it to me!"

"But it cannot be left to you. I have gone to a lawyer, to Mr. Furnival. Why will you not permit that I should act in it as he thinks best? Can you not believe that that will be the best for both of us?"

"If you wish it, I will see Mr. Furnival."

Lady Mason did not wish that, but she was obliged so far to yield as to say that he might do so if he would. Her wish was that he should bear it all and say nothing. It was not that she was indifferent to good repute among her neighbours, or that she was careless as to what the apothecaries and attorneys said of her; but it was easier for her to bear the evil than to combat it. The Ormes and the Furnivals would support her. They and such-like persons would acknowledge her weakness, and would know that from her would not be expected such loud outbursting indignation as might be expected from a man. She had calculated the strength of her own weakness, and thought that she might still be supported by that,—if only her son would so permit.

It was two days after this that Lucius was allowed the honour of a conference by appointment with the great lawyer; and at the expiration of an hour's delay he was shown into the room by Mr. Crabwitz. "And, Crabwitz," said the barrister, before he addressed himself to his young friend, "just run your eye over those papers, and let Mr. Bideawhile have them to-morrow morning; and, Crabwitz—."

"Yes, sir."

"That opinion of Sir Richard's in the Ahatualpaca Mining Company—I have not seen it, have I?"

"It's all ready, Mr. Furnival."

"I will look at it in five minutes. And now, my young friend, what can I do for you?"

It was quite clear from Mr. Furnival's tone and manner that he did not mean to devote much time to Lucius Mason, and that he was not generally anxious to hold any conversation with him on the subject in question. Such, indeed, was the case. Mr. Furnival was determined to pull Lady Mason out of the sea of trouble into which she had fallen, let the effort cost him what it might, but he did not wish to do so by the instrumentality, or even with the aid, of her son.

"Mr. Furnival," began Mason, "I want to ask your advice about these dreadful reports which are being spread on every side in Hamworth about my mother."

"If you will allow me then to say so, I think that the course which you should pursue is very simple. Indeed there is, I think, only one course which you can pursue with proper deference to your mother's feelings."

"And what is that, Mr. Furnival?"

"Do nothing, and say nothing. I fear from what I have heard that you have already done and said much more than was prudent."

"But how am I to hear such things as these spoken of my own mother?"

"That depends on the people by whom the things are spoken. In this world, if we meet a chimney-sweep in the path we do not hustle with him for the right of way. Your mother is going next week to The Cleeve. It was only yesterday that I heard that the Noningsby people are going to call on her. You can hardly, I suppose, desire for your mother better friends than such as these. And can you not understand why such people gather to her at this moment? If you can understand it you will not trouble yourself to interfere much more with Mr. Dockwrath."

There was a rebuke in this which Lucius Mason was forced to endure; but nevertheless as he retreated disconcerted from the barrister's chambers, he could not bring himself to think it right that such calumny should be borne without resistance. He knew but little as yet of the ordinary life of gentlemen in England; but he did know,—so at least he thought,—that it was the duty of a son to shield his mother from insult and libel.

CHAPTER XXI
CHRISTMAS IN HARLEY STREET

It seems singular to me myself, considering the idea which I have in my own mind of the character of Lady Staveley, that I should be driven to declare that about this time she committed an unpardonable offence, not only against good nature, but also against the domestic proprieties. But I am driven so to say, although she herself was of all women the most good-natured and most domestic; for she asked Mr. Furnival to pass his Christmas-day at Noningsby, and I find it impossible to forgive her that offence against the poor wife whom in that case he must leave alone by her desolate hearth. She knew that he was a married man as well as I do. Sophia, who had a proper regard for the domestic peace of her parents, and who could have been happy at Noningsby without a father's care, not unfrequently spoke of her, so that her existence in Harley Street might not be forgotten by the Staveleys—explaining, however, as she did so, that her dear mother never left her own fireside in winter, so that no suspicion might be entertained that an invitation was desired for her also; nevertheless, in spite of all this, on two separate occasions did Lady Staveley say to Mr. Furnival that he might as well prolong his visit over Christmas.

And yet Lady Staveley was not attached to Mr. Furnival with any peculiar warmth of friendship; but she was one of those women whose foolish hearts will not allow themselves to be controlled in the exercise of their hospitality. Her nature demanded of her that she should ask a guest to stay. She would not have allowed a dog to depart from her house at this season of the year, without suggesting to him that he had better take his Christmas bone in her yard. It was for Mr. Furnival to adjust all matters between himself and his wife. He was not bound to accept the invitation because she gave it; but she, finding him there, already present in the house, did feel herself bound to give it;—for which offence, as I have said before, I cannot bring myself to forgive her.

At his sin in staying away from home, or rather—as far as the story has yet carried us—in thinking that he would do so, I am by no means so much surprised. An angry ill-pleased wife is no pleasant companion for a gentleman on a long evening. For those who have managed that things shall run smoothly over the domestic rug there is no happier time of life than these long candlelight hours of home and silence. No spoken content or uttered satisfaction is necessary. The fact that is felt is enough for peace. But when the fact is not felt; when the fact is by no means there; when the thoughts are running in a direction altogether different; when bitter grievances from one to the other fill the heart, rather than memories of mutual kindness; then, I say, those long candlelight hours of home and silence are not easy of endurance. Mr. Furnival was a man who chose to be the master of his own destiny, so at least to himself he boasted; and therefore when he found himself encountered by black looks and occasionally by sullen words, he declared to himself that he was ill-used and that he would not bear it. Since the domestic rose would no longer yield him honey, he would seek his sweets from the stray honeysuckle on which there grew no thorns.

Mr. Furnival was no coward. He was not one of those men who wrong their wives by their absence, and then prolong their absence because they are afraid to meet their wives. His resolve was to be free himself, and to be free without complaint from her. He would have it so, that he might remain out of his own house for a month at the time and then return to it for a week—at any rate without outward bickerings. I have known other men who have dreamed of such a state of things, but at this moment I can remember none who have brought their dream to bear.

Mr. Furnival had written to his wife,—not from Noningsby, but from some provincial town, probably situated among the Essex marshes,—saying various things, and among others that he should not, as he thought, be at home at Christmas-day. Mrs. Furnival had remarked about a fortnight since that Christmas-day was nothing to her now; and the base man, for it was base, had hung upon this poor, sore-hearted word an excuse for remaining away from home. "There are lawyers of repute staying at Noningsby," he had said, "with whom it is very expedient that I should remain at this present crisis."—When yet has there been no crisis present to a man who has wanted an excuse?—"And therefore I may probably stay,"—and so on. Who does not know the false mixture of excuse and defiance which such a letter is sure to maintain; the crafty words which may be taken as adequate reason if the receiver be timid enough so to receive them, or as a noisy gauntlet thrown to the ground if there be spirit there for the picking of it up? Such letter from his little borough in the Essex marshes did Mr. Furnival write to the partner of his cares, and there was still sufficient spirit left for the picking up of the gauntlet. "I shall be home to-morrow," the letter had gone on to say, "but I will not keep you waiting for dinner, as my hours are always so uncertain. I shall be at my chambers till late, and will be with you before tea. I will then return to Alston on the following morning." There was at any rate good courage in this on the part of Mr. Furnival;—great courage; but with it coldness of heart, dishonesty of purpose, and black ingratitude. Had she not given everything to him?

Mrs. Furnival when she got the letter was not alone. "There," said she; throwing it over to a lady who sat on the other side of the fireplace handling a loose sprawling mass of not very clean crochet-work. "I knew he would stay away on Christmas-day. I told you so."

"I didn't think it possible," said Miss Biggs, rolling up the big ball of soiled cotton, that she might read Mr. Furnival's letter at her leisure. "I didn't really think it possible—on Christmas-day! Surely, Mrs. Furnival, he can't mean Christmas-day? Dear, dear, dear! and then to throw it in your face in that way that you said you didn't care about it."

"Of course I said so," answered Mrs. Furnival. "I was not going to ask him to come home as a favour."

"Not to make a favour of it, of course not." This was Miss Biggs from ——. I am afraid if I tell the truth I must say that she came from Red Lion Square! And yet nothing could be more respectable than Miss Biggs. Her father had been a partner with an uncle of Mrs. Furnival's; and when Kitty Blacker had given herself and her young prettinesses to the hardworking lawyer, Martha Biggs had stood at the altar with her, then just seventeen years of age, and had promised to her all manner of success for her coming life. Martha Biggs had never, not even then, been pretty; but she had been very faithful. She had not been a favourite with Mr. Furnival, having neither wit nor grace to recommend her, and therefore in the old happy days of Keppel Street she had been kept in the background; but now, in this present time of her adversity, Mrs. Furnival found the benefit of having a trusty friend.

"If he likes better to be with these people down at Alston, I am sure it is the same to me," said the injured wife.

"But there's nobody special at Alston, is there?" asked Miss Biggs, whose soul sighed for a tale more piquant than one of mere general neglect. She knew that her friend had dreadful suspicions, but Mrs. Furnival had never as yet committed herself by uttering the name of any woman as her rival. Miss Biggs thought that a time had now come in which the strength of their mutual confidence demanded that such name should be uttered. It could not be expected that she should sympathise with generalities for ever. She longed to hate, to reprobate, and to shudder at the actual name of the wretch who had robbed her friend of a husband's heart. And therefore she asked the question, "There's nobody special at Alston, is there?"

Now Mrs. Furnival knew to a furlong the distance from Noningsby to Orley Farm, and knew also that the station at Hamworth was only twenty-five minutes from that at Alston. She gave no immediate answer, but threw up her head and shook her nostrils, as though she were preparing for war; and then Miss Martha Biggs knew that there was somebody special at Alston. Between such old friends why should not the name be mentioned?

On the following day the two ladies dined at six, and then waited tea patiently till ten. Had the thirst of a desert been raging within that drawing-room, and had tea been within immediate call, those ladies would have died ere they would have asked for it before his return. He had said he would be home to tea, and they would have waited for him, had it been till four o'clock in the morning! Let the female married victim ever make the most of such positive wrongs as Providence may vouchsafe to her. Had Mrs. Furnival ordered tea on this evening before her husband's return, she would have been a woman blind to the advantages of her own position. At ten the wheels of Mr. Furnival's cab were heard, and the faces of both the ladies prepared themselves for the encounter.

"Well, Kitty, how are you?" said Mr. Furnival, entering the room with his arms prepared for a premeditated embrace. "What, Miss Biggs with you? I did not know. How do you do, Miss Biggs?" and Mr. Furnival extended his hand to the lady. They both looked at him, and they could tell from the brightness of his eye and from the colour of his nose that he had been dining at his club, and that the bin with the precious cork had been visited on his behalf.

"Yes, my dear, it's rather lonely being here in this big room all by oneself so long; so I asked Martha Biggs to come over to me. I suppose there's no harm in that."

"Oh, if I'm in the way," began Miss Biggs, "or if Mr. Furnival is going to stay at home for long —"

"You are not in the way, and I am not going to stay at home for long," said Mr. Furnival, speaking with a voice that was perhaps a little thick, — only a very little thick. No wife on good terms with her husband would have deigned to notice, even in her own mind, an amount of thickness of voice which was so very inconsiderable. But Mrs. Furnival at the present moment did notice it.

"Oh, I did not know," said Miss Biggs.

"You know now," said Mr. Furnival, whose ear at once appreciated the hostility of tone which had been assumed.

"You need not be rude to my friend after she has been waiting tea for you till near eleven o'clock," said Mrs. Furnival. "It is nothing to me, but you should remember that she is not used to it."

"I wasn't rude to your friend, and who asked you to wait tea till near eleven o'clock? It is only just ten now, if that signifies."

"You expressly desired me to wait tea, Mr. Furnival. I have got your letter, and will show it you if you wish it."

"Nonsense; I just said I should be home—"

"Of course you just said you would be home, and so we waited; and it's not nonsense; and I declare—! Never mind, Martha, don't mind me, there's a good creature. I shall get over it soon;" and then fat, solid, good-humoured Mrs. Furnival burst out into an hysterical fit of sobbing. There was a welcome for a man on his return to his home after a day's labour!

Miss Biggs immediately got up and came round behind the drawing-room table to her friend's head. "Be calm, Mrs. Furnival," she said; "do be calm, and then you will be better soon. Here is the hartshorn."

"It doesn't matter, Martha: never mind: leave me alone," sobbed the poor woman.

"May I be excused for asking what is really the matter?" said Mr. Furnival, "for I'll be whipped if I know." Miss Biggs looked at him as if she thought that he ought to be whipped.

"I wonder you ever come near the place at all, I do," said Mrs. Furnival.

"What place?" asked Mr. Furnival.

"This house in which I am obliged to live by myself, without a soul to speak to, unless when Martha Biggs comes here."

"Which would be much more frequent, only that I know I am not welcome by everybody."

"I know that you hate it. How can I help knowing it?—and you hate me too; I know you do;—and I believe you would be glad if you need never come back here at all; I do. Don't, Martha; leave me alone. I don't want all that fuss. There; I can bear it now, whatever it is. Do you choose to have your tea, Mr. Furnival? or do you wish to keep the servants waiting out of their beds all night?"

"D— — the servants," said Mr. Furnival.

"Oh laws!" exclaimed Miss Biggs, jumping up out of her chair with her hands and fingers outstretched, as though never, never in her life before, had her ears been wounded by such wicked words as those.

"Mr. Furnival, I am ashamed of you," said his wife with gathered calmness of stern reproach.

Mr. Furnival was very wrong to swear; doubly wrong to swear before his wife; trebly wrong to swear before a lady visitor; but it must be confessed that there was provocation. That he was at this present period of his life behaving badly to his wife must be allowed, but on this special evening he had intended to behave well. The woman had sought a ground of quarrel against him, and had driven him on till he had forgotten himself in his present after-dinner humour. When a man is maintaining a whole household on his own shoulders, and working hard to maintain it well, it is not right that he should be brought to book because he keeps the servants up half an hour later than usual to wash the tea-things. It is very proper that the idle members of the establishment should conform to hours, but these hours must give way to his requirements. In those old days of which we have spoken so often he might have had his tea at twelve, one, two, or three without a murmur. Though their staff of servants then was scanty enough, there was never a difficulty then in supplying any such want for him. If no other pair of hands could boil the kettle, there was one pair of hands there which no amount of such work on his behalf could tire. But now, because he had come in for his tea at ten o'clock, he was asked if he intended to keep the servants out of their beds all night!

"Oh laws!" said Miss Biggs, jumping up from her chair as though she had been electrified.

Mr. Furnival did not think it consistent with his dignity to keep up any dispute in the presence of Miss Biggs, and therefore sat himself down in his accustomed chair without further speech. "Would you wish to have tea now, Mr. Furnival?" asked his wife again, putting considerable stress upon the word now.

"I don't care about it," said he.

"And I am sure I don't at this late hour," said Miss Biggs. "But so tired as you are, dear—"

"Never mind me, Martha; as for myself, I shall take nothing now." And then they all sat without a word for the space of some five minutes. "If you like to go, Martha," said Mrs. Furnival, "don't mind waiting for me."

"Oh, very well," and then Miss Biggs took her bedcandle and left the room. Was it not hard upon her that she should be forced to absent herself at this moment, when the excitement of the battle was about to begin in earnest? Her footsteps lingered as she slowly retreated from the drawing-room door, and for one instant she absolutely paused, standing still with eager ears. It was but for an instant, and then she went on up stairs, out of hearing, and sitting herself down by her bedside allowed the battle to rage in her imagination.

Mr. Furnival would have sat there silent till his wife had gone also, and so the matter would have terminated for that evening,—had she so willed it. But she had been thinking of her miseries; and, having come to some sort of resolution to speak of them openly, what time could she find more appropriate for doing so than the present? "Tom," she said,—and as she spoke there was still a twinkle of the old love in her eye, "we are not going on together as well as we should do,—not lately. Would it not be well to make a change before it is too late?"

"What change?" he asked; not exactly in an ill humour, but with a husky, thick voice. He would have preferred now that she should have followed her friend to bed.

"I do not want to dictate to you, Tom, but—! Oh Tom, if you knew how wretched I am!"

"What makes you wretched?"

"Because you leave me all alone; because you care more for other people than you do for me; because you never like to be at home, never if you can possibly help it. You know you don't. You are always away now upon some excuse or other; you know you are. I don't have you home to dinner not one day in the week through the year. That can't be right, and you know it is not. Oh Tom! you are breaking my heart, and deceiving me,—you are. Why did I go down and find that woman in your chamber with you, when you were ashamed to own to me that she was coming to see you? If it had been in the proper way of law business, you wouldn't have been ashamed. Oh, Tom!"

The poor woman had begun her plaint in a manner that was not altogether devoid of a discreet eloquence. If only she could have maintained that tone, if she could have confined her words to the tale of her own grievances, and have been contented to declare that she was unhappy, only because he was not with her, it might have been well. She might have touched his heart, or at any rate his conscience, and there might have been some enduring result for good. But her feelings had been too many for her, and as her wrongs came to her mind, and the words heaped themselves upon her tongue, she could not keep herself from the one subject which she should have left untouched. Mr. Furnival was not the man to bear any interference such as this, or to permit the privacy of Lincoln's Inn to be invaded even by his wife. His brow grew very black, and his eyes became almost bloodshot. The port wine which might have worked him to softness, now worked him to anger, and he thus burst forth with words of marital vigour:

"Let me tell you once for ever, Kitty, that I will admit of no interference with what I do, or the people whom I may choose to see in my chambers in Lincoln's Inn. If you are such an infatuated simpleton as to believe—"

"Yes; of course I am a simpleton; of course I am a fool; women always are."

"Listen to me, will you?"

"Listen, yes; it's my business to listen. Would you like that I should give this house up for her, and go into lodgings somewhere? I shall have very little objection as matters are going now. Oh dear, oh dear, that things should ever have come to this!"

"Come to what?"

"Tom, I could put up with a great deal,—more I think than most women; I could slave for you like a drudge, and think nothing about it. And now that you have got among grand people, I could see you go out by yourself without thinking much about that either. I am very lonely sometimes,— very; but I could bear that. Nobody has longed to see you rise in the world half so anxious as I have done. But, Tom, when I know what your goings on are with a nasty, sly, false woman like that, I won't bear it; and there's an end." In saying which final words Mrs. Furnival rose from her seat, and thrice struck her hand by no means lightly on the loo table in the middle of the room.

"I did not think it possible that you should be so silly. I did not indeed."

"Oh, yes, silly! very well. Women always are silly when they mind that kind of thing. Have you got anything else to say, sir?"

"Yes, I have; I have this to say, that I will not endure this sort of usage."

"Nor I won't," said Mrs. Furnival; "so you may as well understand it at once. As long as there was nothing absolutely wrong, I would put up with it for the sake of appearances, and because of Sophia. For myself I don't mind what loneliness I may have to bear. If you had been called on to go out to the East Indies or even to China, I could have put up with it. But this sort of thing I won't put up with;—nor I won't be blind to what I can't help seeing. So now, Mr. Furnival, you may know that I have made up my mind." And then, without waiting further parley, having wisked herself in her energy near to the door, she stalked out, and went up with hurried steps to her own room.

Occurrences of a nature such as this are in all respects unpleasant in a household. Let the master be ever so much master, what is he to do? Say that his wife is wrong from the beginning to the end of the quarrel,—that in no way improves the matter. His anxiety is that the world abroad shall not know he has ought amiss at home; but she, with her hot sense of injury, and her loud revolt against supposed wrongs, cares not who hears it. "Hold your tongue, madam," the husband says. But the wife, bound though she be by an oath of obedience, will not obey him, but only screams the louder.

All which, as Mr. Furnival sat there thinking of it, disturbed his mind much. That Martha Biggs would spread the tale through all Bloomsbury and St. Pancras of course he was aware. "If she drives me to it, it must be so," he said to himself at last. And then he also betook himself to his rest. And so it was that preparations for Christmas were made in Harley Street.

CHAPTER XXII
CHRISTMAS AT NONINGSBY

The house at Noningsby on Christmas-day was quite full, and yet it was by no means a small house. Mrs. Arbuthnot, the judge's married daughter, was there, with her three children; and Mr. Furnival was there, having got over those domestic difficulties in which we lately saw him as best he might; and Lucius Mason was there, having been especially asked by Lady Staveley when she heard that his mother was to be at The Cleeve. There could be no more comfortable country-house than Noningsby; and it was, in its own way, pretty, though essentially different in all respects from The Cleeve. It was a new house from the cellar to the ceiling, and as a house was no doubt the better for being so. All the rooms were of the proper proportion, and all the newest appliances for comfort had been attached to it. But nevertheless it lacked that something, in appearance rather than in fact, which age alone can give to the residence of a gentleman in the country. The gardens also were new, and the grounds around them trim, and square, and orderly. Noningsby was a delightful house; no one with money and taste at command could have created for himself one more delightful; but then there are delights which cannot be created even by money and taste.

It was a pleasant sight to see, the long, broad, well-filled breakfast table, with all that company round it. There were some eighteen or twenty gathered now at the table, among whom the judge sat pre-eminent, looming large in an arm-chair and having a double space allotted to him;—some eighteen or twenty, children included. At the bottom of the table sat Lady Staveley, who still chose to preside among her own tea cups as a lady should do; and close to her, assisting in the toils of that presidency, sat her daughter Madeline. Nearest to them were gathered the children, and the rest had formed themselves into little parties, each of which already well knew its own place at the board. In how very short a time will come upon one that pleasant custom of sitting in an accustomed place! But here, at these Noningsby breakfasts, among other customs already established, there was one by which Augustus Staveley was always privileged to sit by the side of Sophia Furnival. No doubt his original object was still unchanged. A match between that lady and his friend Graham was still desirable, and by perseverance he might pique Felix Graham to arouse himself. But hitherto Felix Graham had not aroused himself in that direction, and one or two people among the party were inclined to mistake young Staveley's intentions.

"Gus," his sister had said to him the night before, "I declare I think you are going to make love to Sophia Furnival."

"Do you?" he had replied. "As a rule I do not think there is any one in the world for whose discernment I have so much respect as I have for yours. But in this respect even you are wrong."

"Ah, of course you say so."

"If you won't believe me, ask her. What more can I say?"

"I certainly sha'n't ask her, for I don't know her well enough."

"She's a very clever girl; let me tell you that, whoever falls in love with her."

"I'm sure she is, and she is handsome too, very; but for all that she is not good enough for our Gus."

"Of course she is not, and therefore I am not thinking of her. And now go to bed and dream that you have got the Queen of the Fortunate Islands for your sister-in-law."

But although Staveley was himself perfectly indifferent to all the charms of Miss Furnival, nevertheless he could hardly restrain his dislike to Lucius Mason, who, as he thought, was disposed to admire the lady in question. In talking of Lucius to his own family and to his special friend Graham, he had called him conceited, pedantic, uncouth, unenglish, and detestable. His own family, that is, his mother and sister, rarely contradicted him in anything; but Graham was by no means so cautious, and usually contradicted him in everything. Indeed, there was no sign of sterling worth so plainly marked in Staveley's character as the full conviction which he entertained of the superiority of his friend Felix.

"You are quite wrong about him," Felix had said. "He has not been at an English school, or English university, and therefore is not like other young men that you know; but he is, I think, well educated and clever. As for conceit, what man will do any good who is not conceited? Nobody holds a good opinion of a man who has a low opinion of himself."

"All the same, my dear fellow, I do not like Lucius Mason."

"And some one else, if you remember, did not like Dr. Fell."

"And now, good people, what are you all going to do about church?" said Staveley, while they were still engaged with their rolls and eggs.

"I shall walk," said the judge.

"And I shall go in the carriage," said the judge's wife.

"That disposes of two; and now it will take half an hour to settle for the rest. Miss. Furnival, you no doubt will accompany my mother. As I shall be among the walkers you will see how much I sacrifice by the suggestion."

It was a mile to the church, and Miss Furnival knew the advantage of appearing in her seat unfatigued and without subjection to wind, mud, or rain. "I must confess," she said, "that under all the circumstances, I shall prefer your mother's company to yours;" whereupon Staveley, in the completion of his arrangements, assigned the other places in the carriage to the married ladies of the company.

"But I have taken your sister Madeline's seat in the carriage," protested Sophia with great dismay.

"My sister Madeline generally walks."

"Then of course I shall walk with her;" but when the time came Miss Furnival did go in the carriage whereas Miss Staveley went on foot.

It so fell out, as they started, that Graham found himself walking at Miss Staveley's side, to the great disgust, no doubt, of half a dozen other aspirants for that honour. "I cannot help thinking," he said, as they stepped briskly over the crisp white frost, "that this Christmas-day of ours is a great mistake."

"Oh, Mr. Graham!" she exclaimed

"You need not regard me with horror,—at least not with any special horror on this occasion."

"But what you say is very horrid."

"That, I flatter myself, seems so only because I have not yet said it. That part of our Christmas-day which is made to be in any degree sacred is by no means a mistake."

"I am glad you think that."

"Or rather, it is not a mistake in as far as it is in any degree made sacred. But the peculiar conviviality of the day is so ponderous! Its roast-beefiness oppresses one so thoroughly from the first moment of one's waking, to the last ineffectual effort at a bit of fried pudding for supper!"

"But you need not eat fried pudding for supper. Indeed, here, I am afraid, you will not have any supper offered you at all."

"No; not to me individually, under that name. I might also manage to guard my own self under any such offers. But there is always the flavour of the sweetmeat, in the air, — of all the sweetmeats edible and non-edible."

"You begrudge the children their snap-dragon. That's what it all means, Mr. Graham."

"No; I deny it; unpremeditated snap-dragon is dear to my soul; and I could expend myself in blindman's buff."

"You shall then, after dinner; for of course you know that we all dine early."

"But blindman's buff at three, with snap-dragon at a quarter to four — charades at five, with wine and sweet cake at half-past six, is ponderous. And that's our mistake. The big turkey would be very good; — capital fun to see a turkey twice as big as it ought to be! But the big turkey, and the mountain of beef, and the pudding weighing a hundredweight, oppress one's spirits by their combined gravity. And then they impart a memory of indigestion, a halo as it were of apoplexy, even to the church services."

"I do not agree with you the least in the world."

"I ask you to answer me fairly. Is not additional eating an ordinary Englishman's ordinary idea of Christmas-day?"

"I am only an ordinary Englishwoman and therefore cannot say. It is not my idea."

"I believe that the ceremony, as kept by us, is perpetuated by the butchers and beersellers, with a helping hand from the grocers. It is essentially a material festival; and I would not object to it even on that account if it were not so grievously overdone. How the sun is moistening the frost on the ground. As we come back the road will be quite wet."

"We shall be going home then and it will not signify. Remember, Mr. Graham, I shall expect you to come forward in great strength for blindman's buff." As he gave her the required promise, he thought that even the sports of Christmas-day would be bearable, if she also were to make one of the sportsmen; and then they entered the church.

Christmas at Noningsby—Morning.

I do not know of anything more pleasant to the eye than a pretty country church, decorated for Christmas-day. The effect in a city is altogether different. I will not say that churches there should not be decorated, but comparatively it is a matter of indifference. No one knows who does it. The peculiar munificence of the squire who has sacrificed his holly bushes is not appreciated. The work of the fingers that have been employed is not recognised. The efforts made for hanging the pendent wreaths to each capital have been of no special interest to any large number of the worshippers. It has been done by contract, probably, and even if well done has none of the grace of association. But here at Noningsby church, the winter flowers had been cut by Madeline and the gardener, and the red berries had been grouped by her own hands. She and the vicar's wife had stood together with perilous audacity on the top of the clerk's desk while they fixed the branches beneath the cushion of the old-fashioned turret, from which the sermons were preached. And all this had of course been talked about at the house; and some of the party had gone over to see, including Sophia Furnival, who had declared that nothing could be so delightful, though she had omitted to endanger her fingers by any participation in the work. And the children had regarded the operation as a triumph of all that was wonderful in decoration; and thus many of them had been made happy.

On their return from church, Miss Furnival insisted on walking, in order, as she said, that Miss Staveley might not have all the fatigue; but Miss Staveley would walk also, and the carriage, after a certain amount of expostulation and delay, went off with its load incomplete.

"And now for the plum-pudding part of the arrangement," said Felix Graham.

"Yes, Mr. Graham," said Madeline, "now for the plum-pudding—and the blindman's buff."

"Did you ever see anything more perfect than the church, Mr. Mason?" said Sophia.

"Anything more perfect? no; in that sort of way, perhaps, never. I have seen the choir of Cologne."

"Come, come; that's not fair," said Graham. "Don't import Cologne in order to crush us here down in our little English villages. You never saw the choir of Cologne bright with holly berries."

"No; but I have with cardinal's stockings, and bishop's robes."

"I think I should prefer the holly," said Miss Furnival. "And why should not our churches always look like that, only changing the flowers and the foliage with the season? It would make the service so attractive."

"It would hardly do at Lent," said Madeline, in a serious tone.

"No, perhaps not at Lent exactly."

Peregrine and Augustus Staveley were walking on in front, not perhaps as well satisfied with the day as the rest of the party. Augustus, on leaving the church, had made a little effort to assume his place as usual by Miss Furnival's side, but by some accident of war, Mason was there before him. He had not cared to make one of a party of three, and therefore had gone on in advance with young Orme. Nor was Peregrine himself much more happy. He did not know why, but he felt within his breast a growing aversion to Felix Graham. Graham was a puppy, he thought, and a fellow that talked too much; and then he was such a confoundedly ugly dog, and—and—and—Peregrine Orme did not like him. He was not a man to analyze his own feelings in such matters. He did not ask himself why he should have been rejoiced to hear that instant business had taken Felix Graham off to Hong Kong; but he knew that he would have rejoiced. He knew also that Madeline Staveley was—. No; he did not know what she was; but when he was alone, he carried on with her all manner of imaginary conversations, though when he was in her company he had hardly a word to say to her. Under these circumstances he fraternized with her brother; but even in that he could not receive much satisfaction, seeing that he could not abuse Graham to Graham's special friend, nor could he breathe a sigh as to Madeline's perfections into the ear of Madeline's brother.

The children,—and there were three or four assembled there besides those belonging to Mrs. Arbuthnot, were by no means inclined to agree with Mr. Graham's strictures as to the amusements of Christmas-day. To them it appeared that they could not hurry fast enough into the vortex of its dissipations. The dinner was a serious consideration, especially with reference to certain illuminated mince-pies which were the crowning glory of that banquet; but time for these was almost begrudged in order that the fast handkerchief might be tied over the eyes of the first blindman.

"And now we'll go into the schoolroom," said Marian Arbuthnot, jumping up and leading the way. "Come along, Mr. Felix," and Felix Graham followed her.

Madeline had declared that Felix Graham should be blinded first, and such was his doom. "Now mind you catch me, Mr. Felix; pray do," said Marian, when she had got him seated in a corner of the room. She was a beautiful fair little thing, with long, soft curls, and lips red as a rose, and large, bright blue eyes, all soft and happy and laughing, loving the friends of her childhood with passionate love, and fully expecting an equal devotion from them. It is of such children that our wives and sweethearts should be made.

"But how am I to find you when my eyes are blinded?"

"Oh, you can feel, you know. You can put your hand on the top of my head. I mustn't speak, you know; but I'm sure I shall laugh; and then you must guess that it's Marian." That was her idea of playing blindman's buff according to the strict rigour of the game.

"And you'll give me a big kiss?" said Felix.

"Yes, when we've done playing," she promised with great seriousness.

And then a huge white silk handkerchief, as big as a small sail, was brought down from grandpapa's dressing-room, so that nobody should see the least bit "in the world," as Marian had observed with great energy; and the work of blinding was commenced. "I ain't big enough to reach round," said Marian, who had made an effort, but in vain. "You do it, aunt Mad," and she tendered the handkerchief to Miss Staveley, who, however, did not appear very eager to undertake the task.

"I'll be the executioner," said grandmamma, "the more especially as I shall not take any other share in the ceremony. This shall be the chair of doom. Come here, Mr. Graham, and submit yourself to me." And so the first victim was blinded. "Mind you remember," said Marian, whispering into his ear as he was led away. "Green spirits and white; blue spirits and gray—," and then he was twirled round in the room and left to commence his search as best he might.

Marian Arbuthnot was not the only soft little laughing darling that wished to be caught, and blinded, so that there was great pulling at the blindman's tails, and much grasping at his outstretched arms before the desired object was attained. And he wandered round the room skilfully, as though a thought were in his mind false to his treaty with Marian,—as though he imagined for a moment that some other prize might be caught. But if so, the other prize evaded him carefully, and in due progress of play, Marian's soft curls were within his grasp. "I'm sure I didn't speak, or say a word," said she, as she ran up to her grandmother to have the handkerchief put over her eyes. "Did I, grandmamma?"

"There are more ways of speaking than one," said Lady Staveley. "You and Mr. Graham understand each other, I think."

"Oh, I was caught quite fairly," said Marian—"and now lead me round and round." To her at any rate the festivities of Christmas-day were not too ponderous for real enjoyment.

And then, at last, somebody caught the judge. I rather think it was Madeline; but his time in truth was come, and he had no chance of escape. The whole room was set upon his capture, and though he barricaded himself with chairs and children, he was duly apprehended and named. "That's papa; I know by his watch-chain, for I made it."

"Nonsense, my dears," said the judge. "I will do no such thing. I should never catch anybody, and should remain blind for ever."

"But grandpapa must," said Marian. "It's the game that he should be blinded when he's caught."

"Suppose the game was that we should be whipped when we are caught, and I was to catch you," said Augustus.

"But I would not play that game," said Marian.

"Oh, papa, you must," said Madeline. "Do—and you shall catch Mr. Furnival."

"That would be a temptation," said the judge. "I've never been able to do that yet, though I've been trying it for some years."

"Justice is blind," said Graham. "Why should a judge be ashamed to follow the example of his own goddess?" And so at last the owner of the ermine submitted, and the stern magistrate of the bench was led round with the due incantation of the spirits, and dismissed into chaos to seek for a new victim.

Christmas at Noningsby—Evening.

One of the rules of blindman's buff at Noningsby was this, that it should not be played by candlelight,—a rule that is in every way judicious, as thereby an end is secured for that which might otherwise be unending. And therefore when it became so dark in the schoolroom that there was not much difference between the blind man and the others, the handkerchief was smuggled away, and the game was at an end.

"And now for snap-dragon," said Marian.

"Exactly as you predicted, Mr. Graham," said Madeline: "blindman's buff at a quarter past three, and snap-dragon at five."

"I revoke every word that I uttered, for I was never more amused in my life."

"And you will be prepared to endure the wine and sweet cake when they come."

"Prepared to endure anything, and go through everything. We shall be allowed candles now, I suppose."

"Oh, no, by no means. Snap-dragon by candlelight! who ever heard of such a thing? It would wash all the dragon out of it, and leave nothing but the snap. It is a necessity of the game that it should be played in the dark,—or rather by its own lurid light."

"Oh, there is a lurid light; is there?"

"You shall see;" and then she turned away to make her preparations.

To the game of snap-dragon, as played at Noningsby, a ghost was always necessary, and aunt Madeline had played the ghost ever since she had been an aunt, and there had been any necessity for such a part. But in previous years the spectators had been fewer in number and more closely connected with the family. "I think we must drop the ghost on this occasion," she said, coming up to her brother.

"You'll disgust them all dreadfully if you do," said he. "The young Sebrights have come specially to see the ghost."

"Well, you can do ghost for them."

"I! no; I can't act a ghost. Miss Furnival, you'd make a lovely ghost."

"I shall be most happy to be useful," said Sophia.

"Oh, aunt Mad, you must be ghost," said Marian, following her.

"You foolish little thing, you; we are going to have a beautiful ghost—a divine ghost," said uncle Gus.

"But we want Madeline to be the ghost," said a big Miss Sebright, ten or eleven years old.

"She's always ghost," said Marian.

"To be sure; it will be much better," said Miss Furnival. "I only offered my poor services hoping to be useful. No Banquo that ever lived could leave a worse ghost behind him than I should prove."

It ended in there being two ghosts. It had become quite impossible to rob Miss Furnival of her promised part, and Madeline could not refuse to solve the difficulty in this way without making more of the matter than it deserved. The idea of two ghosts was delightful to the children, more especially as it entailed two large dishes full of raisins, and two blue fires blazing up from burnt brandy. So the girls went out, not without proffered assistance from the gentlemen, and after a painfully long interval of some fifteen or twenty minutes,—for Miss Furnival's back hair would not come down and adjust itself into ghostlike lengths with as much readiness as that of her friend,—they returned bearing the dishes before them on large trays. In each of them the spirit was lighted as they entered the schoolroom door, and thus, as they walked in, they were illuminated by the dark-blue flames which they carried.

"Oh, is it not grand?" said Marian, appealing to Felix Graham.

"Uncommonly grand," he replied.

"And which ghost do you think is the grandest? I'll tell you which ghost I like the best,—in a secret, you know; I like aunt Mad the best, and I think she's the grandest too."

"And I'll tell you in a secret that I think the same. To my mind she is the grandest ghost I ever saw in my life."

"Is she indeed?" asked Marian, solemnly, thinking probably that her new friend's experience in ghosts must be extensive. However that might be, he thought that as far as his experience in women went, he had never seen anything more lovely than Madeline Staveley dressed in a long white sheet, with a long bit of white cambric pinned round her face.

And it may be presumed that the dress altogether is not unbecoming when accompanied by blue flames, for Augustus Staveley and Lucius Mason thought the same thing of Miss Furnival, whereas Peregrine Orme did not know whether he was standing on his head or his feet as he looked at Miss Staveley. Miss Furnival may possibly have had some inkling of this when she offered to undertake the task, but I protest that such was not the case with Madeline. There was no second thought in her mind when she first declined the ghosting, and afterwards undertook the part. No wish to look beautiful in the eyes of Felix Graham had come to her—at any rate as yet; and as to Peregrine Orme, she had hardly thought of his existence. "By heavens!" said Peregrine to himself, "she is the most beautiful creature that I ever saw;" and then he began to speculate within his own mind how the idea might be received at The Cleeve.

But there was no such realised idea with Felix Graham. He saw that Madeline Staveley was very beautiful, and he felt in an unconscious manner that her character was very sweet. He may have thought that he might have loved such a girl, had such love been a thing permitted to him. But this was far from being the case. Felix Graham's lot in this life, as regarded that share which his heart might have in it, was already marked out for him;—marked out for himself and by himself. The future wife of his bosom had already been selected, and was now in course of preparation for the duties of her future life. He was one of those few wise men who have determined not to take a partner in life at hazard, but to mould a young mind and character to those pursuits and modes of thought which may best fit a woman for the duties she will have to perform. What little it may be necessary to know of the earlier years of Mary Snow shall be told hereafter. Here it will be only necessary to say that she was an orphan, that as yet she was little more than a child, and that she owed her maintenance and the advantage of her education to the charity and love of her destined husband. Therefore, as I have said, it was manifest that Felix Graham could not think of falling in love with Miss Staveley, even had not his very low position, in reference to worldly affairs, made any such passion on his part quite hopeless. But with Peregrine Orme the matter was different. There could be no possible reason why Peregrine Orme should not win and wear the beautiful girl whom he so much admired.

But the ghosts are kept standing over their flames, the spirit is becoming exhausted, and the raisins will be burnt. At snap-dragon, too, the ghosts here had something to do. The law of the game is this—a law on which Marian would have insisted had not the flames been so very hot—that the raisins shall become the prey of those audacious marauders only who dare to face the presence of the ghost, and to plunge their hands into the burning dish. As a rule the boys do this, clawing out the raisins, while the girls pick them up and eat them. But here at Noningsby the boys were too little to act thus as pioneers in the face of the enemy, and the raisins might have remained till the flames were burnt out, had not the beneficent ghost scattered abroad the richness of her own treasures.

"Now, Marian," said Felix Graham, bringing her up in his arms.

"But it will burn, Mr. Felix. Look there; see; there are a great many at that end. You do it."

"I must have another kiss then."

"Very well, yes; if you get five." And then Felix dashed his hand in among the flames and brought forth a fistful of fruit, which imparted to his fingers and wristband a smell of brandy for the rest of the evening.

"If you take so many at a time I shall rap your knuckles with the spoon," said the ghost, as she stirred up the flames to keep them alive.

"But the ghost shouldn't speak," said Marian, who was evidently unacquainted with the best ghosts of tragedy.

"But the ghost must speak when such large hands invade the caldron;" and then another raid was effected, and the threatened blow was given. Had any one told her in the morning that she would that day have rapped Mr. Graham's knuckles with a kitchen spoon, she would not have believed that person; but it is thus that hearts are lost and won.

And Peregrine Orme looked on from a distance, thinking of it all. That he should have been stricken dumb by the beauty of any girl was surprising even to himself; for though young and almost boyish in his manners, he had never yet feared to speak out in any presence. The tutor at his college had thought him insolent beyond parallel; and his grandfather, though he loved him for his open face and plain outspoken words, found them sometimes almost too much for him. But now he stood there looking and longing, and could not summon courage to go up and address a few words to this young girl even in the midst of their sports. Twice or thrice during the last few days he had essayed to speak to her, but his words had been dull and vapid, and to himself they had appeared childish. He was quite conscious of his own weakness. More than once, during that period of the snap-dragon, did he say to himself that he would descend into the lists and break a lance in that tourney; but still he did not descend, and his lance remained inglorious in its rest.

At the other end of the long table the ghost also had two attendant knights, and neither of them refrained from the battle. Augustus Staveley, if he thought it worth his while to keep the lists at all, would not be allowed to ride through them unopposed from any backwardness on the part of his rival. Lucius Mason was not likely to become a timid, silent, longing lover. To him it was not possible that he should fear the girl whom he loved. He could not worship that which he wished to obtain for himself. It may be doubted whether he had much faculty of worshipping anything in the truest meaning of that word. One worships that which one feels, through the inner and unexpressed conviction of the mind, to be greater, better, higher than oneself; but it was not probable that Lucius Mason should so think of any woman that he might meet.

Nor, to give him his due, was it probable that he should be in any way afraid of any man that he might encounter. He would fear neither the talent, nor the rank, nor the money influence, nor the dexterity of any such rival. In any attempt that he might make on a woman's heart he would regard his own chance as good against that of any other possible he. Augustus Staveley was master here at Noningsby, and was a clever, dashing, handsome, fashionable young fellow; but Lucius Mason never dreamed of retreating before such forces as those. He had words with which to speak as fair as those of any man, and flattered himself that he as well knew how to use them.

It was pretty to see with what admirable tact and judicious management of her smiles Sophia received the homage of the two young men, answering the compliments of both with ease, and so conducting herself that neither could fairly accuse her of undue favour to the other. But unfairly, in his own mind, Augustus did so accuse her. And why should he have been so venomous, seeing that he entertained no regard for the lady himself? His object was still plain enough,—that, namely, of making a match between his needy friend and the heiress.

His needy friend in the mean time played on through the long evening in thoughtless happiness; and Peregrine Orme, looking at the game from a distance, saw that rap given to the favoured knuckles with a bitterness of heart and an inner groaning of the spirit that will not be incomprehensible to many.

"I do so love that Mr. Felix!" said Marian, as her aunt Madeline kissed her in her little bed on wishing her good night. "Don't you, aunt Mad—?"

And so it was that Christmas-day was passed at Noningsby.

CHAPTER XXIII
CHRISTMAS AT GROBY PARK

Christmas-day was always a time of very great trial to Mrs. Mason of Groby Park. It behoved her, as the wife of an old English country gentleman, to spread her board plenteously at that season, and in some sort to make an open house of it. But she could not bring herself to spread any board with plenty, and the idea of an open house would almost break her heart. Unlimited eating! There was something in the very sounds of such words which was appalling to the inner woman.

And on this Christmas-day she was doomed to go through an ordeal of very peculiar severity. It so happened that the cure of souls in the parish of Groby had been intrusted for the last two or three years to a young, energetic, but not very opulent curate. Why the rector of Groby should be altogether absent, leaving the work in the hands of a curate, whom he paid by the lease of a cottage and garden and fifty-five pounds a year,—thereby behaving as he imagined with extensive liberality,—it is unnecessary here to inquire. Such was the case, and the Rev. Adolphus Green, with Mrs. A. Green and the four children, managed to live with some difficulty on the produce of the garden and the allotted stipend; but could not probably have lived at all in that position had not Mrs. Adolphus Green been blessed with some small fortune.

It had so happened that Mrs. Adolphus Green had been instrumental in imparting some knowledge of singing to two of the Miss Masons, and had continued her instructions over the last three years. This had not been done in any preconcerted way, but the lessons had grown by chance. Mrs. Mason the while had looked on with a satisfied eye at an arrangement that was so much to her taste.

"There are no regular lessons you know," she had said to her husband, when he suggested that some reward for so much work would be expedient. "Mrs. Green finds it convenient to have the use of my drawing-room, and would never see an instrument from year's end to year's end if she were not allowed to come up here. Depend upon it she gets a great deal more than she gives."

But after two years of tuition Mr. Mason had spoken a second time. "My dear," he said, "I cannot allow the girls to accept so great a favour from Mrs. Green without making her some compensation."

"I don't see that it is at all necessary," Mrs. Mason had answered; "but if you think so, we could send her down a hamper of apples,—that is, a basketful." Now it happened that apples were very plentiful that year, and that the curate and his wife were blessed with as many as they could judiciously consume.

"Apples! nonsense!" said Mr. Mason.

"If you mean money, my dear, I couldn't do it. I wouldn't so offend a lady for all the world."

"You could buy them something handsome, in the way of furniture. That little room of theirs that they call the drawing-room has nothing in it at all. Get Jones from Leeds to send them some things that will do for them." And hence, after many inner misgivings, had arisen that purchase of a drawing-room set from Mr. Kantwise,—that set of metallic "Louey Catorse furniture," containing three tables, eight chairs, &c., &c., as to which it may be remembered that Mrs. Mason made such an undoubted bargain, getting them for less than cost price. That they had been "strained," as Mr. Kantwise himself admitted in discoursing on the subject to Mr. Dockwrath, was not matter of much moment. They would do extremely well for a curate's wife.

And now on this Christmas-day the present was to be made over to the happy lady. Mr. and Mrs. Green were to dine at Groby Park,—leaving their more fortunate children to the fuller festivities of the cottage; and the intention was that before dinner the whole drawing-room set should be made over. It was with grievous pangs of heart that Mrs. Mason looked forward to such an operation. Her own house was plenteously furnished from the kitchens to the attics, but still she would have loved to keep that metallic set of painted trumpery. She knew that the table would not screw on; she knew that the pivot of the music stool was bent; she knew that there was no place in the house in which they could stand; she must have known that in no possible way could they be of use to her or hers,—and yet she could not part with them without an agony. Her husband was infatuated in this matter of compensation for the use of Mrs. Green's idle hours; no compensation could be necessary;—and then she paid another visit to the metallic furniture. She knew in her heart of hearts that they could never be of use to anybody, and yet she made up her mind to keep back two out of the eight chairs. Six chairs would be quite enough for Mrs. Green's small room.

As there was to be feasting at five, real roast beef, plum-pudding and mince-pies;—"Mince-pies and plum-pudding together are vulgar, my dear," Mrs. Mason had said to her husband; but in spite of the vulgarity he had insisted;—the breakfast was of course scanty. Mr. Mason liked a slice of cold meat in the morning, or the leg of a fowl, or a couple of fresh eggs as well as any man; but the matter was not worth a continual fight. "As we are to dine an hour earlier to-day I did not think you would eat meat," his wife said to him. "Then there would be less expense in putting it on the table," he had answered; and after that there was nothing more said about it. He always put off till some future day that great contest which he intended to wage and to win, and by which he hoped to bring it about that plenty should henceforward be the law of the land at Groby Park. And then they all went to church. Mrs. Mason would not on any account have missed church on Christmas-day or a Sunday. It was a cheap duty, and therefore rigidly performed. As she walked from her carriage up to the church-door she encountered Mrs. Green, and smiled sweetly as she wished that lady all the compliments of the season.

"We shall see you immediately after church," said Mrs. Mason.

"Oh yes, certainly," said Mrs. Green.

"And Mr. Green with you?"

"He intends to do himself the pleasure," said the curate's wife.

"Mind he comes, because we have a little ceremony to go through before we sit down to dinner," and Mrs. Mason smiled again ever so graciously. Did she think, or did she not think, that she was going to do a kindness to her neighbour? Most women would have sunk into their shoes as the hour grew nigh at which they were to show themselves guilty of so much meanness.

She stayed for the sacrament, and it may here be remarked that on that afternoon she rated both the footman and housemaid because they omitted to do so. She thought, we must presume, that she was doing her duty, and must imagine her to have been ignorant that she was cheating her husband and cheating her friend. She took the sacrament with admirable propriety of demeanour, and then, on her return home, withdrew another chair from the set. There would still be six, including the rocking chair, and six would be quite enough for that little hole of a room.

There was a large chamber up stairs at Groby Park which had been used for the children's lessons, but which now was generally deserted. There was in it an old worn-out pianoforte,—and though Mrs. Mason had talked somewhat grandly of the use of her drawing-room, it was here that the singing had been taught. Into this room the metallic furniture had been brought, and up to that Christmas morning it had remained here packed in its original boxes. Hither immediately after breakfast Mrs. Mason had taken herself, and had spent an hour in her efforts to set the things forth to view. Two of the chairs she then put aside into a cupboard, and a third she added to her private store on her return to her work after church.

But, alas, alas! let her do what she would, she could not get the top on to the table. "It's all smashed, ma'am," said the girl whom she at last summoned to her aid. "Nonsense, you simpleton; how can it be smashed when it's new," said the mistress. And then she tried again, and again, declaring as she did do, that she would have the law of the rogue who had sold her a damaged article. Nevertheless she had known that it was damaged, and had bought it cheap on that account, insisting in very urgent language that the table was in fact worth nothing because of its injuries.

At about four Mr. and Mrs. Green walked up to the house and were shown into the drawing-room. Here was Mrs. Mason supported by Penelope and Creusa. As Diana was not musical, and therefore under no compliment to Mrs. Green, she kept out of the way. Mr. Mason also was absent. He knew that something very mean was about to be done, and would not show his face till it was over. He ought to have taken the matter in hand himself, and would have done so had not his mind been full of other things. He himself was a man terribly wronged and wickedly injured, and could not therefore in these present months interfere much in the active doing of kindnesses. His hours were spent in thinking how he might best obtain justice,—how he might secure his pound of flesh. He only wanted his own, but that he would have;—his own, with due punishment on those who had for so many years robbed him of it. He therefore did not attend at the presentation of the furniture.

"And now we'll go up stairs, if you please," said Mrs. Mason, with that gracious smile for which she was so famous. "Mr. Green, you must come too. Dear Mrs. Green has been so very kind to my two girls; and now I have got a few articles,—they are of the very newest fashion, and I do hope that Mrs. Green will like them." And so they all went up into the schoolroom.

"There's a new fashion come up lately," said Mrs. Mason as she walked along the corridor, "quite new:—of metallic furniture. I don't know whether you have seen any." Mrs. Green said she had not seen any as yet.

"The Patent Steel Furniture Company makes it, and it has got very greatly into vogue for small rooms. I thought that perhaps you would allow me to present you with a set for your drawing-room."

"I'm sure it is very kind of you to think of it," said Mrs. Green.

"Uncommonly so," said Mr. Green. But both Mr. Green and Mrs. Green knew the lady, and their hopes did not run high.

And then the door was opened and there stood the furniture to view. There stood the furniture, except the three subtracted chairs, and the loo table. The claw and leg of the table indeed were standing there, but the top was folded up and lying on the floor beside it. "I hope you'll like the pattern," began Mrs. Mason. "I'm told that it is the prettiest that has yet been brought out. There has been some little accident about the screw of the table, but the smith in the village will put that to rights in five minutes. He lives so close to you that I didn't think it worth while to have him up here."

"It's very nice," said Mrs. Green, looking round her almost in dismay.

"Very nice indeed," said Mr. Green, wondering in his mind for what purpose such utter trash could have been manufactured, and endeavouring to make up his mind as to what they might possibly do with it. Mr. Green knew what chairs and tables should be, and was well aware that the things before him were absolutely useless for any of the ordinary purposes of furniture.

"And they are the most convenient things in the world," said Mrs. Mason, "for when you are going to change house you pack them all up again in those boxes. Wooden furniture takes up so much room, and is so lumbersome."

"Yes, it is," said Mrs. Green.

"I'll have them all put up again and sent down in the cart to-morrow."

"Thank you; that will be very kind," said Mr. Green, and then the ceremony of the presentation was over. On the following day the boxes were sent down, and Mrs. Mason might have abstracted even another chair without detection, for the cases lay unheeded from month to month in the curate's still unfurnished room. "The fact is they cannot afford a carpet," Mrs. Mason afterwards said to one of her daughters, "and with such things as those they are quite right to keep them up till they can be used with advantage. I always gave Mrs. Green credit for a good deal of prudence."

And then, when the show was over, they descended again into the drawing-room,—Mr. Green and Mrs. Mason went first, and Creusa followed. Penelope was thus so far behind as to be able to speak to her friend without being heard by the others.

"You know mamma," she said, with a shrug of her shoulders and a look of scorn in her eye.

"The things are very nice."

"No, they are not, and you know they are not. They are worthless; perfectly worthless."

"But we don't want anything."

"No; and if there had been no pretence of a gift it would all have been very well. What will Mr. Green think?"

"I rather think he likes iron chairs;" and then they were in the drawing-room.

Mr. Mason did not appear till dinner-time, and came in only just in time to give his arm to Mrs. Green. He had had letters to write,—a letter to Messrs. Round and Crook, very determined in its tone; and a letter also to Mr. Dockwrath, for the little attorney had so crept on in the affair that he was now corresponding with the principal. "I'll teach those fellows in Bedford Row to know who I am," he had said to himself more than once, sitting on his high stool at Hamworth.

And then came the Groby Park Christmas dinner. To speak the truth Mr. Mason had himself gone to the neighbouring butcher, and ordered the surloin of beef, knowing that it would be useless to trust to orders conveyed through his wife. He had seen the piece of meat put on one side for him, and had afterwards traced it on to the kitchen dresser. But nevertheless when it appeared at table it had been sadly mutilated. A steak had been cut off the full breadth of it—a monstrous cantle from out its fair proportions. The lady had seen the jovial, thick, ample size of the goodly joint, and her heart had been unable to spare it. She had made an effort and turned away, saying to herself that the responsibility was all with him. But it was of no use. There was that within her which could not do it. "Your master will never be able to carve such a mountain of meat as that," she had said, turning back to the cook. "'Deed, an' it's he that will, ma'am," said the Irish mistress of the spit; for Irish cooks are cheaper than those bred and born in England. But nevertheless the thing was done, and it was by her own fair hands that the envious knife was used. "I couldn't do it, ma'am," the cook had said; "I couldn't railly."

Mr. Mason's face became very black when he saw the raid that had been effected, and when he looked up across the table his wife's eye was on him. She knew what she had to expect, and she knew also that it would not come now. Her eye steadily looked at his, quivering with fear; for Mr. Mason could be savage enough in his anger. And what had she gained? One may as well ask what does the miser gain who hides away his gold in an old pot, or what does that other madman gain who is locked up for long long years because he fancies himself the grandmother of the Queen of England?

But there was still enough beef on the table for all of them to eat, and as Mrs. Mason was not intrusted with the carving of it, their plates were filled. As far as a sufficiency of beef can make a good dinner Mr. and Mrs. Green did have a good dinner on that Christmas-day. Beyond that their comfort was limited, for no one was in a humour for happy conversation.

And over and beyond the beef there was a plum-pudding and three mince-pies. Four mince-pies had originally graced the dish, but before dinner one had been conveyed away to some up stairs receptacle for such spoils. The pudding also was small, nor was it black and rich, and laden with good things as a Christmas pudding should be laden. Let us hope that what the guests so lost was made up to them on the following day, by an absence of those ill effects which sometimes attend upon the consumption of rich viands.

"And now, my dear, we'll have a bit of bread and cheese and a glass of beer," Mr. Green said when he arrived at his own cottage. And so it was that Christmas-day was passed at Groby Park.

CHAPTER XXIV
CHRISTMAS IN GREAT ST. HELENS

We will now look in for a moment at the Christmas doings of our fat friend, Mr. Moulder. Mr. Moulder was a married man living in lodgings over a wine-merchant's vaults in Great St. Helens. He was blessed—or troubled, with no children, and prided himself greatly on the material comfort with which his humble home was surrounded. "His wife," he often boasted, "never wanted for plenty of the best of eating; and for linen and silks and such-like, she could show her drawers and her wardrobes with many a great lady from Russell Square, and not be ashamed, neither!" And then, as for drink,—"tipple," as Mr. Moulder sportively was accustomed to name it among his friends, he opined that he was not altogether behind the mark in that respect. "He had got some brandy—he didn't care what anybody might say about Cognac and eau de vie; but the brandy which he had got from Betts' private establishment seventeen years ago, for richness of flavour and fullness of strength, would beat any French article that anybody in the city could show. That at least was his idea. If anybody didn't like it, they needn't take it. There was whisky that would make your hair stand on end." So said Mr. Moulder, and I can believe him; for it has made my hair stand on end merely to see other people drinking it.

And if comforts of apparel, comforts of eating and drinking, and comforts of the feather-bed and easy-chair kind can make a woman happy, Mrs. Moulder was no doubt a happy woman. She had quite fallen in to the mode of life laid out for her. She had a little bit of hot kidney for breakfast at about ten; she dined at three, having seen herself to the accurate cooking of her roast fowl, or her bit of sweetbread, and always had her pint of Scotch ale. She turned over all her clothes almost every day. In the evening she read Reynolds's Miscellany, had her tea and buttered muffins, took a thimbleful of brandy and water at nine, and then went to bed. The work of her life consisted in sewing buttons on to Moulder's shirts, and seeing that his things were properly got up when he was at home. No doubt she would have done better as to the duties of the world, had the world's duties come to her. As it was, very few such had come in her direction. Her husband was away from home three-fourths of the year, and she had no children that required attention. As for society, some four or five times a year she would drink tea with Mrs. Hubbles at Clapham. Mrs. Hubbles was the wife of the senior partner in the firm, and on such occasions Mrs. Moulder dressed herself in her best, and having travelled to Clapham in an omnibus, spent the evening in dull propriety on one corner of Mrs. Hubbles's sofa. When I have added to this that Moulder every year took her to Broadstairs for a fortnight, I think that I have described with sufficient accuracy the course of Mrs. Moulder's life.

On the occasion of this present Christmas-day Mr. Moulder entertained a small party. And he delighted in such occasional entertainments, taking extraordinary pains that the eatables should be of the very best; and he would maintain an hospitable good humour to the last,—unless anything went wrong in the cookery, in which case he could make himself extremely unpleasant to Mrs. M. Indeed, proper cooking for Mr. M. and the proper starching of the bands of his shirts were almost the only trials that Mrs. Moulder was doomed to suffer. "What the d—— are you for?" he would say, almost throwing the displeasing viands at her head across the table, or tearing the rough linen from off his throat. "It ain't much I ask of you in return for your keep;" and then he would scowl at her with bloodshot eyes till she shook in her shoes. But this did not happen often, as experiences had made her careful.

But on this present Christmas festival all went swimmingly to the end. "Now, bear a hand, old girl," was the harshest word he said to her; and he enjoyed himself like Duncan, shut up in measureless content. He had three guests with him on this auspicious day. There was his old friend Snengkeld, who had dined with him on every Christmas since his marriage; there was his wife's brother, of whom we will say a word or two just now;—and there was our old friend, Mr. Kantwise. Mr. Kantwise was not exactly the man whom Moulder would have chosen as his guest, for they were opposed to each other in all their modes of thought and action; but he had come across the travelling agent of the Patent Metallic Steel Furniture Company on the previous day, and finding that he was to be alone in London on this general holiday, he had asked him out of sheer good nature. Moulder could be very good natured, and full of pity when the sorrow to be pitied arose from some such source as the want of a Christmas dinner. So Mr. Kantwise had been asked, and precisely at four o'clock he made his appearance at Great St. Helens.

But now, as to this brother-in-law. He was no other than that John Kenneby whom Miriam Usbech did not marry,—whom Miriam Usbech might, perhaps, have done well to marry. John Kenneby, after one or two attempts in other spheres of life, had at last got into the house of Hubbles and Grease, and had risen to be their book-keeper. He had once been tried by them as a traveller, but in that line he had failed. He did not possess that rough, ready, self-confident tone of mind which is almost necessary for a man who is destined to move about quickly from one circle of persons to another. After a six months' trial he had given that up, but during the time, Mr. Moulder, the senior traveller of the house, had married his sister. John Kenneby was a good, honest, painstaking fellow, and was believed by his friends to have put a few pounds together in spite of the timidity of his character.

When Snengkeld and Kenneby were shown up into the room, they found nobody there but Kantwise. That Mrs. Moulder should be down stairs looking after the roast turkey was no more than natural; but why should not Moulder himself be there to receive his guests? He soon appeared, however, coming up without his coat.

"Well, Snengkeld, how are you, old fellow; many happy returns, and all that; the same to you, John. I'll tell you what, my lads; it's a prime 'un. I never saw such a bird in all my days."

"What, the turkey?" said Snengkeld.

"You didn't think it'd be a ostrich, did you?"

"Ha, ha, ha!" laughed Snengkeld. "No, I didn't expect nothing but a turkey here on Christmas-day."

"And nothing but a turkey you'll have, my boys. Can you eat turkey, Kantwise?"

Mr. Kantwise declared that his only passion in the way of eating was for a turkey.

"As for John, I'm sure of him. I've seen him at the work before." Whereupon John grinned but said nothing.

"I never see such a bird in my life, certainly."

"From Norfolk, I suppose," said Snengkeld, with a great appearance of interest.

"Oh, you may swear to that. It weighed twenty-four pounds, for I put it into the scales myself, and old Gibbetts let me have it for a guinea. The price marked on it was five-and-twenty, for I saw it. He's had it hanging for a fortnight, and I've been to see it wiped down with vinegar regular every morning. And now, my boys, it's done to a turn. I've been in the kitchen most of the time myself; and either I or Mrs. M. has never left it for a single moment."

"How did you manage about divine service?" said Kantwise; and then, when he had spoken, closed his eyes and sucked his lips.

Mr. Moulder looked at him for a minute, and then said, "Gammon."

"Ha, ha, ha!" laughed Snengkeld. And then Mrs. Moulder appeared, bringing the turkey with her; for she would trust it to no hands less careful than her own.

"By George, it is a bird," said Snengkeld, standing over it and eyeing it minutely.

"Uncommon nice it looks," said Kantwise.

"All the same, I wouldn't eat none, if I were you," said Moulder, "seeing what sinners have been a basting it." And then they all sat down to dinner, Moulder having first resumed his coat.

For the next three or four minutes Moulder did not speak a word. The turkey was on his mind, with the stuffing, the gravy, the liver, the breast, the wings, and the legs. He stood up to carve it, and while he was at the work he looked at it as though his two eyes were hardly sufficient. He did not help first one person and then another, so ending by himself; but he cut up artistically as much as might probably be consumed, and located the fragments in small heaps or shares in the hot gravy; and then, having made a partition of the spoils, he served it out with unerring impartiality. To have robbed any one of his or her fair slice of the breast would, in his mind, have been gross dishonesty. In his heart he did not love Kantwise, but he dealt by him with the utmost justice in the great affair of the turkey's breast. When he had done all this, and his own plate was laden, he gave a long sigh. "I shall never cut up such another bird as that, the longest day that I have to live," he said; and then he took out his large red silk handkerchief and wiped the perspiration from his brow.

"Deary me, M.; don't think of that now," said the wife.

"What's the use?" said Snengkeld. "Care killed a cat."

"And perhaps you may," said John Kenneby, trying to comfort him; "who knows?"

"It's all in the hands of Providence," said Kantwise, "and we should look to him."

"And how does it taste?" asked Moulder, shaking the gloomy thoughts from his mind.

"Uncommon," said Snengkeld, with his mouth quite full. "I never eat such a turkey in all my life."

"Like melted diamonds," said Mrs. Moulder, who was not without a touch of poetry.

"Ah, there's nothing like hanging of 'em long enough, and watching of 'em well. It's that vinegar as done it;" and then they went seriously to work, and there was nothing more said of any importance until the eating was nearly over.

And now Mrs. M. had taken away the cloth, and they were sitting cozily over their port wine. The very apple of the eye of the evening had not arrived even yet. That would not come till the pipes were brought out, and the brandy was put on the table, and the whisky was there that made the people's hair stand on end. It was then that the floodgates of convivial eloquence would be unloosed. In the mean time it was necessary to sacrifice something to gentility, and therefore they sat over their port wine.

"Did you bring that letter with you, John?" said his sister. John replied that he had done so, and that he had also received another letter that morning from another party on the same subject.

"Do show it to Moulder, and ask him," said Mrs. M.

"I've got 'em both on purpose," said John; and then he brought forth two letters, and handed one of them to his brother-in-law. It contained a request, very civilly worded, from Messrs. Round and Crook, begging him to call at their office in Bedford Row on the earliest possible day, in order that they might have some conversation with him regarding the will of the late Sir Joseph Mason, who died in 18—.

"Why, this is law business," said Moulder, who liked no business of that description. "Don't you go near them, John, if you ain't obliged."

And then Kenneby gave his explanation on the matter, telling how in former years,—many years ago, he had been a witness in a lawsuit. And then as he told it he sighed, remembering Miriam Usbech, for whose sake he had remained unmarried even to this day. And he went on to narrate how he had been bullied in the court, though he had valiantly striven to tell the truth with exactness; and as he spoke, an opinion of his became manifest that old Usbech had not signed the document in his presence. "The girl signed it certainly," said he, "for I handed her the pen. I recollect it, as though it were yesterday."

"They are the very people we were talking of at Leeds," said Moulder, turning to Kantwise. "Mason and Martock; don't you remember how you went out to Groby Park to sell some of them iron gimcracks? That was old Mason's son. They are the same people."

"Ah, I shouldn't wonder," said Kantwise, who was listening all the while. He never allowed intelligence of this kind to pass by him idly.

"And who's the other letter from?" asked Moulder. "But, dash my wigs, it's past six o'clock. Come, old girl, why don't you give us the tobacco and stuff?"

"It ain't far to fetch," said Mrs. Moulder. And then she put the tobacco and "stuff" upon the table.

"The other letter is from an enemy of mine," said John Kenneby, speaking very solemnly; "an enemy of mine, named Dockwrath, who lives at Hamworth. He's an attorney too."

"Dockwrath!" said Moulder.

Mr. Kantwise said nothing, but he looked round over his shoulder at Kenneby, and then shut his eyes.

"That was the name of the man whom we left in the commercial room at the Bull," said Snengkeld.

"He went out to Mason's at Groby Park that same day," said Moulder.

"Then it's the same man," said Kenneby; and there was as much solemnity in the tone of his voice as though the unravelment of all the mysteries of the iron mask was now about to take place. Mr. Kantwise still said nothing, but he also perceived that it was the same man.

"Let me tell you, John Kenneby," said Moulder, with the air of one who understood well the subject that he was discussing, "if they two be the same man, then the man who wrote that letter to you is as big a blackguard as there is from this to hisself." And Mr. Moulder in the excitement of the moment puffed hard at his pipe, took a long pull at his drink, and dragged open his waistcoat. "I don't know whether Kantwise has anything to say upon that subject," added Moulder.

"Not a word at present," said Kantwise. Mr. Kantwise was a very careful man, and usually calculated with accuracy the value which he might extract from any circumstances with reference to his own main chance. Mr. Dockwrath had not as yet paid him for the set of metallic furniture, and therefore he also might well have joined in that sweeping accusation; but it might be that by a judicious use of what he now heard he might obtain the payment of that little bill,—and perhaps other collateral advantages.

And then the letter from Dockwrath to Kenneby was brought forth and read. "My dear John," it began,—for the two had known each other when they were lads together,—and it went on to request Kenneby's attendance at Hamworth for the short space of a few hours,—"I want to have a little conversation with you about a matter of considerable interest to both of us; and as I cannot expect you to undertake expense I enclose a money order for thirty shillings."

"He's in earnest at any rate," said Mr. Moulder.

"No mistake about that," said Snengkeld.

But Mr. Kantwise spoke never a word.

It was at last decided that John Kenneby should go both to Hamworth and to Bedford Row, but that he should go to Hamworth first. Moulder would have counselled him to have gone to neither, but Snengkeld remarked that there were too many at work to let the matter sleep, and John himself observed that "anyways he hadn't done anything to be ashamed of."

"Then go," said Moulder at last, "only don't say more than you are obliged to."

"I does not like these business talkings on Christmas night," said Mrs. Moulder, when the matter was arranged.

"What can one do?" asked Moulder.

"It's a tempting of Providence in my mind," said Kantwise, as he replenished his glass, and turned his eyes up to the ceiling.

"Now that's gammon," said Moulder. And then there arose among them a long and animated discussion on matters theological.

"I'll tell you what my idea of death is," said Moulder, after a while. "I ain't a bit afeard of it. My father was an honest man as did his duty by his employers, and he died with a bottom of brandy before him and a pipe in his mouth. I sha'n't live long myself—"

"Gracious, Moulder, don't!" said Mrs. M.

"No, more I sha'n't, 'cause I'm fat as he was; and I hope I may die as he did. I've been honest to Hubbles and Grease. They've made thousands of pounds along of me, and have never lost none. Who can say more than that? When I took to the old girl there, I insured my life, so that she shouldn't want her wittles and drink—"

"Oh, M., don't!"

"And I ain't afeard to die. Snengkeld, my old pal, hand us the brandy."

Such is the modern philosophy of the Moulders, pigs out of the sty of Epicurus. And so it was they passed Christmas-day in Great St. Helens.

CHAPTER XXV
MR. FURNIVAL AGAIN AT HIS CHAMBERS

The Christmas doings at The Cleeve were not very gay. There was no visitor there, except Lady Mason, and it was known that she was in trouble. It must not, however, be supposed that she constantly bewailed herself while there, or made her friends miserable by a succession of hysterical tears. By no means. She made an effort to be serene, and the effort was successful—as such efforts usually are. On the morning of Christmas-day they duly attended church, and Lady Mason was seen by all Hamworth sitting in The Cleeve pew. In no way could the baronet's friendship have been shown more plainly than in this, nor could a more significant mark of intimacy have been given;—all which Sir Peregrine well understood. The people of Hamworth had chosen to talk scandal about Lady Mason, but he at any rate would show how little attention he paid to the falsehoods that there were circulated. So he stood by her at the pew door as she entered, with as much deference as though she had been a duchess; and the people of Hamworth, looking on, wondered which would be right, Mr. Dockwrath or Sir Peregrine.

After dinner Sir Peregrine gave a toast. "Lady Mason, we will drink the health of the absent boys. God bless them! I hope they are enjoying themselves."

"God bless them!" said Mrs. Orme, putting her handkerchief to her eyes.

"God bless them both!" said Lady Mason, also putting her handkerchief to her eyes. Then the ladies left the room, and that was the extent of their special festivity. "Robert," said Sir Peregrine immediately afterwards to his butler, "let them have what port wine they want in the servants' hall— within measure."

"Yes, Sir Peregrine."

"And Robert, I shall not want you again."

"Thank you, Sir Peregrine."

From all which it may be imagined that the Christmas doings at The Cleeve were chiefly maintained below stairs.

"I do hope they are happy," said Mrs. Orme, when the two ladies were together in the drawing-room. "They have a very nice party at Noningsby."

"Your boy will be happy, I'm sure," said Lady Mason.

"And why not Lucius also?"

It was sweet in Lady Mason's ear to hear her son called by his Christian name. All these increasing signs of interest and intimacy were sweet, but especially any which signified some favour shown to her son. "This trouble weighs heavy on him," she replied. "It is only natural that he should feel it."

"Papa does not seem to think much of it," said Mrs. Orme. "If I were you, I would strive to forget it."

"I do strive," said the other; and then she took the hand which Mrs. Orme had stretched out to her, and that lady got up and kissed her.

"Dearest friend," said Mrs. Orme, "if we can comfort you we will." And then they sobbed in each other's arms.

In the mean time Sir Peregrine was sitting alone, thinking. He sat thinking, with his glass of claret untouched by his side, and with the biscuit which he had taken lying untouched upon the table. As he sat he had raised one leg upon the other, placing his foot on his knee, and he held it there with his hand upon his instep. And so he sat without moving for some quarter of an hour, trying to use all his mind on the subject which occupied it. At last he roused himself, almost with a start, and leaving his chair, walked three or four times the length of the room. "Why should I not?" at last he said to himself, stopping suddenly and placing his hand upon the table. "Why should I not, if it pleases me? It shall not injure him—nor her." And then he walked again. "But I will ask Edith," he said, still speaking to himself. "If she says that she disapproves of it, I will not do it." And then he left the room, while the wine still remained untasted on the table.

"Why should I not?"

On the day following Christmas Mr. Furnival went up to town, and Mr. Round junior,—Mat Round, as he was called in the profession,—came to him at his chambers. A promise had been made to the barrister by Round and Crook that no active steps should be taken against Lady Mason on the part of Joseph Mason of Groby, without notice being given to Mr. Furnival. And this visit by appointment was made in consequence of that promise.

"You see," said Matthew Round, when that visit was nearly brought to a close, "that we are pressed very hard to go on with this, and if we do not, somebody else will."

"Nevertheless, if I were you, I should decline," said Mr. Furnival.

"You're looking to your client, not to ours, sir," said the attorney. "The fact is that the whole case is very queer. It was proved on the last trial that Bolster and Kenneby were witnesses to a deed on the 14th of July, and that was all that was proved. Now we can prove that they were on that day witnesses to another deed. Were they witnesses to two?"

"Why should they not be?"

"That is for us to see. We have written to them both to come up to us, and in order that we might be quite on the square I thought it right to tell you."

"Thank you; yes; I cannot complain of you. And what form do you think that your proceedings will take?"

"Joseph Mason talks of indicting her for—forgery," said the attorney, pausing a moment before he dared to pronounce the dread word.

"Indict her for forgery!" said Furnival, with a start. And yet the idea was one which had been for some days present to his mind's eye.

"I do not say so," said Round. "I have as yet seen none of the witnesses myself. If they are prepared to prove that they did sign two separate documents on that day, the thing must pass off." It was clear to Mr. Furnival that even Mr. Round junior would be glad that it should pass off. And then he also sat thinking. Might it not be probable that, with a little judicious exercise of their memory, those two witnesses would remember that they had signed two documents; or at any rate, looking to the lapse of the time, that they might be induced to forget altogether whether they had signed one, two, or three? Or even if they could be mystified so that nothing could be proved, it would still be well with his client. Indeed no magistrate would commit such a person as Lady Mason, especially after so long an interval, and no grand jury would find a bill against her, except upon evidence that was clear, well defined, and almost indubitable. If any point of doubt could be shown, she might be brought off without a trial, if only she would be true to herself. At the former trial there was the existing codicil, and the fact also that the two surviving reputed witnesses would not deny their signatures. These signatures—if they were genuine signatures—had been attached with all proper formality, and the form used went to state that the testator had signed the instrument in the presence of them all, they all being present together at the same time. The survivors had both asserted that when they did affix their names the three were then present, as was also Sir Joseph; but there had been a terrible doubt even then as to the identity of the document; and a doubt also as to there having been any signature made by one of the reputed witnesses—by that one, namely, who at the time of that trial was dead. Now another document was forthcoming, purporting to have been witnessed, on the same day, by these two surviving witnesses! If that document were genuine, and if these two survivors should be clear that they had written their names but once on that 14th of July, in such case could it be possible to quash further public inquiry? The criminal prosecution might not be possible as a first proceeding, but if the estate were recovered at common law, would not the criminal prosecution follow as a matter of course? And then Mr. Furnival thought it all over again and again.

If this document were genuine,—this new document which the man Dockwrath stated that he had found,—this deed of separation of partnership which purported to have been executed on that 14th of July! That was now the one important question. If it were genuine! And why should there not be as strong a question of the honesty of that document as of the other? Mr. Furnival well knew that no fraudulent deed would be forged and produced without a motive; and that if he impugned this deed he must show the motive. Motive enough there was, no doubt. Mason might have had it forged in order to get the property, or Dockwrath to gratify his revenge. But in such case it would be a forgery of the present day. There could have been no motive for such a forgery twenty years ago. The paper, the writing, the attested signature of Martock, the other party to it, would prove that it had not been got up and manufactured now. Dockwrath would not dare to bring forward such a forgery as that. There was no hope of any such result.

But might not he, Furnival, if the matter were pushed before a jury, make them think that the two documents stood balanced against each other? and that Lady Mason's respectability, her long possession, together with the vile malignity of her antagonists, gave the greater probability of honesty to the disputed codicil? Mr. Furnival did think that he might induce a jury to acquit her; but he terribly feared that he might not be able to induce the world to acquit her also. As he thought of all the case, he seemed to put himself apart from the world at large. He did not question himself as to his own belief, but seemed to feel that it would suffice for him if he could so bring it about that her other friends should think her innocent. It would by no means suffice for him to secure for her son the property, and for her a simple acquittal. It was not that he dreaded the idea of thinking her guilty himself; perhaps he did so think her now—he half thought her so, at any rate; but he greatly dreaded the idea of others thinking so. It might be well to buy up Dockwrath, if it were possible. If it were possible! But then it was not possible that he himself could have a hand in such a matter. Could Crabwitz do it? No; he thought not. And then, at this moment, he was not certain that he could depend on Crabwitz.

And why should he trouble himself in this way? Mr. Furnival was a man loyal to his friends at heart. Had Lady Mason been a man, and had he pulled that man through great difficulties in early life, he would have been loyally desirous of carrying him through the same or similar difficulties at any after period. In that cause which he had once battled he was always ready to do battle, without reference to any professional consideration of triumph or profit. It was to this feeling of loyalty that he had owed much of his success in life. And in such a case as this it may be supposed that that feeling would be strong. But then such a feeling presumed a case in which he could sympathise—in which he could believe. Would it be well that he should allow himself to feel the same interest in this case, to maintain respecting it the same personal anxiety, if he ceased to believe in it? He did ask himself the question, and he finally answered it in the affirmative. He had beaten Joseph Mason once in a good stand-up fight; and having done so, having thus made the matter his own, it was necessary to his comfort that he should beat him again, if another fight were to be fought. Lady Mason was his client, and all the associations of his life taught him to be true to her as such.

And as we are thus searching into his innermost heart we must say more than this. Mrs. Furnival perhaps had no sufficient grounds for those terrible fears of hers; but nevertheless the mistress of Orley Farm was very comely in the eyes of the lawyer. Her eyes, when full of tears, were very bright, and her hand, as it lay in his, was very soft. He laid out for himself no scheme of wickedness with reference to her; he purposely entertained no thoughts which he knew to be wrong; but, nevertheless, he did feel that he liked to have her by him, that he liked to be her adviser and friend, that he liked to wipe the tears from those eyes—not by a material handkerchief from his pocket, but by immaterial manly sympathy from his bosom; and that he liked also to feel the pressure of that hand. Mrs. Furnival had become solid, and heavy, and red; and though he himself was solid, and heavy, and red also—more so, indeed, in proportion than his poor wife, for his redness, as I have said before, had almost reached a purple hue; nevertheless his eye loved to look upon the beauty of a lovely woman, his ear loved to hear the tone of her voice, and his hand loved to meet the soft ripeness of her touch. It was very wrong that it should have been so, but the case is not without a parallel.

And therefore he made up his mind that he would not desert Lady Mason. He would not desert her; but how would he set about the fighting that would be necessary in her behalf? He was well aware of this, that if he fought at all, he must fight now. It would not do to let the matter go on till she should be summoned to defend herself. Steps which might now be available would be altogether unavailable in two or three months' time— would be so, perhaps, if he allowed two or three weeks to pass idly by him. Mr. Round, luckily, was not disposed to hurry his proceedings; nor, as far as he was concerned, was there any bitterness of antagonism. But with both Mason and Dockwrath there would be hot haste, and hotter malice. From those who were really her enemies she could expect no quarter.

He was to return on that evening to Noningsby, and on the following day he would go over to The Cleeve. He knew that Lady Mason was staying there; but his object in making that visit would not be merely that he might see her, but also that he might speak to Sir Peregrine, and learn how far the baronet was inclined to support his neighbour in her coming tribulation. He would soon be able to ascertain what Sir Peregrine really thought—whether he suspected the possibility of any guilt; and he would ascertain also what was the general feeling in the neighbourhood of Hamworth. It would be a great thing if he could spread abroad a conviction that she was an injured woman. It would be a great thing even if he could make it known that the great people of the neighbourhood so thought. The jurymen of Alston would be mortal men; and it might be possible that they should be imbued with a favourable bias on the subject before they assembled in their box for its consideration.

He wished that he knew the truth in the matter; or rather he wished he could know whether or no she were innocent, without knowing whether or no she were guilty. The fight in his hands would be conducted on terms so much more glorious if he could feel sure of her innocence. But then if he attempted that, and she were not innocent, all might be sacrificed by the audacity of his proceedings. He could not venture that, unless he were sure of his ground. For a moment or two he thought that he would ask her the question. He said to himself that he could forgive the fault. That it had been repented ere this he did not doubt, and it would be sweet to say to her that it was very grievous, but that yet it might be forgiven. It would be sweet to feel that she was in his hands, and that he would treat her with mercy and kindness. But then a hundred other thoughts forbade him to think more of this. If she had been, guilty,—if she declared her guilt to him,—would not restitution be necessary? In that case her son must know it, and all the world must know it. Such a confession would be incompatible with that innocence before the world which it was necessary that she should maintain. Moreover, he must be able to proclaim aloud his belief in her innocence; and how could he do that, knowing her to be guilty—knowing that she also knew that he had such knowledge? It was impossible that he should ask any such question, or admit of any such confidence.

It would be necessary, if the case did come to a trial, that she should employ some attorney. The matter must come into the barrister's hands in the usual way, through a solicitor's house, and it would be well that the person employed should have a firm faith in his client. What could he say—he, as a barrister—if the attorney suggested to him that the lady might possibly be guilty? As he thought of all these things he almost dreaded the difficulties before him.

He rang the bell for Crabwitz,—the peculiar bell which Crabwitz was bound to answer,—having first of all gone through a little ceremony with his cheque-book. Crabwitz entered, still sulky in his demeanour, for as yet the old anger had not been appeased, and it was still a doubtful matter in the clerk's mind whether or no it might not be better for him to seek a master who would better appreciate his services. A more lucrative position it might be difficult for him to find; but money is not everything, as Crabwitz said to himself more than once.

"Crabwitz," said Mr. Furnival, looking with a pleasant face at his clerk, "I am leaving town this evening, and I shall be absent for the next ten days. If you like you can go away for a holiday."

"It's rather late in the season now, sir," said Crabwitz, gloomily, as though he were determined not to be pleased.

"It is a little late, as you say; but I really could not manage it earlier. Come, Crabwitz, you and I should not quarrel. Your work has been a little hard, but then so has mine also."

"I fancy you like it, sir."

"Ha! ha! Like it, indeed! But so do you like it—in its way. Come, Crabwitz, you have been an excellent servant to me; and I don't think that, on the whole, I have been a bad master to you."

"I am making no complaint, sir."

"But you're cross because I've kept you in town a little too long. Come, Crabwitz, you must forget all that. You have worked very hard this year past. Here is a cheque for fifty pounds. Get out of town for a fortnight or so, and amuse yourself."

"I'm sure I'm very much obliged, sir," said Crabwitz, putting out his hand and taking the cheque. He felt that his master had got the better of him, and he was still a little melancholy on that account. He would have valued his grievance at that moment almost more than the fifty pounds, especially as by the acceptance of it he surrendered all right to complain for some considerable time to come.

"By-the-by, Crabwitz," said Mr. Furnival, as the clerk was about to leave the room.

"Yes, sir," said Crabwitz.

"You have never chanced to hear of an attorney named Dockwrath, I suppose?"

"What! in London, Mr. Furnival?"

"No; I fancy he has no place of business in town. He lives I know at Hamworth."

"It's he you mean, sir, that is meddling in this affair of Lady Mason's."

"What! you have heard of that; have you?"

"Oh! yes, sir. It's being a good deal talked about in the profession. Messrs. Round and Crook's leading young man was up here with me the other day, and he did say a good deal about it. He's a very decent young man, considering his position, is Smart."

"And he knows Dockwrath, does he?"

"Well, sir, I can't say that he knows much of the man; but Dockwrath has been at their place of business pretty constant of late, and he and Mr. Matthew seem thick enough together."

"Oh! they do; do they?"

"So Smart tells me. I don't know how it is myself, sir. I don't suppose this Dockwrath is a very—"

"No, no; exactly. I dare say not. You've never seen him yourself, Crabwitz?"

"Who, sir? I, sir? No, sir, I've never set eyes on the man, sir. From all I hear it's not very likely he should come here; and I'm sure it is not at all likely that I should go to him."

Mr. Furnival sat thinking awhile, and the clerk stood waiting opposite to him, leaning with both his hands upon the table. "You don't know any one in the neighbourhood of Hamworth, I suppose?" Mr. Furnival said at last.

"Who, sir? I, sir? Not a soul, sir. I never was there in my life."

— "I'll tell you why I ask. I strongly suspect that that man Dockwrath is at some very foul play." And then he told to his clerk so much of the whole story of Lady Mason and her affairs as he chose that he should know. "It is plain enough that he may give Lady Mason a great deal of annoyance," he ended by saying.

"There's no doubting that, sir," said Crabwitz. "And, to tell the truth, I believe his mind is made up to do it."

"You don't think that anything could be done by seeing him? Of course Lady Mason has got nothing to compromise. Her son's estate is as safe as my hat; but—"

"The people at Round's think it isn't quite so safe, sir."

"Then the people at Round's know nothing about it. But Lady Mason is so averse to legal proceedings that it would be worth her while to have matters settled. You understand?"

"Yes, sir; I understand. Would not an attorney be the best person, sir?"

"Not just at present, Crabwitz. Lady Mason is a very dear friend of mine—"

"Yes, sir; we know that," said Crabwitz.

"If you could make any pretence for running down to Hamworth—change of air, you know, for a week or so. It's a beautiful country; just the place you like. And you might find out whether anything could be done, eh?"

Mr. Crabwitz was well aware, from the first, that he did not get fifty pounds for nothing.

CHAPTER XXVI
WHY SHOULD I NOT?

A day or two after his conversation with Crabwitz, as described in the last chapter, Mr. Furnival was driven up to the door of Sir Peregrine Orme's house in a Hamworth fly. He had come over by train from Alston on purpose to see the baronet, whom he found seated in his library. At that very moment he was again asking himself those questions which he had before asked as he was walking up and down his own dining-room. "Why should I not?" he said to himself,—"unless, indeed, it will make her unhappy." And then the barrister was shown into his room, muffled up to his eyes in his winter clothing.

Sir Peregrine and Mr. Furnival were well known to each other, and had always met as friends. They had been interested on the same side in the first Orley Farm Case, and possessed a topic of sympathy in their mutual dislike to Joseph Mason of Groby Park. Sir Peregrine therefore was courteous, and when he learned the subject on which he was to be consulted he became almost more than courteous.

"Oh! yes; she's staying here, Mr. Furnival. Would you like to see her?"

"Before I leave I shall be glad to see her, Sir Peregrine; but if I am justified in regarding you as specially her friend, it may perhaps be well that I should first have some conversation with you." Sir Peregrine in answer to this declared that Mr. Furnival certainly would be so justified; that he did regard himself as Lady Mason's special friend, and that he was ready to hear anything that the barrister might have to say to him.

Many of the points of this case have already been named so often, and will, I fear, be necessarily named so often again that I will spare the repetition when it is possible. Mr. Furnival on this occasion told Sir Peregrine—not all that he had heard, but all that he thought it necessary to tell, and soon became fully aware that in the baronet's mind there was not the slightest shadow of suspicion that Lady Mason could have been in any way to blame. He, the baronet, was thoroughly convinced that Mr. Mason was the great sinner in this matter, and that he was prepared to harass an innocent and excellent lady from motives of disappointed cupidity and long-sustained malice, which made him seem in Sir Peregrine's eyes a being almost too vile for humanity. And of Dockwrath he thought almost as badly—only that Dockwrath was below the level of his thinking. Of Lady Mason he spoke as an excellent and beautiful woman driven to misery by unworthy persecution; and so spoke with an enthusiasm that was surprising to Mr. Furnival. It was very manifest that she would not want for friendly countenance, if friendly countenance could carry her through her difficulties.

There was no suspicion against Lady Mason in the mind of Sir Peregrine, and Mr. Furnival was careful not to arouse any such feeling. When he found that the baronet spoke of her as being altogether pure and good, he also spoke of her in the same tone; but in doing so his game was very difficult. "Let him do his worst, Mr. Furnival," said Sir Peregrine; "and let her remain tranquil; that is my advice to Lady Mason. It is not possible that he can really injure her."

"It is possible that he can do nothing—very probable that he can do nothing; but nevertheless, Sir Peregrine—"

"I would have no dealing with him or his. I would utterly disregard them. If he, or they, or any of them choose to take steps to annoy her, let her attorney manage that in the usual way. I am no lawyer myself, Mr. Furnival, but that I think is the manner in which things of this kind should be arranged. I do not know whether they have still the power of disputing the will, but if so, let them do it."

Gradually, by very slow degrees, Mr. Furnival made Sir Peregrine understand that the legal doings now threatened were not of that nature;—that Mr. Mason did not now talk of proceeding at law for the recovery of the property, but for the punishment of his father's widow as a criminal; and at last the dreadful word "forgery" dropped from his lips.

"Who dares to make such a charge as that?" demanded the baronet, while fire literally flashed from his eyes in his anger. And when he was told that Mr. Mason did make such a charge he called him "a mean, unmanly dastard." "I do not believe that he would dare to make it against a man," said Sir Peregrine.

But there was the fact of the charge—the fact that it had been placed in the hands of respectable attorneys, with instructions to them to press it on—and the fact also that the evidence by which that charge was to be supported possessed at any rate a *primâ facie* appearance of strength. All that it was necessary to explain to Sir Peregrine, as it would also be necessary to explain it to Lady Mason.

"Am I to understand, then, that you also think—?" began Sir Peregrine.

"You are not to understand that I think anything injurious to the lady; but I do fear that she is in a position of much jeopardy, and that great care will be necessary."

"Good heavens! Do you mean to say that an innocent person can under such circumstances be in danger in this country?"

"An innocent person, Sir Peregrine, may be in danger of very great annoyance, and also of very great delay in proving that innocence. Innocent people have died under the weight of such charges. We must remember that she is a woman, and therefore weaker than you or I."

"Yes, yes; but still—. You do not say that you think she can be in any real danger?" It seemed, from the tone of the old man's voice, as though he were almost angry with Mr. Furnival for supposing that such could be the case. "And you intend to tell her all this?" he asked.

"I fear that, as her friend, neither you nor I will be warranted in keeping her altogether in the dark. Think what her feelings would be if she were summoned before a magistrate without any preparation!"

"No magistrate would listen to such a charge," said Sir Peregrine.

"In that he must be guided by the evidence."

"I would sooner throw up my commission than lend myself in any way to a proceeding so iniquitous."

This was all very well, and the existence of such a feeling showed great generosity, and perhaps also poetic chivalry on the part of Sir Peregrine Orme; but it was not the way of the world, and so Mr. Furnival was obliged to explain. Magistrates would listen to the charge—would be forced to listen to the charge,—if the evidence were apparently sound. A refusal on the part of a magistrate to do so would not be an act of friendship to Lady Mason, as Mr. Furnival endeavoured to explain. "And you wish to see her?" Sir Peregrine asked at last.

"I think she should be told; but as she is in your house, I will, of course, do nothing in which you do not concur." Upon which Sir Peregrine rang the bell and desired the servant to take his compliments to Lady Mason and beg her attendance in the library if it were quite convenient. "Tell her," said Sir Peregrine, "that Mr. Furnival is here."

When the message was given to her she was seated with Mrs. Orme, and at the moment she summoned strength to say that she would obey the invitation, without displaying any special emotion while the servant was in the room; but when the door was shut, her friend looked at her and saw that she was as pale as death. She was pale and her limbs quivered, and that look of agony, which now so often marked her face, was settled on her brow. Mrs. Orme had never yet seen her with such manifest signs of suffering as she wore at this instant.

"I suppose I must go to them," she said, slowly rising from her seat; and it seemed to Mrs. Orme that she was forced to hold by the table to support herself.

"Mr. Furnival is a friend, is he not?"

"Oh, yes! a kind friend, but—"

"They shall come in here if you like it better, dear."

"Oh, no! I will go to them. It would not do that I should seem so weak. What must you think of me to see me so?"

"I do not wonder at it, dear," said Mrs. Orme, coming round to her; "such cruelty would kill me. I wonder at your strength rather than your weakness." And then she kissed her. What was there about the woman that had made all those fond of her that came near her?

Mrs. Orme walked with her across the hall, and left her only at the library door. There she pressed her hand and again kissed her, and then Lady Mason turned the handle of the door and entered the room. Mr. Furnival, when he looked at her, was startled by the pallor of her face, but nevertheless he thought that she had never looked so beautiful. "Dear Lady Mason," said he, "I hope you are well."

Sir Peregrine advanced to her and handed her over to his own arm-chair. Had she been a queen in distress she could not have been treated with more gentle deference. But she never seemed to count upon this, or in any way to assume it as her right. I should accuse her of what I regard as a sin against all good taste were I to say that she was humble in her demeanour; but there was a soft meekness about her, an air of feminine dependence, a proneness to lean and almost to cling as she leaned, which might have been felt as irresistible by any man. She was a woman to know in her deep sorrow rather than in her joy and happiness; one with whom one would love to weep rather than to rejoice. And, indeed, the present was a time with her for weeping, not for rejoicing.

Sir Peregrine looked as though he were her father as he took her hand, and the barrister immediately comforted himself with the remembrance of the baronet's great age. It was natural, too, that Lady Mason should hang on him in his own house. So Mr. Furnival contented himself at the first moment with touching her hand and hoping that she was well. She answered hardly a word to either of them, but she attempted to smile as she sat down, and murmured something about the trouble she was giving them.

"Mr. Furnival thinks it best that you should be made aware of the steps which are being taken by Mr. Mason of Groby Park," began Sir Peregrine. "I am no lawyer myself, and therefore of course I cannot put my advice against his."

"I am sure that both of you will tell me for the best," she said.

"In such a matter as this it is right that you should be guided by him. That he is as firmly your friend as I am there can be no doubt."

"I believe Lady Mason trusts me in that," said the lawyer.

"Indeed I do; I would trust you both in anything," she said.

"And there can be no doubt that he must be able to direct you for the best. I say so much at the first, because I myself so thoroughly despise that man in Yorkshire,—I am so convinced that anything which his malice may prompt him to do must be futile, that I could not myself have thought it needful to pain you by what must now be said."

This was a dreadful commencement, but she bore it, and even was relieved by it. Indeed, no tale that Mr. Furnival could have to tell after such an exordium would be so bad as that which she had feared as the possible result of his visit. He might have come there to let her know that she was at once to be carried away—immediately to be taken to her trial—perhaps to be locked up in gaol. In her ignorance of the law she could only imagine what might or might not happen to her at any moment, and therefore the words which Sir Peregrine had spoken relieved her rather than added to her fears.

And then Mr. Furnival began his tale, and gradually put before her the facts of the matter. This he did with a choice of language and a delicacy of phraseology which were admirable, for he made her clearly understand the nature of the accusation which was brought against her without using any word which was in itself harsh in its bearing. He said nothing about fraud, or forgery, or false evidence, but he made it manifest to her that Joseph Mason had now instructed his lawyer to institute a criminal proceeding against her for having forged a codicil to her husband's will.

"I must bear it as best I may," she said. "May the Lord give me strength to bear it!"

"It is terrible to think of," said Sir Peregrine; "but nobody can doubt how it will end. You are not to suppose that Mr. Furnival intends to express any doubt as to your ultimate triumph. What we fear for you is the pain you must endure before this triumph comes."

Ah, if that were all! As the baronet finished speaking she looked furtively into the lawyer's face to see how far the meaning of these smooth words would be supported by what she might read there. Would he also think that a final triumph did certainly await her? Sir Peregrine's real opinion was easily to be learned, either from his countenance or from his words; but it was not so with Mr. Furnival. In Mr. Furnival's face, and from Mr. Furnival's words, could be learned only that which Mr. Furnival wished to declare. He saw that glance, and fully understood it; and he knew instinctively, on the spur of the moment, that he must now either assure her by a lie, or break down all her hopes by the truth. That final triumph was not certain to her—was very far from certain! Should he now be honest to his friend, or dishonest? One great object with him was to secure the support which Sir Peregrine could give by his weight in the county; and therefore, as Sir Peregrine was present, it was needful that he should be dishonest. Arguing thus he looked the lie, and Lady Mason derived more comfort from that look than from all Sir Peregrine's words.

And then those various details were explained to her which Mr. Furnival understood that Mr. Dockwrath had picked up. They went into that matter of the partnership deed, and questions were asked as to the man Kenneby and the woman Bolster. They might both, Lady Mason said, have been witnesses to half a dozen deeds on that same day, for aught she knew to the contrary. She had been present with Sir Joseph, as far as she could now remember, during the whole of that morning, "in and out, Sir Peregrine, as you can understand." Sir Peregrine said that he did understand perfectly. She did know that Mr. Usbech had been there for many hours that day, probably from ten to two or three, and no doubt therefore much business was transacted. She herself remembered nothing but the affair of the will; but then that was natural, seeing that there was no other affair in which she had specially interested herself.

"No doubt these people did witness both the deeds," said Sir Peregrine. "For myself, I cannot conceive how that wretched man can be so silly as to spend his money on such a case as this."

"He would do anything for revenge," said Mr. Furnival.

And then Lady Mason was allowed to go back to the drawing-room, and what remained to be said was said between the two gentlemen alone. Sir Peregrine was very anxious that his own attorneys should be employed, and he named Messrs. Slow and Bideawhile, than whom there were no more respectable men in the whole profession. But then Mr. Furnival feared that they were too respectable. They might look at the matter in so straightforward a light as to fancy their client really guilty; and what might happen then? Old Slow would not conceal the truth for all the baronets in England—no, nor for all the pretty women. The touch of Lady Mason's hand and the tear in her eye would be nothing to old Slow. Mr. Furnival, therefore, was obliged to explain that Slow and Bideawhile did not undertake that sort of business.

"But I should wish it to be taken up through them. There must be some expenditure, Mr. Furnival, and I should prefer that they should arrange about that."

Mr. Furnival made no further immediate objection, and consented at last to having an interview with one of the firm on the subject, provided, of course, that that member of the firm came to him at his chambers. And then he took his leave. Nothing positive had been done, or even settled to be done, on this morning; but the persons most interested in the matter had been made to understand that the affair was taking an absolute palpable substance, and that steps must be taken—indeed would be taken almost immediately. Mr. Furnival, as he left the house, resolved to employ the attorneys whom he might think best adapted for the purpose. He would settle that matter with Slow and Bideawhile afterwards.

And then, as he returned to Noningsby, he wondered at his persistence in the matter. He believed that his client had been guilty; he believed that this codicil was no real instrument made by Sir Joseph Mason. And so believing, would it not be better for him to wash his hands of the whole affair? Others did not think so, and would it not be better that such others should be her advisers? Was he not taking up for himself endless trouble and annoyance that could have no useful purpose? So he argued with himself, and yet by the time that he had reached Noningsby he had determined that he would stand by Lady Mason to the last. He hated that man Mason, as he declared to himself when providing himself with reasons for his resolve, and regarded his bitter, malicious justice as more criminal than any crime of which Lady Mason might have been guilty. And then as he leaned back in the railway carriage he still saw her pale face before him, still heard the soft tone of her voice, and was still melted by the tear in her eye. Young man, young friend of mine, who art now filled to the overflowing of thy brain with poetry, with chivalry, and love, thou seest seated opposite to thee there that grim old man, with long snuffy nose, with sharp piercing eyes, with scanty frizzled hairs. He is rich and cross, has been three times married, and has often quarrelled with his children. He is fond of his wine, and snores dreadfully after dinner. To thy seeming he is a dry, withered stick, from which all the sap of sentiment has been squeezed by the rubbing and friction of years. Poetry, the feeling if not the words of poetry,—is he not dead to it, even as the pavement is dead over which his wheels trundle? Oh, my young friend! thou art ignorant in this—as in most other things. He may not twitter of sentiment, as thou doest; nor may I trundle my hoop along the high road as do the little boys. The fitness of things forbids it. But that old man's heart is as soft as thine, if thou couldst but read it. The body dries up and withers away, and the bones grow old; the brain, too, becomes decrepit, as do the sight, the hearing, and the soul. But the heart that is tender once remains tender to the last.

Lady Mason, when she left the library, walked across the hall towards the drawing-room, and then she paused. She would fain remain alone for a while if it were possible, and therefore she turned aside into a small breakfast parlour, which was used every morning, but which was rarely visited afterwards during the day. Here she sat, leaving the door slightly open, so that she might know when Mr. Furnival left the baronet. Here she sat for a full hour, waiting—waiting—waiting. There was no sofa or lounging-chair in the room, reclining in which she could remain there half sleeping, sitting comfortably at her ease; but she placed herself near the table, and leaning there with her face upon her hand, she waited patiently till Mr. Furnival had gone. That her mind was full of thoughts I need hardly say, but yet the hour seemed very long to her. At last she heard the library door open, she heard Sir Peregrine's voice as he stood in the hall and shook hands with his departing visitor, she heard the sound of the wheels as the fly moved upon the gravel, and then she heard Sir Peregrine again shut the library door behind him.

She did not immediately get up from her chair; she still waited awhile, perhaps for another period of ten minutes, and then she noiselessly left the room, and moving quickly and silently across the hall she knocked at Sir Peregrine's door. This she did so gently that at first no answer was made to her. Then she knocked again, hardly louder but with a repeated rap, and Sir Peregrine summoned her to come in. "May I trouble you once more—for one moment?" she said.

"Certainly, certainly; it is no trouble. I am glad that you are here in the house at this time, that you may see me at any moment that you may wish."

"I do not know why you should be so good to me."

"Because you are in great grief, in undeserved grief, because—. Lady Mason, my services are at your command. I will act for you as I would for a—daughter."

"You hear now of what it is that they accuse me."

"Yes, he said; I do hear;" and as he spoke he came round so that he was standing near to her, but with his back to the fireplace. "I do hear, and I blush to think that there is a man in England, holding the position of a county magistrate, who can so forget all that is due to honesty, to humanity, and to self-respect."

"You do not then think that I have been guilty of this thing?"

"Guilty—I think you guilty! No, nor does he think so. It is impossible that he should think so. I am no more sure of my own innocence than of yours;" and as he spoke he took both her hands and looked into her face, and his eyes also were full of tears. "You may be sure of this, that neither I nor Edith will ever think you guilty."

"Dearest Edith," she said; she had never before called Sir Peregrine's daughter-in-law by her Christian name, and as she now did so she almost felt that she had sinned. But Sir Peregrine took it in good part. "She is dearest," he said; "and be sure of this, that she will be true to you through it all."

And so they stood for a while without further speech. He still held both her hands, and the tears still stood in his eyes. Her eyes were turned to the ground, and from them the tears were running fast. At first they ran silently, without audible sobbing, and Sir Peregrine, with his own old eyes full of salt water, hardly knew that she was weeping. But gradually the drops fell upon his hand, one by one at first, and then faster and faster; and soon there came a low sob, a sob all but suppressed, but which at last forced itself forth, and then her head fell upon his shoulder. "My dear," he said, himself hardly able to speak; "my poor dear, my ill-used dear!" and as she withdrew one hand from his, that she might press a handkerchief to her face, his vacant arm passed itself round her waist. "My poor, ill-used dear!" he said again, as he pressed her to his old heart, and leaning over her he kissed her lips.

So she stood for some few seconds, feeling that she was pressed close by the feeble pressure of his arm, and then she gradually sank through from his embrace, and fell upon her knees at his feet. She knelt at his feet, supporting herself with one arm upon the table, and with the other hand she still held his hand over which her head was bowed. "My friend," she said, still sobbing, and sobbing loudly now; "my friend, that God has sent me in my trouble." And then, with words that were wholly inaudible, she murmured some prayer on his behalf.

"I am better now," she said, raising herself quickly to her feet when a few seconds had passed. "I am better now," and she stood erect before him. "By God's mercy I will endure it; I think I can endure it now."

"If I can lighten the load —"

"You have lightened it—of half its weight; but, Sir Peregrine, I will leave this—"

"Leave this! go away from The Cleeve!"

"Yes; I will not destroy the comfort of your home by the wretchedness of my position. I will not—"

"Lady Mason, my house is altogether at your service. If you will be led by me in this matter, you will not leave it till this cloud shall have passed by you. You will be better to be alone now;" and then before she could answer him further, he led her to the door. She felt that it was better for her to be alone, and she hastened up the stairs to her own chamber.

"And why should I not?" said Sir Peregrine to himself, as he again walked the length of the library.

CHAPTER XXVII
COMMERCE

Lucius Mason was still staying at Noningsby when Mr. Furnival made his visit to Sir Peregrine, and on that afternoon he received a note from his mother. Indeed, there were three notes passed between them on that afternoon, for he wrote an answer to his mother, and then received a reply to that answer. Lady Mason told him that she did not intend to return home to the Farm quite immediately, and explained that her reason for not doing so was the necessity that she should have assistance and advice at this period of her trouble. She did not say that she misdoubted the wisdom of her son's counsels; but it appeared to him that she intended to signify to him that she did so, and he answered her in words that were sore and almost bitter. "I am sorry," he said, "that you and I cannot agree about a matter that is of such vital concern to both of us; but as it is so, we can only act as each thinks best, you for yourself and I for myself. I am sure, however, that you will believe that my only object is your happiness and your fair name, which is dearer to me than anything else in the world." In answer to this, she had written again immediately, filling her letter with sweet words of motherly love, telling him that she was sure, quite sure, of his affection and kind spirit, and excusing herself for not putting the matter altogether in his hands by saying that she was forced to lean on those who had supported her from the beginning—through that former trial which had taken place when he, Lucius, was yet a baby. "And, dearest Lucius, you must not be angry with me," she went on to say; "I am suffering much under this cruel persecution, but my sufferings would be more than doubled if my own boy quarrelled with me." Lucius, when he received this, flung up his head. "Quarrel with her," he said to himself; "nothing on earth would make me quarrel with her; but I cannot say that that is right which I think to be wrong." His feelings were good and honest, and kindly too in their way; but tenderness of heart was not his weakness. I should wrong him if I were to say that he was hard-hearted, but he flattered himself that he was just-hearted, which sometimes is nearly the same—as had been the case with his father before him, and was now the case with his half-brother Joseph.

The day after this was his last at Noningsby. He had told Lady Staveley that he intended to go, and though she had pressed his further stay, remarking that none of the young people intended to move till after twelfth-night, nevertheless he persisted. With the young people of the house themselves he had not much advanced himself; and altogether he did not find himself thoroughly happy in the judge's house. They were more thoughtless than he—as he thought; they did not understand him, and therefore he would leave them. Besides, there was a great day of hunting coming on, at which everybody was to take a part, and as he did not hunt that gave him another reason for going. "They have nothing to do but amuse themselves," he said to himself; "but I have a man's work before me, and a man's misfortunes. I will go home and face both."

In all this there was much of conceit, much of pride, much of deficient education,—deficiency in that special branch of education which England has imparted to the best of her sons, but which is now becoming out of fashion. He had never learned to measure himself against others,—I do not mean his knowledge or his book-acquirements, but the every-day conduct of his life,—and to perceive that that which is insignificant in others must be insignificant in himself also. To those around him at Noningsby his extensive reading respecting the Iapetidæ recommended him not at all, nor did his agricultural ambitions;—not even to Felix Graham, as a companion, though Felix Graham could see further into his character than did the others. He was not such as they were. He had not the unpretentious, self-controlling humour, perfectly free from all conceit, which was common to them. Life did not come easy to him, and the effort which he was ever making was always visible. All men should ever be making efforts, no doubt; but those efforts should not be conspicuous. But yet Lucius Mason was not a bad fellow, and young Staveley showed much want of discernment when he called him empty-headed and selfish. Those epithets were by no means applicable to him. That he was not empty-headed is certain; and he was moreover capable of a great self-sacrifice.

That his talents and good qualities were appreciated by one person in the house, seemed evident to Lady Staveley and the other married ladies of the party. Miss Furnival, as they all thought, had not found him empty-headed. And, indeed, it may be doubted whether Lady Staveley would have pressed his stay at Noningsby, had Miss Furnival been less gracious. Dear Lady Staveley was always living in a fever lest her only son, the light of her eyes, should fall irrevocably in love with some lady that was by no means good enough for him. Revocably in love he was daily falling; but some day he would go too deep, and the waters would close over his well-loved head. Now in her dear old favouring eyes Sophia Furnival was by no means good enough, and it had been quite clear that Augustus had become thoroughly lost in his attempts to bring about a match between Felix Graham and the barrister's daughter. In preparing the bath for his friend he had himself fallen bodily into the water. He was always at Miss Furnival's side as long as Miss Furnival would permit it. But it seemed to Lady Staveley that Miss Furnival, luckily, was quite as fond of having Lucius Mason at her side;—that of the two she perhaps preferred Lucius Mason. That her taste and judgment should be so bad was wonderful to Lady Staveley; but this depravity though wonderful was useful; and therefore Lucius Mason might have been welcome to remain at Noningsby.

It may, however, be possible that Miss Furnival knew what she was doing quite as well as Lady Staveley could know for her. In the first place she may possibly have thought it indiscreet to admit Mr. Staveley's attentions with too much freedom. She may have doubted their sincerity; or feared to give offence to the family, or Mr. Mason may in her sight have been the preferable suitor. That his gifts of intellect were at any rate equal to those of the other there can be no doubt. Then, his gifts of fortune were already his own, and for ought that Miss Furnival knew, might be equal to any that would ever appertain to the other gentleman. That Lady Staveley should think her swan better looking than Lady Mason's goose was very natural; but then Lady Mason would no doubt have regarded the two birds in an exactly opposite light. It is only fair to conceive that Miss Furnival was a better judge than either of them.

On the evening before his departure the whole party had been playing commerce; for the rule of the house during these holidays was this, that all the amusements brought into vogue were to be adapted to the children. If the grown-up people could adapt themselves to them, so much the better for them; if not, so much the worse; they must in such case provide for themselves. On the whole, the grown-up people seemed to live nearly as jovial a life as did the children. Whether the judge himself was specially fond of commerce I cannot say; but he persisted in putting in the whole pool, and played through the entire game, rigidly fighting for the same pool on behalf of a very small grandchild, who sat during the whole time on his knee. There are those who call cards the devil's books, but we will presume that the judge was of a different way of thinking.

On this special evening Sophia had been sitting next to Augustus,—a young man can always arrange these matters in his own house,—but had nevertheless lost all her lives early in the game. "I will not have any cheating to-night," she had said to her neighbour; "I will take my chance, and if I die, I die. One can die but once." And so she had died, three times indeed instead of once only, and had left the table. Lucius Mason also had died.

He generally did die the first, having no aptitude for a collection of kings or aces, and so they two came together over the fire in the second drawing-room, far away from the card-players. There was nothing at all remarkable in this, as Mr. Furnival and one or two others who did not play commerce were also there; but nevertheless they were separated from those of the party who were most inclined to criticise their conduct.

"So you are leaving to-morrow, Mr. Mason," said Sophia.

"Yes. I go home to-morrow after breakfast; to my own house, where for some weeks to come I shall be absolutely alone."

"Your mother is staying at The Cleeve, I think."

"Yes,—and intends remaining there as she tells me. I wish with all my heart she were at Orley Farm."

"Papa saw her yesterday. He went over to The Cleeve on purpose to see her; and this morning he has been talking to me about her. I cannot tell you how I grieve for her."

"It is very sad; very sad. But I wish she were in her own house. Under the circumstances as they now are, I think it would be better for her to be there than elsewhere. Her name has been disgraced—"

"No, Mr. Mason; not disgraced."

"Yes; disgraced. Mark you; I do not say that she has been disgraced; and pray do not suppose it possible that I should think so. But a great opprobrium has been thrown on her name, and it would be better, I think, that she should remain at home till she has cast it off from her. Even for myself, I feel it almost wrong to be here; nor would I have come had I known when I did come as much as I do know now."

"But no one can for a moment think that your mother has done anything that she should not have done."

"Then why do so many people talk of her as though she had committed a great crime? Miss Furnival, I know that she is innocent. I know it as surely as I know the fact of my own existence—"

"And we all feel the same thing."

"But if you were in my place,—if it were your father whose name was so bandied about in people's mouths, you would think that it behoved him to do nothing, to go nowhere, till he had forced the world to confess his innocence. And this is ten times stronger with regard to a woman. I have given my mother my counsel, and I regret to say that she differs from me."

"Why do you not speak to papa?"

"I did once. I went to him at his chambers, and he rebuked me."

"Rebuked you, Mr. Mason! He did not do that intentionally I am sure. I have heard him say that you are an excellent son."

"But nevertheless he did rebuke me. He considered that I was travelling beyond my own concerns, in wishing to interfere for the protection of my mother's name. He said that I should leave it to such people as the Staveleys and the Ormes to guard her from ignominy and disgrace."

"Oh, he did not mean that!"

"But to me it seems that it should be a son's first duty. They are talking of trouble and of cost. I would give every hour I have in the day, and every shilling I own in the world to save her from one week of such suffering as she now endures; but it cuts me to the heart when she tells me that because she is suffering, therefore she must separate herself from me. I think it would be better for her, Miss Furnival, to be staying at home with me, than to be at The Cleeve."

"The kindness of Mrs. Orme must be a great support to her."

"And why should not my kindness be a support to her,—or rather my affection? We know from whom all these scandals come. My desire is to meet that man in a court of law and thrust these falsehoods down his throat."

"Ah! but you are a man."

"And therefore I would take the burden from her shoulders. But no; she will not trust to me. The truth, Miss Furnival, is this, that she has not yet learned to think of me as a man. To her I am still the boy for whom she is bound to provide, not the son who should bear for her all her cares. As it is I feel that I do not dare again to trouble her with my advice."

"Grandmamma is dead," shouted out a shrill small voice from the card-table. "Oh, grandmamma, do have one of my lives. Look! I've got three," said another.

"Thank you, my dears; but the natural term of my existence has come, and I will not rebel against fate."

"Oh, grandmamma,—we'll let you have another grace."

"By no means, Charley. Indeed I am not clear that I am entitled to Christian burial, as it is."

"A case of felo de se, I rather think," said her son. "About this time of the night suicide does become common among the elders. Unfortunately for me, the pistol that I have been snapping at my own head for the last half-hour always hangs fire."

There was not much of love-making in the conversation which had taken place between young Mason and Sophia; not much at least up to this point; but a confidence had been established, and before he left her he did say a word or two that was more tender in its nature. "You must not be in dudgeon with me," he said, "for speaking to you of all this. Hitherto I have kept it all to myself, and perhaps I should still have done so."

"Oh no; do not say that."

"I am in great grief. It is dreadful to me to hear these things said, and as yet I have found no sympathy."

"I can assure you, Mr. Mason, that I do sympathise with you most sincerely. I only wish my sympathy could be of more value."

"It will be invaluable," he said, not looking at her, but fixing his eyes upon the fire, "if it be given with constancy from the first to the last of this sad affair."

"It shall be so given," said Miss Furnival, also looking at the fire.

"It will be tolerably long, and men will say cruel things of us. I can foresee this, that it will be very hard to prove to the world with certainty that there is no foundation whatever for these charges. If those who are now most friendly to us turn away from us—"

"I will never turn away from you, Mr. Mason."

"Then give me your hand on that, and remember that such a promise in my ears means much." He in his excitement had forgotten that there were others in the room who might be looking at them, and that there was a vista open upon them direct from all the eyes at the card-table; but she did not forget it. Miss Furnival could be very enthusiastic, but she was one of those who in her enthusiasm rarely forgot anything. Nevertheless, after a moment's pause, she gave him her hand. "There it is," she said; "and you may be sure of this, that with me also such a promise does mean something.

And now I will say good night." And so, having received the pressure of her hand, she left him.

"I will get you your candle," he said, and so he did.

"Good night, papa," she said, kissing her father. And then, with a slight muttered word to Lady Staveley, she withdrew, having sacrificed the remainder of that evening for the sake of acceding to Mr. Mason's request respecting her pledge. It could not be accounted strange that she should give her hand to the gentleman with whom she was immediately talking as she bade him good night.

"And now grandpapa is dead too," said Marian, "and there's nobody left but us three."

"And we'll divide," said Fanny Sebright; and so the game of commerce was brought to an end.

CHAPTER XXVIII
MONKTON GRANGE

During these days Peregrine Orme—though he was in love up to his very chin, seriously in love, acknowledging this matter to himself openly, pulling his hair in the retirement of his bedroom, and resolving that he would do that which he had hitherto in life always been successful in doing—ask, namely, boldly for that he wanted sorely—Peregrine Orme, I say, though he was in this condition, did not in these days neglect his hunting. A proper attendance upon the proceedings of the H. H. was the only duty which he had hitherto undertaken in return for all that his grandfather had done for him, and I have no doubt that he conceived that he was doing a duty in going hither and thither about the county to their most distant meets. At this period of the present season it happened that Noningsby was more central to the proceedings of the hunt than The Cleeve, and therefore he was enabled to think that he was remaining away from home chiefly on business. On one point, however, he had stoutly come to a resolution. That question should be asked of Madeline Staveley before he returned to his grandfather's house.

And now had arrived a special hunting morning,—special, because the meet was in some degree a show meet, appropriate for ladies, at a comfortable distance from Noningsby, and affording a chance of amusement to those who sat in carriages as well as to those on horseback. Monkton Grange was the well-known name of the place, a name perhaps dearer to the ladies than to the gentlemen of the country, seeing that show meets do not always give the best sport. Monkton Grange is an old farm-house, now hardly used as such, having been left, as regards the habitation, in the hands of a head labourer; but it still possesses the marks of ancient respectability and even of grandeur. It is approached from the high road by a long double avenue of elms, which still stand in all their glory. The road itself has become narrow, and the space between the side row of trees is covered by soft turf, up which those coming to the meet love to gallop, trying the fresh metal of their horses. And the old house itself is surrounded by a moat, dry indeed now for the most part, but nevertheless an evident moat, deep and well preserved, with a bridge over it which Fancy tells us must once have been a drawbridge. It is here, in front of the bridge, that the old hounds sit upon their haunches, resting quietly round the horses of the huntsmen, while the young dogs move about, and would wander if the whips allowed them—one of the fairest sights to my eyes that this fair country of ours can show. And here the sportsmen and ladies congregate by degrees, men from a distance in dog-carts generally arriving first, as being less able to calculate the time with accuracy. There is room here too in the open space for carriages, and there is one spot on which always stands old Lord Alston's chariot with the four posters; an ancient sportsman he, who still comes to some few favourite meets; and though Alston Court is but eight miles from the Grange, the post-horses always look as though they had been made to do their best, for his lordship likes to move fast even in his old age. He is a tall thin man, bent much with age, and apparently too weak for much walking; he is dressed from head to foot in a sportsman's garb, with a broad stiffly starched coloured handkerchief tied rigidly round his neck. One would say that old as he is he has sacrificed in no way to comfort. It is with difficulty that he gets into his saddle, his servant holding his rein and stirrup and giving him perhaps some other slight assistance; but when he is there, there he will remain all day, and when his old blood warms he will gallop along the road with as much hot fervour as his grandson. An old friend he of Sir Peregrine's. "And why is not your grandfather here to-day?" he said on this occasion to young Orme. "Tell him from me that if he fails us in this way, I shall think he is getting old." Lord Alston was in truth five years older than Sir Peregrine, but Sir Peregrine at this time was thinking of other things.

Monkton Grange.

And then a very tidy little modern carriage bustled up the road, a brougham made for a pair of horses which was well known to all hunting men in these parts. It was very unpretending in its colour and harness; but no vehicle more appropriate to its purpose ever carried two thorough-going sportsmen day after day about the country. In this as it pulled up under the head tree of the avenue were seated the two Miss Tristrams. The two Miss Tristrams were well known to the Hamworth Hunt—I will not merely say as fearless riders,—of most girls who hunt as much can be said as that; but they were judicious horsewomen; they knew when to ride hard, and when hard riding, as regarded any necessary for the hunt, would be absolutely thrown away. They might be seen for half the day moving about the roads as leisurely, or standing as quietly at the covert's side as might the seniors of the fields. But when the time for riding did come, when the hounds were really running—when other young ladies had begun to go home—then the Miss Tristrams were always there;—there or thereabouts, as their admirers would warmly boast.

Nor did they commence their day's work as did other girls who came out on hunting mornings. With most such it is clear to see that the object is pretty much the same here as in the ballroom. "Spectatum veniunt; veniunt spectentur ut ipsæ," as it is proper, natural, and desirable that they should do. By that word "spectatum" I would wish to signify something more than the mere use of the eyes. Perhaps an occasional word dropped here and there into the ears of a cavalier may be included in it; and the "spectentur" also may include a word so received. But the Miss Tristrams came for hunting. Perhaps there might be a slight shade of affectation in the manner by which they would appear to come for that and that only. They would talk of nothing else, at any rate during the earlier portion of the day, when many listeners were by. They were also well instructed as to the country to be drawn, and usually had a word of import to say to the huntsman. They were good-looking, fair-haired girls, short in size, with bright gray eyes, and a short decisive mode of speaking. It must not be imagined that they were altogether indifferent to such matters as are dear to the hearts of other girls. They were not careless as to admiration, and if report spoke truth of them were willing enough to establish themselves in the world; but all their doings of that kind had a reference to their favourite amusement, and they would as soon have thought of flirting with men who did not hunt as some other girls would with men who did not dance.

I do not know that this kind of life had been altogether successful with them, or that their father had been right to permit it. He himself had formerly been a hunting man, but he had become fat and lazy, and the thing had dropped away from him. Occasionally he did come out with them, but when he did not do so some other senior of the field would have them nominally under charge; but practically they were as independent when going across the country as the young men who accompanied them. I have expressed a doubt whether this life was successful with them, and indeed such doubt was expressed by many of their neighbours. It had been said of each of them for the last three years that she was engaged, now to this man, and then to that other; but neither this man nor that other had yet made good the assertion, and now people were beginning to say that no man was engaged to either of them. Hunting young ladies are very popular in the hunting-field; I know no place in which girls receive more worship and attention; but I am not sure but they may carry their enthusiasm too far for their own interests, let their horsemanship be as perfect as it may be.

The two girls on this occasion sat in their carriage till the groom brought up their horses, and then it was wonderful to see with what ease they placed themselves in their saddles. On such occasions they admitted no aid from the gentlemen around them, but each stepping for an instant on a servant's hand, settled herself in a moment on horseback. Nothing could be more perfect than the whole thing, but the wonder was that Mr. Tristram should have allowed it.

The party from Noningsby consisted of six or seven on horseback, besides those in the carriage. Among the former there were the two young ladies, Miss Furnival and Miss Staveley, and our friends Felix Graham, Augustus Staveley, and Peregrine Orme. Felix Graham was not by custom a hunting man, as he possessed neither time nor money for such a pursuit; but to-day he was mounted on his friend Staveley's second horse, having expressed his determination to ride him as long as they two, the man and the horse, could remain together.

"I give you fair warning," Felix had said, "if I do not spare my own neck, you cannot expect me to spare your horse's legs."

"You may do your worst," Staveley had answered. "If you give him his head, and let him have his own way, he won't come to grief, whatever you may do."

On their road to Monkton Grange, which was but three miles from Noningsby, Peregrine Orme had ridden by the side of Miss Staveley, thinking more of her than of the affairs of the hunt, prominent as they were generally in his thoughts. How should he do it, and when, and in what way should he commence the deed? He had an idea that it might be better for him if he could engender some closer intimacy between himself and Madeline before he absolutely asked the fatal question; but the closer intimacy did not seem to produce itself readily. He had, in truth, known Madeline Staveley for many years, almost since they were children together; but lately, during these Christmas holidays especially, there had not been between them that close conversational alliance which so often facilitates such an overture as that which Peregrine was now desirous of making. And, worse again, he had seen that there was such close conversational alliance between Madeline and Felix Graham. He did not on that account dislike the young barrister, or call him, even within his own breast, a snob or an ass. He knew well that he was neither the one nor the other; but he knew as well that he could be no fit match for Miss Staveley, and, to tell the truth, he did not suspect that either Graham or Miss Staveley would think of such a thing.

It was not jealousy that tormented him, so much as a diffidence in his own resources. He made small attempts which did not succeed, and therefore he determined that he would at once make a grand attempt. He would create himself an opportunity before he left Noningsby, and would do it even to-day on horseback, if he could find sufficient opportunity. In taking a determined step like that, he knew that he would not lack the courage.

"Do you mean to ride to-day," he said to Madeline, as they were approaching the bottom of the Grange avenue. For the last half-mile he had been thinking what he would say to her, and thinking in vain; and now, at the last moment, he could summon no words to his assistance more potent for his purpose than these.

"If you mean by riding, Mr. Orme, going across the fields with you and the Miss Tristrams, certainly not. I should come to grief, as you call it, at the first ditch."

"And that is just what I shall do," said Felix Graham, who was at her other side.

"Then, if you take my advice, you'll remain with us in the wood, and act as squire of dames. What on earth would Marian do if aught but good was to befall you?"

"Dear Marian! She gave me a special commission to bring her the fox's tail. Foxes' tails are just like ladies."

"Thank you, Mr. Graham. I've heard you make some pretty compliments, and that is about the prettiest."

"A faint heart will never win either the one or the other, Miss Staveley."

"Oh, ah, yes. That will do very well. Under these circumstances I will accept the comparison."

All of which very innocent conversation was overheard by Peregrine Orme, riding on the other side of Miss Staveley's horse. And why not? Neither Graham nor Miss Staveley had any objection. But how was it that he could not join in and take his share in it? He had made one little attempt at conversation, and that having failed he remained perfectly silent till they reached the large circle at the head of the avenue. "It's no use, this sort of thing," he said to himself. "I must do it at a blow, if I do it at all;" and then he rode away to the master of the hounds.

As our party arrived at the open space the Miss Tristrams were stepping out of their carriage, and they came up to shake hands with Miss Staveley.

"I am so glad to see you," said the eldest; "it is so nice to have some ladies out besides ourselves."

"Do keep up with us," said the second. "It's a very open country about here, and anybody can ride it." And then Miss Furnival was introduced to them. "Does your horse jump, Miss Furnival?"

"I really do not know," said Sophia; "but I sincerely trust that if he does, he will refrain to-day."

"Don't say so," said the eldest sportswoman. "If you'll only begin it will come as easy to you as going along the road;" and then, not being able to spare more of these idle moments, they both went off to their horses, walking as though their habits were no impediments to them, and in half a minute they were seated.

"What is Harriet on to-day?" asked Staveley of a constant member of the hunt. Now Harriet was the eldest Miss Tristram.

"A little brown mare she got last week. That was a terrible brush we had on Friday. You weren't out, I think. We killed in the open, just at the edge of Rotherham Common. Harriet was one of the few that was up, and I don't think the chestnut horse will be the better of it this season."

"That was the horse she got from Griggs?"

"Yes; she gave a hundred and fifty for him; and I'm told he was as nearly done on Friday as any animal you ever put your eyes on. They say Harriet cried when she got home." Now the gentleman who was talking about Harriet on this occasion was one with whom she would no more have sat down to table than with her own groom.

But though Harriet may have cried when she got home on that fatal Friday evening, she was full of the triumph of the hunt on this morning. It is not often that the hounds run into a fox and absolutely surround and kill him on the open ground, and when this is done after a severe run, there are seldom many there to see it. If a man can fairly take a fox's brush on such an occasion as that, let him do it; otherwise let him leave it to the huntsman. On the occasion in question it seems that Harriet Tristram might have done so, and some one coming second to her had been gallant enough to do it for her.

"Oh, my lord, you should have been out on Friday," she said to Lord Alston. "We had the prettiest thing I ever saw."

"A great deal too pretty for me, my dear."

"Oh, you who know the roads so well would certainly have been up. I suppose it was thirteen miles from Cobbleton's Bushes to Rotherham Common."

"Not much less, indeed," said his lordship, unwilling to diminish the lady's triumph. Had a gentleman made the boast his lordship would have demonstrated that it was hardly more than eleven.

"I timed it accurately from the moment he went away," said the lady, "and it was exactly fifty-seven minutes. The first part of it was awfully fast. Then we had a little check at Moseley Bottom. But for that, nobody could have lived through it. I never shall forget how deep it was coming up from there to Cringleton. I saw two men get off to ease their horses up the deep bit of plough; and I would have done so too, only my horse would not have stood for me to get up."

"I hope he was none the worse for it," said the sporting character who had been telling Staveley just now how she had cried when she got home that night.

"To tell the truth, I fear it has done him no good. He would not feed, you know, that night at all."

"And broke out into cold sweats," said the gentleman.

"Exactly," said the lady, not quite liking it, but still enduring with patience.

"Rather groggy on his pins the next morning?" suggested her friend.

"Very groggy," said Harriet, regarding the word as one belonging to fair sporting phraseology.

"And inclined to go very much on the points of his toes. I know all about it, Miss Tristram, as well as though I'd seen him."

"There's nothing but rest for it, I suppose."

"Rest and regular exercise—that's the chief thing; and I should give him a mash as often as three times a week. He'll be all right again in three or four weeks,—that is if he's sound, you know."

"Oh, as sound as a bell," said Miss Tristram.

"He'll never be the same horse on a road though," said the sporting gentlemen, shaking his head and whispering to Staveley.

And now the time had come at which they were to move. They always met at eleven; and at ten minutes past, to the moment, Jacob the huntsman would summons the old hounds from off their haunches. "I believe we may be moving, Jacob," said Mr. Williams, the master.

"The time be up," said Jacob, looking at a ponderous timekeeper that might with truth be called a hunting-watch; and then they all moved slowly away back from the Grange, down a farm-road which led to Monkton Wood, distant from the old house perhaps a quarter of a mile.

"May we go as far as the wood?" said Miss Furnival to Augustus. "Without being made to ride over hedges, I mean."

"Oh, dear, yes; and ride about the wood half the day. It will be an hour and a half before a fox will break—even if he ever breaks."

"Dear me! how tired you will be of us. Now do say something pretty, Mr. Staveley."

"It's not my *métier*. We shall be tired, not of you, but of the thing. Galloping up and down the same cuts in the wood for an hour and a half is not exciting; nor does it improve the matter much if we stand still, as one should do by rights."

"That would be very slow."

"You need not be afraid. They never do here. Everybody will be rushing about as though the very world depended on their galloping."

"I'm so glad; that's just what I like."

"Everybody except Lord Alston, Miss Tristram, and, the other old stagers. They will husband their horses, and come out as fresh at two o'clock as though they were only just out. There is nothing so valuable as experience in hunting."

"Do you think it nice seeing a young lady with so much hunting knowledge?"

"Now you want me to talk slander, but I won't do it. I admire the Miss Tristrams exceedingly, and especially Julia."

"And which is Julia?"

"The youngest; that one riding by herself."

"And why don't you go and express your admiration?"

"Ah, me! why don't we all express the admiration that we feel, and pour sweet praises into the ears of the lady that excites it? Because we are cowards, Miss Furnival, and are afraid even of such a weak thing as a woman."

"Dear me! I should hardly have thought that you would suffer from such terror as that."

"Because you don't quite know me, Miss Furnival."

"And Miss Julia Tristram is the lady that has excited it?"

"If it be not she, it is some other fair votary of Diana at present riding into Monkton Wood."

"Ah, now you are giving me a riddle to guess, and I never guess riddles. I won't even try at it. But they all seem to be stopping."

"Yes, they are putting the hounds into covert. Now if you want to show yourself a good sportsman, look at your watch. You see that Julia Tristram has got hers in her hand."

"What's that for?"

"To time the hounds; to see how long they'll be before they find. It's very pretty work in a small gorse, but in a great wood like this I don't care much for being so accurate. But for heaven's sake don't tell Julia Tristram; I should not have a chance if she thought I was so slack."

And now the hounds were scattering themselves in the wood, and the party rode up the centre roadway towards a great circular opening in the middle of it. Here it was the recognised practice of the horsemen to stand, and those who properly did their duty would stand there; but very many lingered at the gate, knowing that there was but one other exit from the wood, without overcoming the difficulty of a very intricate and dangerous fence.

"There be a gap, bain't there?" said one farmer to another, as they were entering.

"Yes, there be a gap, and young Grubbles broke his 'orse's back a getting over of it last year," said the second farmer.

"Did he though?" said the first; and so they both remained at the gate.

And others, a numerous body, including most of the ladies, galloped up and down the cross ways, because the master of the hounds and the huntsman did so. "D— — those fellows riding up and down after me wherever I go," said the master. "I believe they think I'm to be hunted." This seemed to be said more especially to Miss Tristram, who was always in the master's confidence; and I fear that the fellows alluded to included Miss Furnival and Miss Staveley.

And then there came the sharp, eager sound of a hound's voice; a single, sharp, happy opening bark, and Harriet Tristram was the first to declare that the game was found. "Just five minutes and twenty seconds, my lord," said Julia Tristram to Lord Alston. "That's not bad in a large wood like this."

"Uncommonly good," said his lordship. "And when are we to get out of it?"

"They'll be here for the next hour, I'm afraid," said the lady, not moving her horse from the place where she stood, though many of the more impetuous of the men were already rushing away to the gates. "I have seen a fox go away from here without resting a minute; but that was later in the season, at the end of February. Foxes are away from home then." All which observations showed a wonderfully acute sporting observation on the part of Miss Tristram.

And then the music of the dogs became fast and frequent, as they drove the brute across and along from one part of the large wood to another. Sure there is no sound like it for filling a man's heart with an eager desire to be at work. What may be the trumpet in battle I do not know, but I can imagine that it has the same effect. And now a few of them were standing on that wide circular piece of grass, when a sound the most exciting of them all reached their ears. "He's away!" shouted a whip from a corner of the wood. The good-natured beast, though as yet it was hardly past Christmas-time, had consented to bless at once so many anxious sportsmen, and had left the back of the covert with the full pack at his heels.

"There is no gate that way, Miss Tristram," said a gentleman.

"There's a double ditch and bank that will do as well," said she, and away she went directly after the hounds, regardless altogether of the gates. Peregrine Orme and Felix Graham, who were with her, followed close upon her track.

CHAPTER XXIX
BREAKING COVERT

"There's a double ditch and bank that will do as well," Miss Tristram had said when she was informed that there was no gate out of the wood at the side on which the fox had broken. The gentleman who had tendered the information might as well have held his tongue, for Miss Tristram knew the wood intimately, was acquainted with the locality of all its gates, and was acquainted also with the points at which it might be left, without the assistance of any gate at all, by those who were well mounted and could ride their horses. Therefore she had thus replied, "There's a double ditch and bank that will do as well." And for the double ditch and bank at the end of one of the grassy roadways Miss Tristram at once prepared herself.

"That's the gap where Grubbles broke his horse's back," said a man in a red coat to Peregrine Orme, and so saying he made up his wavering mind and galloped away as fast as his nag could carry him. But Peregrine Orme would not avoid a fence at which a lady was not afraid to ride; and Felix Graham, knowing little but fearing nothing, followed Peregrine Orme.

At the end of the roadway, in the middle of the track, there was the gap. For a footman it was doubtless the easiest way over the fence, for the ditch on that side was half filled up, and there was space enough left of the half-broken bank for a man's scrambling feet; but Miss Tristram at once knew that it was a bad place for a horse. The second or further ditch was the really difficult obstacle, and there was no footing in the gap from which a horse could take his leap. To the right of this the fence was large and required a good horse, but Miss Tristram knew her animal and was accustomed to large fences. The trained beast went well across on to the bank, poised himself there for a moment, and taking a second spring carried his mistress across into the further field apparently with ease. In that field the dogs were now running, altogether, so that a sheet might have covered them; and Miss Tristram, exulting within her heart and holding in her horse, knew that she had got away uncommonly well.

Peregrine Orme followed,—a little to the right of the lady's passage, so that he might have room for himself, and do no mischief in the event of Miss Tristram or her horse making any mistake at the leap. He also got well over. But, alas! in spite of such early success he was destined to see nothing of the hunt that day! Felix Graham, thinking that he would obey instructions by letting his horse do as he pleased, permitted the beast to come close upon Orme's track and to make his jump before Orme's horse had taken his second spring.

"Have a care," said Peregrine, feeling that the two were together on the bank, "or you'll shove me into the ditch." He however got well over.

Felix, attempting to "have a care" just when his doing so could be of no avail, gave his horse a pull with the curb as he was preparing for his second spring. The outside ditch was broad and deep and well banked up, and required that an animal should have all his power. It was at such a moment as this that he should have been left to do his work without injudicious impediment from his rider. But poor Graham was thinking only of Orme's caution, and attempted to stop the beast when any positive and absolute stop was out of the question. The horse made his jump, and, crippled as he was, jumped short. He came with his knees against the further bank, threw his rider, and then in his struggle to right himself rolled over him.

Felix felt at once that he was much hurt—that he had indeed come to grief; but still he was not stunned nor did he lose his presence of mind. The horse succeeded in gaining his feet, and then Felix also jumped up and even walked a step or two towards the head of the animal with the object of taking the reins. But he found that he could not raise his arm, and he found also that he could hardly breathe.

Both Peregrine and Miss Tristram looked back. "There's nothing wrong I hope," said the lady; and then she rode on. And let it be understood that in hunting those who are in advance generally do ride on. The lame and the halt and the wounded, if they cannot pick themselves up, have to be picked up by those who come after them. But Peregrine saw that there was no one else coming that way. The memory of young Grubbles' fate had placed an interdict on that pass out of the wood, which nothing short of the pluck and science of Miss Tristram was able to disregard. Two cavaliers she had carried with her. One she had led on to instant slaughter, and the other remained to look after his fallen brother-in-arms. Miss Tristram in the mean time was in the next field and had settled well down to her work.

"Are you hurt, old fellow?" said Peregrine, turning back his horse, but still not dismounting.

"Not much, I think," said Graham, smiling. "There's something wrong about my arm,—but don't you wait." And then he found that he spoke with difficulty.

"Can you mount again?"

"I don't think I'll mind that. Perhaps I'd better sit down." Then Peregrine Orme knew that Graham was hurt, and jumping off his own horse he gave up all hope of the hunt.

"Here, you fellow, come and hold these horses." So invoked, a boy who in following the sport had got as far as this ditch did as he was bid, and scrambled over. "Sit down, Graham: there; I'm afraid you are hurt. Did he roll on you?" But Felix merely looked up into his face,—still smiling. He was now very pale, and for the moment could not speak. Peregrine came close to him, and gently attempted to raise the wounded limb; whereupon Graham shuddered, and shook his head.

"I fear it is broken," said Peregrine. Graham nodded his head, and raised his left hand to his breast; and Peregrine then knew that something else was amiss also.

I don't know any feeling more disagreeable than that produced by being left alone in a field, when out hunting, with a man who has been very much hurt and who is incapable of riding or walking. The hurt man himself has the privilege of his infirmities and may remain quiescent; but you, as his only attendant, must do something. You must for the moment do all, and if you do wrong the whole responsibility lies on your shoulders. If you leave a wounded man on the damp ground, in the middle of winter, while you run away, five miles perhaps, to the next doctor, he may not improbably— as you then think—be dead before you come back. You don't know the way; you are heavy yourself, and your boots are very heavy. You must stay therefore; but as you are no doctor you don't in the least know what is the amount of the injury. In your great trouble you begin to roar for assistance; but the woods re-echo your words, and the distant sound of the huntsman's horn, as he summons his hounds at a check, only mocks your agony.

But Peregrine had a boy with him. "Get upon that horse," he said at last; "ride round to Farmer Griggs, and tell them to send somebody here with a spring cart. He has got a spring cart I know;—and a mattress in it."

"But I hain't no gude at roiding like," said the boy, looking with dismay at Orme's big horse.

"Then run; that will be better, for you can go through the wood. You know where Farmer Griggs lives. The first farm the other side of the Grange."

"Ay, ay, I knows where Farmer Griggs lives well enough."

"Run, then; and if the cart is here in half an hour I'll give you a sovereign."

Inspirited by the hopes of such wealth, golden wealth, wealth for a lifetime, the boy was quickly back over the fence, and Peregrine was left alone with Felix Graham. He was now sitting down, with his feet hanging into the ditch, and Peregrine was kneeling behind him. "I am sorry I can do nothing more," said he; "but I fear we must remain here till the cart comes."

"I am—so—vexed—about your hunt," said Felix, gasping as he spoke. He had in fact broken his right arm which had been twisted under him as the horse rolled, and two of his ribs had been staved in by the pommel of his saddle. Many men have been worse hurt and have hunted again before the end of the season, but the fracture of three bones does make a man uncomfortable for the time. "Now the cart—is—sent for, couldn't you—go on?" But it was not likely that Peregrine Orme would do that. "Never mind me," he said. "When a fellow is hurt he has always to do as he's told. You'd better have a drop of sherry. Look here: I've got a flask at my saddle. There; you can support yourself with that arm a moment. Did you ever see horses stand so quiet. I've got hold of yours, and now I'll fasten them together. I say, Whitefoot, you don't kick, do you?" And then he contrived to picket the horses to two branches, and having got out his case of sherry, poured a small modicum into the silver mug which was attached to the apparatus and again supported Graham while he drank. "You'll be as right as a trivet by-and-by; only you'll have to make Noningsby your headquarters for the next six weeks." And then the same idea passed through the mind of each of them;—how little a man need be pitied for such a misfortune if Madeline Staveley would consent to be his nurse.

Felix Graham in trouble.

No man could have less surgical knowledge than Peregrine Orme, but nevertheless he was such a man as one would like to have with him if one came to grief in such a way. He was cheery and up-hearted, but at the same time gentle and even thoughtful. His voice was pleasant and his touch could be soft. For many years afterwards Felix remembered how that sherry had been held to his lips, and how the young heir of The Cleeve had knelt behind him in his red coat, supporting him as he became weary with waiting, and saying pleasant words to him through the whole. Felix Graham was a man who would remember such things.

In running through the wood the boy first encountered three horsemen. They were the judge, with his daughter Madeline and Miss Furnival. "There be a mon there who be a'most dead," said the boy, hardly able to speak from want of breath. "I be agoing for Farmer Griggs' cart." And then they stopped him a moment to ask for some description, but the boy could tell them nothing to indicate that the wounded man was one of their friends. It might however be Augustus, and so the three rode on quickly towards the fence, knowing nothing of the circumstances of the ditches which would make it out of their power to get to the fallen sportsman.

But Peregrine heard the sound of the horses and the voices of the horsemen. "By Jove, there's a lot of them coming down here," said he. "It's the judge and two of the girls. Oh, Miss Staveley, I'm so glad you've come. Graham has had a bad fall and hurt himself. You haven't a shawl, have you? the ground is so wet under him."

"It doesn't signify at all," said Felix, looking round and seeing the faces of his friends on the other side of the bank.

Madeline Staveley gave a slight shriek which her father did not notice, but which Miss Furnival heard very plainly. "Oh papa," she said, "cannot you get over to him?" And then she began to bethink herself whether it were possible that she should give up something of her dress to protect the man who was hurt from the damp muddy ground on which he lay.

"Can you hold my horse, dear," said the judge, slowly dismounting; for the judge, though he rode every day on sanitary considerations, had not a sportsman's celerity in leaving and recovering his saddle. But he did get down, and burdened as he was with a great-coat, he did succeed in crossing that accursed fence. Accursed it was from henceforward in the annals of the H. H., and none would ride it but dare-devils who professed themselves willing to go at anything. Miss Tristram, however, always declared that there was nothing in it—though she avoided it herself, whispering to her friends that she had led others to grief there, and might possibly do so again if she persevered.

"Could you hold the horse?" said Madeline to Miss Furnival; "and I will go for a shawl to the carriage." Miss Furnival declared that to the best of her belief she could not, but nevertheless the animal was left with her, and Madeline turned round and galloped back towards the carriage. She made her horse do his best though her eyes were nearly blinded with tears, and went straight on for the carriage, though she would have given much for a moment to hide those tears before she reached it.

"Oh, mamma! give me a thick shawl; Mr. Graham has hurt himself in the field, and is lying on the grass." And then in some incoherent and quick manner she had to explain what she knew of the accident before she could get a carriage-cloak out of the carriage. This, however, she did succeed in doing, and in some manner, very unintelligible to herself afterwards, she did gallop back with her burden. She passed the cloak over to Peregrine, who clambered up the bank to get it, while the judge remained on the ground, supporting the young barrister. Felix Graham, though he was weak, was not stunned or senseless, and he knew well who it was that had procured for him that comfort.

And then the carriage followed Madeline, and there was quite a concourse of servants and horses and ladies on the inside of the fence. But the wounded man was still unfortunately on the other side. No cart from Farmer Griggs made its appearance, though it was now more than half an hour since the boy had gone. Carts, when they are wanted in such sudden haste, do not make their appearance. It was two miles through the wood to Mr. Griggs's farm-yard, and more than three miles back by any route which the cart could take. And then it might be more than probable that in Farmer Griggs's establishment there was not always a horse ready in harness, or a groom at hand prepared to yoke him. Peregrine had become very impatient, and had more than once invoked a silent anathema on the farmer's head; but nevertheless there was no appearance of the cart.

"We must get him across the ditches into the carriage," said the judge.

"If Lady Staveley will let us do that," said Peregrine.

"The difficulty is not with Lady Staveley but with these nasty ditches," said the judge, for he had been up to his knees in one of them, and the water had penetrated his boots. But the task was at last done. Mrs. Arbuthnot stood up on the back seat of the carriage so that she might hold the horses, and the coachman and footman got across into the field. "It would be better to let me lie here all day," said Felix, as three of them struggled back with their burden, the judge bringing up the rear with two hunting-whips and Peregrine's cap. "How on earth any one would think of riding over such a place as that!" said the judge. But then, when he had been a young man it had not been the custom for barristers to go out hunting.

Madeline, as she saw the wounded man carefully laid on the back seat of the carriage, almost wished that she could have her mother's place that she might support him. Would they be careful enough with him? Would they remember how terrible must be the pain of that motion to one so hurt as he was? And then she looked into his face as he was made to lean back, and she saw that he still smiled. Felix Graham was by no means a handsome man; I should hardly sin against the truth if I were to say that he was ugly. But Madeline, as she looked at him now lying there utterly without colour but always with that smile on his countenance, thought that no face to her liking had ever been more gracious. She still rode close to him as they went down the grassy road, saying never a word. And Miss Furnival rode there also, somewhat in the rear, condoling with the judge as to his wet feet.

"Miss Furnival," he said, "when a judge forgets himself and goes out hunting he has no right to expect anything better. What would your father have said had he seen me clambering up the bank with young Orme's hunting-cap between my teeth? I positively did."

"He would have rushed to assist you," said Miss Furnival, with a little burst of enthusiasm which was hardly needed on the occasion. And then Peregrine came after them leading Graham's horse. He had been compelled to return to the field and ride both the horses back into the wood; one after the other, while the footman held them. That riding back over fences in cold blood is the work that really tries a man's nerve. And a man has to do it too when no one is looking on. How he does crane and falter and look about for an easy place at such a moment as that! But when the blood is cold, no places are easy.

The procession got back to Noningsby without adventure, and Graham as a matter of course was taken up to his bed. One of the servants had been despatched to Alston for a surgeon, and in an hour or two the extent of the misfortune was known. The right arm was broken—"very favourably," as the doctor observed. But two ribs were broken—"rather unfavourably." There was some talk of hæmorrhage and inward wounds, and Sir Jacob from Saville Row was suggested by Lady Staveley. But the judge, knowing the extent of Graham's means, made some further preliminary inquiries, and it was considered that Sir Jacob would not be needed—at any rate not as yet.

"Why don't they send for him?" said Madeline to her mother with rather more than her wonted energy.

"Your papa does not think it necessary, my dear. It would be very expensive, you know."

"But, mamma, would you let a man die because it would cost a few pounds to cure him?"

"My dear, we all hope that Mr. Graham won't die—at any rate not at present. If there be any danger you may be sure that your papa will send for the best advice."

But Madeline was by no means satisfied. She could not understand economy in a matter of life and death. If Sir Jacob's coming would have cost fifty pounds, or a hundred, what would that have signified, weighed in such a balance? Such a sum would be nothing to her father. Had Augustus fallen and broken his arm all the Sir Jacobs in London would not have been considered too costly could their joint coming have mitigated any danger. She did not however dare to speak to her mother again, so she said a word or two to Peregrine Orme, who was constant in his attendance on Felix. Peregrine had been very kind, and she had seen it, and her heart therefore warmed towards him.

"Don't you think he ought to have more advice, Mr. Orme?"

"Well, no; I don't know. He's very jolly, you know; only he can't talk. One of the bones ran into him, but I believe he's all right."

"Oh, but that is so frightful!" and the tears were again in her eyes.

"If I were him I should think one doctor enough. But it's easy enough having a fellow down from London, you know, if you like it."

"If he should get worse, Mr. Orme—." And then Peregrine made her a sort of promise, but in doing so an idea shot through his poor heart of what the truth might really be. He went back and looked at Felix who was sleeping. "If it is so I must bear it," he said to himself; "but I'll fight it on;" and a quick thought ran through his brain of his own deficiencies. He knew that he was not clever and bright in talk like Felix Graham. He could not say the right thing at the right moment without forethought. How he wished that he could! But still he would fight it on, as he would have done any losing match,—to the last. And then he sat down by Felix's head, and resolved that he would be loyal to his new friend all the same—loyal in all things needful. But still he would fight it on.

CHAPTER XXX
ANOTHER FALL

Felix Graham had plenty of nurses, but Madeline was not one of them. Augustus Staveley came home while the Alston doctor was still busy at the broken bones, and of course he would not leave his friend. He was one of those who had succeeded in the hunt, and consequently had heard nothing of the accident till the end of it. Miss Tristram had been the first to tell him that Mr. Graham had fallen in leaving the covert, but having seen him rise to his legs she had not thought he was seriously hurt.

"I do not know much about your friend," she had said; "but I think I may comfort you by an assurance that your horse is none the worse. I could see as much as that."

"Poor Felix!" said, Staveley. "He has lost a magnificent run. I suppose we are nine or ten miles from Monkton Grange now?"

"Eleven if we are a yard," said the lady. "It was an ugly country, but the pace was nothing wonderful." And then others dropped in, and at last came tidings about Graham. At first there was a whisper that he was dead. He had ridden over Orme, it was said; had nearly killed him, and had quite killed himself. Then the report became less fatal. Both horses were dead, but Graham was still living though with most of his bones broken.

"Don't believe it," said Miss Tristram. "In what condition Mr. Graham may be I won't say; but that your horse was safe and sound after he got over the fence, of that you may take my word." And thus, in a state of uncertainty, obtaining fresh rumours from every person he passed, Staveley hurried home. "Right arm and two ribs," Peregrine said to him, as he met him in the hall. "Is that all?" said Augustus. It was clear therefore that he did not think so much about it as his sister.

"If you'd let her have her head she'd never have come down like that," Augustus said, as he sat that evening by his friend's bedside.

"But he pulled off, I fancy, to avoid riding over me," said Peregrine.

"Then he must have come too quick at his leap," said Augustus. "You should have steadied him as he came to it." From all which Graham perceived that a man cannot learn how to ride any particular horse by two or three words of precept.

"If you talk any more about the horse, or the hunt, or the accident, neither of you shall stay in the room," said Lady Staveley, who came in at that moment. But they both did stay in the room, and said a great deal more about the hunt, and the horse, and the accident before they left it; and even became so far reconciled to the circumstance that they had a hot glass of brandy and water each, sitting by Graham's fire.

"But, Augustus, do tell me how he is," Madeline said to her brother, as she caught him going to his room. She had become ashamed of asking any more questions of her mother.

"He's all right; only he'll be as fretful as a porcupine, shut up there. At least I should be. Are there lots of novels in the house? Mind you send for a batch to-morrow. Novels are the only chance a man has when he's laid up like that." Before breakfast on the following morning Madeline had sent off to the Alston circulating library a list of all the best new novels of which she could remember the names.

No definite day had hitherto been fixed for Peregrine's return to The Cleeve, and under the present circumstances he still remained at Noningsby assisting to amuse Felix Graham. For two days after the accident such seemed to be his sole occupation; but in truth he was looking for an opportunity to say a word or two to Miss Staveley, and paving his way as best he might for that great speech which he was fully resolved that he would make before he left the house. Once or twice he bethought himself whether he would not endeavour to secure for himself some confidant in the family, and obtain the sanction and special friendship either of Madeline's mother, or her sister, or her brother. But what if after that she should reject him? Would it not be worse for him then that any one should have known of his defeat? He could, as he thought, endure to suffer alone; but on such a matter as that pity would be unendurable. So as he sat there by Graham's fireside, pretending to read one of poor Madeline's novels for the sake of companionship, he determined that he would tell no one of his intention;—no one till he could make the opportunity for telling her.

And when he did meet her, and find, now and again, some moment for saying a word alone to her, she was very gracious to him. He had been so kind and gentle with Felix, there was so much in him that was sweet and good and honest, so much that such an event as this brought forth and made manifest, that Madeline, and indeed the whole family, could not but be gracious to him. Augustus would declare that he was the greatest brick he had ever known, repeating all Graham's words as to the patience with which the embryo baronet had knelt behind him on the cold muddy ground, supporting him for an hour, till the carriage had come up. Under such circumstances how could Madeline refrain from being gracious to him?

"But it is all from favour to Graham!" Peregrine would say to himself with bitterness; and yet though he said so he did not quite believe it. Poor fellow! It was all from favour to Graham. And could he have thoroughly believed the truth of those words which he repeated to himself so often, he might have spared himself much pain. He might have spared himself much pain, and possibly some injury; for if aught could now tend to mature in Madeline's heart an affection which was but as yet nascent, it would be the offer of some other lover. But such reasoning on the matter was much too deep for Peregrine Orme. "It may be," he said to himself, "that she only pities him because he is hurt. If so, is not this time better for me than any other? If it be that she loves him, let me know it, and be out of my pain." It did not then occur to him that circumstances such as those in question could not readily be made explicit;—that Madeline might refuse his love, and yet leave him no wiser than he now was as to her reasons for so refusing;—perhaps, indeed, leave him less wise, with increased cause for doubt and hopeless hope, and the green melancholy of a rejected lover.

Madeline during these two days said no more about the London doctor; but it was plain to all who watched her that her anxiety as to the patient was much more keen than that of the other ladies of the house. "She always thinks everybody is going to die," Lady Staveley said to Miss Furnival, intending, not with any consummate prudence, to account to that acute young lady for her daughter's solicitude. "We had a cook here, three months since, who was very ill, and Madeline would never be easy till the doctor assured her that the poor woman's danger was altogether past."

"She is so very warm-hearted," said Miss Furnival in reply. "It is quite delightful to see her. And she will have such pleasure when she sees him come down from his room."

Lady Staveley on this immediate occasion said nothing to her daughter, but Mrs. Arbuthnot considered that a sisterly word might perhaps be spoken in due season.

"The doctor says he is doing quite well now," Mrs. Arbuthnot said to her, as they were sitting alone.

"But does he indeed? Did you hear him?" said Madeline, who was suspicious.

"He did so, indeed. I heard him myself. But he says also that he ought to remain here, at any rate for the next fortnight,—if mamma can permit it without inconvenience."

"Of course she can permit it. No one would turn any person out of their house in such a condition as that!"

"Papa and mamma both will be very happy that he should stay here;—of course they would not do what you call turning him out. But, Mad, my darling,"—and then she came up close and put her arm round her sister's waist. "I think mamma would be more comfortable in his remaining here if your charity towards him were—what shall I say?—less demonstrative."

"What do you mean, Isabella?"

"Dearest, dearest; you must not be angry with me. Nobody has hinted to me a word on the subject, nor do I mean to hint anything that can possibly be hurtful to you."

"But what do you mean?"

"Don't you know, darling? He is a young man—and—and—people see with such unkind eyes, and hear with such scandal-loving ears. There is that Miss Furnival—"

"If Miss Furnival can think such things, I for one do not care what she thinks."

"No, nor do I;—not as regards any important result. But may it not be well to be careful? You know what I mean, dearest?"

"Yes—I know. At least I suppose so. And it makes me know also how very cold and shallow and heartless people are! I won't ask any more questions, Isabella; but I can't know that a fellow-creature is suffering in the house,—and a person like him too, so clever, whom we all regard as a friend,—the most intimate friend in the world that Augustus has,—and the best too, as I heard papa himself say—without caring whether he is going to live or die."

"There is no danger now, you know."

"Very well; I am glad to hear it. Though I know very well that there must be danger after such a terrible accident as that."

"The doctor says there is none."

"At any rate I will not—" And then instead of finishing her sentence she turned away her head and put up her handkerchief to wipe away a tear.

"You are not angry with me, dear?" said Mrs. Arbuthnot.

"Oh, no," said Madeline; and then they parted.

For some days after that Madeline asked no question whatever about Felix Graham, but it may be doubted whether this did not make the matter worse. Even Sophia Furnival would ask how he was at any rate twice a day, and Lady Staveley continued to pay him regular visits at stated intervals. As he got better she would sit with him, and brought back reports as to his sayings. But Madeline never discussed any of these; and refrained alike from the conversation, whether his broken bones or his unbroken wit were to be the subject of it. And then Mrs. Arbuthnot, knowing that she would still be anxious, gave her private bulletins as to the state of the sick man's progress;—all which gave an air of secrecy to the matter, and caused even Madeline to ask herself why this should be so.

On the whole I think that Mrs. Arbuthnot was wrong. Mrs. Arbuthnot and the whole Staveley family would have regarded a mutual attachment between Mr. Graham and Madeline as a great family misfortune. The judge was a considerate father to his children, holding that a father's control should never be brought to bear unnecessarily. In looking forward to the future prospects of his sons and daughters it was his theory that they should be free to choose their life's companions for themselves. But nevertheless it could not be agreeable to him that his daughter should fall in love with a man who had nothing, and whose future success at his own profession seemed to be so very doubtful. On the whole I think that Mrs. Arbuthnot was wrong, and that the feeling that did exist in Madeline's bosom might more possibly have died away, had no word been said about it—even by a sister.

And then another event happened which forced her to look into her own heart. Peregrine Orme did make his proposal. He waited patiently during those two or three days in which the doctor's visits were frequent, feeling that he could not talk about himself while any sense of danger pervaded the house. But then at last a morning came on which the surgeon declared that he need not call again till the morrow; and Felix himself, when the medical back was turned, suggested that it might as well be to-morrow week. He began also to scold his friends, and look bright about the eyes, and drink his glass of sherry in a pleasant dinner-table fashion, not as if he were swallowing his physic. And Peregrine, when he saw all this, resolved that the moment had come for the doing of his deed of danger. The time would soon come at which he must leave Noningsby, and he would not leave Noningsby till he had learned his fate.

Lady Staveley, who with a mother's eye had seen her daughter's solicitude for Felix Graham's recovery,—had seen it, and animadverted on it to herself,—had seen also, or at any rate had suspected, that Peregrine Orme looked on her daughter with favouring eyes. Now Peregrine Orme would have satisfied Lady Staveley as a son-in-law. She liked his ways and manners of thought—in spite of those rumours as to the rat-catching which had reached her ears. She regarded him as quite clever enough to be a good husband, and no doubt appreciated the fact that he was to inherit his title and The Cleeve from an old grandfather instead of a middle-aged father. She therefore had no objection to leave Peregrine alone with her one ewe-lamb, and therefore the opportunity which he sought was at last found.

"I shall be leaving Noningsby to-morrow, Miss Staveley," he said one day, having secured an interview in the back drawing-room—in that happy half-hour which occurs in winter before the world betakes itself to dress. Now I here profess my belief, that out of every ten set offers made by ten young lovers, nine of such offers are commenced with an intimation that the lover is going away. There is a dash of melancholy in such tidings well suited to the occasion. If there be any spark of love on the other side it will be elicited by the idea of a separation. And then, also, it is so frequently the actual fact. This making of an offer is in itself a hard piece of business,—a job to be postponed from day to day. It is so postponed, and thus that dash of melancholy, and that idea of separation are brought in at the important moment with so much appropriate truth.

"I shall be leaving Noningsby to-morrow, Miss Staveley," Peregrine said.

"Oh dear! we shall be so sorry. But why are you going? What will Mr. Graham and Augustus do without you? You ought to stay at least till Mr. Graham can leave his room."

"Poor Graham!—not that I think he is much to be pitied either; but he won't be about for some weeks to come yet."

"You do not think he is worse; do you?"

"Oh, dear, no; not at all." And Peregrine was unconsciously irritated against his friend by the regard which her tone evinced. "He is quite well; only they will not let him be moved. But, Miss Staveley, it was not of Mr. Graham that I was going to speak."

"No—only I thought he would miss you so much." And then she blushed, though the blush in the dark of the evening was lost upon him. She remembered that she was not to speak about Felix Graham's health, and it almost seemed as though Mr. Orme had rebuked her for doing so in saying that he had not come there to speak of him.

"Lady Staveley's house has been turned up side down since this affair, and it is time now that some part of the trouble should cease."

"Oh! mamma does not mind it at all."

"I know how good she is; but nevertheless, Miss Staveley, I must go to-morrow." And then he paused a moment before he spoke again. "It will depend entirely upon you," he said, "whether I may have the happiness of returning soon to Noningsby."

"On me, Mr. Orme!"

"Yes, on you. I do not know how to speak properly that which I have to say; but I believe I may as well say it out at once. I have come here now to tell you that I love you and to ask you to be my wife." And then he stopped as though there were nothing more for him to say upon the matter.

It would be hardly extravagant to declare that Madeline's breath was taken away by the very sudden manner in which young Orme had made his proposition. It had never entered her head that she had an admirer in him. Previously to Graham's accident she had thought nothing about him. Since that event she had thought about him a good deal; but altogether as of a friend of Graham's. He had been good and kind to Graham, and therefore she had liked him and had talked to him. He had never said a word to her that had taught her to regard him as a possible lover; and now that he was an actual lover, a declared lover standing before her, waiting for an answer, she was so astonished that she did not know how to speak. All her ideas too, as to love,—such ideas as she had ever formed, were confounded by his abruptness. She would have thought, had she brought herself absolutely to think upon it, that all speech of love should be very delicate; that love should grow slowly, and then be whispered softly, doubtingly, and with infinite care. Even had she loved him, or had she been in the way towards loving him, such violence as this would have frightened her and scared her love away. Poor Peregrine! His intentions had been so good and honest! He was so true and hearty, and free from all conceit in the matter! It was a pity that he should have marred his cause by such ill judgment.

But there he stood waiting an answer,—and expecting it to be as open, definite, and plain as though he had asked her to take a walk with him. "Madeline," he said, stretching out his hand when he perceived that she did not speak to him at once. "There is my hand. If it be possible give me yours."

"Oh, Mr. Orme!"

"I know that I have not said what I had to say very—very gracefully. But you will not regard that I think. You are too good, and too true."

She had now seated herself, and he was standing before her. She had retreated to a sofa in order to avoid the hand which he had offered her; but he followed her, and even yet did not know that he had no chance of success. "Mr. Orme," she said at last, speaking hardly above her breath, "what has made you do this?"

"What has made me do it? What has made me tell you that I love you?"

"You cannot be in earnest!"

"Not in earnest! By heavens, Miss Staveley, no man who has said the same words was ever more in earnest. Do you doubt me when I tell you that I love you?"

"Oh, I am so sorry!" And then she hid her face upon the arm of the sofa and burst into tears.

Peregrine stood there, like a prisoner on his trial, waiting for a verdict. He did not know how to plead his cause with any further language; and indeed no further language could have been of any avail. The judge and jury were clear against him, and he should have known the sentence without waiting to have it pronounced in set terms. But in plain words he had made his offer, and in plain words he required that an answer should be given to him. "Well," he said, "will you not speak to me? Will you not tell me whether it shall be so?"

"No,—no,—no," she said.

"You mean that you cannot love me." And as he said this the agony of his tone struck her ear and made her feel that he was suffering. Hitherto she had thought only of herself, and had hardly recognised it as a fact that he could be thoroughly in earnest.

"Mr. Orme, I am very sorry. Do not speak as though you were angry with me. But—"

"But you cannot love me?" And then he stood again silent, for there was no reply. "Is it that, Miss Staveley, that you mean to answer? If you say that with positive assurance, I will trouble you no longer." Poor Peregrine! He was but an unskilled lover!

"No!" she sobbed forth through her tears; but he had so framed his question that he hardly knew what No meant.

"Do you mean that you cannot love me, or may I hope that a day will come—? May I speak to you again—?"

"Oh, no, no! I can answer you now. It grieves me to the heart. I know you are so good. But, Mr. Orme—"

"Well—"

"It can never, never be."

"And I must take that as answer?"

"I can make no other." He still stood before her,—with gloomy and almost angry brow, could she have seen him; and then he thought he would ask her whether there was any other love which had brought about her scorn for him. It did not occur to him, at the first moment, that in doing so he would insult and injure her.

"At any rate I am not flattered by a reply which is at once so decided," he began by saying.

"Oh! Mr. Orme, do not make me more unhappy—"

"But perhaps I am too late. Perhaps—" Then he remembered himself and paused. "Never mind," he said, speaking to himself rather than to her. "Good-bye, Miss Staveley. You will at any rate say good-bye to me. I shall go at once now."

"Go at once! Go away, Mr. Orme?"

"Yes; why should I stay here? Do you think that I could sit down to table with you all after that? I will ask your brother to explain my going; I shall find him in his room. Good-bye."

She took his hand mechanically, and then he left her. When she came down to dinner she looked furtively round to his place and saw that it was vacant.

CHAPTER XXXI
FOOTSTEPS IN THE CORRIDOR

"Upon my word I am very sorry," said the judge. "But what made him go off so suddenly? I hope there's nobody ill at The Cleeve!" And then the judge took his first spoonful of soup.

"No, no; there is nothing of that sort," said Augustus. "His grandfather wants him, and Orme thought he might as well start at once. He was always a sudden harum-scarum fellow like that."

"He's a very pleasant, nice young man," said Lady Staveley; "and never gives himself any airs. I like him exceedingly."

Poor Madeline did not dare to look either at her mother or her brother, but she would have given much to know whether either of them were aware of the cause which had sent Peregrine Orme so suddenly away from the house. At first she thought that Augustus surely did know, and she was wretched as she thought that he might probably speak to her on the subject. But he went on talking about Orme and his abrupt departure till she became convinced that he knew nothing and suspected nothing of what had occurred.

But her mother said never a word after that eulogium which she had uttered, and Madeline read that eulogium altogether aright. It said to her ears that if ever young Orme should again come forward with his suit, her mother would be prepared to receive him as a suitor; and it said, moreover, that if that suitor had been already sent away by any harsh answer, she would not sympathise with that harshness.

The dinner went on much as usual, but Madeline could not bring herself to say a word. She sat between her brother-in-law, Mr. Arbuthnot, on one side, and an old friend of her father's, of thirty years' standing, on the other. The old friend talked exclusively to Lady Staveley, and Mr. Arbuthnot, though he now and then uttered a word or two, was chiefly occupied with his dinner. During the last three or four days she had sat at dinner next to Peregrine Orme, and it seemed to her now that she always had been able to talk to him. She had liked him so much too! Was it not a pity that he should have been so mistaken! And then as she sat after dinner, eating five or six grapes, she felt that she was unable to recall her spirits and look and speak as she was wont to do: a thing had happened which had knocked the ground from under her—had thrown her from her equipoise, and now she lacked the strength to recover herself and hide her dismay.

After dinner, while the gentlemen were still in the dining-room, she got a book, and nobody disturbed her as she sat alone pretending to read it. There never had been any intimate friendship between her and Miss Furnival, and that young lady was now employed in taking the chief part in a general conversation about wools. Lady Staveley got through a good deal of wool in the course of the year, as also did the wife of the old thirty-years' friend; but Miss Furnival, short as her experience had been, was able to give a few hints to them both, and did not throw away the occasion. There was another lady there, rather deaf, to whom Mrs. Arbuthnot devoted herself, and therefore Madeline was allowed to be alone.

Then the men came in, and she was obliged to come forward and officiate at the tea-table. The judge insisted on having the teapot and urn brought into the drawing-room, and liked to have his cup brought to him by one of his own daughters. So she went to work and made the tea; but still she felt that she scarcely knew how to go through her task. What had happened to her that she should be thus beside herself, and hardly capable of refraining from open tears? She knew that her mother was looking at her, and that now and again little things were done to give her ease if any ease were possible.

"Is anything the matter with my Madeline?" said her father, looking up into her face, and holding the hand from which he had taken his cup.

"No, papa; only I have got a headache."

"A headache, dear; that's not usual with you."

"I have seen that she has not been well all the evening," said Lady Staveley; "but I thought that perhaps she might shake it off. You had better go, my dear, if you are suffering. Isabella, I'm sure, will pour out the tea for us."

And so she got away, and skulked slowly up stairs to her own room. She felt that it was skulking. Why should she have been so weak as to have fled in that way? She had no headache—nor was it heartache that had now upset her. But a man had spoken to her openly of love, and no man had ever so spoken to her before.

She did not go direct to her own chamber, but passed along the corridor towards her mother's dressing-room. It was always her custom to remain there some half-hour before she went to bed, doing little things for her mother, and chatting with any other girl who might be intimate enough to be admitted there. Now she might remain there for an hour alone without danger of being disturbed; and she thought to herself that she would remain there till her mother came, and then unburthen herself of the whole story.

As she went along the corridor she would have to pass the room which had been given up to Felix Graham. She saw that the door was ajar, and as she came close up to it, she found the nurse in the act of coming out from the room. Mrs. Baker had been a very old servant in the judge's family, and had known Madeline from the day of her birth. Her chief occupation for some years had been nursing when there was anybody to nurse, and taking a general care and surveillance of the family's health when there was no special invalid to whom she could devote herself. Since Graham's accident she had been fully employed, and had greatly enjoyed the opportunities it had given her.

Mrs. Baker was in the doorway as Madeline attempted to pass by on tiptoe. "Oh, he's a deal better now, Miss Madeline, so that you needn't be afeard of disturbing;—ain't you, Mr. Graham?" So she was thus brought into absolute contact with her friend, for the first time since he had hurt himself.

Footsteps in the corridor.

"Indeed I am," said Felix; "I only wish they'd let me get up and go down stairs. Is that Miss Staveley, Mrs. Baker?"

"Yes, sure. Come, my dear, he's got his dressing-gown on, and you may just come to the door and ask him how he does."

"I am very glad to hear that you are so much better, Mr. Graham," said Madeline, standing in the doorway with averted eyes, and speaking with a voice so low that it only just reached his ears.

"Thank you, Miss Staveley; I shall never know how to express what I feel for you all."

"And there's none of 'em have been more anxious about you than she, I can tell you; and none of 'em ain't kinder-hearteder," said Mrs. Baker.

"I hope you will be up soon and be able to come down to the drawing-room," said Madeline. And then she did glance round, and for a moment saw the light of his eye as he sat upright in the bed. He was still pale and thin, or at least she fancied so, and her heart trembled within her as she thought of the danger he had passed.

"I do so long to be able to talk to you again; all the others come and visit me, but I have only heard the sounds of your footsteps as you pass by."

"And yet she always walks like a mouse," said Mrs. Baker.

"But I have always heard them," he said. "I hope Marian thanked you for the books. She told me how you had gotten them for me."

"She should not have said anything about them; it was Augustus who thought of them," said Madeline.

"Marian comes to me four or five times a day," he continued; "I do not know what I should do without her."

"I hope she is not noisy," said Madeline.

"Laws, miss, he don't care for noise now, only he ain't good at moving yet, and won't be for some while."

"Pray take care of yourself, Mr. Graham," she said; "I need not tell you how anxious we all are for your recovery. Good night, Mr. Graham." And then she passed on to her mother's dressing-room, and sitting herself down in an arm-chair opposite to the fire began to think—to think, or else to try to think.

And what was to be the subject of her thoughts? Regarding Peregrine Orme there was very little room for thinking. He had made her an offer, and she had rejected it as a matter of course, seeing that she did not love him. She had no doubt on that head, and was well aware that she could never accept such an offer. On what subject then was it necessary that she should think?

How odd it was that Mr. Graham's room door should have been open on this especial evening, and that nurse should have been standing there, ready to give occasion for that conversation! That was the idea that first took possession of her brain. And then she recounted all those few words which had been spoken as though they had had some special value—as though each word had been laden with interest. She felt half ashamed of what she had done in standing there and speaking at his bedroom door, and yet she would not have lost the chance for worlds. There had been nothing in what had passed between her and the invalid. The very words, spoken elsewhere, or in the presence of her mother and sister, would have been insipid and valueless; and yet she sat there feeding on them as though they were of flavour so rich that she could not let the sweetness of them pass from her. She had been stunned at the idea of poor Peregrine's love, and yet she never asked herself what was this new feeling. She did not inquire—not yet at least—whether there might be danger in such feelings.

She remained there, with eyes fixed on the burning coals, till her mother came up. "What, Madeline," said Lady Staveley, "are you here still? I was in hopes you would have been in bed before this."

"My headache is gone now, mamma; and I waited because—"

"Well, dear; because what?" and her mother came and stood over her and smoothed her hair. "I know very well that something has been the matter. There has been something; eh, Madeline?"

"Yes, mamma."

"And you have remained up that we may talk about it. Is that it, dearest?"

"I did not quite mean that, but perhaps it will be best. I can't be doing wrong, mamma, in telling you."

"Well; you shall judge of that yourself;" and Lady Staveley sat down on the sofa so that she was close to the chair which Madeline still occupied. "As a general rule I suppose you could not be doing wrong; but you must decide. If you have any doubt, wait till to-morrow."

"No, mamma; I will tell you now. Mr. Orme—"

"Well, dearest. Did Mr. Orme say anything specially to you before he went away?"

"He—he—"

"Come to me, Madeline, and sit here. We shall talk better then." And the mother made room beside her on the sofa for her daughter, and Madeline, running over, leaned with her head upon her mother's shoulder. "Well, darling; what did he say? Did he tell you that he loved you?"

"Yes, mamma."

"And you answered him—"

"I could only tell him—"

"Yes, I know. Poor fellow! But, Madeline, is he not an excellent young man;—one, at any rate, that is lovable? Of course in such a matter the heart must answer for itself. But I, looking at the offer as a mother—I could have been well pleased—"

"But, mamma, I could not—"

"Well, love, there shall be an end of it; at least for the present. When I heard that he had gone suddenly away I thought that something had happened."

"I am so sorry that he should be unhappy, for I know that he is good."

"Yes, he is good; and your father likes him, and Augustus. In such a matter as this, Madeline, I would never say a word to persuade you. I should think it wrong to do so. But it may be, dearest, that he has flurried you by the suddenness of his offer; and that you have not yet thought much about it."

"But, mamma, I know that I do not love him."

"Of course. That is natural. It would have been a great misfortune if you had loved him before you had reason to know that he loved you;—a great misfortune. But now,—now that you cannot but think of him, now that you know what his wishes are, perhaps you may learn—"

"But I have refused him, and he has gone away."

"Young gentlemen under such circumstances sometimes come back again."

"He won't come back, mamma, because—because I told him so plainly—I am sure he understands that it is all to be at an end."

"But if he should, and if you should then think differently towards him—"

"Oh, no!"

"But if you should, it may be well that you should know how all your friends esteem him. In a worldly view the marriage would be in all respects prudent; and as to disposition and temper, which I admit are much more important, I confess I think that he has all the qualities best adapted to make a wife happy. But, as I said before, the heart must speak for itself."

"Yes; of course. And I know that I shall never love him;—not in that way."

"You may be sure, dearest, that there will be no constraint put upon you. It might be possible that I or your papa should forbid a daughter's marriage, if she had proposed to herself an imprudent match; but neither he nor I would ever use our influence with a child to bring about a marriage because we think it prudent in a worldly point of view." And then Lady Staveley kissed her daughter.

"Dear mamma, I know how good you are to me." And she answered her mother's embrace by the pressure of her arm. But nevertheless she did not feel herself to be quite comfortable. There was something in the words which her mother had spoken which grated against her most cherished feelings;—something, though she by no means knew what. Why had her mother cautioned her in that way, that there might be a case in which she would refuse her sanction to a proposed marriage? Isabella's marriage had been concluded with the full agreement of the whole family; and she, Madeline, had certainly never as yet given cause either to father or mother to suppose that she would be headstrong and imprudent. Might not the caution have been omitted?—or was it intended to apply in any way to circumstances as they now existed?

"You had better go now, dearest," said Lady Staveley, "and for the present we will not think any more about this gallant young knight." And then Madeline, having said good night, went off rather crestfallen to her own room. In doing so she again had to pass Graham's door, and as she went by it, walking not quite on tiptoe, she could not help asking herself whether or no he would really recognise the sound of her footsteps.

It is hardly necessary to say that Lady Staveley had conceived to herself a recognised purpose in uttering that little caution to her daughter; and she would have been quite as well pleased had circumstances taken Felix Graham out of her house instead of Peregrine Orme. But Felix Graham must necessarily remain for the next fortnight, and there could be no possible benefit in Orme's return, at any rate till Graham should have gone.

CHAPTER XXXII
WHAT BRIDGET BOLSTER HAD TO SAY

It has been said in the earlier pages of this story that there was no prettier scenery to be found within thirty miles of London than that by which the little town of Hamworth was surrounded. This was so truly the case that Hamworth was full of lodgings which in the autumn season were always full of lodgers. The middle of winter was certainly not the time for seeing the Hamworth hills to advantage; nevertheless it was soon after Christmas that two rooms were taken there by a single gentleman who had come down for a week, apparently with no other view than that of enjoying himself. He did say something about London confinement and change of air; but he was manifestly in good health, had an excellent appetite, said a great deal about fresh eggs,—which at that time of the year was hardly reasonable, and brought with him his own pale brandy. This gentleman was Mr. Crabwitz.

The house at which he was to lodge had been selected with considerable judgment. It was kept by a tidy old widow known as Mrs. Trump; but those who knew anything of Hamworth affairs were well aware that Mrs. Trump had been left without a shilling, and could not have taken that snug little house in Paradise Row and furnished it completely, out of her own means. No. Mrs. Trump's lodging-house was one of the irons which Samuel Dockwrath ever kept heating in the fire, for the behoof of those fourteen children. He had taken a lease of the house in Paradise Row, having made a bargain and advanced a few pounds while it was yet being built; and he then had furnished it and put in Mrs. Trump. Mrs. Trump received from him wages and a percentage; but to him were paid over the quota of shillings per week in consideration for which the lodgers were accommodated. All of which Mr. Crabwitz had ascertained before he located himself in Paradise Row.

And when he had so located himself he soon began to talk to Mrs. Trump about Mr. Dockwrath. He himself, as he told her in confidence, was in the profession of the law; he had heard of Mr. Dockwrath, and should be very glad if that gentleman would come over and take a glass of brandy and water with him some evening.

"And a very clever sharp gentleman he is," said Mrs. Trump.

"With a tolerably good business, I suppose?" asked Crabwitz.

"Pretty fair for that, sir. But he do be turning his hand to everything. He's a mortal long family of his own, and he has need of it all, if it's ever so much. But he'll never be poor for the want of looking after it."

But Mr. Dockwrath did not come near his lodger on the first evening, and Mr. Crabwitz made acquaintance with Mrs. Dockwrath before he saw her husband. The care of the fourteen children was not supposed to be so onerous but that she could find a moment now and then to see whether Mrs. Trump kept the furniture properly dusted, and did not infringe any of the Dockwrathian rules. These were very strict; and whenever they were broken it was on the head of Mrs. Dockwrath that the anger of the ruler mainly fell.

"I hope you find everything comfortable, sir," said poor Miriam, having knocked at the sitting-room door when Crabwitz had just finished his dinner.

"Yes, thank you; very nice. Is that Mrs. Dockwrath?"

"Yes, sir. I'm Mrs. Dockwrath. As it's we who own the room I looked in to see if anything's wanting."

"You are very kind. No; nothing is wanting. But I should be delighted to make your acquaintance if you would stay for a moment. Might I ask you to take a chair?" and Mr. Crabwitz handed her one.

"Thank you; no, sir I won't intrude."

"Not at all, Mrs. Dockwrath. But the fact is, I'm a lawyer myself, and I should be so glad to become known to your husband. I have heard a great deal of his name lately as to a rather famous case in which he is employed."

"Not the Orley Farm case?" said Mrs. Dockwrath immediately.

"Yes, yes; exactly."

"And is he going on with that, sir?" asked Mrs. Dockwrath with great interest.

"Is he not? I know nothing about it myself, but I always supposed that such was the case. If I had such a wife as you, Mrs. Dockwrath, I should not leave her in doubt as to what I was doing in my own profession."

"I know nothing about it, Mr. Cooke;"—for it was as Mr. Cooke that he now sojourned at Hamworth. Not that it should be supposed he had received instructions from Mr. Furnival to come down to that place under a false name. From Mr. Furnival he had received no further instructions on that matter than those conveyed at the end of a previous chapter. "I know nothing about it, Mr. Cooke; and don't want to know generally. But I am anxious about this Orley Farm case. I do hope that he's going to drop it." And then Mr. Crabwitz elicited her view of the case with great ease.

On that evening, about nine, Mr. Dockwrath did go over to Paradise Row, and did allow himself to be persuaded to mix a glass of brandy and water and light a cigar. "My missus tells me, sir, that you belong to the profession as well as myself."

"Oh yes; I'm a lawyer, Mr. Dockwrath."

"Practising in town as an attorney, sir?"

"Not as an attorney on my own hook exactly. I chiefly employ my time in getting up cases for barristers. There's a good deal done in that way."

"Oh, indeed," said Mr. Dockwrath, beginning to feel himself the bigger man of the two; and from that moment he patronised his companion instead of allowing himself to be patronised.

This went against the grain with Mr. Crabwitz, but, having an object to gain, he bore it. "We hear a great deal up in London just at present about this Orley Farm case, and I always hear your name as connected with it. I had no idea when I was taking these lodgings that I was coming into a house belonging to that Mr. Dockwrath."

"The same party, sir," said Mr. Dockwrath, blowing the smoke out of his mouth as he looked up to the ceiling.

And then by degrees Mr. Crabwitz drew him into conversation. Dockwrath was by nature quite as clever a man as Crabwitz, and in such a matter as this was not one to be outwitted easily; but in truth he had no objection to talk about the Orley Farm case. "I have taken it up on public motives, Mr. Cooke," he said, "and I mean to go through with it."

"Oh, of course; in such a case as that you will no doubt go through with it?"

"That's my intention, I assure you. And I tell you what; young Mason,— that's the son of the widow of the old man who made the will—"

"Or rather who did not make it, as you say."

"Yes, yes; he made the will; but he did not make the codicil—and that young Mason has no more right to the property than you have."

"Hasn't he now?"

"No; and I can prove it too."

"Well; the general opinion in the profession is that Lady Mason will stand her ground and hold her own. I don't know what the points are myself, but I have heard it discussed, and that is certainly what people think."

"Then people will find that they are very much mistaken."

"I was talking to one of Round's young men about it, and I fancy they are not very sanguine."

"I do not care a fig for Round or his young men. It would be quite as well for Joseph Mason if Round and Crook gave up the matter altogether. It lies in a nutshell, and the truth must come out whatever Round and Crook may choose to say. And I'll tell you more—old Furnival, big a man as he thinks himself, cannot save her."

"Has he anything to do with it?" asked Mr. Cooke.

"Yes; the sly old fox. My belief is that only for him she'd give up the battle, and be down on her marrow-bones asking for mercy."

"She'd have little chance of mercy, from what I hear of Joseph Mason."

"She'd have to give up the property of course. And even then I don't know whether he'd let her off. By heavens! he couldn't let her off unless I chose." And then by degrees he told Mr. Cooke some of the circumstances of the case.

But it was not till the fourth evening that Mr. Dockwrath spent with his lodger that the intimacy had so far progressed as to enable Mr. Crabwitz to proceed with his little scheme. On that day Mr. Dockwrath had received a notice that at noon on the following morning Mr. Joseph Mason and Bridget Bolster would both be at the house of Messrs. Round and Crook in Bedford Row, and that he could attend at that hour if it so pleased him. It certainly would so please him, he said to himself when he got that letter; and in the evening he mentioned to his new friend the business which was taking him to London.

"If I might advise you in the matter, Mr. Dockwrath," said Crabwitz, "I should stay away altogether."

"And why so?"

"Because that's not your market. This poor devil of a woman—for she is a poor devil of a woman—"

"She'll be poor enough before long."

"It can't be any gratification to you running her down."

"Ah, but the justice of the thing."

"Bother. You're talking now to a man of the world. Who can say what is the justice or the injustice of anything after twenty years of possession? I have no doubt the codicil did express the old man's wish,—even from your own story. But of course you are looking for your market. Now it seems to me that there's a thousand pounds in your way as clear as daylight."

"I don't see it myself, Mr. Cooke."

"No; but I do. The sort of thing is done every day. You have your father-in-law's office journal?"

"Safe enough."

"Burn it;—or leave it about in these rooms like;—so that somebody else may burn it."

"I'd like to see the thousand pounds first."

"Of course you'd do nothing till you knew about that;—nothing except keeping away from Round and Crook to-morrow. The money would be forthcoming if the trial were notoriously dropped by next assizes."

Dockwrath sat thinking for a minute or two, and every moment of thought made him feel more strongly that he could not now succeed in the manner pointed out by Mr. Cooke. "But where would be the market you are talking of?" said he.

"I could manage that," said Crabwitz.

"And go shares in the business?"

"No, no; nothing of the sort." And then he added, remembering that he must show that he had some personal object, "If I got a trifle in the matter it would not come out of your allowance."

The attorney again sat silent for a while, and now he remained so for full five minutes, during which Mr. Crabwitz puffed the smoke from between his lips with a look of supreme satisfaction. "May I ask," at last Mr. Dockwrath said, "whether you have any personal interest in this matter?"

"None in the least;—that is to say, none as yet."

"You did not come down here with any view—"

"Oh dear no; nothing of the sort. But I see at a glance that it is one of those cases in which a compromise would be the most judicious solution of difficulties. I am well used to this kind of thing, Mr. Dockwrath."

"It would not do, sir," said Mr. Dockwrath, after some further slight period of consideration. "It wouldn't do. Round and Crook have all the dates, and so has Mason too. And the original of that partnership deed is forthcoming; and they know what witnesses to depend on. No, sir; I've begun this on public grounds, and I mean to carry it on. I am in a manner bound to do so as the representative of the attorney of the late Sir Joseph Mason;—and by heavens, Mr. Cooke, I'll do my duty."

"I dare say you're right," said Mr. Crabwitz, mixing a quarter of a glass more brandy and water.

"I know I'm right, sir," said Dockwrath. "And when a man knows he's right, he has a deal of inward satisfaction in the feeling." After that Mr. Crabwitz was aware that he could be of no use at Hamworth, but he stayed out his week in order to avoid suspicion.

On the following day Mr. Dockwrath did proceed to Bedford Row, determined to carry out his original plan, and armed with that inward satisfaction to which he had alluded. He dressed himself in his best, and endeavoured as far as was in his power to look as though he were equal to the Messrs. Round. Old Crook he had seen once, and him he already despised. He had endeavoured to obtain a private interview with Mrs. Bolster before she could be seen by Matthew Round; but in this he had not succeeded. Mrs. Bolster was a prudent woman, and, acting doubtless under advice, had written to him, saying that she had been summoned to the office of Messrs. Round and Crook, and would there declare all that she knew about the matter. At the same time she returned to him a money order which he had sent to her.

Punctually at twelve he was in Bedford Row, and there he saw a respectable-looking female sitting at the fire in the inner part of the outer office. This was Bridget Bolster, but he would by no means have recognised her. Bridget had risen in the world and was now head chambermaid at a large hotel in the west of England. In that capacity she had laid aside whatever diffidence may have afflicted her earlier years, and was now able to speak out her mind before any judge or jury in the land. Indeed she had never been much afflicted by such diffidence, and had spoken out her evidence on that former occasion, now twenty years since, very plainly. But as she now explained to the head clerk, she had at that time been only a poor ignorant slip of a girl, with no more than eight pounds a year wages.

Dockwrath bowed to the head clerk, and passed on to Mat Round's private room. "Mr. Matthew is inside, I suppose," said he, and hardly waiting for permission he knocked at the door, and then entered. There he saw Mr. Matthew Round, sitting in his comfortable arm-chair, and opposite to him sat Mr. Mason of Groby Park.

Mr. Mason got up and shook hands with the Hamworth attorney, but Round junior made his greeting without rising, and merely motioned his visitor to a chair.

"Mr. Mason and the young ladies are quite well, I hope?" said Mr. Dockwrath, with a smile.

"Quite well, I thank you," said the county magistrate.

"This matter has progressed since I last had the pleasure of seeing them. You begin to think I was right; eh, Mr. Mason?"

"Don't let us triumph till we are out of the wood," said Mr. Round. "It is a deal easier to spend money in such an affair as this than it is to make money by it. However we shall hear to-day more about it."

"I do not know about making money," said Mr. Mason, very solemnly. "But that I have been robbed by that woman out of my just rights in that estate for the last twenty years, — that I may say I do know."

"Quite true, Mr. Mason; quite true," said Mr. Dockwrath with considerable energy.

"And whether I make money or whether I lose money I intend to proceed in this matter. It is dreadful to think that in this free and enlightened country so abject an offender should have been able to hold her head up so long without punishment and without disgrace."

"That is exactly what I feel," said Dockwrath. "The very stones and trees of Hamworth cry out against her."

"Gentlemen," said Mr. Round, "we have first to see whether there has been any injustice or not. If you will allow me I will explain to you what I now propose to do."

"Proceed, sir," said Mr. Mason, who was by no means satisfied with his young attorney.

"Bridget Bolster is now in the next room, and as far as I can understand the case at present, she would be the witness on whom your case, Mr. Mason, would most depend. The man Kenneby I have not yet seen; but from what I understand he is less likely to prove a willing witness than Mrs. Bolster."

"I cannot go along with you there, Mr. Round," said Dockwrath.

"Excuse me, sir, but I am only stating my opinion. If I should find that this woman is unable to say that she did not sign two separate documents on that day—that is, to say so with a positive and point blank assurance, I shall recommend you, as my client, to drop the prosecution."

"I will never drop it," said Mr. Mason.

"You will do as you please," continued Round; "I can only say what under such circumstances will be the advice given to you by this firm. I have talked the matter over very carefully with my father and with our other partner, and we shall not think well of going on with it unless I shall now find that your view is strongly substantiated by this woman."

Then outspoke Mr. Dockwrath, "Under these circumstances, Mr. Mason, if I were you, I should withdraw from the house at once. I certainly would not have my case blown upon."

"Mr. Mason, sir, will do as he pleases about that. As long as the business with which he honours us is straight-forward, we will do it for him, as for an old client, although it is not exactly in our own line. But we can only do it in accordance with our own judgment. I will proceed to explain what I now propose to do. The woman Bolster is in the next room, and I, with the assistance of my head clerk, will take down the headings of what evidence she can give."

"In our presence, sir," said Mr. Dockwrath; "or if Mr. Mason should decline, at any rate in mine."

"By no means, Mr. Dockwrath," said Round.

"I think Mr. Dockwrath should hear her story," said Mr. Mason.

"He certainly will not do so in this house or in conjunction with me. In what capacity should he be present, Mr. Mason?"

"As one of Mr. Mason's legal advisers," said Dockwrath.

"If you are to be one of them, Messrs. Round and Crook cannot be the others. I think I explained that to you before. It now remains for Mr. Mason to say whether he wishes to employ our firm in this matter or not. And I can tell him fairly," Mr. Round added this after a slight pause, "that we shall be rather pleased than otherwise if he will put the case into other hands."

"Of course I wish you to conduct it," said Mr. Mason, who, with all his bitterness against the present holders of Orley Farm, was afraid of throwing himself into the hands of Dockwrath. He was not an ignorant man, and he knew that the firm of Round and Crook bore a high reputation before the world.

"Then," said Round, "I must do my business in accordance with my own views of what is right. I have reason to believe that no one has yet tampered with this woman," and as he spoke he looked hard at Dockwrath, "though probably attempts may have been made."

"I don't know who should tamper with her," said Dockwrath, "unless it be Lady Mason—whom I must say you seem very anxious to protect."

"Another word like that, sir, and I shall be compelled to ask you to leave the house. I believe that this woman has been tampered with by no one. I will now learn from her what is her remembrance of the circumstances as they occurred twenty years since, and I will then read to you her deposition. I shall be sorry, gentlemen, to keep you here, perhaps for an hour or so, but you will find the morning papers on the table." And then Mr. Round, gathering up certain documents, passed into the outer office, and Mr. Mason and Mr. Dockwrath were left alone.

"He is determined to get that woman off," said Mr. Dockwrath, in a whisper.

"I believe him to be an honest man," said Mr. Mason, with some sternness.

"Honesty, sir! It is hard to say what is honesty and what is dishonesty. Would you believe it, Mr. Mason, only last night I had a thousand pounds offered me to hold my tongue about this affair?"

Mr. Mason at the moment did not believe this, but he merely looked hard into his companion's face, and said nothing.

"By the heavens above us what I tell you is true! a thousand pounds, Mr. Mason! Only think how they are going it to get this thing stifled. And where should the offer come from but from those who know I have the power?"

"Do you mean to say that the offer came from this firm?"

"Hush-sh, Mr. Mason. The very walls hear and talk in such a place as this. I'm not to know who made the offer, and I don't know. But a man can give a very good guess sometimes. The party who was speaking to me is up to the whole transaction, and knows exactly what is going on here—here, in this house. He let it all out, using pretty nigh the same words as Round used just now. He was full about the doubt that Round and Crook felt—that they'd never pull it through. I'll tell you what it is, Mr. Mason, they don't mean to pull it through."

"What answer did you make to the man?"

"What answer! why I just put my thumb this way over my shoulder. No, Mr. Mason, if I can't carry on without bribery and corruption, I won't carry on at all. He'd called at the wrong house with that dodge, and so he soon found."

"And you think he was an emissary from Messrs. Round and Crook?"

"Hush-sh-sh. For heaven's sake, Mr. Mason, do be a little lower. You can put two and two together as well as I can, Mr. Mason. I find they make four. I don't know whether your calculation will be the same. My belief is, that these people are determined to save that woman. Don't you see it in that young fellow's eye—that his heart is all on the other side. Now he's got hold of that woman Bolster, and he'll teach her to give such evidence as will upset us. But I'll be even with him yet, Mr. Mason. If you'll only trust me, we'll both be even with him yet."

Mr. Mason at the present moment said nothing further, and when Dockwrath pressed him to continue the conversation in whispers, he distinctly said that he would rather say no more upon the subject just then. He would wait for Mr. Round's return. "Am I at liberty," he asked, "to mention that offer of the thousand pounds?"

"What—to Mat Round?" said Dockwrath. "Certainly not, Mr. Mason. It wouldn't be our game at all."

"Very well, sir." And then Mr. Mason took up a newspaper, and no further words were spoken till the door opened and Mr. Round re-entered the room.

This he did with slow, deliberate step, and stopping on the hearth-rug, he stood leaning with his back against the mantelpiece. It was clear from his face to see that he had much to tell, and clear also that he was not pleased at the turn which affairs were taking.

"Well, gentlemen, I have examined the woman," he said, "and here is her deposition."

"And what does she say?" asked Mr. Mason.

"Come, out with it, sir," said Dockwrath. "Did she, or did she not sign two documents on that day?"

"Mr. Mason," said Round, turning to that gentleman, and altogether ignoring Dockwrath and his question; "I have to tell you that her statement, as far as it goes, fully corroborates your view of the case. As far as it goes, mind you."

"Oh, it does; does it?" said Dockwrath.

"And she is the only important witness?" said Mr. Mason with great exultation.

"I have never said that; what I did say was this—that your case must break down unless her evidence supported it. It does support it—strongly; but you will want more than that."

"And now if you please, Mr. Round, what is it that she has deposed?" asked Dockwrath.

"She remembers it all then?" said Mason.

"She is a remarkably clear-headed woman, and apparently does remember a great deal. But her remembrance chiefly and most strongly goes to this—that she witnessed only one deed."

"She can prove that, can she?" said Mason, and the tone of his voice was loudly triumphant.

"She declares that she never signed but one deed in the whole of her life—either on that day or on any other; and over and beyond this she says now—now that I have explained to her what that other deed might have been—that old Mr. Usbech told her that it was about a partnership."

"He did, did he?" said Dockwrath, rising from his chair and clapping his hands. "Very well. I don't think we shall want more than that, Mr. Mason."

There was a tone of triumph in the man's voice, and a look of gratified malice in his countenance which disgusted Mr. Round and irritated him almost beyond his power of endurance. It was quite true that he would much have preferred to find that the woman's evidence was in favour of Lady Mason. He would have been glad to learn that she actually had witnessed the two deeds on the same day. His tone would have been triumphant, and his face gratified, had he returned to the room with such tidings. His feelings were all on that side, though his duty lay on the other. He had almost expected that it would be so. As it was, he was prepared to go on with his duty, but he was not prepared to endure the insolence of Mr. Dockwrath. There was a look of joy also about Mr. Mason which added to his annoyance. It might be just and necessary to prosecute that unfortunate woman at Orley Farm, but he could not gloat over such work.

"Mr. Dockwrath," he said, "I will not put up with such conduct here. If you wish to rejoice about this, you must go elsewhere."

"And what are we to do now?" said Mr. Mason. "I presume there need be no further delay."

"I must consult with my partner. If you can make it convenient to call this day week—"

"But she will escape."

"No, she will not escape. I shall not be ready to say anything before that. If you are not in town, then I can write to you." And so the meeting was broken up, and Mr. Mason and Mr. Dockwrath left the lawyer's office together.

Mr. Mason and Mr. Dockwrath left the office in Bedford Row together, and thus it was almost a necessity that they should walk together for some distance through the streets. Mr. Mason was going to his hotel in Soho Square, and Mr. Dockwrath turned with him through the passage leading into Red Lion Square, linking his own arm in that of his companion. The Yorkshire county magistrate did not quite like this, but what was he to do?

"Did you ever see anything like that, sir?" said Mr. Dockwrath; "for by heavens I never did."

"Like what?" said Mr. Mason.

"Like that fellow there;—that Round. It is my opinion that he deserves to have his name struck from the rolls. Is it not clear that he is doing all in his power to bring that wretched woman off? And I'll tell you what, Mr. Mason, if you let him play his own game in that way, he will bring her off."

"But he expressly admitted that this woman Bolster's evidence is conclusive."

"Yes; he was so driven into a corner that he could not help admitting that. The woman had been too many for him, and he found that he couldn't cushion her. But do you mind my words, Mr. Mason. He intends that you shall be beaten. It's as plain as the nose on your face. You can read it in the very look of him, and in every tone of his voice. At any rate I can. I'll tell you what it is"—and then he squeezed very close to Mr. Mason—"he and old Furnival understand each other in this matter like two brothers. Of course Round will have his bill against you. Win or lose, he'll get his costs out of your pocket. But he can make a deuced pretty thing out of the other side as well. Let me tell you, Mr. Mason, that when notes for a thousand pounds are flying here and there, it isn't every lawyer that will see them pass by him without opening his hand."

"I do not think that Mr. Round would take a bribe," said Mr. Mason very stiffly.

"Wouldn't he? Just as a hound would a pat of butter. It's your own look-out, you know, Mr. Mason. I haven't got an estate of twelve hundred a year depending on it. But remember this;—if she escapes now, Orley Farm is gone for ever."

All this was extremely disagreeable to Mr. Mason. In the first place he did not at all like the tone of equality which the Hamworth attorney had adopted; he did not like to acknowledge that his affairs were in any degree dependent on a man of whom he thought so badly as he did of Mr. Dockwrath; he did not like to be told that Round and Crook were rogues,— Round and Crook whom he had known all his life; but least of all did he like the feeling of suspicion with which, in spite of himself, this man had imbued him, or the fear that his victim might at last escape him. Excellent, therefore, as had been the evidence with which Bridget Bolster had declared herself ready to give in his favour, Mr. Mason was not a contented man when he sat down to his solitary beefsteak in Soho Square.

CHAPTER XXXIII
THE ANGEL OF LIGHT

In speaking of the character and antecedents of Felix Graham I have said that he was moulding a wife for himself. The idea of a wife thus moulded to fit a man's own grooves, and educated to suit matrimonial purposes according to the exact views of the future husband was by no means original with him. Other men have moulded their wives, but I do not know that as a rule the practice has been found to answer. It is open, in the first place, to this objection, — that the moulder does not generally conceive such idea very early in life, and the idea when conceived must necessarily be carried out on a young subject. Such a plan is the result of much deliberate thought, and has generally arisen from long observation, on the part of the thinker, of the unhappiness arising from marriages in which there has been no moulding. Such a frame of mind comes upon a bachelor, perhaps about his thirty-fifth year, and then he goes to work with a girl of fourteen. The operation takes some ten years, at the end of which the moulded bride regards her lord as an old man. On the whole I think that the ordinary plan is the better, and even the safer. Dance with a girl three times, and if you like the light of her eye and the tone of voice with which she, breathless, answers your little questions about horseflesh and music—about affairs masculine and feminine, — then take the leap in the dark. There is danger, no doubt; but the moulded wife is, I think, more dangerous.

With Felix Graham the matter was somewhat different, seeing that he was not yet thirty, and that the lady destined to be the mistress of his family had already passed through three or four years of her noviciate. He had begun to be prudent early in life; or had become prudent rather by force of sentiment than by force of thought. Mary Snow was the name of his bride-elect; and it is probable that, had not circumstances thrown Mary Snow in his way, he would not have gone out of his way to seek a subject for his experiment. Mary Snow was the daughter of an engraver, — not of an artist who receives four or five thousand pounds for engraving the chef-d'œuvre of a modern painter, — but of a man who executed flourishes on ornamental cards for tradespeople, and assisted in the illustration of circus playbills. With this man Graham had become acquainted through certain transactions of his with the press, and had found him to be a widower, drunken, dissolute, and generally drowned in poverty. One child the man had, and that child was Mary Snow.

How it came to pass that the young barrister first took upon himself the charge of maintaining and educating this poor child need not now be told. His motives had been thoroughly good, and in the matter he had endeavoured to act the part of a kind Samaritan. He had found her pretty, half starved, dirty, ignorant, and modest; and so finding her had made himself responsible for feeding, cleaning, and teaching her,—and ultimately for marrying her. One would have said that in undertaking a task of such undoubted charity as that comprised in the three first charges, he would have encountered no difficulty from the drunken, dissolute, impoverished engraver. But the man from the beginning was cunning; and before Graham had succeeded in obtaining the custody of the child, the father had obtained a written undertaking from him that he would marry her at a certain age if her conduct up to that age had been becoming. As to this latter stipulation no doubt had arisen; and indeed Graham had so acted by her that had she fallen away the fault would have been all her own. There wanted now but one year to the coming of that day on which he was bound to make himself a happy man, and hitherto he himself had never doubted as to the accomplishment of his undertaking.

He had told his friends,—those with whom he was really intimate, Augustus Staveley and one or two others,—what was to be his matrimonial lot in life; and they had ridiculed him for his quixotic chivalry. Staveley especially had been strong in his conviction that no such marriage would ever take place, and had already gone so far as to plan another match for his friend.

"You know you do not love her," he had said, since Felix had been staying on this occasion at Noningsby.

"I know no such thing," Felix had answered, almost in anger. "On the contrary I know that I do love her."

"Yes, as I love my niece Marian, or old Aunt Bessy, who always supplied me with sugar-candy when I was a boy."

"It is I that have supplied Mary with her sugar-candy, and the love thus engendered is the stronger."

"Nevertheless you are not in love with her, and never will be, and if you marry her you will commit a great sin."

"How moral you have grown!"

"No, I'm not. I'm not a bit moral. But I know very well when a man is in love with a girl, and I know very well that you're not in love with Mary Snow. And I tell you what, my friend, if you do marry her you are done for life. There will absolutely be an end of you."

"You mean to say that your royal highness will drop me."

"I mean to say nothing about myself. My dropping you or not dropping you won't alter your lot in life. I know very well what a poor man wants to give him a start; and a fellow like you who has such quaint ideas on so many things requires all the assistance he can get. You should look out for money and connection."

"Sophia Furnival, for instance."

"No; she would not suit you. I perceive that now."

"So I supposed. Well, my dear fellow, we shall not come to loggerheads about that. She is a very fine girl, and you are welcome to the hatful of money—if you can get it."

"That's nonsense. I'm not thinking of Sophia Furnival any more than you are. But if I did it would be a proper marriage. Now—" And then he went on with some further very sage remarks about Miss Snow.

All this was said as Felix Graham was lying with his broken bones in the comfortable room at Noningsby; and to tell the truth, when it was so said his heart was not quite at ease about Mary Snow. Up to this time, having long since made up his mind that Mary should be his wife, he had never allowed his thoughts to be diverted from that purpose. Nor did he so allow them now,—as long as he could prevent them from wandering.

But, lying there at Noningsby, thinking of those sweet Christmas evenings, how was it possible that they should not wander? His friend had told him that he did not love Mary Snow; and then, when alone, he asked himself whether in truth he did love her. He had pledged himself to marry her, and he must carry out that pledge. But nevertheless did he love her? And if not her, did he love any other?

Mary Snow knew very well what was to be her destiny, and indeed had known it for the last two years. She was now nineteen years old,— and Madeline Staveley was also nineteen; she was nineteen, and at twenty she was to become a wife, as by agreement between Felix Graham and Mr. Snow, the drunken engraver. They knew their destiny,—the future husband and the future wife,—and each relied with perfect faith on the good faith and affection of the other.

Graham, while he was thus being lectured by Staveley, had under his pillow a letter from Mary. He wrote to her regularly—on every Sunday, and on every Tuesday she answered him. Nothing could be more becoming than the way she obeyed all his behests on such matters; and it really did seem that in his case the moulded wife would turn out to have been well moulded. When Staveley left him he again read Mary's letter. Her letters were always of the same length, filling completely the four sides of a sheet of note paper. They were excellently well written; and as no one word in them was ever altered or erased, it was manifest enough to Felix that the original composition was made on a rough draft. As he again read through the four sides of the little sheet of paper, he could not refrain from conjecturing what sort of a letter Madeline Staveley might write. Mary Snow's letter ran as follows:—

3 Bloomfield Terrace, Peckham,
Tuesday, 10 January, 18—.

My dearest Felix,

—she had so called him for the last twelvemonth by common consent between Graham and the very discreet lady under whose charge she at present lived. Previously to that she had written to him as, My dear Mr. Graham.

My dearest Felix,

> I am very glad to hear that your arm and your two ribs are getting so much better. I received your letter yesterday, and was glad to hear that you are so comfortable in the house of the very kind people with whom you are staying. If I knew them I would send them my respectful remembrances, but as I do not know them I suppose it would not be proper. But I remember them in my prayers.—

This last assurance was inserted under the express instruction of Mrs. Thomas, who however did not read Mary's letters, but occasionally, on some subjects, gave her hints as to what she ought to say. Nor was there hypocrisy in this, for under the instruction of her excellent mentor she had prayed for the kind people. —

> I hope you will be well enough to come and pay me a visit before long, but pray do not come before you are well enough to do so without giving yourself any pain. I am glad to hear that you do not mean to go hunting any more, for it seems to me to be a dangerous amusement.

And then the first paragraph came to an end.

> My papa called here yesterday. He said he was very badly off indeed, and so he looked. I did not know what to say at first, but he asked me so much to give him some money, that I did give him at last all that I had. It was nineteen shillings and sixpence. Mrs. Thomas was angry, and told me I had no right to give away your money, and that I should not have given more than half a crown. I hope you will not be angry with me. I do not want any more at present. But indeed he was very bad, especially about his shoes.

> I do not know that I have any more to say except that I put back thirty lines of Télémaque into French every morning before breakfast. It never comes near right, but nevertheless M. Grigaud says it is well done. He says that if it came quite right I should compose French as well as M. Fénelon, which of course I cannot expect.

> I will now say good-bye, and I am yours most affectionately,

> Mary Snow.

There was nothing in this letter to give any offence to Felix Graham, and so he acknowledged to himself. He made himself so acknowledge, because on the first reading of it he had felt that he was half angry with the writer. It was clear that there was nothing in the letter which would justify censure; — nothing which did not, almost, demand praise. He would have been angry with her had she limited her filial donation to the half-crown which Mrs. Thomas had thought appropriate. He was obliged to her for that attention to her French which he had specially enjoined. Nothing could be more proper than her allusion to the Staveleys; — and altogether the letter was just what it ought to be. Nevertheless it made him unhappy and irritated him. Was it well that he should marry a girl whose father was "indeed very bad, but especially about his shoes?" Staveley had told him that connection would be necessary for him, and what sort of a connection would this be? And was there one word in the whole letter that showed a spark of true love? Did not the footfall of Madeline Staveley's step as she passed along the passage go nearer to his heart than all the outspoken assurance of Mary Snow's letter?

Nevertheless he had undertaken to do this thing, and he would do it, — let the footfall of Madeline Staveley's step be ever so sweet in his ear. And then, lying back in his bed, he began to think whether it would have been as well that he should have broken his neck instead of his ribs in getting out of Monkton Grange covert.

Mrs. Thomas was a lady who kept a school consisting of three little girls and Mary Snow. She had in fact not been altogether successful in the line of life she had chosen for herself, and had hardly been able to keep her modest door-plate on her door, till Graham, in search of some home for his bride, then in the first noviciate of her moulding, had come across her. Her means were now far from plentiful; but as an average number of three children still clung to her, and as Mary Snow's seventy pounds per annum — to include clothes — were punctually paid, the small house at Peckham was maintained. Under these circumstances Mary Snow was somebody in the eyes of Mrs. Thomas, and Felix Graham was a very great person indeed.

Graham had received his letter on a Wednesday, and on the following Monday Mary, as usual, received one from him. These letters always came to her in the evening, as she was sitting over her tea with Mrs. Thomas, the three children having been duly put to bed. Graham's letters were very short, as a man with a broken right arm and two broken ribs is not fluent with his pen. But still a word or two did come to her. "Dearest Mary, I am doing better and better, and I hope I shall see you in about a fortnight. Quite right in giving the money. Stick to the French. Your own F. G." But as he signed himself her own, his mind misgave him that he was lying.

"It is very good of him to write to you while he is in such a state," said Mrs. Thomas.

"Indeed it is," said Mary — "very good indeed." And then she went on with the history of "Rasselas" in his happy valley, by which study Mrs. Thomas intended to initiate her into that course of novel-reading which has become necessary for a British lady. But Mrs. Thomas had a mind to improve the present occasion. It was her duty to inculcate in her pupil love and gratitude towards the beneficent man who was doing so much for her.

Gratitude for favours past and love for favours to come; and now, while that scrap of a letter was lying on the table, the occasion for doing so was opportune.

"Mary, I do hope you love Mr. Graham with all your heart and all your strength." She would have thought it wicked to say more; but so far she thought she might go, considering the sacred tie which was to exist between her pupil and the gentleman in question.

"Oh, yes, indeed I do;" and then Mary's eyes fell wishfully on the cover of the book which lay in her lap while her finger kept the place. Rasselas is not very exciting, but it was more so than Mrs. Thomas.

"You would be very wicked if you did not. And I hope you think sometimes of the very responsible duties which a wife owes to her husband. And this will be more especially so with you than with any other woman— almost that I ever heard of."

There was something in this that was almost depressing to poor Mary's spirit, but nevertheless she endeavoured to bear up against it and do her duty. "I shall do all I can to please him, Mrs. Thomas;—and indeed I do try about the French. And he says I was right to give papa that money."

"But there will be many more things than that when you've stood at the altar with him and become his wife;—bone of his bone, Mary." And she spoke these last words in a very solemn tone, shaking her head, and the solemn tone almost ossified poor Mary's heart as she heard it.

"Yes; I know there will. But I shall endeavour to find out what he likes."

"I don't think he is so particular about his eating and drinking as some other gentlemen; though no doubt he will like his things nice."

"I know he is fond of strong tea, and I sha'n't forget that."

"And about dress. He is not very rich you know, Mary; but it will make him unhappy if you are not always tidy. And his own shirts—I fancy he has no one to look after them now, for I so often see the buttons off. You should never let one of them go into his drawers without feeling them all to see that they're on tight."

"I'll remember that," said Mary, and then she made another little furtive attempt to open the book.

"And about your own stockings, Mary. Nothing is so useful to a young woman in your position as a habit of darning neat. I'm sometimes almost afraid that you don't like darning."

"Oh yes I do." That was a fib; but what could she do, poor girl, when so pressed?

"Because I thought you would look at Jane Robinson's and Julia Wright's which are lying there in the basket. I did Rebecca's myself before tea, till my old eyes were sore."

"Oh, I didn't know," said Mary, with some slight offence in her tone. "Why didn't you ask me to do them downright if you wanted?"

"It's only for the practice it will give you."

"Practice! I'm always practising something." But nevertheless she laid down the book, and dragged the basket of work up on to the table. "Why, Mrs. Thomas, it's impossible to mend these; they're all darn."

"Give them to me," said Mrs. Thomas. And then there was silence between them for a quarter of an hour during which Mary's thoughts wandered away to the events of her future life. Would his stockings be so troublesome as these?

But Mrs. Thomas was at heart an honest woman, and as a rule was honest also in practice. Her conscience told her that Mr. Graham might probably not approve of this sort of practice for conjugal duties, and in spite of her failing eyes she resolved to do her duty. "Never mind them, Mary," said she. "I remember now that you were doing your own before dinner."

"Of course I was," said Mary sulkily. "And as for practice, I don't suppose he'll want me to do more of that than anything else."

"Well, dear, put them by." And Miss Snow did put them by, resuming Rasselas as she did so. Who darned the stockings of Rasselas and felt that the buttons were tight on his shirts? What a happy valley must it have been if a bride expectant were free from all such cares as these!

"I suppose, Mary, it will be some time in the spring of next year." Mrs. Thomas was not reading, and therefore a little conversation from time to time was to her a solace.

"What will be, Mrs. Thomas?"

"Why, the marriage."

"I suppose it will. He told father it should be early in 18—, and I shall be past twenty then."

"I wonder where you'll go to live."

"I don't know. He has never said anything about that."

"I suppose not; but I'm sure it will be a long way away from Peckham." In answer to this Mary said nothing, but could not help wishing that it might be so. Peckham to her had not been a place bright with happiness, although she had become in so marked a way a child of good fortune. And then, moreover, she had a deep care on her mind with which the streets and houses and pathways of Peckham were closely connected. It would be very expedient that she should go far, far away from Peckham when she had become, in actual fact, the very wife of Felix Graham.

"Miss Mary," whispered the red-armed maid of all work, creeping up to Mary's bedroom door, when they had all retired for the night, and whispering through the chink. "Miss Mary. I've somethink to say." And Mary opened the door. "I've got a letter from him;" and the maid of all work absolutely produced a little note enclosed in a green envelope.

"Sarah, I told you not," said Mary, looking very stern and hesitating with her finger whether or no she would take the letter.

"But he did so beg and pray. Besides, miss, as he says hisself he must have his answer. Any gen'leman, he says, 'as a right to a answer. And if you'd a seed him yourself I'm sure you'd have took it. He did look so nice with a blue and gold hankercher round his neck. He was a-going to the the-a-tre he said."

"And who was going with him, Sarah?"

"Oh, no one. Only his mamma and sister, and them sort. He's all right— he is." And then Mary Snow did take the letter.

"And I'll come for the answer when you're settling the room after breakfast to-morrow?" said the girl.

"No; I don't know. I sha'n't send any answer at all. But, Sarah, for heaven's sake, do not say a word about it!"

"Who, I? Laws love you, miss. I wouldn't;—not for worlds of gold." And then Mary was left alone to read a second letter from a second suitor.

"Angel of light!" it began, "but cold as your own fair name." Poor Mary thought it was very nice and very sweet, and though she was so much afraid of it that she almost wished it away, yet she read it a score of times. Stolen pleasures always are sweet. She had not cared to read those two lines from her own betrothed lord above once, or at the most twice; and yet they had been written by a good man,—a man superlatively good to her, and written too with considerable pain.

The Angel of Light.

She sat down all trembling to think of what she was doing; and then, as she thought, she read the letter again. "Angel of light! but cold as your own fair name." Alas, alas! it was very sweet to her!

CHAPTER XXXIV
MR. FURNIVAL LOOKS FOR ASSISTANCE

"And you think that nothing can be done down there?" said Mr. Furnival to his clerk, immediately after the return of Mr. Crabwitz from Hamworth to London.

"Nothing at all, sir," said Mr. Crabwitz, with laconic significance.

"Well; I dare say not. If the matter could have been arranged at a reasonable cost, without annoyance to my friend Lady Mason, I should have been glad; but, on the whole, it will perhaps be better that the law should take its course. She will suffer a good deal, but she will be the safer for it afterwards."

"Mr. Furnival, I went so far as to offer a thousand pounds!"

"A thousand pounds! Then they'll think we're afraid of them."

"Not a bit more than they did before. Though I offered the money, he doesn't know the least that the offer came from our side. But I'll tell you what it is, Mr. Furnival—. I suppose I may speak my mind."

"Oh, yes! But remember this, Crabwitz; Lady Mason is no more in danger of losing the property than you are. It is a most vexatious thing, but there can be no doubt as to what the result will be."

"Well, Mr. Furnival,—I don't know."

"In such matters, I am tolerably well able to form an opinion."

"Oh, certainly!"

"And that's my opinion. Now I shall be very glad to hear yours."

"My opinion is this, Mr. Furnival, that Sir Joseph never made that codicil."

"And what makes you think so?"

"The whole course of the evidence. It's quite clear there was another deed executed that day, and witnessed by Bolster and Kenneby. Had there been two documents for them to witness, they would have remembered it so soon after the occurrence."

"Well, Crabwitz, I differ from you,—differ from you in toto. But keep your opinion to yourself, that's all. I've no doubt you did the best for us you could down at Hamworth, and I'm much obliged to you. You'll find we've got our hands quite full again,—almost too full." Then he turned round to his table, and to the papers upon it; whereupon, Crabwitz took the hint, and left the room.

But when he had gone, Mr. Furnival again raised his eyes from the papers on the table, and leaning back in his chair, gave himself up to further consideration of the Orley Farm case. Crabwitz he knew was a sharp, clever man, and now the opinion formed by Crabwitz, after having seen this Hamworth attorney, tallied with his own opinion. Yes; it was his own opinion. He had never said as much, even to himself, with those inward words which a man uses when he assures himself of the result of his own thoughts; but he was aware that it was his own opinion. In his heart of hearts, he did believe that that codicil had been fraudulently manufactured by his friend and client, Lady Mason.

Under these circumstances, what should he do? He had the handle of his pen between his teeth, as was his habit when he was thinking, and tried to bring himself to some permanent resolution.

How beautiful had she looked while she stood in Sir Peregrine's library, leaning on the old man's arm—how beautiful and how innocent! That was the form which his thoughts chiefly took. And then she had given him her hand, and he still felt the soft silken touch of her cool fingers. He would not be a man if he could desert a woman in such a strait. And such a woman! If even guilty, had she not expiated her guilt by deep sorrow? And then he thought of Mr. Mason of Groby Park; and he thought of Sir Peregrine's strong conviction, and of Judge Staveley's belief; and he thought also of the strong hold which public opinion and twenty years of possession would still give to the cause he favoured. He would still bring her through! Yes; in spite of her guilt, if she were guilty; on the strength of her innocency, if she were innocent; but on account of her beauty, and soft hand, and deep liquid eye. So at least he would have owned, could he have been honest enough to tell himself the whole truth.

But he must prepare himself for the battle in earnest. It was not as though he had been briefed in this case, and had merely to perform the duty for which he had been hired. He was to undertake the whole legal management of the affair. He must settle what attorney should have the matter in hand, and instruct that attorney how to reinstruct him, and how to reinstruct those other barristers who must necessarily be employed on the defence, in a case of such magnitude. He did not yet know under what form the attack would be made; but he was nearly certain that it would be done in the shape of a criminal charge. He hoped that it might take the direct form of an accusation of forgery. The stronger and more venomous the charge made, the stronger also would be public opinion in favour of the accused, and the greater the chance of an acquittal. But if she were to be found guilty on any charge, it would matter little on what. Any such verdict of guilty would be utter ruin and obliteration of her existence.

He must consult with some one, and at last he made up his mind to go to his very old friend, Mr. Chaffanbrass. Mr. Chaffanbrass was safe, and he might speak out his mind to him without fear of damaging the cause. Not that he could bring himself to speak out his real mind, even to Mr. Chaffanbrass. He would so speak that Mr. Chaffanbrass should clearly understand him; but still, not even to his ears, would he say that he really believed Lady Mason to have been guilty. How would it be possible that he should feign before a jury his assured, nay, his indignant conviction of his client's innocence, if he had ever whispered to any one his conviction of her guilt?

On that same afternoon he sent to make an appointment with Mr. Chaffanbrass, and immediately after breakfast, on the following morning, had himself taken to that gentleman's chambers. The chambers of this great guardian of the innocence—or rather not-guiltiness of the public—were not in any so-named inn, but consisted of two gloomy, dark, panelled rooms in Ely Place. The course of our story, however, will not cause us to make many visits to Ely Place, and any closer description of them may be spared. I have said that Mr. Chaffanbrass and Mr. Furnival were very old friends. So they were. They had known each other for more than thirty years, and each knew the whole history of the other's rise and progress in the profession; but any results of their friendship at present were but scanty. They might meet each other in the streets, perhaps, once in the year; and occasionally—but very seldom—might be brought together on subjects connected with their profession; as was the case when they travelled together down to Birmingham. As to meeting in each other's houses, or coming together for the sake of the friendship which existed,—the idea of doing so never entered the head of either of them.

All the world knows Mr. Chaffanbrass—either by sight or by reputation. Those who have been happy enough to see the face and gait of the man as, in years now gone, he used to lord it at the Old Bailey, may not have thought much of the privilege which was theirs. But to those who have only read of him, and know of his deeds simply by their triumphs, he was a man very famous and worthy to be seen. "Look; that's Chaffanbrass. It was he who cross-examined —— at the Old Bailey, and sent him howling out of London, banished for ever into the wilderness." "Where, where? Is that Chaffanbrass? What a dirty little man!"

To this dirty little man in Ely Place, Mr. Furnival now went in his difficulty. Mr. Furnival might feel himself sufficient to secure the acquittal of an innocent person, or even of a guilty person, under ordinary circumstances; but if any man in England could secure the acquittal of a guilty person under extraordinary circumstances, it would be Mr. Chaffanbrass. This had been his special line of work for the last thirty years.

Mr. Chaffanbrass was a dirty little man; and when seen without his gown and wig, might at a first glance be thought insignificant. But he knew well how to hold his own in the world, and could maintain his opinion, unshaken, against all the judges in the land. "Well, Furnival, and what can I do for you?" he said, as soon as the member for the Essex Marshes was seated opposite to him. "It isn't often that the light of your countenance shines so far east as this. Somebody must be in trouble, I suppose?"

"Somebody is in trouble," said Mr. Furnival; and then he began to tell his story. Mr. Chaffanbrass listened almost in silence throughout. Now and then he asked a question by a word or two, expressing no opinion whatever as he did so; but he was satisfied to leave the talking altogether in the hands of his visitor till the whole tale was told. "Ah," he said then, "a clever woman!"

"An uncommonly sweet creature too," said Mr. Furnival.

"I dare say," said Mr. Chaffanbrass; and then there was a pause.

"And what can I do for you?" said Mr. Chaffanbrass.

"In the first place I should be very glad to have your advice; and then—. Of course I must lead in defending her,—unless it were well that I should put the case altogether in your hands."

"Oh no! don't think of that. I couldn't give the time to it. My heart is not in it, as yours is. Where will it be?"

"At Alston, I suppose."

"At the Spring assizes. That will be—. Let me see; about the 10th of March."

"I should think we might get it postponed till the summer. Round is not at all hot about it."

"Should we gain anything by that? If a prisoner be innocent why torment him by delay. He is tolerably sure of escape. If he be guilty, extension of time only brings out the facts the clearer. As far as my experience goes, the sooner a man is tried the better,—always."

"And you would consent to hold a brief?"

"Under you? Well; yes. I don't mind it at Alston. Anything to oblige an old friend. I never was proud, you know."

"And what do you think about it, Chaffanbrass?"

"Ah! that's the question."

"She must be pulled through. Twenty years of possession! Think of that."

"That's what Mason, the man down in Yorkshire, is thinking of. There's no doubt of course about that partnership deed?"

"I fear not. Round would not go on with it if that were not all true."

"It depends on those two witnesses, Furnival. I remember the case of old, though it was twenty years ago, and I had nothing to do with it. I remember thinking that Lady Mason was a very clever woman, and that Round and Crook were rather slow."

"He's a brute; is that fellow, Mason of Groby Park."

"A brute; is he? We'll get him into the box and make him say as much for himself. She's uncommonly pretty, isn't she?"

"She is a pretty woman."

"And interesting? It will all tell, you know. A widow with one son, isn't she?"

"Yes, and she has done her duty admirably since her husband's death. You will find too that she has the sympathies of all the best people in her neighbourhood. She is staying now at the house of Sir Peregrine Orme, who would do anything for her."

"Anything, would he?"

"And the Staveleys know her. The judge is convinced of her innocence."

"Is he? He'll probably have the Home Circuit in the summer. His conviction expressed from the bench would be more useful to her. You can make Staveley believe everything in a drawing-room or over a glass of wine; but I'll be hanged if I can ever get him to believe anything when he's on the bench."

"But, Chaffanbrass, the countenance of such people will be of great use to her down there. Everybody will know that she's been staying with Sir Peregrine."

"I've no doubt she's a clever woman."

"But this new trouble has half killed her."

"I don't wonder at that either. These sort of troubles do vex people. A pretty woman like that should have everything smooth; shouldn't she? Well, we'll do the best we can. You'll see that I'm properly instructed. By-the-by, who is her attorney? In such a case as that you couldn't have a better man than old Solomon Aram. But Solomon Aram is too far east from you, I suppose?"

"Isn't he a Jew?"

"Upon my word I don't know. He's an attorney, and that's enough for me."

And then the matter was again discussed between them, and it was agreed that a third counsel would be wanting. "Felix Graham is very much interested in the case," said Mr. Furnival, "and is as firmly convinced of her innocence as—as I am." And he managed to look his ally in the face and to keep his countenance firmly.

"Ah," said Mr. Chaffanbrass. "But what if he should happen to change his opinion about his own client?"

"We could prevent that, I think."

"I'm not so sure. And then he'd throw her over as sure as your name's Furnival."

"I hardly think he'd do that."

"I believe he'd do anything." And Mr. Chaffanbrass was quite moved to enthusiasm. "I've heard that man talk more nonsense about the profession in one hour, than I ever heard before since I first put a cotton gown on my back. He does not understand the nature of the duty which a professional man owes to his client."

"But he'd work well if he had a case at heart himself. I don't like him, but he is clever."

"You can do as you like, of course. I shall be out of my ground down at Alston, and of course I don't care who takes the fag of the work. But I tell you this fairly;—if he does go into the case and then turns against us or drops it,—I shall turn against him and drop into him."

"Heaven help him in such a case as that!" And then these two great luminaries of the law shook hands and parted.

One thing was quite clear to Mr. Furnival as he had himself carried in a cab from Ely Place to his own chambers in Lincoln's Inn. Mr. Chaffanbrass was fully convinced of Lady Mason's guilt. He had not actually said so, but he had not even troubled himself to go through the little ceremony of expressing a belief in her innocence. Mr. Furnival was well aware that Mr. Chaffanbrass would not on this account be less likely to come out strongly with such assurances before a jury, or to be less severe in his cross-examination of a witness whose evidence went to prove that guilt; but nevertheless the conviction was disheartening. Mr. Chaffanbrass would know, almost by instinct, whether an accused person was or was not guilty; and he had already perceived, by instinct, that Lady Mason was guilty. Mr. Furnival sighed as he stepped out of his cab, and again wished that he could wash his hands of the whole affair. He wished it very much;—but he knew that his wish could not be gratified.

"Solomon Aram!" he said to himself, as he again sat down in his arm-chair. "It will sound badly to those people down at Alston. At the Old Bailey they don't mind that kind of thing." And then he made up his mind that Solomon Aram would not do. It would be a disgrace to him to take a case out of Solomon Aram's hands. Mr. Chaffanbrass did not understand all this. Mr. Chaffanbrass had been dealing with Solomon Arams all his life. Mr. Chaffanbrass could not see the effect which such an alliance would have on the character of a barrister holding Mr. Furnival's position. Solomon Aram was a good man in his way no doubt;—perhaps the best man going. In taking every dodge to prevent a conviction no man could be better than Solomon Aram. All this Mr. Furnival felt;—but he felt also that he could not afford it. "It would be tantamount to a confession of guilt to take such a man as that down into the country," he said to himself, trying to excuse himself.

And then he also made up his mind that he would sound Felix Graham. If Felix Graham could be induced to take up the case thoroughly believing in the innocence of his client, no man would be more useful as a junior. Felix Graham went the Home Circuit on which Alston was one of the assize towns.

CHAPTER XXXV
LOVE WAS STILL THE LORD OF ALL

Why should I not? Such had been the question which Sir Peregrine Orme had asked himself over and over again, in these latter days, since Lady Mason had been staying at his house; and the purport of the question was this:—Why should he not make Lady Mason his wife?

I and my readers can probably see very many reasons why he should not do so; but then we are not in love with Lady Mason. Her charms and her sorrows,—her soft, sad smile and her more lovely tears have not operated upon us. We are not chivalrous old gentlemen, past seventy years of age, but still alive, keenly alive, to a strong feeling of romance. That visit will perhaps be remembered which Mr. Furnival made at The Cleeve, and the subsequent interview between Lady Mason and the baronet. On that day he merely asked himself the question, and took no further step. On the subsequent day and the day after, it was the same. He still asked himself the question, sitting alone in his library; but he did not ask it as yet of any one else. When he met Lady Mason in these days his manner to her was full of the deference due to a lady and of the affection due to a dear friend; but that was all. Mrs. Orme, seeing this, and cordially concurring in this love for her guest, followed the lead which her father-in-law gave, and threw herself into Lady Mason's arms. They two were fast and bosom friends.

And what did Lady Mason think of all this? In truth there was much in it that was sweet to her, but there was something also that increased that idea of danger which now seemed to envelop her whole existence. Why had Sir Peregrine so treated her in the library, behaving towards her with such tokens of close affection? He had put his arm round her waist and kissed her lips and pressed her to his old bosom. Why had this been so? He had assured her that he would be to her as a father, but her woman's instinct had told her that the pressure of his hand had been warmer than that which a father accords to his adopted daughter. No idea of anger had come upon her for a moment; but she had thought about it much, and had thought about it almost in dismay. What if the old man did mean more than a father's love? It seemed to her as though it must be a dream that he should do so; but what if he did? How should she answer him? In such circumstances what should she do or say? Could she afford to buy his friendship,—even his warmest love at the cost of the enmity of so many others? Would not Mrs. Orme hate her, Mrs. Orme, whom she truly, dearly, eagerly loved? Mrs. Orme's affection was, of all personal gratifications, the sweetest to her. And the young heir,—would not he hate her? Nay, would he not interfere and with some strong hand prevent so mean a deed on the part of his grandfather? And if so, would she not thus have lost them altogether? And then she thought of that other friend whose aid would be so indispensable to her in this dreadful time of tribulation. How would Mr. Furnival receive such tidings, if it should come to pass that such tidings were to be told?

Lady Mason was rich with female charms, and she used them partly with the innocence of the dove, but partly also with the wisdom of the serpent. But in such use as she did make of these only weapons which Providence had given to her, I do not think that she can be regarded as very culpable. During those long years of her young widowhood in which nothing had been wanting to her, her conduct had been free from any hint of reproach. She had been content to find all her joy in her duties and in her love as a mother. Now a great necessity for assistance had come upon her. It was necessary that she should bind men to her cause, men powerful in the world and able to fight her battle with strong arms. She did so bind them with the only chains at her command,—but she had no thought, nay, no suspicion of evil in so doing. It was very painful to her when she found that she had caused unhappiness to Mrs. Furnival; and it caused her pain now, also, when she thought of Sir Peregrine's new love. She did wish to bind these men to her by a strong attachment; but she would have stayed this feeling at a certain point had it been possible for her so to manage it.

In the mean time Sir Peregrine still asked himself that question. He had declared to himself when first the idea had come to him, that none of those whom he loved should be injured. He would even ask his daughter-in-law's consent, condescending to plead his cause before her, making her understand his motives, and asking her acquiescence as a favour. He would be so careful of his grandson that this second marriage—if such event did come to pass—should not put a pound out of his pocket, or at any rate should not hamper the succession of the estate with a pound of debt. And then he made excuses to himself as to the step which he proposed to take, thinking how he would meet his friends, and how he would carry himself before his old servants.

Old men have made more silly marriages than this which he then desired. Gentlemen such as Sir Peregrine in age and station have married their housemaids,—have married young girls of eighteen years of age,—

have done so and faced their friends and servants afterwards. The bride that he proposed to himself was a lady, an old friend, a woman over forty, and one whom by such a marriage he could greatly assist in her deep sorrow. Why should he not do it?

After much of such thoughts as these, extended over nearly a week, he resolved to speak his mind to Mrs. Orme. If it were to be done it should be done at once. The incredulous unromantic readers of this age would hardly believe me if I said that his main object was to render assistance to Lady Mason in her difficulty; but so he assured himself, and so he believed. This assistance to be of true service must be given at once;—and having so resolved he sent for Mrs. Orme into the library.

"Edith, my darling," he said, taking her hand and pressing it between both his own as was often the wont with him in his more affectionate moods. "I want to speak to you—on business that concerns me nearly; may perhaps concern us all nearly. Can you give me half an hour?"

"Of course I can—what is it, sir? I am a bad hand at business; but you know that."

"Sit down, dear; there; sit there, and I will sit here. As to this business, no one can counsel me as well as you."

"Dearest father, I should be a poor councillor in anything."

"Not in this, Edith. It is about Lady Mason that I would speak to you. We both love her dearly; do we not?"

"I do."

"And are glad to have her here?"

"Oh, so glad. When this trial is only over, it will be so sweet, to have her for a neighbour. We really know her now. And it will be so pleasant to see much of her."

There was nothing discouraging in this, but still the words in some slight degree grated against Sir Peregrine's feelings. At the present moment he did not wish to think of Lady Mason as living at Orley Farm, and would have preferred that his daughter-in-law should have spoken of her as being there, at The Cleeve.

"Yes; we know her now," he said. "And believe me in this, Edith; no knowledge obtained of a friend in happiness is at all equal to that which is obtained in sorrow. Had Lady Mason been prosperous, had she never become subject to the malice and avarice of wicked people, I should never have loved her as I do love her."

"Nor should I, father."

"She is a cruelly ill-used woman, and a woman worthy of the kindest usage. I am an old man now, but it has never before been my lot to be so anxious for a fellow-creature as I am for her. It is dreadful to think that innocence in this country should be subject to such attacks."

"Indeed it is; but you do not think that there is any danger?"

This was all very well, and showed that Mrs. Orme's mind was well disposed towards the woman whom he loved. But he had known that before, and he began to feel that he was not approaching the object which he had in view. "Edith," at last he said abruptly, "I love her with my whole heart. I would fain make her—my wife." Sir Peregrine Orme had never in his course through life failed in anything for lack of courage; and when the idea came home to him that he was trembling at the task which he had imposed on himself, he dashed at it at once. It is so that forlorn hopes are led, and become not forlorn; it is so that breaches are taken.

"Your wife!" said Mrs. Orme. She would not have breathed a syllable to pain him if she could have helped it, but the suddenness of the announcement overcame her for a moment.

"Yes, Edith, my wife. Let us discuss the matter before you condemn it. But in the first place I would have you to understand this—I will not marry her if you say that it will make you unhappy. I have not spoken to her as yet, and she knows nothing of this project." Sir Peregrine, it may be presumed, had not himself thought much of that kiss which he had given her. "You," he continued to say, "have given up your whole life to me. You are my angel. If this thing will make you unhappy it shall not be done."

Sir Peregrine had not so considered it, but with such a woman as Mrs. Orme this was, of course, the surest way to overcome opposition. On her own behalf, thinking only of herself, she would stand in the way of nothing that could add to Sir Peregrine's happiness. But nevertheless the idea was strong in her mind that such a marriage would be imprudent. Sir Peregrine at present stood high before the world. Would he stand so high if he did this thing? His gray hair and old manly bearing were honoured and revered by all who knew him. Would this still be so if he made himself the husband of Lady Mason? She loved so dearly, she valued so highly the honour that was paid to him! She was so proud of her own boy in that he was the grandson of so perfect a gentleman! Would not this be a sad ending to such a career? Such were the thoughts which ran through her mind at the moment.

"Make me unhappy!" she said getting up and going over to him. "It is your happiness of which I would think. Will it make you more happy?"

"It will enable me to befriend her more effectually."

"But, dearest father, you must be the first consideration to us,—to me and Peregrine. Will it make you more happy?"

"I think it will," he answered slowly.

"Then I, for one, will say nothing against it," she answered. She was very weak, it will be said. Yes, she was weak. Many of the sweetest, kindest, best of women are weak in this way. It is not every woman that can bring herself to say hard, useful, wise words in opposition to the follies of those they love best. A woman to be useful and wise no doubt should have such power. For myself I am not so sure that I like useful and wise women. "Then I for one will say nothing against it," said Mrs. Orme, deficient in utility, wanting in wisdom, but full of the sweetest affection.

"You are sure that you will not love her the less yourself?" said Sir Peregrine.

"Yes; I am sure of that. If it were to be so, I should endeavour to love her the more."

"Dearest Edith. I have only one other person to tell."

"Do you mean Peregrine?" she said in her softest voice.

"Yes. Of course he must be told. But as it would not be well to ask his consent,—as I have asked yours—" and then as he said this she kissed his brow.

"But you will let him know it?"

"Yes; that is if she accepts my proposition. Then he shall know it immediately. And, Edith, my dear, you may be sure of this; nothing that I do shall be allowed in any way to injure his prospects or to hamper him as regards money when I am gone. If this marriage takes place I cannot do very much for her in the way of money; she will understand that. Something I can of course."

And then Mrs. Orme stood over the fire, looking at the hot coals, and thinking what Lady Mason's answer would be. She esteemed Lady Mason very highly, regarding her as a woman sensible and conscientious at all points, and she felt by no means certain that the offer would be accepted. What if Lady Mason should say that such an arrangement would not be possible for her. Mrs. Orme felt that under such circumstances she at any rate would not withdraw her love from Lady Mason.

"And now I may as well speak to her at once," said Sir Peregrine. "Is she in the drawing-room?"

"I left her there."

"Will you ask her to come to me—with my love?"

"I had better not say anything I suppose?"

Sir Peregrine, in his heart of hearts wished that his daughter-in-law could say it all, but he would not give her such a commission. "No; perhaps not." And then Mrs. Orme was going to leave him.

"One word more, Edith. You and I, darling, have known each other so long and loved each other so well, that I should be unhappy if I were to fall in your estimation."

"There is no fear of that, father."

"Will you believe me when I assure you that my great object in doing this is to befriend a good and worthy woman whom I regard as ill used—beyond all ill usage of which I have hitherto known anything?"

She then assured him that she did so believe, and she assured him truly; after that she left him and went away to send in Lady Mason for her interview. In the mean time Sir Peregrine got up and stood with his back to the fire. He would have been glad that the coming scene could be over, and yet I should be wronging him to say that he was afraid of it. There would be a pleasure to him in telling her that he loved her so dearly and trusted her with such absolute confidence. There would be a sort of pleasure to him in speaking even of her sorrow, and in repeating his assurance that he would fight the battle for her with all the means at his command. And perhaps also there would be some pleasure in the downcast look of her eye, as she accepted the tender of his love. Something of that pleasure he had known already. And then he remembered the other alternative. It was quite upon the cards that she should decline his offer. He did not by any means shut his eyes to that. Did she do so, his friendship should by no means be withdrawn from her. He would be very careful from the onset that she should understand so much as that. And then he heard the light footsteps in the hall; the gentle hand was raised to the door, and Lady Mason was standing in the room.

"Dear Lady Mason," he said, meeting her half way across the room, "it is very kind of you to come to me when I send for you in this way."

"It would be my duty to come to you, if it were half across the kingdom;—and my pleasure also."

"Would it?" said he, looking into her face with all the wishfulness of a young lover. From that moment she knew what was coming. Strange as was the destiny which was to be offered to her at this period of her life, yet she foresaw clearly that the offer was to be made. What she did not foresee, what she could not foretell, was the answer which she might make to it!

"It would certainly be my sweetest pleasure to send for you if you were away from us,—to send for you or to follow you," said he.

"I do not know how to make return for all your kind regard to me;—to you and to dear Mrs. Orme."

"Call her Edith, will you not? You did so call her once."

"I call her so often when we are alone together, now; and yet I feel that I have no right."

"You have every right. You shall have every right if you will accept it. Lady Mason, I am an old man,—some would say a very old man. But I am not too old to love you. Can, you accept the love of an old man like me?"

Lady Mason was, as we are aware, not taken in the least by surprise; but it was quite necessary that she should seem to be so taken. This is a little artifice which is excusable in almost any lady at such a period. "Sir Peregrine," she said, "you do not mean more than the love of a most valued friend?"

"Yes, much more. I mean the love of a husband for his wife; of a wife for her husband."

"Sir Peregrine! Ah me! You have not thought of this, my friend. You have not remembered the position in which I am placed. Dearest, dearest friend; dearest of all friends,"—and then she knelt before him, leaning on his knees, as he sat in his accustomed large arm-chair. "It may not be so. Think of the sorrow that would come to you and yours, if my enemies should prevail."

"By — — they shall not prevail!" swore Sir Peregrine, roundly; and as he swore the oath he put his two hands upon her shoulders.

"No; we will hope not. I should die here at your feet if I thought that they could prevail. But I should die twenty deaths were I to drag you with me into disgrace. There will be disgrace even in standing at that bar."

"Who will dare to say so, when I shall stand there with you?" said Sir Peregrine.

There was a feeling expressed in his face as he spoke these words, which made it glorious, and bright, and beautiful. She, with her eyes laden with tears, could not see it; but nevertheless, she knew that it was bright and beautiful. And his voice was full of hot eager assurance,—that assurance which had the power to convey itself from one breast to another. Would it not be so? If he stood there with her as her husband and lord, would it not be the case that no one would dare to impute disgrace to her?

And yet she did not wish it. Even yet, thinking of all this as she did think of it, according to the truth of the argument which he himself put before her, she would still have preferred that it should not be so. If she only knew with what words to tell him so;—to tell him so and yet give no offence! For herself, she would have married him willingly. Why should she not? Nay, she could and would have loved him, and been to him a wife, such as he could have found in no other woman. But she said within her heart that she owed him kindness and gratitude—that she owed them all kindness, and that it would be bad to repay them in such a way as this. She also thought of Sir Peregrine's gray hairs, and of his proud standing in the county, and the respect in which men held him. Would it be well in her to drag him down in his last days from the noble pedestal on which he stood, and repay him thus for all that he was doing for her?

"Well," said he, stroking her soft hair with his hands—the hair which appeared in front of the quiet prim cap she wore, "shall it be so? Will you give me the right to stand there with you and defend you against the tongues of wicked men? We each have our own weakness, and we also have each our own strength. There I may boast that I should be strong."

She thought again for a moment or two without rising from her knees, and also without speaking. Would such strength suffice? And if it did suffice, would it then be well with him? As for herself, she did love him. If she had not loved him before, she loved him now. Who had ever been to her so noble, so loving, so gracious as he? In her ears no young lover's vows had ever sounded. In her heart such love as all the world knows had never been known. Her former husband had been kind to her in his way, and she had done her duty by him carefully, painfully, and with full acceptance of her position. But there had been nothing there that was bright, and grand, and noble. She would have served Sir Peregrine on her knees in the smallest offices, and delighted in such services. It was not for lack of love that she must refuse him. But still she did not answer him, and still he stroked her hair.

"It would be better that you had never seen me," at last she said; and she spoke with truth the thought of her mind. That she must do his bidding, whatever that bidding might be, she had in a certain way acknowledged to herself. If he would have it so, so it must be. How could she refuse him anything, or be disobedient in aught to one to whom she owed so much? But still it would be wiser otherwise, wiser for all—unless it were for herself alone. "It would be better that you had never seen me," she said.

"Nay, not so, dearest. That it would not be better for me,—for me and Edith I am quite sure. And I would fain hope that for you—"

"Oh, Sir Peregrine! you know what I mean. You know how I value your kindness. What should I be if it were withdrawn from me?"

"It shall not be withdrawn. Do not let that feeling actuate you. Answer me out of your heart, and however your heart may answer, remember this, that my friendship and support shall be the same. If you will take me for your husband, as your husband will I stand by you. If you cannot,—then I will stand by you as your father."

What could she say? A word or two she did speak as to Mrs. Orme and her feelings, delaying her absolute reply—and as to Peregrine Orme and his prospects; but on both, as on all other points, the baronet was armed with his answer. He had spoken to his darling Edith, and she had gladly given her consent. To her it would be everything to have so sweet a friend. And then as to his heir, every care should be taken that no injury should be done to him; and speaking of this, Sir Peregrine began to say a few words, plaintively, about money. But then Lady Mason stopped him. "No," she said, "she could not, and would not, listen to that. She would have no settlement. No consideration as to money should be made to weigh with her. It was in no degree for that—" And then she wept there till she would have fallen had he not supported her.

What more is there to be told. Of course she accepted him. As far as I can see into such affairs no alternative was allowed to her. She also was not a wise woman at all points. She was one whose feelings were sometimes too many for her, and whose feelings on this occasion had been much too many for her. Had she been able to throw aside from her his offer, she would have done so; but she had felt that she was not able. "If you wish it, Sir Peregrine," she said at last.

"And can you love an old man?" he had asked. Old men sometimes will ask questions such as these. She did not answer him, but stood by his side; and, then again he kissed her, and was happy.

He resolved from that moment that Lady Mason should no longer be regarded as the widow of a city knight, but as the wife elect of a country baronet. Whatever ridicule he might incur in this matter, he would incur at once. Men and women had dared to speak of her cruelly, and they should now learn that any such future speech would be spoken of one who was exclusively his property. Let any who chose to be speakers under such circumstances look to it. He had devoted himself to her that he might be her knight and bear her scathless through the fury of this battle. With God's help he would put on his armour at once for that fight. Let them who would now injure her look to it. As soon as might be she should bear his name; but all the world should know at once what was her right to claim his protection. He had never been a coward, and he would not now be guilty of the cowardice of hiding his intentions. If there were those who chose to smile at the old man's fancy, let them smile. There would be many, he knew, who would not understand an old man's honour and an old man's chivalry.

"My own one," he then said, pressing her again to his side, "will you tell Edith, or shall I? She expects it." But Lady Mason begged that he would tell the tale. It was necessary, she said, that she should be alone for a while. And then, escaping, she went to her own chamber.

"Ask Mrs. Orme if she will kindly step to me," said Sir Peregrine, having rang his bell for the servant.

Lady Mason escaped across the hall to the stairs, and succeeded in reaching her room without being seen by any one. Then she sat herself down, and began to look her future world in the face. Two questions she had to ask. Would it be well for her that this marriage should take place? and would it be well for him? In an off-hand way she had already answered both questions; but she had done so by feeling rather than by thought.

No doubt she would gain much in the coming struggle by such a position as Sir Peregrine would give her. It did seem to her that Mr. Dockwrath and Joseph Mason would hardly dare to bring such a charge as that threatened against the wife of Sir Peregrine Orme. And then, too, what evidence as to character would be so substantial as the evidence of such a marriage? But how would Mr. Furnival bear it, and if he were offended would it be possible that the fight should be fought without him? No; that would be impossible. The lawyer's knowledge, experience, and skill were as necessary to her as the baronet's position and character. But why should Mr. Furnival be offended by such a marriage? "She did not know," she said to herself. "She could not see that there should be cause of offence." But yet some inner whisper of her conscience told her that there would be offence. Must Mr. Furnival be told; and must he be told at once? And then what would Lucius say and think, and how should she answer the strong words which her son would use to her? He would use strong words she knew, and would greatly dislike this second marriage of his mother. What grown-up son is ever pleased to hear that his mother is about to marry? The Cleeve must be her home now—that is, if she did this deed. The Cleeve must be her home, and she must be separated in all things from Orley Farm. As she thought of this her mind went back, and back to those long gone days in which she had been racked with anxiety that Orley Farm should be the inheritance of the little baby that was lying at her feet. She remembered how she had pleaded to the father, pointing out the rights of her son—declaring, and with justice, that for herself she had asked for nothing; but that for him—instead of asking might she not demand? Was not that other son provided for, and those grown-up women with their rich husbands? "Is he not your child as well as they?" she had pleaded. "Is he not your own, and as well worthy of your love?" She had succeeded in getting the inheritance for the baby at her feet;—but had his having it made her happy, or him? Then her child had been all in all to her; but now she felt that that child was half estranged from her about this very property, and would become wholly estranged by the method she was taking to secure it! "I have toiled for him," she said to herself, "rising up early, and going to bed late; but the thief cometh in the night and despoileth it." Who can guess the bitterness of her thoughts as she said this?

But her last thoughts, as she sat there thinking, were of him—Sir Peregrine. Would it be well for him that he should do this? And in thus considering she did not turn her mind chiefly to the usual view in which such a marriage would be regarded. Men might call Sir Peregrine an old fool and laugh at him; but for that she would, with God's help, make him amends. In those matters, he could judge for himself; and should he judge it right thus to link his life to hers, she would be true and leal to him in all things.

But then, about this trial. If there came disgrace and ruin, and an utter overthrow? If—? Would it not be well at any rate that no marriage should take place till that had been decided? She could not find it in her heart to bring down his old gray hairs with utter sorrow to the grave.

CHAPTER XXXVI
WHAT THE YOUNG MEN THOUGHT ABOUT IT

Lucius Mason at this time was living at home at Orley Farm, not by any means in a happy frame of mind. It will be perhaps remembered that he had at one time had an interview with Mr. Furnival in that lawyer's chambers, which was by no means consoling to him, seeing that Mr. Furnival had pooh-poohed him and his pretensions in a very off-hand way; and he had since paid a very memorable visit to Mr. Dockwrath in which he had hardly been more successful. Nevertheless, he had gone to another lawyer. He had felt it impossible to remain tranquil, pursuing the ordinary avocations of his life, while such dreadful charges were being made openly against his mother, and being so made without any authorised contradiction. He knew that she was innocent. No doubt on that matter ever perplexed his mind for a moment. But why was she such a coward that she would not allow him to protect her innocence in the only way which the law permitted? He could hardly believe that he had no power of doing so even without her sanction; and therefore he went to another lawyer.

The other lawyer did him no good. It was not practicable that he, the son, should bring an action for defamatory character on the part of the mother, without that mother's sanction. Moreover, as this new lawyer saw in a moment, any such interference on the part of Lucius, and any interposition of fresh and new legal proceedings would cripple and impede the advisers to whom Lady Mason had herself confided her own case. The new lawyer could do nothing, and thus Lucius, again repulsed, betook himself to Orley Farm in no happy frame of mind.

For some day or two after this he did not see his mother. He would not go down to The Cleeve, though they sent up and asked him; and she was almost afraid to go across to the house and visit him. "He will be in church on Sunday," she had said to Mrs. Orme. But he was not in church on Sunday, and then on Sunday afternoon she did go to him. This, it will be understood, was before Sir Peregrine had made his offer, and therefore as to that, there was as yet no embarrassment on the widow's mind.

"I cannot help feeling, mother," he said, after she had sat there with him for a short time, "that for the present there is a division between you and me."

"Oh, Lucius!"

"It is no use our denying it to ourselves. It is so. You are in trouble, and you will not listen to my advice. You leave my house and take to the roof of a new and an untried friend."

"No, Lucius; not that."

"Yes. I say a new friend. Twelve months ago, though you might call there, you never did more than that—and even that but seldom. They are new friends; and yet, now that you are in trouble, you choose to live with them."

"Dear Lucius, is there any reason why I should not visit at The Cleeve?"

"Yes; if you ask me—yes;" and now he spoke very sternly. "There is a cloud upon you, and you should know nothing of visitings and of new friendships till that cloud has been dispersed. While these things are being said of you, you should set at no other table than this, and drink of no man's cup but mine. I know your innocence," and as he went on to speak, he stood up before her and looked down fully into her face, "but others do not. I know how unworthy are these falsehoods with which wicked men strive to crush you, but others believe that they are true accusations. They cannot be disregarded, and now it seems,—now that you have allowed them to gather to a head, they will result in a trial, during which you will have to stand at the bar charged with a dreadful crime."

"Oh, Lucius!" and she hid her eyes in her hands. "I could not have helped it. How could I have helped it?"

"Well; it must be so now. And till that trial is over, here should be your place. Here, at my right hand; I am he who am bound to stand by you. It is I whose duty it is to see that your name be made white again, though I spend all I have, ay, and my life in doing it. I am the one man on whose arm you have a right to lean. And yet, in such days as these, you leave my house and go to that of a stranger."

"He is not a stranger, Lucius."

"He cannot be to you as a son should be. However, it is for you to judge. I have no control in this matter, but I think it right that you should know what are my thoughts."

And then she had crept back again to The Cleeve. Let Lucius say what he might, let this additional sorrow be ever so bitter, she could not obey her son's behests. If she did so in one thing she must do so in all. She had chosen her advisers with her best discretion, and by that choice she must abide—even though it separated her from her son. She could not abandon Sir Peregrine Orme and Mr. Furnival. So she crept back and told all this to Mrs. Orme. Her heart would have utterly sunk within her could she not have spoken openly to some one of this sorrow.

"But he loves you," Mrs. Orme had said, comforting her. "It is not that he does not love you."

"But he is so stern to me." And then Mrs. Orme had kissed her, and promised that none should be stern to her, there, in that house. On the morning after this Sir Peregrine had made his offer, and then she felt that the division between her and her boy would be wider than ever. And all this had come of that inheritance which she had demanded so eagerly for her child.

And now Lucius was sitting alone in his room at Orley Farm, having, for the present, given up all idea of attempting anything himself by means of the law. He had made his way into Mr. Dockwrath's office, and had there insulted the attorney in the presence of witnesses. His hope now was that the attorney might bring an action against him. If that were done he would thus have the means of bringing out all the facts of the case before a jury and a judge. It was fixed in his mind that if he could once drag that reptile before a public tribunal, and with loud voice declare the wrong that was being done, all might be well. The public would understand and would speak out, and the reptile would be scorned and trodden under foot. Poor Lucius! It is not always so easy to catch public sympathy, and it will occur sometimes that the wrong reptile is crushed by the great public heel.

Lucius Mason in his Study.

He had his books before him as he sat there—his Latham and his Pritchard, and he had the jawbone of one savage and the skull of another. His Liverpool bills for unadulterated guano were lying on the table, and a philosophical German treatise on agriculture which he had resolved to study. It became a man, he said to himself, to do a man's work in spite of any sorrow. But, nevertheless, as he sat there, his studies were but of little service to him. How many men have declared to themselves the same thing, but have failed when the trial came! Who, can command the temper and the mind? At ten I will strike the lyre and begin my poem. But at ten the poetic spirit is under a dark cloud—because the water for the tea had not boiled when it was brought in at nine. And so the lyre remains unstricken.

And Lucius found that he could not strike his lyre. For days he had sat there and no good note had been produced. And then he had walked over his land, having a farming man at his heels, thinking that he could turn his mind to the actual and practical working of his land. But little good had come of that either. It was January, and the land was sloppy and half frozen. There was no useful work to be done on it. And then what farmer Greenwood had once said of him was true enough, "The young maister's spry and active surely, but he can't let unself down to stable doong and the loik o' that." He had some grand idea of farming—a conviction that the agricultural world in general was very backward, and that he would set it right. Even now in his sorrow, as he walked through his splashy, frozen fields, he was tormented by a desire to do something, he knew not what, that might be great.

He had no such success on the present occasion and returned disconsolate to the house. This happened about noon on the day after that on which Sir Peregrine had declared himself. He returned as I have said to the house, and there at the kitchen door he met a little girl whom he knew well as belonging to The Cleeve. She was a favourite of Mrs. Orme's, was educated and clothed by her, and ran on her messages. Now she had brought a letter up to Lucius from his mother. Curtsying low she so told him, and he at once went into the sitting-room where he found it lying on his table. His hand was nervous as he opened it; but if he could have seen how tremulous had been the hand that wrote it! The letter was as follows:—

> Dearest Lucius,
>
> I know you will be very much surprised at what I am going to tell you, but I hope you will not judge me harshly. If I know myself at all I would take no step of any kind for my own advantage which could possibly injure you. At the present moment we unfortunately do not agree about a subject which is troubling us both, and I cannot therefore consult you as I should otherwise have done. I trust that by God's mercy these troubles may come to an end, and that there may be no further differences between you and me.
>
> Sir Peregrine Orme has made me an offer of marriage and I have accepted it—

Lucius Mason when he had read so far threw down the letter upon the table, and rising suddenly from his chair walked rapidly up and down the room. "Marry him!" he said out loud, "marry him!" The idea that their fathers and mothers should marry and enjoy themselves is always a thing horrible to be thought of in the minds of the rising generation. Lucius Mason now began to feel against his mother the same sort of anger which Joseph Mason had felt when his father had married again. "Marry him!" And then he walked rapidly about the room, as though some great injury had been threatened to him.

And so it had, in his estimation. Was it not her position in life to be his mother? Had she not had her young days? But it did not occur to him to think what those young days had been. And this then was the meaning of her receding from his advice and from his roof! She had been preparing for herself in the world new hopes, a new home, and a new ambition. And she had so prevailed upon the old man that he was about to do this foolish thing! Then again he walked up and down the room, injuring his mother much in his thoughts. He gave her credit for none of those circumstances which had truly actuated her in accepting the hand which Sir Peregrine had offered her. In that matter touching the Orley Farm estate he could acquit his mother instantly,—with acclamation. But in this other matter he had pronounced her guilty before she had been allowed to plead. Then he took up the letter and finished it.

> Sir Peregrine Orme has made me an offer of marriage and I have accepted it. It is very difficult to explain in a letter all the causes that have induced me to do so. The first perhaps is this, that I feel myself so bound to him by love and gratitude, that I think it my duty to fall in with all his wishes. He has pointed out to me that as my husband he can do more for me than would be possible for him without that name. I have explained to him that I would rather perish than that he should sacrifice himself; but he is pleased to say that it is no sacrifice. At any rate he so wishes it, and as Mrs. Orme has cordially assented, I feel myself bound to fall in with his views. It was only yesterday that Sir Peregrine made his offer. I mention this that you may know that I have lost no time in telling you.
>
> Dearest Lucius, believe that I shall be as ever
> Your most affectionate mother,
>
> Mary Mason.
>
> The little girl will wait for an answer if she finds that you are at the farm.

"No," he said to himself, still walking about the room. "She can never be to me the same mother that she was. I would have sacrificed everything for her. She should have been the mistress of my house, at any rate till she herself should have wished it otherwise. But now—" And then his mind turned away suddenly to Sophia Furnival.

I cannot myself but think that had that affair of the trial been set at rest Lady Mason would have been prudent to look for another home. The fact that Orley Farm was his house and not hers occurred almost too frequently to Lucius Mason; and I am not certain that it would have been altogether comfortable as a permanent residence for his mother after he should have brought home to it some such bride as her he now proposed to himself.

It was necessary that he should write an answer to his mother, which he did at once.

Orley Farm, — January.

Dear Mother,

It is I fear too late for me to offer any counsel on the subject of your letter. I cannot say that I think you are right.

Your affectionate son,

Lucius Mason.

And then, having finished this, he again walked the room. "It is all up between me and her," he said, "as real friends in life and heart. She shall still have the respect of a son, and I shall have the regard of a mother. But how can I trim my course to suit the welfare of the wife of Sir Peregrine Orme?" And then he lashed himself into anger at the idea that his mother should have looked for other solace than that which he could have given.

Nothing more from The Cleeve reached him that day; but early on the following morning he had a visitor whom he certainly had not expected. Before he sat down to his breakfast he heard the sound of a horse's feet before the door, and immediately afterwards Peregrine Orme entered the sitting-room. He was duly shown in by the servant, and in his ordinary way came forward quickly and shook hands. Then he waited till the door was closed, and at once began upon the subject which had brought him there.

"Mason," he said, "you have heard of this that is being done at The Cleeve?"

Lucius immediately fell back a step or two, and considered for a moment how he should answer. He had pressed very heavily on his mother in his own thoughts, but he was not prepared to hear her harshly spoken of by another.

"Yes," said he, "I have heard."

"And I understand from your mother that you do not approve of it."

"Approve of it! No; I do not approve of it."

"Nor by heavens do I!"

"I do not approve of it," said Mason, speaking with deliberation; "but I do not know that I can take any steps towards preventing it."

"Cannot you see her, and talk to her, and tell her how wrong it is?"

"Wrong! I do not know that she is wrong in that sense. I do not know that you have any right to blame her. Why do not you speak to your grandfather?"

"So I have—as far as it was possible for me. But you do not know Sir Peregrine. No one has any influence over him, but my mother;—and now also your mother."

"And what does Mrs. Orme say?"

"She will say nothing. I know well that she disapproves of it. She must disapprove of it, though she will not say so. She would rather burn off both her hands than displease my grandfather. She says that he asked her and that she consented."

"It seems to me that it is for her and you to prevent this."

"No; it is for your mother to prevent it. Only think of it, Mason. He is over seventy, and, as he says himself, he will not burden the estate with a new jointure. Why should she do it?"

"You are wronging her there. It is no affair of money. She is not going to marry him for what she can get."

"Then why should she do it?"

"Because he tells her. These troubles about the lawsuit have turned her head, and she has put herself entirely into his hands. I think she is wrong. I could have protected her from all this evil, and would have done so. I could have done more, I think, than Sir Peregrine can do. But she has thought otherwise, and I do not know that I can help it."

"But will you speak to her? Will make her perceive that she is injuring a family that is treating her with kindness?"

"If she will come here I will speak to her. I cannot do it there. I cannot go down to your grandfather's house with such an object as that."

"All the world will turn against her if she marries him," said Peregrine. And then there was silence between them for a moment or two.

"It seems to me," said Lucius at last, "that you wrong my mother very much in this matter, and lay all the blame where but the smallest part of the blame is deserved. She has no idea of money in her mind, or any thought of pecuniary advantage. She is moved solely by what your grandfather has said to her,—and by an insane dread of some coming evil which she thinks may be lessened by his assistance. You are in the house with them, and can speak to him,—and if you please to her also. I do not see that I can do either."

"And you will not help me to break it off?"

"Certainly,—if I can see my way."

"Will you write to her?"

"Well; I will think about it."

"Whether she be to blame or not it must be your duty as well as mine to prevent such a marriage if it be possible. Think what people will say of it?"

After some further discussion Peregrine remounted his horse, and rode back to The Cleeve, not quite satisfied with young Mason.

"If you do speak to her,—to my mother, do it gently." Those were the last words whispered by Lucius as Peregrine Orme had his foot in the stirrup.

Young Peregrine Orme, as he rode home, felt that the world was using him very unkindly. Everything was going wrong with him, and an idea entered his head that he might as well go and look for Sir John Franklin at the North Pole, or join some energetic traveller in the middle of Central Africa. He had proposed to Madeline Staveley and had been refused. That in itself caused a load to lie on his heart which was almost unendurable;— and now his grandfather was going to disgrace himself. He had made his little effort to be respectable and discreet, devoting himself to the county hunt and county drawing-rooms, giving up the pleasures of London and the glories of dissipation. And for what?

Then Peregrine began to argue within himself as some others have done before him—

"Were it not better done as others use—" he said to himself, in that or other language; and as he rode slowly into the courtyard of The Cleeve, he thought almost with regret of his old friend Carroty Bob.

CHAPTER XXXVII
PEREGRINE'S ELOQUENCE

In the last chapter Peregrine Orme called at Orley Farm with the view of discussing with Lucius Mason the conduct of their respective progenitors; and, as will be remembered, the young men agreed in a general way that their progenitors were about to make fools of themselves. Poor Peregrine, however, had other troubles on his mind. Not only had his grandfather been successful in love, but he had been unsuccessful. As he had journeyed home from Noningsby to The Cleeve in a high-wheeled vehicle which he called his trap, he had determined, being then in a frame of mind somewhat softer than was usual with him, to tell all his troubles to his mother. It sounds as though it were lack-a-daisical—such a resolve as this on the part of a dashing young man, who had been given to the pursuit of rats, and was now a leader among the sons of Nimrod in the pursuit of foxes. Young men of the present day, when got up for the eyes of the world, look and talk as though they could never tell their mothers anything,—as though they were harder than flint, and as little in want of a woman's counsel and a woman's help as a colonel of horse on the morning of a battle. But the rigid virility of his outward accoutrements does in no way alter the man of flesh and blood who wears them; the young hero, so stern to the eye, is, I believe, as often tempted by stress of sentiment to lay bare the sorrow of his heart as is his sister. On this occasion Peregrine said to himself that he would lay bare the sorrow of his heart. He would find out what others thought of that marriage which he had proposed to himself; and then, if his mother encouraged him, and his grandfather approved, he would make another attack, beginning on the side of the judge, or perhaps on that of Lady Staveley.

But he found that others, as well as he, were labouring under a stress of sentiment; and when about to tell his own tale, he had learned that a tale was to be told to him. He had dined with Lady Mason, his mother, and his grandfather, and the dinner had been very silent. Three of the party were in love, and the fourth was burdened with the telling of the tale. The baronet himself said nothing on the subject as he and his grandson sat over their wine; but later in the evening Peregrine was summoned to his mother's room, and she, with considerable hesitation and much diffidence, informed him of the coming nuptials.

"Marry Lady Mason!" he had said.

"Yes, Peregrine. Why should he not do so if they both wish it?"

Peregrine thought that there were many causes and impediments sufficiently just why no such marriage should take place, but he had not his arguments ready at his fingers' ends. He was so stunned by the intelligence that he could say but little about it on that occasion. By the few words that he did say, and by the darkness of his countenance, he showed plainly enough that he disapproved. And then his mother said all that she could in the baronet's favour, pointing out that in a pecuniary way Peregrine would receive benefit rather than injury.

"I'm not thinking of the money, mother."

"No, my dear; but it is right that I should tell you how considerate your grandfather is."

"All the same, I wish he would not marry this woman."

"Woman, Peregrine! You should not speak in that way of a friend whom I dearly love."

"She is a woman all the same." And then he sat sulkily looking at the fire. His own stress of sentiment did not admit of free discussion at the present moment, and was necessarily postponed. On that other affair he was told that his grandfather would be glad to see him on the following morning; and then he left his mother.

"Your grandfather, Peregrine, asked for my assent," said Mrs. Orme; "and I thought it right to give it." This she said to make him understand that it was no longer in her power to oppose the match. And she was thoroughly glad that this was so, for she would have lacked the courage to oppose Sir Peregrine in anything.

On the next morning Peregrine saw his grandfather before breakfast. His mother came to his room door while he was dressing to whisper a word of caution to him. "Pray, be courteous to him," she said. "Remember how good he is to you—to us both! Say that you congratulate him."

"But I don't," said Peregrine.

"Ah, but, Peregrine—"

"I'll tell you what I'll do, mother. I'll leave the house altogether and go away, if you wish it."

"Oh, Peregrine! How can you speak in that way? But he's waiting now. Pray, pray, be kind in your manner to him."

He descended with the same sort of feeling which had oppressed him on his return home after his encounter with Carroty Bob in Smithfield. Since then he had been on enduring good terms with his grandfather, but now again all the discomforts of war were imminent.

"Good morning, sir," he said, on going into his grandfather's dressing-room.

"Good morning, Peregrine." And then there was silence for a moment or two.

"Did you see your mother last night?"

"Yes; I did see her."

"And she told you what it is that I propose to do?"

"Yes, sir; she told me."

"I hope you understand, my boy, that it will not in any way affect your own interests injuriously."

"I don't care about that, sir—one way or the other."

"But I do, Peregrine. Having seen to that I think that I have a right to please myself in this matter."

"Oh, yes, sir; I know you have the right."

"Especially as I can benefit others. Are you aware that your mother has cordially given her consent to the marriage?"

"She told me that you had asked her, and that she had agreed to it. She would agree to anything."

"Peregrine, that is not the way in which you should speak of your mother."

And then the young man stood silent, as though there was nothing more to be said. Indeed, he had nothing more to say. He did not dare to bring forward in words all the arguments against the marriage which were now crowding themselves into his memory, but he could not induce himself to wish the old man joy, or to say any of those civil things which are customary on such occasions. The baronet sat for a while, silent also, and a cloud of anger was coming across his brow; but he checked that before he spoke. "Well, my boy," he said, and his voice was almost more than usually kind, "I can understand your thoughts, and we will say nothing of them at present. All I will ask of you is to treat Lady Mason in a manner befitting the position in which I intend to place her."

"If you think it will be more comfortable, sir, I will leave The Cleeve for a time."

"I hope that may not be necessary—Why should it? Or at any rate, not as yet," he added, as a thought as to his wedding day occurred to him. And then the interview was over, and in another half-hour they met again at breakfast.

In the breakfast-room Lady Mason was also present. Peregrine was the last to enter, and as he did so his grandfather was already standing in his usual place, with the book of Prayers in his hand, waiting that the servants should arrange themselves at their chairs before he knelt down. There was no time then for much greeting, but Peregrine did shake hands with her as he stept across to his accustomed corner. He shook hands with her, and felt that her hand was very cold; but he did not look at her, nor did he hear any answer given to his muttered words. When they all got up she remained close to Mrs. Orme, as though she might thus be protected from the anger which she feared from Sir Peregrine's other friends. And at breakfast also she sat close to her, far away from the baronet, and almost hidden by the urn from his grandson. Sitting there she said nothing; neither in truth did she eat anything. It was a time of great suffering to her, for she knew that her coming could not be welcomed by the young heir. "It must not be," she said to herself over and over again. "Though he turn me out of the house, I must tell him that it cannot be so."

After breakfast Peregrine had ridden over to Orley Farm, and there held his consultation with the other heir. On his returning to The Cleeve, he did not go into the house, but having given up his horse to a groom, wandered away among the woods. Lucius Mason had suggested that he, Peregrine Orme, should himself speak to Lady Mason on this matter. He felt that his grandfather would be very angry, should he do so. But he did not regard that much. He had filled himself full with the theory of his duties, and he would act up to it. He would see her, without telling any one what was his purpose, and put it to her whether she would bring down this destruction on so noble a gentleman. Having thus resolved, he returned to the house, when it was already dark, and making his way into the drawing-room, sat himself down before the fire, still thinking of his plan. The room was dark, as such rooms are dark for the last hour or two before dinner in January, and he sat himself in an arm-chair before the fire, intending to sit there till it would be necessary that he should go to dress. It was an unaccustomed thing with him so to place himself at such a time, or to remain in the drawing-room at all till he came down for a few minutes before dinner; but he did so now, having been thrown out of his usual habits by the cares upon his mind. He had been so seated about a quarter of an hour, and was already nearly asleep, when he heard the rustle of a woman's garment, and looking round, with such light as the fire gave him, perceived that Lady Mason was in the room. She had entered very quietly, and was making her way in the dark to a chair which she frequently occupied, between the fire and one of the windows, and in doing so she passed so near Peregrine as to touch him with her dress.

"Lady Mason," he said, speaking, in the first place, in order that she might know that she was not alone, "it is almost dark; shall I ring for candles for you?"

She started at hearing his voice, begged his pardon for disturbing him, declined his offer of light, and declared that she was going up again to her own room immediately. But it occurred to him that if it would be well that he should speak to her, it would be well that he should do so at once; and what opportunity could be more fitting than the present? "If you are not in a hurry about anything," he said, "would you mind staying here for a few minutes?"

"Oh no, certainly not." But he could perceive that her voice trembled in uttering even these few words.

"I think I'd better light a candle," he said; and then he did light one of those which stood on the corner of the mantelpiece,—a solitary candle, which only seemed to make the gloom of the large room visible. She, however, was standing close to it, and would have much preferred that the room should have been left to its darkness.

"Won't you sit down for a few minutes?" and then she sat down. "I'll just shut the door, if you don't mind." And then, having done so, he returned to his own chair and again faced the fire. He saw that she was pale and nervous, and he did not like to look at her as he spoke. He began to reflect also that they might probably be interrupted by his mother, and he wished that they could adjourn to some other room. That, however, seemed to be impossible; so he summoned up all his courage, and began his task.

"I hope you won't think me uncivil, Lady Mason, for speaking to you about this affair."

"Oh no, Mr. Orme; I am sure that you will not be uncivil to me."

"Of course I cannot help feeling a great concern in it, for it's very nearly the same, you know, as if he were my father. Indeed, if you come to that, it's almost worse; and I can assure you it is nothing about money that I mind. Many fellows in my place would be afraid about that, but I don't care twopence what he does in that respect. He is so honest and so noble-hearted, that I am sure he won't do me a wrong."

"I hope not, Mr. Orme; and certainly not in respect to me."

"I only mention it for fear you should misunderstand me. But there are other reasons, Lady Mason, why this marriage will make me—make me very unhappy."

"Are there? I shall be so unhappy if I make others unhappy."

"You will then,—I can assure you of that. It is not only me, but your own son. I was up with him to-day, and he thinks of it the same as I do."

"What did he say, Mr. Orme?"

"What did he say? Well, I don't exactly remember his words; but he made me understand that your marriage with Sir Peregrine would make him very unhappy. He did indeed. Why do you not see him yourself, and talk to him?"

"I thought it best to write to him in the first place."

"Well, now you have written; and don't you think it would be well that you should go up and see him? You will find that he is quite as strong against it as I am,—quite."

Peregrine, had he known it, was using the arguments which were of all the least likely to induce Lady Mason to pay a visit to Orley Farm. She dreaded the idea of a quarrel with her son, and would have made almost any sacrifice to prevent such a misfortune; but at the present moment she feared the anger of his words almost more than the anger implied by his absence. If this trial could be got over, she would return to him and almost throw herself at his feet; but till that time, might it not be well that they should be apart? At any rate, these tidings of his discontent could not be efficacious in inducing her to seek him.

"Dear Lucius!" she said, not addressing herself to her companion, but speaking her thoughts. "I would not willingly give him cause to be discontented with me."

"He is, then, very discontented. I can assure you of that."

"Yes; he and I think differently about all this."

"Ah, but don't you think you had better speak to him before you quite make up your mind? He is your son, you know; and an uncommon clever fellow too. He'll know how to say all this much better than I do."

"Say what, Mr. Orme?"

"Why, of course you can't expect that anybody will like such a marriage as this;—that is, anybody except you and Sir Peregrine."

"Your mother does not object to it."

"My mother! But you don't know my mother yet. She would not object to have her head cut off if anybody wanted it that she cared about. I do not know how it has all been managed, but I suppose Sir Peregrine asked her. Then of course she would not object. But look at the common sense of it, Lady Mason. What does the world always say when an old man like my grandfather marries a young woman?"

"But I am not—." So far she got, and then she stopped herself.

"We have all liked you very much. I'm sure I have for one; and I'll go in for you, heart and soul, in this shameful law business. When Lucius asked me, I didn't think anything of going to that scoundrel in Hamworth; and all along I've been delighted that Sir Peregrine took it up. By heavens! I'd be glad to go down to Yorkshire myself, and walk into that fellow that wants to do you this injury. I would indeed; and I'll stand by you as strong as anybody. But, Lady Mason, when it comes to one's grandfather marrying, it—it—it—. Think what people in the county will say of him. If it was your father, and if he had been at the top of the tree all his life, how would you like to see him get a fall, and be laughed at as though he were in the mud just when he was too old ever to get up again?"

I am not sure whether Lucius Mason, with all his cleverness, could have put the matter much better, or have used a style of oratory more efficacious to the end in view. Peregrine had drawn his picture with a coarse pencil, but he had drawn it strongly, and with graphic effect. And then he paused; not with self-confidence, or as giving his companion time to see how great had been his art, but in want of words, and somewhat confused by the strength of his own thoughts. So he got up and poked the fire, turning his back to it, and then sat down again. "It is such a deuce of a thing, Lady Mason," he said, "that you must not be angry with me for speaking out."

"Oh, Mr. Orme, I am not angry, and I do not know what to say to you."

"Why don't you speak to Lucius?"

"What could he say more than you have said? Dear Mr. Orme, I would not injure him,—your grandfather, I mean,—for all that the world holds."

"You will injure him;—in the eyes of all his friends."

"Then I will not do it. I will go to him, and beg him that it may not be so. I will tell him that I cannot. Anything will be better than bringing him to sorrow or disgrace."

"By Jove! but will you really?" Peregrine was startled and almost frightened at the effect of his own eloquence. What would the baronet say when he learned that he had been talked out of his wife by his grandson?

"Mr. Orme," continued Lady Mason, "I am sure you do not understand how this matter has been brought about. If you did, however much it might grieve you, you would not blame me, even in your thoughts. From the first to the last my only desire has been to obey your grandfather in everything."

"But you would not marry him out of obedience?"

"I would—and did so intend. I would, certainly; if in doing so I did him no injury. You say that your mother would give her life for him. So would I;—that or anything else that I could give, without hurting him or others. It was not I that sought for this marriage; nor did I think of it. If you were in my place, Mr. Orme, you would know how difficult it is to refuse."

Peregrine again got up, and standing with his back to the fire, thought over it all again. His soft heart almost relented towards the woman who had borne his rough words with so much patient kindness. Had Sir Peregrine been there then, and could he have condescended so far, he might have won his grandson's consent without much trouble. Peregrine, like some other generals, had expended his energy in gaining his victory, and was more ready now to come to easy terms than he would have been had he suffered in the combat.

Peregrine's Eloquence.

"Well," he said after a while, "I'm sure I'm very much obliged to you for the manner in which you have taken what I said to you. Nobody knows about it yet, I suppose; and perhaps, if you will talk to the governor—"

"I will talk to him, Mr. Orme."

"Thank you; and then perhaps all things may turn out right. I'll go and dress now." And so saying he took his departure, leaving her to consider how best she might act at this crisis of her life, so that things might go right, if such were possible. The more she thought of it, the less possible it seemed that her affairs should be made to go right.

CHAPTER XXXVIII
OH, INDEED!

The dinner on that day at The Cleeve was not very dull. Peregrine had some hopes that the idea of the marriage might be abandoned, and was at any rate much better disposed towards Lady Mason than he had been. He spoke to her, asking her whether she had been out, and suggesting roast mutton or some such creature comfort. This was lost neither on Sir Peregrine nor on Mrs. Orme, and they both exerted themselves to say a few words in a more cheery tone than had been customary in the house for the last day or two. Lady Mason herself did not say much; but she had sufficient tact to see the effort which was being made; and though she spoke but little she smiled and accepted graciously the courtesies that were tendered to her.

Then the two ladies went away, and Peregrine was again left with his grandfather. "That was a nasty accident that Graham had going out of Monkton Grange," said he, speaking on the moment of his closing the dining-room door after his mother. "I suppose you heard all about it, sir?" Having fought his battle so well before dinner, he was determined to give some little rest to his half-vanquished enemy.

"The first tidings we heard were that he was dead," said Sir Peregrine, filling his glass.

"No; he wasn't dead. But of course you know that now. He broke an arm and two ribs, and got rather a bad squeeze. He was just behind me, you know, and I had to wait for him. I lost the run, and had to see Harriet Tristram go away with the best lead any one has had to a fast thing this year. That's an uncommon nasty place at the back of Monkton Grange."

"I hope, Peregrine, you don't think too much about Harriet Tristram."

"Think of her! who? I? Think of her in what sort of a way? I think she goes uncommonly well to hounds."

"That may be, but I should not wish to see you pin your happiness on any lady that was celebrated chiefly for going well to hounds."

"Do you mean marry her?" and Peregrine immediately made a strong comparison in his mind between Miss Tristram and Madeline Staveley.

"Yes; that's what I did mean."

"I wouldn't have her if she owned every fox-cover in the county. No, by Jove! I know a trick worth two of that. It's jolly enough to see them going, but as to being in love with them—in that sort of way—"

"You are quite right, my boy; quite right. It is not that that a man wants in a wife."

"No," said Peregrine, with a melancholy cadence in his voice, thinking of what it was that he did want. And so they sat sipping their wine. The turn which the conversation had taken had for the moment nearly put Lady Mason out of the young man's head.

"You would be very young to marry yet," said the baronet.

"Yes, I should be young; but I don't know that there is any harm in that."

"Quite the contrary, if a young man feels himself to be sufficiently settled. Your mother I know would be very glad that you should marry early;—and so should I, if you married well."

What on earth could all this mean? It could not be that his grandfather knew that he was in love with Miss Staveley; and had this been known his grandfather would not have talked of Harriet Tristram. "Oh yes; of course a fellow should marry well. I don't think much of marrying for money."

"Nor do I, Peregrine;—I think very little of it."

"Nor about being of very high birth."

"Well; it would make me unhappy—very unhappy if you were to marry below your own rank."

"What do you call my own rank?"

"I mean any girl whose father is not a gentleman, and whose mother is not a lady; and of whose education among ladies you could not feel certain."

"I could be quite certain about her," said Peregrine, very innocently.

"Her! what her?"

"Oh, I forgot that we were talking about nobody."

"You don't mean Harriet Tristram?"

"No, certainly not."

"Of whom were you thinking, Peregrine? May I ask—if it be not too close a secret?" And then again there was a pause, during which Peregrine emptied his glass and filled it again. He had no objection to talk to his grandfather about Miss Staveley, but he felt ashamed of having allowed the matter to escape him in this sort of way. "I will tell you why I ask, my boy," continued the baronet. "I am going to do that which many people will call a very foolish thing."

"You mean about Lady Mason."

"Yes; I mean my own marriage with Lady Mason. We will not talk about that just at present, and I only mention it to explain that before I do so, I shall settle the property permanently. If you were married I should at once divide it with you. I should like to keep the old house myself, till I die—"

"Oh, Sir!"

"But sooner than give you cause of offence I would give that up."

"I would not consent to live in it unless I did so as your guest."

"Until your marriage I think of settling on you a thousand a year;—but it would add to my happiness if I thought it likely that you would marry soon. Now may I ask of whom were you thinking?"

Peregrine paused for a second or two before he made any reply, and then he brought it out boldly. "I was thinking of Madeline Staveley."

"Then, my boy, you were thinking of the prettiest girl and the best-bred lady in the county. Here's her health;" and he filled for himself a bumper of claret. "You couldn't have named a woman whom I should be more proud to see you bring home. And your mother's opinion of her is the same as mine. I happen to know that;" and with a look of triumph he drank his glass of wine, as though much that was very joyful to him had been already settled.

"Yes," said Peregrine mournfully, "she is a very nice girl; at least I think so."

"The man who can win her, Peregrine, may consider himself to be a lucky fellow. You were quite right in what you were saying about money. No man feels more sure of that than I do. But if I am not mistaken Miss Staveley will have something of her own. I rather think that Arbuthnot got ten thousand pounds."

"I'm sure I don't know, sir," said Peregrine; and his voice was by no means as much elated as that of his grandfather.

"I think he did; or if he didn't get it all, the remainder is settled on him. And the judge is not a man to behave better to one child than to another."

"I suppose not."

And then the conversation flagged a little, for the enthusiasm was all one side. It was moreover on that side which naturally would have been the least enthusiastic. Poor Peregrine had only told half his secret as yet, and that not the most important half. To Sir Peregrine the tidings, as far as he had heard them, were very pleasant. He did not say to himself that he would purchase his grandson's assent to his own marriage by giving his consent to his grandson's marriage. But it did seem to him that the two affairs, acting upon each other, might both be made to run smooth. His heir could have made no better choice in selecting the lady of his love. Sir Peregrine had feared much that some Miss Tristram or the like might have been tendered to him as the future Lady Orme, and he was agreeably surprised to find that a new mistress for The Cleeve had been so well chosen. He would be all kindness to his grandson and win from him, if it might be possible, reciprocal courtesy and complaisance. "Your mother will be very pleased when she hears this," he said.

"I meant to tell my mother," said Peregrine, still very dolefully, "but I do not know that there is anything in it to please her. I only said that I—I admired Miss Staveley."

"My dear boy, if you'll take my advice you'll propose to her at once. You have been staying in the same house with her, and—"

"But I have."

"Have what?"

"I have proposed to her."

"Well?"

"And she has refused me. You know all about it now, and there's no such great cause for joy."

"Oh, you have proposed to her. Have you spoken to her father or mother?"

"What was the use when she told me plainly that she did not care for me? Of course I should have asked her father. As to Lady Staveley, she and I got on uncommonly well. I'm almost inclined to think that she would not have objected."

"It would be a very nice match for them, and I dare say she would not have objected." And then for some ten minutes they sat looking at the fire. Peregrine had nothing more to say about it, and the baronet was thinking how best he might encourage his grandson.

"You must try again, you know," at last he said.

"Well; I fear not. I do not think it would be any good. I'm not quite sure she does not care for some one else."

"Who is he?"

"Oh, a fellow that's there. The man who broke his arm. I don't say she does, you know, and of course you won't mention it."

Sir Peregrine gave the necessary promises, and then endeavoured to give encouragement to the lover. He would himself see the judge, if it were thought expedient, and explain what liberal settlement would be made on the lady in the event of her altering her mind. "Young ladies, you know, are very prone to alter their minds on such matters," said the old man. In answer to which Peregrine declared his conviction that Madeline Staveley would not alter her mind. But then do not all despondent lovers hold that opinion of their own mistresses?

Sir Peregrine had been a great gainer by what had occurred, and so he felt it. At any rate all the novelty of the question of his own marriage was over, as between him and Peregrine; and then he had acquired a means of being gracious which must almost disarm his grandson of all power of criticism. When he, an old man, was ready to do so much to forward the views of a young man, could it be possible that the young man should oppose his wishes? And Peregrine was aware that his power of opposition was thus lessened.

In the evening nothing remarkable occurred between them. Each had his or her own plans; but these plans could not be furthered by anything to be said in a general assembly. Lady Mason had already told to Mrs. Orme all that had passed in the drawing-room before dinner, and Sir Peregrine had determined that he would consult Mrs. Orme as to that matter regarding Miss Staveley. He did not think much of her refusal. Young ladies always do refuse—at first.

On the day but one following this there came another visit from Mr. Furnival, and he was for a long time closeted with Sir Peregrine. Matthew Round had, he said, been with him, and had felt himself obliged in the performance of his duty to submit a case to counsel on behalf of his client Joseph Mason. He had not as yet received the written opinion of Sir Richard Leatherham, to whom he had applied; but nevertheless, as he wished to give every possible notice, he had called to say that his firm were of opinion that an action must be brought either for forgery or for perjury.

"For perjury!" Mr. Furnival had said.

"Well; yes. We would wish to be as little harsh as possible. But if we convict her of having sworn falsely when she gave evidence as to having copied the codicil herself, and having seen it witnessed by the pretended witnesses;—why in that case of course the property would go back."

"I can't give any opinion as to what might be the result in such a case," said Mr. Furnival.

Mr. Round had gone on to say that he thought it improbable that the action could be tried before the summer assizes.

"The sooner the better as far as we are concerned," said Mr. Furnival.

"If you really mean that, I will see that there shall be no unnecessary delay." Mr. Furnival had declared that he did really mean it, and so the interview had ended.

Mr. Furnival had really meant it, fully concurring in the opinion which Mr. Chaffanbrass had expressed on this matter; but nevertheless the increasing urgency of the case had almost made him tremble. He still carried himself with a brave outside before Mat Round, protesting as to the utter absurdity as well as cruelty of the whole proceeding; but his conscience told him that it was not absurd. "Perjury!" he said to himself, and then he rang the bell for Crabwitz. The upshot of that interview was that Mr. Crabwitz received a commission to arrange a meeting between that great barrister, the member for the Essex Marshes, and Mr. Solomon Aram.

"Won't it look rather, rather—rather—; you know what I mean, sir?" Crabwitz had asked.

"We must fight these people with their own weapons," said Mr. Furnival;—not exactly with justice, seeing that Messrs. Round and Crook were not at all of the same calibre in the profession as Mr. Solomon Aram.

Mr. Furnival had already at this time seen Mr. Slow, of the firm of Slow and Bideawhile, who were Sir Peregrine's solicitors. This he had done chiefly that he might be able to tell Sir Peregrine that he had seen him.

Mr. Slow had declared that the case was one which his firm would not be prepared to conduct, and he named a firm to which he should recommend his client to apply. But Mr. Furnival, carefully considering the whole matter, had resolved to take the advice and benefit by the experience of Mr. Chaffanbrass.

And then he went down once more to The Cleeve. Poor Mr. Furnival! In these days he was dreadfully buffeted about both as regards his outer man and his inner conscience by this unfortunate case, giving up to it time that would otherwise have turned itself into heaps of gold; giving up domestic conscience—for Mrs. Furnival was still hot in her anger against poor Lady Mason; and giving up also much peace of mind, for he felt that he was soiling his hands by dirty work. But he thought of the lady's pale sweet face, of her tear-laden eye, of her soft beseeching tones, and gentle touch; he thought of these things—as he should not have thought of them;—and he persevered.

On this occasion he was closeted with Sir Peregrine for a couple of hours, and each heard much from the other that surprised him very much. Sir Peregrine, when he was told that Mr. Solomon Aram from Bucklersbury, and Mr. Chaffanbrass from the Old Bailey, were to be retained for the defence of his future wife, drew himself up and said that he could hardly approve of it. The gentlemen named were no doubt very clever in criminal concerns; he could understand as much as that, though he had not had great opportunity of looking into affairs of that sort. But surely, in Lady Mason's case, assistance of such a description would hardly be needed. Would it not be better to consult Messrs. Slow and Bideawhile?

And then it turned out that Messrs. Slow and Bideawhile had been consulted; and Mr. Furnival, not altogether successfully, endeavoured to throw dust into the baronet's eyes, declaring that in a combat with the devil one must use the devil's weapons. He assured Sir Peregrine that he had given the matter his most matured and indeed most painful professional consideration; there were unfortunate circumstances which required peculiar care; it was a matter which would depend entirely on the evidence of one or two persons who might be suborned; and in such a case it would be well to trust to those who knew how to break down and crush a lying witness. In such work as that Slow and Bideawhile would be innocent and ignorant as babes. As to breaking down and crushing a witness anxious to speak the truth, Mr. Furnival at that time said nothing.

"I will not think that falsehood and fraud can prevail," said Sir Peregrine proudly.

"But they do prevail sometimes," said Mr. Furnival. And then with much outer dignity of demeanour, but with some shame-faced tremblings of the inner man hidden under the guise of that outer dignity, Sir Peregrine informed the lawyer of his great purpose.

"Indeed!" said Mr. Furnival, throwing himself back into his chair with a start.

"Yes, Mr. Furnival. I should not have taken the liberty to trouble you with a matter so private in its nature, but for your close professional intimacy and great friendship with Lady Mason."

"Oh, indeed!" said Mr. Furnival; and the baronet could understand from the lawyer's tone that even he did not approve.

CHAPTER XXXIX
WHY SHOULD HE GO?

"I am well aware, Mr. Staveley, that you are one of those gentlemen who amuse themselves by frequently saying such things to girls. I had learned your character in that respect before I had been in the house two days."

"Then, Miss Furnival, you learned what was very false. May I ask who has blackened me in this way in your estimation?" It will be easily seen from this that Mr. Augustus Staveley and Miss Furnival were at the present moment alone together in one of the rooms at Noningsby.

"My informant," she replied, "has been no one special sinner whom you can take by the throat and punish. Indeed, if you must shoot anybody, it should be chiefly yourself, and after that your father, and mother, and sisters. But you need not talk of being black. Such sins are venial now-a-days, and convey nothing deeper than a light shade of brown."

"I regard a man who can act in such a way as very base."

"Such a way as what, Mr. Staveley?"

"A man who can win a girl's heart for his own amusement."

"I said nothing about the winning of hearts. That is treachery of the worst dye; but I acquit you of any such attempt. When there is a question of the winning of hearts men look so different."

"I don't know how they look," said Augustus, not altogether satisfied as to the manner in which he was being treated—"but such has been my audacity,—my too great audacity on the present occasion."

"You are the most audacious of men, for your audacity would carry you to the feet of another lady to-morrow without the slightest check."

"And that is the only answer I am to receive from you?"

"It is quite answer enough. What would you have me do? Get up and decline the honour of being Mrs. Augustus Staveley with a curtsy?"

"No—I would have you do nothing of the kind. I would have you get up and accept the honour,—with a kiss."

"So that you might have the kiss, and I might have the—; I was going to say disappointment, only that would be untrue. Let me assure you that I am not so demonstrative in my tokens of regard."

"I wonder whether you mean that you are not so honest?"

"No, Mr. Staveley; I mean nothing of the kind; and you are very impertinent to express such a supposition. What have I done or said to make you suppose that I have lost my heart to you?"

"As you have mine, it is at any rate human nature in me to hope that I might have yours."

"Psha! your heart! You have been making a shuttlecock of it till it is doubtful whether you have not banged it to pieces. I know two ladies who carry in their caps two feathers out of it. It is so easy to see when a man is in love. They all go cross-gartered like Malvolio;—cross-gartered in their looks and words and doings."

"And there is no touch of all this in me?"

"You cross-gartered! You have never got so far yet as a lack-a-daisical twist to the corner of your mouth. Did you watch Mr. Orme before he went away?"

"Why; was he cross-gartered?"

"But you men have no eyes; you never see anything. And your idea of love-making is to sit under a tree wishing, wondering whether the ripe fruit will fall down into your mouth. Ripe fruit does sometimes fall, and then it is all well with you. But if it won't, you pass on and say that it is sour. As for climbing—"

"The fruit generally falls too fast to admit of such exercise," said Staveley, who did not choose that all the sharp things should be said on the other side.

"And that is the result of your very extended experience? The orchards which have been opened to you have not, I fear, been of the first quality. Mr. Staveley, my hand will do very well by itself. Such is not the sort of climbing that is required. That is what I call stooping to pick up the fruit that has fallen." And as she spoke, she moved a little away from him on the sofa.

"And how is a man to climb?"

"Do you really mean that you want a lesson? But if I were to tell you, my words would be thrown away. Men will not labour who have gotten all that they require without work. Why strive to deserve any woman, when women are plenty who do not care to be deserved? That plan of picking up the fallen apples is so much the easier."

The lesson might perhaps have been given, and Miss Furnival might have imparted to Mr. Staveley her idea of "excelsior" in the matter of love-making, had not Mr. Staveley's mother come into the room at that moment. Mrs. Staveley was beginning to fear that the results of her Christmas hospitality would not be satisfactory. Peregrine Orme, whom she would have been so happy to welcome to the warmest corner of her household temple as a son, had been sent away in wretchedness and disappointment. Madeline was moping about the house, hardly making an effort to look like herself; attributing, in her mother's ears, all her complaint to that unexpected interview with Peregrine Orme, but not so attributing it—as her mother fancied—with correctness. And there was Felix Graham still in the room up stairs, the doctor having said that he might be moved in a day or two;—that is, such movement might possibly be effected without detriment;—but having said also that another ten days of uninterrupted rest would be very desirable. And now, in addition to this, her son Augustus was to be found on every wet morning closeted somewhere with Sophia Furnival;—on every wet morning, and sometimes on dry mornings also!

Lady Stavely interrupting her Son and Sophia Furnival.

And then, on this very day, Lady Staveley had discovered that Felix Graham's door in the corridor was habitually left open. She knew her child too well, and was too clear and pure in her own mind, to suppose that there was anything wrong in this;—that clandestine talkings were arranged, or anything planned in secret. What she feared was that which really occurred. The door was left open, and as Madeline passed Felix would say a word, and then Madeline would pause and answer him. Such words as they were might have been spoken before all the household, and if so spoken would have been free from danger. But they were not free from danger when spoken in that way, in the passage of a half-closed doorway;—all which Lady Staveley understood perfectly.

"Baker," she had said, with more of anger in her voice than was usual with her, "why do you leave that door open?"

"I think it sweetens the room, my lady;" and, indeed, Felix Graham sometimes thought so too.

"Nonsense; every sound in the house must be heard. Keep it shut, if you please."

"Yes, my lady," said Mrs. Baker—who also understood perfectly.

"He is better, my darling," said Mrs. Baker to Madeline, the same day; "and, indeed, for that he is well enough as regards eating and drinking. But it would be cruelty to move him yet. I heard what the doctor said."

"Who talks of moving him?"

"Well, he talks of it himself; and the doctor said it might be possible. But I know what that means."

"What does it mean?"

"Why, just this: that if we want to get rid of him, it won't quite be the death of him."

"But who wants to get rid of him?"

"I'm sure I don't. I don't mind my trouble the least in life. He's as nice a young gentleman as ever I sat beside the bed of; and he's full of spirit—he is."

And then Madeline appealed to her mother. Surely her mother would not let Mr. Graham be sent out of the house in his present state, merely because the doctor said it might be possible to move him without causing his instant death! And tears stood in poor Madeline's eyes as she thus pleaded the cause of the sick and wounded. This again tormented Lady Staveley, who found it necessary to give further caution to Mrs. Baker. "Baker," she said, "how can you be so foolish as to be talking to Miss Madeline about Mr. Graham's arm?"

"Who, my lady? I, my lady?"

"Yes, you; when you know that the least thing frightens her. Don't you remember how ill it made her when Roger"—Roger was an old family groom—"when Roger had that accident?" Lady Staveley might have saved herself the trouble of the reminiscence as to Roger, for Baker knew more about it than that. When Roger's scalp had been laid bare by a fall, Miss Madeline had chanced to see it, and had fainted; but Miss Madeline was not fainting now. Baker knew all about it, almost better than Lady Staveley herself. It was of very little use talking to Baker about Roger the groom. Baker thought that Mr. Felix Graham was a very nice young man, in spite of his "not being exactly handsomelike about the physgognomy," as she remarked to one of the younger maids, who much preferred Peregrine Orme.

Coming away from this last interval with Mrs. Baker, Lady Staveley interrupted her son and Sophia Furnival in the back drawing-room, and began to feel that her solicitude for her children would be almost too much for her. Why had she asked that nasty girl to her house, and why would not the nasty girl go away? As for her going away, there was no present hope; for it had been arranged that she should stay for another fortnight. Why could not the Fates have been kind, and have allowed Felix Graham and Miss Furnival to fall in love with each other? "I can never make a daughter of her if he does marry her," Lady Staveley said to herself, as she looked at them.

Augustus looked as though he were detected, and stammered out some question about his mother and the carriage; but Miss Furnival did not for a moment lose her easy presence of mind. "Lady Staveley," said she, "why does not your son go and hunt, or shoot, or fish, instead of staying in the house all day? It seems to me that his time is so heavy on his hands that he will almost have to hang himself."

"I'm sure I can't tell," said Lady Staveley, who was not so perfect an actor as her guest.

"I do think gentlemen in the house in the morning always look so unfortunate. You have been endeavouring to make yourself agreeable, but you know you've been yawning."

"Do you suppose then that men never sit still in the morning?" said Augustus.

"Oh, in their chambers, yes; or on the bench, and perhaps also behind counters; but they very seldom do so in a drawing-room. You have been fidgeting about with the poker till you have destroyed the look of the fireplace."

"Well, I'll go and fidget up stairs with Graham," said he; and so he left the room.

"Nasty, sly girl," said Lady Staveley to herself as she took up her work and sat herself down in her own chair.

Augustus did go up to his friend and found him reading letters. There was no one else in the room, and the door when Augustus reached it was properly closed. "I think I shall be off to-morrow, old boy," said Felix.

"Then I think you'll do no such thing," said Augustus. "What's in the wind now?"

"The doctor said this morning that I could be moved without danger."

"He said that it might possibly be done in two or three days—that was all. What on earth makes you so impatient? You've nothing to do. Nobody else wants to see you; and nobody here wants to get rid of you."

"You're wrong in all your three statements."

"The deuce I am! Who wants to get rid of you?"

"That shall come last. I have something to do, and somebody else does want to see me. I've got a letter from Mary here, and another from Mrs. Thomas;" and he held up to view two letters which he had received, and which had, in truth, startled him.

"Mary's duenna;—the artist who is supposed to be moulding the wife."

"Yes; Mary's duenna, or Mary's artist, whichever you please."

"And which of them wants to see you? It's just like a woman, to require a man's attendance exactly when he is unable to move."

Then Felix, though he did not give up the letters to be read, described to a certain extent their contents. "I don't know what on earth has happened," he said. "Mary is praying to be forgiven, and saying that it is not her fault; and Mrs. Thomas is full of apologies, declaring that her conscience forces her to tell everything; and yet, between them both, I do not know what has happened."

"Miss Snow has probably lost the key of the workbox you gave her."

"I have not given her a workbox."

"Then the writing-desk. That's what a man has to endure when he will make himself head schoolmaster to a young lady. And so you're going to look after your charge with your limbs still in bandages?"

"Just so;" and then he took up the two letters and read them again, while Staveley still sat on the foot of the bed. "I wish I knew what to think about it," said Felix.

"About what?" said the other. And then there was another pause, and another reading of a portion of the letters.

"There seems something—something almost frightful to me," said Felix gravely, "in the idea of marrying a girl in a few months' time, who now, at so late a period of our engagement, writes to me in that sort of cold, formal way."

"It's the proper moulded-wife style, you may depend," said Augustus.

"I'll tell you what, Staveley, if you can talk to me seriously for five minutes, I shall be obliged to you. If that is impossible to you, say so, and I will drop the matter."

"Well, go on; I am serious enough in what I intend to express, even though I may not be so in my words."

"I'm beginning to have my doubts about this dear girl."

"I've had my doubts for some time."

"Not, mark you, with regard to myself. The question is not now whether I can love her sufficiently for my own happiness. On that side I have no longer the right to a doubt."

"But you wouldn't marry her if you did not love her."

"We need not discuss that. But what if she does not love me? What if she would think it a release to be freed from this engagement? How am I to find that out?"

Augustus sat for a while silent, for he did feel that the matter was serious. The case as he looked at it stood thus:—His friend Graham had made a very foolish bargain, from which he would probably be glad to escape, though he could not now bring himself to say as much. But this bargain, bad for him, would probably be very good for the young lady. The young lady, having no shilling of her own, and no merits of birth or early breeding to assist her outlook in the world, might probably regard her ready-made engagement to a clever, kind-hearted, high-spirited man, as an advantage not readily to be abandoned. Staveley, as a sincere friend, was very anxious that the match should be broken off; but he could not bring himself to tell Graham that he thought that the young lady would so wish. According to his idea the young lady must undergo a certain amount of disappointment, and receive a certain amount of compensation. Graham had been very foolish, and must pay for his folly. But in preparing to do so, it would be better that he should see and acknowledge the whole truth of the matter.

"Are you sure that you have found out your own feelings?" Staveley said at last; and his tone was then serious enough even for his friend.

"It hardly matters whether I have or have not," said Felix.

"It matters above all things;—above all things, because as to them you may come to something like certainty. Of the inside of her heart you cannot know so much. The fact I take it is this—that you would wish to escape from this bondage."

"No; not unless I thought she regarded it as bondage also. It may be that she does. As for myself, I believe that at the present moment such a marriage would be for me the safest step that I could take."

"Safe as against what danger?"

"All dangers. How, if I should learn to love another woman,—some one utterly out of my reach,—while I am still betrothed to her?"

"I rarely flatter you, Graham, and don't mean to do it now; but no girl ought to be out of your reach. You have talent, position, birth, and gifts of nature, which should make you equal to any lady. As for money, the less you have the more you should look to get. But if you would cease to be mad, two years would give you command of an income."

"But I shall never cease to be mad."

"Who is it that cannot be serious, now?"

"Well, I will be serious—serious enough. I can afford to be so, as I have received my medical passport for to-morrow. No girl, you say, ought to be out of my reach. If the girl were one Miss Staveley, should she be regarded as out of my reach?"

"A man doesn't talk about his own sister," said Staveley, having got up from the bed and walked to the window, "and I know you don't mean anything."

"But, by heavens! I do mean a great deal."

"What is it you mean, then?"

"I mean this—What would you say if you learned that I was a suitor for her hand?"

Staveley had been right in saying that a man does not talk about his own sister. When he had declared, with so much affectionate admiration for his friend's prowess, that he might aspire to the hand of any lady, that one retiring, modest-browed girl had not been thought of by him. A man in talking to another man about women is always supposed to consider those belonging to himself as exempt from the incidents of the conversation. The dearest friends do not talk to each other about their sisters when they have once left school; and a man in such a position as that now taken by Graham has to make fight for his ground as closely as though there had been no former intimacies. My friend Smith in such a matter as that, though I have been hail fellow with him for the last ten years, has very little advantage over Jones, who was introduced to the house for the first time last week. And therefore Staveley felt himself almost injured when Felix Graham spoke to him about Madeline.

"What would I say? Well—that is a question one does not understand, unless—unless you really meant to state it as a fact that it was your intention to propose to her."

"But I mean rather to state it as a fact that it is not my intention to propose to her."

"Then we had better not speak of her."

"Listen to me a moment. In order that I may not do so, it will be better for me—better for us all, that I should leave the house."

"Do you mean to say—?"

"Yes, I do mean to say! I mean to say all that your mind is now suggesting to you. I quite understand your feelings when you declare that a man does not like to talk of his own sister, and therefore we will talk of your sister no more. Old fellow, don't look at me as though you meant to drop me."

Augustus came back to the bedside, and again seating himself, put his hand almost caressingly over his friend's shoulder. "I did not think of this," he said.

"No; one never does think of it," Graham replied.

"And she?"

"She knows no more of it than that bed-post," said Graham. "The injury, such as there is, is all on one side. But I'll tell you who suspects it."

"Baker?"

"Your mother. I am much mistaken if you will not find that she, with all her hospitality, would prefer that I should recover my strength elsewhere."

"But you have done nothing to betray yourself."

"A mother's ears are very sharp. I know that it is so. I cannot explain to you how. Do you tell her that I think of getting up to London to-morrow, and see how she will take it. And, Staveley, do not for a moment suppose that I am reproaching her. She is quite right. I believe that I have in no way committed myself—that I have said no word to your sister with which Lady Staveley has a right to feel herself aggrieved; but if she has had the wit to read the thoughts of my bosom, she is quite right to wish that I were out of the house."

Poor Lady Staveley had been possessed of no such wit at all. The sphynx which she had read had been one much more in her own line. She had simply read the thoughts in her daughter's bosom—or rather, the feelings in her daughter's heart.

Augustus Staveley hardly knew what he ought to say. He was not prepared to tell his friend that he was the very brother-in-law for whose connection he would be desirous. Such a marriage for Madeline, even should Madeline desire it, would not be advantageous. When Augustus told Graham that he had gifts of nature which made him equal to any lady, he did not include his own sister. And yet the idea of acquiescing in his friend's sudden departure was very painful to him. "There can be no reason why you should not stay up here, you know," at last he said;—and in so saying he pronounced an absolute verdict against poor Felix.

On few matters of moment to a man's own heart can he speak out plainly the whole truth that is in him. Graham had intended so to do, but had deceived himself. He had not absolutely hoped that his friend would say, "Come among us, and be one of us; take her, and be my brother." But yet there came upon his heart a black load of disappointment, in that the words which were said were the exact opposite of these. Graham had spoken of himself as unfit to match with Madeline Staveley, and Madeline Staveley's brother had taken him at his word. The question which Augustus asked himself was this—Was it, or was it not practicable that Graham should remain there without danger of intercourse with his sister? To Felix the question came in a very different shape. After having spoken as he had spoken— might he be allowed to remain there, enjoying such intercourse, or might he not? That was the question to which he had unconsciously demanded an answer;—and unconsciously he had still hoped that the question might be answered in his favour. He had so hoped, although he was burdened with Mary Snow, and although he had spoken of his engagement with that lady in so rigid a spirit of self-martyrdom. But the question had been answered against him. The offer of a further asylum in the seclusion of that bedroom had been made to him by his friend with a sort of proviso that it would not be well that he should go further than the bedroom, and his inner feelings at once grated against each other, making him wretched and almost angry.

"Thank you, no; I understand how kind you are, but I will not do that. I will write up to-night, and shall certainly start to-morrow."

"My dear fellow—"

"I should get into a fever, if I were to remain in this house after what I have told you. I could not endure to see you, or your mother, or Baker, or Marian, or any one else. Don't talk about it. Indeed, you ought to feel that it is not possible. I have made a confounded ass of myself, and the sooner I get away the better. I say—perhaps you would not be angry if I was to ask you to let me sleep for an hour or so now. After that I'll get up and write my letters."

He was very sore. He knew that he was sick at heart, and ill at ease, and cross with his friend; and knew also that he was unreasonable in being so. Staveley's words and manner had been full of kindness. Graham was aware of this, and was therefore the more irritated with himself. But this did not prevent his being angry and cross with his friend.

"Graham," said the other, "I see clearly enough that I have annoyed you."

"Not in the least. A man falls into the mud, and then calls to another man to come and see him. The man in the mud of course is not comfortable."

"But you have called to me, and I have not been able to help you."

"I did not suppose you would, so there has been no disappointment. Indeed, there was no possibility for help. I shall follow out the line of life which I have long since chalked out for myself, and I do not expect that I shall be more wretched than other poor devils around me. As far as my idea goes, it all makes very little difference. Now leave me; there's a good fellow."

"Dear old fellow, I would give my right hand if it would make you happy!"

"But it won't. Your right hand will make somebody else happy, I hope."

"I'll come up to you again before dinner."

"Very well. And, Staveley, what we have now said cannot be forgotten between us; but when we next meet, and ever after, let it be as though it were forgotten." Then he settled himself down on the bed, and Augustus left the room.

It will not be supposed that Graham did go to sleep, or that he had any thought of doing so. When he was alone those words of his friend rang over and over again in his ears, "No girl ought to be out of your reach." Why should Madeline Staveley be out of his reach, simply because she was his friend's sister? He had been made welcome to that house, and therefore he was bound to do nothing unhandsome by the family. But then he was bound by other laws, equally clear, to do nothing unhandsome by any other family—or by any other lady. If there was anything in Staveley's words, they applied as strongly to Staveley's sister as to any other girl. And why should not he, a lawyer, marry a lawyer's daughter? Sophia Furnival, with her hatful of money, would not be considered too high for him; and in what respect was Madeline Staveley above Sophia Furnival? That the one was immeasurably above the other in all those respects which in his estimation tended towards female perfection, he knew to be true enough; but the fruit which he had been forbidden to gather hung no higher on the social tree than that other fruit which he had been specially invited to pluck and garner.

And then Graham was not a man to think any fruit too high for him. He had no overweening idea of his own deserts, either socially or professionally, nor had he taught himself to expect great things from his own genius; but he had that audacity of spirit which bids a man hope to compass that which he wishes to compass,—that audacity which is both the father and mother of success,—that audacity which seldom exists without the inner capability on which it ought to rest.

But then there was Mary Snow! Augustus Staveley thought but little of Mary Snow. According to his theory of his friend's future life, Mary Snow might be laid aside without much difficulty. If this were so, why should not Madeline be within his reach? But then was it so? Had he not betrothed himself to Mary Snow in the presence of the girl's father, with every solemnity and assurance, in a manner fixed beyond that of all other betrothals? Alas, yes; and for this reason it was right that he should hurry away from Noningsby.

Then he thought of Mary's letter, and of Mrs. Thomas's letter. What was it that had been done? Mary had written as though she had been charged with some childish offence; but Mrs. Thomas talked solemnly of acquitting her own conscience. What could have happened that had touched Mrs. Thomas in the conscience?

But his thoughts soon ran away from the little house at Peckham, and settled themselves again at Noningsby. Should he hear more of Madeline's footsteps?—and if not, why should they have been banished from the corridor? Should he hear her voice again at the door,—and if not, why should it have been hushed? There is a silence which may be more eloquent than the sounds which it follows. Had no one in that house guessed the feelings in his bosom, she would have walked along the corridor as usual, and spoken a word with her sweet voice in answer to his word. He felt sure that this would be so no more; but who had stopped it, and why should such sounds be no more heard?

At last he did go to sleep, not in pursuance of any plan formed for doing so; for had he been asked he would have said that sleep was impossible for him. But he did go to sleep, and when he awoke it was dark. He had intended to have got up and dressed on that afternoon, or to have gone through such ceremony of dressing as was possible for him,—in preparation of his next day's exercise; and now he rose up in his bed with a start, angry with himself in having allowed the time to pass by him.

"Lord love you, Mr. Graham, why how you have slept!" said Mrs. Baker. "If I haven't just sent your dinner down again to keep hot. Such a beautiful pheasant, and the bread sauce'll be lumpy now, for all the world like pap."

"Never mind the bread sauce, Mrs. Baker;—the pheasant's the thing."

"And her ladyship's been here, Mr. Graham, only she wouldn't have you woke. She won't hear of your being moved to-morrow, nor yet won't the judge. There was a rumpus down stairs when Mr. Augustus as much as mentioned it. I know one who—"

"You know one who—you were saying?"

"Never mind.—It ain't one more than another, but it's all. You ain't to leave this to-morrow, so you may just give it over. And indeed your things is all at the wash, so you can't;—and now I'll go down for the pheasant."

Felix still declared very positively that he should go, but his doing so did not shake Mrs. Baker. The letter-bag he knew did not leave till eight, and as yet it was not much past five. He would see Staveley again after his dinner, and then he would write.

When Augustus left the room in the middle of the day he encountered Madeline wandering about the house. In these days she did wander about the house, as though there were something always to be done in some place apart from that in which she then was. And yet the things which she did were but few. She neither worked nor read, and as for household duties, her share in them was confined almost entirely to the morning and evening teapot.

"It isn't true that he's to go to-morrow morning, Augustus, is it?" said she.

"Who, Graham? Well; he says that he will. He is very anxious to get to London; and no doubt he finds it stupid enough lying there and doing nothing."

"But he can do as much there as he can lying by himself in his own chambers, where I don't suppose he would have anybody to look after him. He thinks he's a trouble and all that, and therefore he wants to go. But you know mamma doesn't mind about trouble of that kind; and what should we think of it afterwards if anything bad was to happen to your friend because we allowed him to leave the house before he was in a fit state to be moved? Of course Mr. Pottinger says so—" Mr. Pottinger was the doctor. "Of course Mr. Pottinger says so, because he thinks he has been so long here, and he doesn't understand."

"But Mr. Pottinger would like to keep a patient."

"Oh no; he's not at all that sort of man. He'd think of mamma,—the trouble I mean of having a stranger in the house. But you know mamma would think nothing of that, especially for such an intimate friend of yours."

Augustus turned slightly round so as to look more fully into his sister's face, and he saw that a tear was gathered in the corner of her eye. She perceived his glance and partly shrank under it, but she soon recovered herself and answered it. "I know what you mean," she said, "and if you choose to think so, I can't help it. But it is horrible—horrible—" and then she stopped herself, finding that a little sob would become audible if she trusted herself to further words.

"You know what I mean, Mad?" he said, putting his arm affectionately round her waist. "And what is it that I mean? Come; you and I never have any secrets;—you always say so when you want to get at mine. Tell me what it is that I mean."

"I haven't got any secret."

"But what did I mean?"

"You looked at me, because I don't want you to let them send Mr. Graham away. If it was old Mr. Furnival I shouldn't like them to turn him out of this house when he was in such a state as that."

"Poor Mr. Furnival; no; I think he would bear it worse than Felix."

"Then why should he go? And why—should you look at me in that way?"

"Did I look at you, Mad? Well, I believe I did. We are to have no secrets; are we?"

"No," said she. But she did not say it in the same eager voice with which hitherto she had declared that they would always tell each other everything.

"Felix Graham is my friend," said he, "my special friend; and I hope you will always like my friends. But—"

"Well?" she said.

"You know what I mean, Mad"

"Yes," she said.

"That is all, dearest." And then she knew that he also had cautioned her not to fall in love with Felix Graham, and she felt angry with him for the caution. "Why—why—why—?" But she hardly knew as yet how to frame the question which she desired to ask herself.

CHAPTER XL
I CALL IT AWFUL

"Oh indeed!" Those had been the words with which Mr. Furnival had received the announcement made by Sir Peregrine as to his proposed nuptials. And as he uttered them the lawyer drew himself up stiffly in his chair, looking much more like a lawyer and much less like an old family friend than he had done the moment before.

Whereupon Sir Peregrine drew himself up also. "Yes," he said. "I should be intrusive if I were to trouble you with my motives, and therefore I need only say further as regards the lady, that I trust that my support, standing as I shall do in the position of her husband, will be more serviceable to her than it could otherwise have been in this trial which she will, I presume, be forced to undergo."

"No doubt; no doubt," said Mr. Furnival; and then the interview had ended. The lawyer had been anxious to see his client, and had intended to ask permission to do so; but he had felt on hearing Sir Peregrine's tidings that it would be useless now to make any attempt to see her alone, and that he could speak to her with no freedom in Sir Peregrine's presence. So he left The Cleeve, having merely intimated to the baronet the fact of his having engaged the services of Mr. Chaffanbrass and Mr. Solomon Aram. "You will not see Lady Mason?" Sir Peregrine had asked. "Thank you; I do not know that I need trouble her," Mr. Furnival had answered. "You of course will explain to her how the case at present stands. I fear she must reconcile herself to the fact of a trial. You are aware, Sir Peregrine, that the offence imputed is one for which bail will be taken. I should propose yourself and her son. Of course I should be happy to lend my own name, but as I shall be on the trial, perhaps it may be as well that this should be avoided."

Bail will be taken! These words were dreadful in the ears of the expectant bridegroom. Had it come to this; that there was a question whether or no she should be locked up in a prison, like a felon? But nevertheless his heart did not misgive him. Seeing how terribly she was injured by others, he felt himself bound by the stronger law to cling to her himself. Such was the special chivalry of the man.

Mr. Furnival on his return to London thought almost more of Sir Peregrine than he did either of Lady Mason or of himself. Was it not a pity? Was it not a thousand pities that that aged noble gentleman should be sacrificed? He had felt angry with Sir Peregrine when the tidings were first communicated to him; but now, as he journeyed up to London this feeling of anger was transferred to his own client. This must be her doing, and such doing on her part, while she was in her present circumstances, was very wicked. And then he remembered her guilt,—her probable guilt, and his brow became very black. Her supposed guilt had not been horrible to him while he had regarded it as affecting herself alone, and in point of property affecting Joseph Mason and her son Lucius. He could look forward, sometimes almost triumphantly, to the idea of washing her—so far as this world's washing goes—from that guilt, and setting her up again clear before the world, even though in doing so he should lend a hand in robbing Joseph Mason of his estate. But this dragging down of another— and such another—head into the vortex of ruin and misery was horrible to him. He was not straitlaced, or mealy-mouthed, or overburthened with scruples. In the way of his profession he could do many a thing at which—I express a single opinion with much anxious deference—at which an honest man might be scandalized if it came beneath his judgment unprofessionally. But this he could not stand. Something must be done in the matter. The marriage must be stayed till after the trial,—or else he must himself retire from the defence and explain both to Lady Mason and to Sir Peregrine why he did so.

And then he thought of the woman herself, and his spirit within him became very bitter. Had any one told him that he was jealous of the preference shown by his client to Sir Peregrine, he would have fumed with anger, and thought that he was fuming justly. But such was in truth the case. Though he believed her to have been guilty of this thing, though he believed her to be now guilty of the worse offence of dragging the baronet to his ruin, still he was jealous of her regard. Had she been content to lean upon him, to trust to him as her great and only necessary friend, he could have forgiven all else, and placed at her service the full force of his professional power,—even though by doing so he might have lowered himself in men's minds. And what reward did he expect? None. He had formed no idea that the woman would become his mistress. All that was as obscure before his mind's eye, as though she had been nineteen and he five-and-twenty.

He was to dine at home on this day, that being the first occasion of his doing so for—as Mrs. Furnival declared—the last six months. In truth, however, the interval had been long, though not so long as that. He had a hope that having announced his intention, he might find the coast clear and hear Martha Biggs spoken of as a dear one lately gone. But when he arrived at home Martha Biggs was still there. Under circumstances as they now existed Mrs. Furnival had determined to keep Martha Biggs by her, unless any special edict for her banishment should come forth. Then, in case of such special edict, Martha Biggs should go, and thence should arise the new casus belli. Mrs. Furnival had made up her mind that war was expedient,—nay, absolutely necessary. She had an idea, formed no doubt from the reading of history, that some allies require a smart brush now and again to blow away the clouds of distrust which become engendered by time between them; and that they may become better allies than ever afterwards. If the appropriate time for such a brush might ever come, it had come now. All the world,—so she said to herself,—was talking of Mr. Furnival and Lady Mason. All the world knew of her injuries.

Martha Biggs was second cousin to Mr. Crook's brother's wife—I speak of that Mr. Crook who had been professionally known for the last thirty years as the partner of Mr. Round. It had been whispered in the office in Bedford Row—such whisper I fear originating with old Round—that Mr. Furnival admired his fair client. Hence light had fallen upon the eyes of Martha Biggs, and the secret of her friend was known to her. Need I trace the course of the tale with closer accuracy?

"Oh, Kitty," she had said to her friend with tears that evening—"I cannot bear to keep it to myself any more! I cannot when I see you suffering so. It's awful."

"Cannot bear to keep what, Martha?"

"Oh, I know. Indeed all the town knows it now."

"Knows what? You know how I hate that kind of thing. If you have anything to say, speak out."

This was not kind to such a faithful friend as Martha Biggs; but Martha knew what sacrifices friendship such as hers demanded, and she did not resent it.

"Well then;—if I am to speak out, it's—Lady Mason. And I do say that it's shameful, quite shameful;—and awful; I call it awful."

Mrs. Furnival had not said much at the time to encourage the fidelity of her friend, but she was thus justified in declaring to herself that her husband's goings on had become the talk of all the world;—and his goings on especially in that quarter in which she had long regarded them with so much dismay. She was not therefore prepared to welcome him on this occasion of his coming home to dinner by such tokens of friendly feeling as the dismissal of her friend to Red Lion Square. When the moment for absolute war should come Martha Biggs should be made to depart.

Mr. Furnival when he arrived at his own house was in a thoughtful mood, and disposed for quiet and domestic meditation. Had Miss Biggs not been there he could have found it in his heart to tell everything about Lady Mason to his wife, asking her counsel as to what he should do with reference to that marriage. Could he have done so, all would have been well; but this was not possible while that red-faced lump of a woman from Red Lion Square sat in his drawing-room, making everything uncomfortable.

The three sat down to dinner together, and very little was said between them. Mr. Furnival did try to be civil to his wife, but wives sometimes have a mode of declining such civilities without committing themselves to overt acts of war. To Miss Biggs Mr. Furnival could not bring himself to say anything civil, seeing that he hated her; but such words as he did speak to her she received with grim griffin-like austerity, as though she were ever meditating on the awfulness of his conduct. And so in truth she was. Why his conduct was more awful in her estimation since she had heard Lady Mason's name mentioned, than when her mind had been simply filled with general ideas of vague conjugal infidelity, I cannot say; but such was the case. "I call it awful," were the first words she again spoke when she found herself once more alone with Mrs. Furnival in the drawing-room. And then she sat down over the fire, thinking neither of her novel nor her knitting, with her mind deliciously filled with the anticipation of coming catastrophes.

"If I sit up after half-past ten would you mind going to bed?" said Mrs. Furnival, when they had been in the drawing-room about ten minutes.

"Oh no, not in the least," said Miss Biggs. "I'll be sure to go." But she thought it very unkind, and she felt as a child does who is deceived in a matter of being taken to the play. If no one goes the child can bear it. But to see others go, and to be left behind, is too much for the feelings of any child,—or of Martha Biggs.

Mr. Furnival had no inclination for sitting alone over his wine on this occasion. Had it been possible for him he would have preferred to have gone quickly up stairs, and to have taken his cup of coffee from his wife's hand with some appreciation of domestic comfort. But there could be no such comfort to him while Martha Biggs was there, so he sat down stairs, sipping his port according to his custom, and looking into the fire for a solution of his difficulties about Lady Mason. He began to wish that he had never seen Lady Mason, and to reflect that the intimate friendship of pretty women often brings with it much trouble. He was resolved on one thing.

He would not go down into court and fight that battle for Lady Orme. Were he to do so the matter would have taken quite a different phase,—one that he had not at all anticipated. In case that his present client should then have become Lady Orme, Mr. Chaffanbrass and Mr. Solomon Aram might carry on the battle between them, with such assistance as they might be able to get from Messrs. Slow and Bideawhile. He became angry as he drank his port, and in his anger he swore that it should be so. And then as his anger became hot at the close of his libations, he remembered that Martha Biggs was up stairs, and became more angry still. And thus when he did go into the drawing-room at some time in the evening not much before ten, he was not in a frame of mind likely to bring about domestic comfort.

He walked across the drawing-room, sat down in an arm-chair by the table, and took up the last number of a review, without speaking to either of them. Whereupon Mrs. Furnival began to ply her needle which had been lying idly enough upon her work, and Martha Biggs fixed her eyes intently upon her book. So they sat twenty minutes without a word being spoken, and then Mrs. Furnival inquired of her lord whether he chose to have tea.

"Of course I shall,—when you have it," said he.

"Don't mind us," said Mrs. Furnival.

"Pray don't mind me," said Martha Biggs. "Don't let me be in the way."

"No, I won't," said Mr. Furnival. Whereupon Miss Biggs again jumped up in her chair as though she had been electrified. It may be remembered that on a former occasion Mr. Furnival had sworn at her—or at least in her presence.

"You need not be rude to a lady in your own house, because she is my friend," said Mrs. Furnival.

"Bother," said Mr. Furnival. "And now if we are going to have any tea, let us have it."

"I don't think I'll mind about tea to-night, Mrs. Furnival," said Miss Biggs, having received a notice from her friend's eye that it might be well for her to depart. "My head aches dreadful, and I shall be better in bed. Good-night, Mrs. Furnival." And then she took her candle and went away.

For the next five minutes there was not a word said. No tea had been ordered, although it had been mentioned. Mrs. Furnival had forgotten it among the hot thoughts that were running through her mind, and Mr. Furnival was indifferent upon the subject. He knew that something was coming, and he resolved that he would have the upper hand let that something be what it might. He was being ill used,—so he said to himself—and would not put up with it.

At last the battle began. He was not looking, but he heard her first movement as she prepared herself. "Tom!" she said, and then the voice of the war goddess was again silent. He did not choose to answer her at the instant, and then the war goddess rose from her seat and again spoke. "Tom!" she said, standing over him and looking at him.

"What is it you mean?" said he, allowing his eyes to rise to her face over the top of his book.

"Tom!" she said for the third time.

"I'll have no nonsense, Kitty," said he. "If you have anything to say, say it."

Even then she had intended to be affectionate,—had so intended at the first commencement of her address. She had no wish to be a war goddess. But he had assisted her attempt at love by no gentle word, by no gentle look, by no gentle motion. "I have this to say," she replied; "you are disgracing both yourself and me, and I will not remain in this house to be a witness to it."

"Then you may go out of the house." These words, be it remembered, were uttered not by the man himself, but by the spirit of port wine within the man.

"Tom, do you say that;—after all?"

"By heavens I do say it! I'll not be told in my own drawing-room, even by you, that I am disgracing myself."

"Then why do you go after that woman down to Hamworth? All the world is talking of you. At your age too! You ought to be ashamed of yourself."

"I can't stand this," said he, getting up and throwing the book from him right across the drawing-room floor; "and, by heavens! I won't stand it."

"Then why do you do it, sir?"

"Kitty, I believe the devil must have entered into you to drive you mad."

"Oh, oh, oh! very well, sir. The devil in the shape of drink and lust has entered into you. But you may understand this; I—will—not—consent to live with you while such deeds as these are being done." And then without waiting for another word, she stormed out of the room.